Praise for the sexy novels of

JENNIFER PROBST

"Witty dialogue and passionate characters."
—*RT Book Reviews*

EMMA CHASE

"Witty, endearing, laugh-out-loud funny."
—Bestselling author K. Bromberg

KRISTEN PROBY

"Knows how to draw the audience and keep them there."
—*Morning After a Good Book*

MELODY ANNE

"If you like drama, angst, graphic hot sex . . , and a story that ends in the sweetest, most lovely happily ever after, you're in for a really great read."
—*Tipsy Lit*

KATE MEADER

"Will have readers drooling over the hero and heroine."
—*RT Book Reviews*

JENNIFER PROBST

Searching For series

Searching for Someday
Searching for Perfect

And coming in 2015 . . .

Searching for Beautiful
Searching for Always

Marriage to a Billionaire series

The Marriage Bargain
The Marriage Trap
The Marriage Mistake
The Marriage Merger

❅ ❅ ❅

EMMA CHASE

Tangled series

Tangled
Twisted
Tamed
Tied

❅ ❅ ❅

KRISTEN PROBY

Love Under the Big Sky series

Loving Cara
Seducing Lauren

❅ ❅ ❅

And watch for these sizzling books
in spring 2015 . . .

MELODY ANNE

Her Unexpected Hero

KATE MEADER

Flirting with Fire

JENNIFER
PROBST

EMMA
CHASE

Baby, It's Cold Outside

KRISTEN
PROBY

MELODY
ANNE

KATE
MEADER

POCKET BOOKS

New York   London   Toronto   Sydney   New Delhi

Pocket Books
A Division of Simon & Schuster, Inc.
1230 Avenue of the Americas
New York, NY 10020

This book is a work of fiction. Any references to historical events, real people, or real places are used fictitiously. Other names, characters, places, and events are products of the author's imagination, and any resemblance to actual events or places or persons, living or dead, is entirely coincidental.

Searching For You copyright © 2014 by Jennifer Probst
It's a Wonderful Tangled Christmas Carol copyright © 2014 by Emma Chase
Saving Grace copyright © 2014 by Kristen Proby
Safe in His Arms copyright © 2014 by Melody Anne Null
Rekindle the Flame copyright © 2014 by Kate Meader

First Pocket Books paperback edition November 2014

POCKET and colophon are registered trademarks of Simon & Schuster, Inc.

For information about special discounts for bulk purchases, please contact Simon & Schuster Special Sales at 1-866-506-1949 or business@simonandschuster.com.

The Simon & Schuster Speakers Bureau can bring authors to your live event. For more information or to book an event contact the Simon & Schuster Speakers Bureau at 1-866-248-3049 or visit our website at www.simonspeakers.com.

Interior design by Leydiana Rodríguez-Ovalles
Cover design © Eileen Carey
Cover images © Jim Craigmyle/Corbis; © Tomasz Pietryszek/Getty Images; © t_kimura/Getty Images

Manufactured in the United States of America

10 9 8 7 6 5 4 3 2 1

ISBN 978-1-4767-8383-3
ISBN 978-1-4767-8619-3 (ebook)

Contents

· · · · · · · · · · · · ·

Searching for You
BY JENNIFER PROBST
1

It's a Wonderful Tangled Christmas Carol
BY EMMA CHASE
107

Saving Grace
BY KRISTEN PROBY
181

Safe in His Arms
BY MELODY ANNE
279

Rekindle the Flame
BY KATE MEADER
405

Searching for You

....

JENNIFER PROBST

chapter 1

. . . .

$\mathcal{K}$ate Seymour studied the computer in front of her, squinted, and read the entry again.

And again.

Her heart beat faster and that familiar electrical buzz tingled under her skin. Impossible. They were completely different—a match made in literal hell, not heaven. Yet numbers like this didn't lie. Time to bring in the troops.

She hit the intercom button. "Hey, Arilyn? Can you come in here? And bring Kennedy."

"Sure."

A few minutes later, her business partners and best friends joined her in the office. Her face softened into a smile at their presence. Their drunken plans years ago to start their own matchmaking agency in Verily, upstate New York, sounded impossible, but they'd made it work. More so. With over a dozen marriages, and endless statistically proven committed happy relationships, they'd made the dream a reality. Kinnections was an exclusive matchmaking agency that catered to the twenty-five-to-forty crowd, and had already been featured in local newspapers and television stations as the new "hot" way to meet a mate. Hell, it had actually worked for her and Kennedy. Now if only they could find Arilyn her match.

Kennedy Ashe, the social recruiter and makeover expert, slid into the chair and let out a sigh. Her burnished hair, whiskey eyes, and plum Donna Karan suit screamed polish and success. "Please let this be good news. I've already depleted my hotel bottles of liquor. Is it Friday yet?"

Arilyn shook her head in sympathy, her strawberry hair streaming down her back in pin straight strands. Green eyes shone with concern. She was both counselor and computer guru, and dedicated her life to living a natural, healthy pathway to happiness. She wore her usual outfit of organic cottons, and spent her free time in yoga classes or with the rescue shelter. "Do you need some chocolate, sweets? I have a Kashi bar in my purse."

Kennedy flashed her a grateful smile. "No, thanks. I'm saving my calories. I'm bummed over the breakup with Sally and Tom. I thought they were perfect together. I hate when I screw up."

Kate tapped her finger against the desk. "We can't be one hundred percent all the time. We'll rematch them and maybe find a better fit."

"I guess." Kennedy pouted. She hated when one of her own matches failed. They all took their jobs seriously, knowing the journey to love was filled with a mix of emotions that included heartbreak too many times.

"Which brings me to why I asked you in here." She swiveled her Apple screen around so her friends could look. "Remember I told you about my neighbor Riley Fox?"

Arilyn nodded. "CEO of Chic Publishing. Named *Fortune*'s woman of the year, gorgeous, smart, and completely kick-ass. Can't believe she still lives in Verily. Aren't her offices in Manhattan?"

"Yes, but Riley prefers to stay out of the limelight. She's been a longtime resident here. I've been trying to convince her for years to sign up with Kinnections, but she always refused."

Kennedy cocked her head. "Riley probably doesn't need us. With her background, I bet finding men isn't a problem."

"Guess again."

Arilyn let out a small sigh as an inner lightbulb cranked on. "Ah, that's the problem, isn't it? Plenty of quantity but little quality?"

Kate grinned. "Her last date drove her to the Ben & Jerry's and a weekend marathon of *Top Chef.* She's thirty-three, and her biological clock just turned on."

"Ticktock," Kennedy said. "Rotten piece of machinery if you ask me. If it was up to me, I would've pulled the batteries long ago."

Kate's lips tugged in a grin. "How many times has Nate proposed this month?"

Her friend grunted. "A few."

Kennedy had found her soul mate and the love of her life in Nate Dunkle, but she was still refusing to surrender to the final step of marriage. Kate was enjoying watching her friend's barriers crash down one by one as Nate first moved in, then dedicated himself to proving marriage wasn't a deadly trap for females.

"Well, Riley has a different approach. I've done her intake, and she's refused counseling and makeover."

"The woman was on the cover of *Fortune*. She doesn't need a trip to the mall," Kennedy pointed out.

Arilyn pursed her lips. "But everyone could use some counseling. What is she looking for, Kate?"

This was where it got delicate. Kate steepled her fingers and stared at her friends. "She was the most thorough client I've ever met with. Knows everything she wants, everything she doesn't, and is so specific I thought we'd never be able to match her. I used that new computer profiling system you built, A, and the craziest thing happened. I got a full match."

Kennedy leaned forward. "Full? You mean, one hundred percent?"

The room grew quiet. The system of matching people with the computer was a delicate balance of science, gut instincts, and social networking. A top-rated match was 80 percent, and they already had three marriages from the statistic. But this time it was different.

Arilyn's face lit up. "That's wonderful. We found her perfect match. Who is he?"

Kate tapped a key and pointed to the screen.

Arilyn and Kennedy gasped in unison.

"Full name: Ryan Dylan McCray," Kate announced. "Preferred to be known as, and called, Dylan."

Arilyn looked pale. "There must be a bug. That's impossible."

Kennedy let out a humorless laugh. "Arilyn's right. Dylan's been with us for over two years now. He's had twelve mixers, five socials, thirty-two dates, and multiple sessions of counseling. He's a Peter Pan billionaire playboy who says he wants a wife, but calls us within twenty-four hours of the first date and tells us there's no chemistry. That's a disaster waiting to happen."

Kate motioned again to the screen. "I know! I checked it numerous times, pulled their files, and manually went over each point. Their personalities are completely contradictory, yet the computer assigns them a perfect match."

Arilyn shivered. "Maybe there's something bigger going on here. The universe is trying to tell us something."

Kennedy walked over to the screen, dropped into the chair near the desk, and began studying the charts and data. "I don't trust the universe, I trust Kate. Why don't you bring them both to the office, lay your hands on them, and confirm whether they're a match?"

Kate groaned. Her ability she termed the "touch" had been passed from generation to generation. She was able to sense an immediate electrical connection between two soul mates. It had been more of a curse in her endless dating years, until she touched Slade Montgomery, a client of Kinnections and her total opposite, and realized they were meant to be together. "Ken, I told you we don't run our business like that. I'm not going to touch every couple and try to match people that way. We rely on our all assets here—we agreed on that point when we opened."

Arilyn chimed in. "She's right. No using Kate for a shortcut. I say we set them both up on a date. They have nothing to lose. If it doesn't work, we know there's a glitch in the system and I'll rework it. If they fall for each other, it's a win-win."

Kennedy scrolled through the numerous pages and finally leaned back in surrender. "Agreed. I've never seen this before. It's almost by being completely opposite they're a perfect match. Bizarre."

"I know. They both attended Cornell the same years, too. Think they know each other?"

Kennedy seemed to ponder the information. "Could be. This gets more and more mysterious, doesn't it?"

"Yeah. My instincts say to go ahead and schedule the date but not give them much information. They both tend to make assumptions early on, and I think meeting blind would be better. No full names or background details. I think they both trust me enough to take the leap."

Her friends both agreed and Kate relaxed. "Good, that was what I figured, but I wanted to check with you both first. I was thinking of setting them up this weekend. Ice-skating in Rinker's Park. It's romantic around the holidays."

"I love ice-skating," Arilyn said dreamily. "It forces couples to be intimate in a natural way."

"Like yoga?" Kennedy quipped.

Arilyn shot her a glare. "Don't knock it till you try it,

Ken. I've reached levels you never even heard of. In and out of the studio." She paused. "And the bedroom."

Kennedy laughed. "I know a challenge when I hear one." She slid off her chair and headed for the door. "Maybe I'll have Nate study Tantric sex and give me a full demonstration. The man is a walking fountain of knowledge." Her grin turned wicked. "In and out of the bedroom."

Kate shook her head as her friend blew them kisses and disappeared. Arilyn fought a grin and got up. "Let me know if you need any help with this one."

"Thanks. Hey, A, when you counseled Dylan, did you find any huge issues I should know about?"

Arilyn looked thoughtful. "No. Weird, because usually billionaire playboys have issues and angst galore. Dylan is charming, funny, and smart. But he seems to be looking for something I can't pinpoint. Has a strong family background and seems like he'd make a great husband or father. I just don't know what's holding him back."

Kate nodded. "Okay, thanks. Girls' night Friday at Mugs?"

"Absolutely."

She watched Arilyn retreat and swiveled back her computer screen. She'd set up the date and hope for the best. Her instincts hummed, as if something big was about to happen. Unfortunately, it could be a premonition of either great circumstance or complete disaster.

Kate prayed for the former and reached for her phone.

chapter 2

. . . .

*R*iley Fox was late.

She despised tardiness.

Trying not to freak out and get all OCD before she went on her first official matchmaking date, she dragged in a breath for calm, and methodically clicked down her list of items to take. Purse. iPhone. Charger. Water. Check, check, check, check.

The snow was steadily falling so she tugged on her leather gloves, buttoned her coat to the neck, and locked the door. Her sleek silver Infiniti was already warmed, and she sighed when her rear slid into the heated seat. Hmm, she knew the general direction, but never made the trek up the mountain. Better get Google Maps ready. The GPS in the car sucked and usually gave her the wrong directions. She clicked on the app, tapped in the address, and buckled her seat belt. Easing the car onto the snow-covered road, Riley headed for her ice-skating date.

Deciding to forgo music for her thoughts, she ignored the slight twinge of nerves in her stomach and wondered if she'd been crazy to agree to this. Riley expected photos, full name, date of birth, social security number, and a checklist of traits her date copped to. Instead, Kate informed her it was a total blind encounter. Meaning she knew his first name was Ryan, he would meet her at exactly 7 p.m. by the gate of Rinker's Park, and he was safe, sane, and cute.

Kate refused to give her anything else.

Normally, that would challenge Riley's competitive instincts to shine and compel Kate to give her more information, but Arilyn backed Kate up by gently reminding her of her inability to take risks in her love life, and how going in without any prior information would open her mind.

Finally, she agreed. But if the man exhibited any violations of her rules she was outta there.

Riley drove through Verily, relaxing slightly as the cheerful lights and festive atmosphere on a cold December night made her feel alive. She'd fallen in love with the upstate river town's artsy appeal and quiet demeanor. Working in Manhattan was amazing—there wasn't a city in the world as vibrant and fast paced, and she thrived on a career level. But personally, she gravitated toward a quirky, calmer type of atmosphere, where she could sip a coffee, window-shop, talk to her neighbors, and pretend she wasn't living for sales reports, auctions, and networking.

Pathetic.

Normally, she wouldn't have cared. Her drive for achievement was something she now lived with and never questioned. Valedictorian in college, a coveted internship in Manhattan at graduation, and years of learning from the best in the business. Finally, she'd been ready to take the leap to create her own publishing business focused on women.

Everyone called her crazy. Laughed. Refused to take her seriously.

Now that same line of rotten men lined up to kiss her ass.

Score.

Riley held back a giggle and took the next turn slow. Her rear wheels slid, adjusted, and pushed on. Damn, this was gonna be a bitch of a snowstorm. The initial reports had called for a dusting, but already huge flakes hit her windshield in kamikaze form, and the faint sound of tinkling ice warned her of the road conditions.

Crap. She was still fifteen minutes late.

Knowing her car could handle it, she calmly pressed the accelerator to make up for some time, keeping her senses sharp to the surroundings around her. She was an excellent driver and had never gotten into an accident. She drove like she did everything else in her life: with a firm capability and a goal toward one thing.

Success.

Men said she had issues. Who didn't? She'd plunged ahead, and except for the occasional sexual affair she carefully plotted out to meet her bodily needs, she never felt lonely. Until recently. Stupid female clock screwed everything up. She was going along quite happily when she'd caught sight of a pregnant woman stroking her belly.

She'd stopped in the middle of a crowded street. The hit of emotion drained her breath and an ache in her heart made her want to wail like a toddler. From that moment, everything changed. Riley looked at couples around her, baby strollers, flashing diamond rings, and she *wanted*. Wanted with her heart, soul, and gut, like she'd never wanted anything before.

She'd called Kate and decided to do something about it.

Work had been the element to drive her forward, but now she was ready to attack her personal life. Finally at the stage she always dreamed to be in her career, she realized lately she was lonely. An empty ache pulsed in her gut. She craved cooking in her gourmet kitchen for someone other than herself. Her three-hundred-count Egyptian cotton sheets were cold with no one to snuggle with. Wasn't it time she finally focused on finding love? Wasn't it finally her turn?

Her past dates had been bitterly disappointing. Always lacking in certain qualities, exhibiting characteristics she refused to bend on. Too lazy, or arrogant, or needy. Not father material. Not husband material. Lacking character or humor or intelligence.

She yearned for a companion to share her life with. Raise a family. Grow old together. Riley knew the exact type of man who'd complement her lifestyle. A man who was serious, hardworking, family oriented. Perhaps a bit conservative, with an ability to be calm and even tempered. She despised fighting or disagreements. She pictured living in harmony with a man who was also her friend.

He needed to fit.

Kinnections was the right choice for her. The detailed questionnaire she filled out confirmed the match would be based entirely on her checklist and requirements. Science, not the fickle dream of fate where lust was mistaken for love and sex for commitment.

She reached the foot of the mountain. The car fishtailed, then straightened. Riley clenched and unclenched her fingers around the wheel. Call and cancel? Was he running late, too, from the weather? She peered through the whipping windshield wipers and judged how much farther up the rink was. Probably not far. Her car was topnotch in bad weather, and maybe it was going to stop soon.

This date could be the *one*. Kinnections was successful, and boasted an extremely high percentage of marriages. Her husband could be waiting on top of that mountain and a bit of snow was not going to stop her from finally meeting him.

She inched her way up and came to a fork in the road. Where was the sign? Why was her iPhone suddenly silent? With a disgusted mutter, Riley grabbed her phone.

No signal.

Crap. Okay, the rink couldn't be far. She mentally recited *eeney meeney miney moe* and took the right. The road emptied and twisted before her, flanked by thick woods.

Huge, gnarled trees bent over and shook in the wind. Icicles dripped from branches and pelted ice drops at her windshield. Why did she suddenly feel like she'd dropped into Narnia? Riley downshifted, curving around another bend, and almost hit the brake at the sight before her.

Massive wrought-iron gates rivaling those in *King Kong* towered before her. Wicked spikes lined the top and blocked a row of ice-encrusted privacy bushes. She caught a glimpse of a towering, multitiered brick fortress as she reached the top of the road, and gently pumped the brake.

The tires caught, spun, and slid to the right. She pulled the wheel in the opposite direction but it was too late.

The rear end fishtailed and dropped her backward over the side incline.

The last thought Riley had was how pissed off she was that she'd miss meeting her future husband.

Then everything went black.

chapter 3

· · · · · · · · · · · · · ·

𝒟ylan McCray stared at the unconscious woman on his couch and wondered if someone was playing a joke on him. After all, he'd just been hand delivered the woman he hadn't been able to get off his mind or his dick for the past decade.

He swore softly and lay a damp washcloth over her forehead. He had no idea if it was the right thing to do, but he'd seen the move in enough films to figure it worked. Thank God she'd been lucky. Other than the bruise on her cheek, she didn't have any bumps or breaks. The car was banged up, but her seat belt and the open ditch filled with snow had softened the blow. He shuddered to think of the circumstances if she'd hit the trees.

Her breathing was deep and even. Her heart rate steady. What the hell was she doing here? He'd decided to close the park once the snow began, so he hadn't expected anyone. He assumed his blind date was canceled. The cell lines were down so he couldn't call Kate, and in some weird type of power move Kate refused to give him a last name, so it wasn't like he could even try and track down the mysterious woman.

He was getting ready to close up the gates when he caught the crash on his security camera. Thank God he'd seen it or Riley could've been trapped overnight. He hoped she didn't have a concussion. He figured worst-case scenario he'd get the snowplow and drive her to the hospital. First, he'd try to wake her up and work from there.

What was the woman doing out in a blizzard? Anger twisted with fear and burned through his system, though he kept his touch gentle. For God's sake, no one was out in this weather. The radio blasted the quick movement of the storm heading their way, and warned everyone to stay home. Of course, if Riley Fox was the same stubborn, frustrating woman she'd always been, no wonder she hadn't listened. She had a God complex. It both fascinated and irritated him.

Besides getting him hot.

His gaze took in her softened features. She hadn't changed. Dark hair with burgundy highlights was swept back from her high forehead and fell in long silky waves to her shoulders. She used to wear it scooped up in a no-nonsense ponytail that bobbed when she walked. Her face was well-defined, which made for an arresting vision that held a man's attention and entranced him to look deeper. He remembered eyes the color of a soft violet, snapping with command and control. Her lips were thin but perfectly formed to a bow shape. Her jaw was too square, her cheekbones too blunt, her nose too sharp, her brows too arched. But all the features put together made her impossible to ignore.

Just as she liked it.

They'd shared a dormitory at Cornell for four years. He still pictured the way she marched down the hallways, backpack swinging, gaze directed ahead with a tunnel vision no beginning college students exhibited. She avoided sororities, beer pong parties, sporting events, and generally any social activity where there was alcohol, sex, and distraction. She graduated with a double major in business management and marketing, a minor in English, worked for the Junior Executive League, school newspaper, and published three articles in featured mass-market magazines.

She was a force of nature, but Dylan suspected underneath she was one big hot mess. Total control freak meets uptight workaholic. They'd almost killed each other when Professor Tagg paired them for the final project in sophomore year. Fifty percent of their grade and he almost quit. Almost.

He was too stubborn to let her win.

Even more so because of the heat between them.

Dylan shook his head at the memory. Unbelievable. One moment he wanted to strangle her, the next back her up against the wall, release the ponytail, and strip off that white prim blouse she always favored. It was almost as if the fighting was a crazy form of foreplay, but she'd die rather than admit it.

So would he.

Still, he'd fantasized that he could push her proper boundaries to make her scream. Beg. Come. For him.

His dick hardened but he shook it off and began pacing. Why the hell did it have to be Riley Fox to turn him into a horn dog? He had tons of money, a good disposition, looks, and a sense of humor. He'd dated so many women it must be in the triple digits, bedded many along the way, and not once had he found the lightning strike.

Maybe he never would.

But already, the air hummed like a live presence, and his blood warmed in his veins. Her scent swam in his nostrils and in his memory. Oranges and jasmine. Some intoxicating mingle of images involving juicy, ripe fruit trickling down his chin, soft floral blossoms, and pure sweetness.

The ridiculous poetry of his thoughts made him groan. Stupid. Her presence just brought back memories and surprised him. The moment she opened her mouth he'd be reminded of their inability to get through a two-minute conversation without wanting to kill each other.

She stirred in her sleep. Dylan walked back over and stared down at her. Was she sleeping too long? Should he wake her? He cursed under his breath and decided to shake her gently. Maybe help her along. He reached over.

Her eyes flew open.

Dylan jerked back from the sudden awakening like a vampire in a coffin. He watched her gorgeous eyes flicker, obviously trying to remember where she was and what had happened. He opened his mouth to calm her. Explain what happened in a soothing voice so she didn't freak out on him.

He never got a chance.

She shot up to a sitting position, hair sliding over one eye, a scowl marring her brows. Her mouth twisted as if she'd either tasted or smelled something bad.

"You."

Her voice slammed him with disdain and ice.

And just like that, Dylan was back in college with a woman who'd pushed every single button he owned and a few he never knew he had.

He treated her to a slow, insolent smile.

"Hey, darlin'. Long time, no see."

The fury on her face from the familiar greeting made him feel a hell of a lot better.

Yeah. Maybe this would be more fun than he expected.

❆   ❆   ❆

When Riley woke, she was struck by blinding white.

At first, she thought she'd died. Heaven was really pretty in a clean Rachel Zoe way. The vaulted ceiling, walls, and lush shag carpet were pure white. An elaborate four-tier chandelier dripped crystals and pearls, adding to the effect of elegance. A huge fireplace framed in marble took up the far end of the room. The sound of snapping logs drifted in the air. She rolled to her side and noticed she lay on a long white sofa, with matching wing chairs of the same color. At least heaven was color coordinated. She'd be so disappointed to be stuck in tie-dye.

Her gaze rose and collided with a pair of stunning eyes. One pure blue. The other a rich brown. A memory deep inside unfurled, and heat bloomed in her belly, spreading through her veins. Impossible. She knew this man.

Dylan McCray.

She struggled for composure, and bolted upright. Dear God, it was him. How was it possible to look better after a whole decade? His hair was still a delicious mix of wheat-colored strands with streaks of white peppered throughout. With that thick and unruly hair, he gave off a surfer vibe. The deceiving halo was a wicked contradiction to his hypnotic gaze that could command a woman to drop her panties in 2.2 seconds. His face was a dance of graceful lines that set off his lips, which had a delicious natural sulky curve. He sported dimples that emphasized his mischievous charm rather than caused him to look boyish. He reminded her of an angel, with a lean, muscled physique. He was Michael and Gabriel reincarnated to seduce women and master men on Earth.

"You."

The word blasted from her mouth in pure shock, horror, and frustration.

Riley stared back helplessly at the man she'd never been able to forget. Heir to McCray Technologies—the billion-dollar computer giant rivaling Sony and Apple for market share with cutting-edge electronics. A playboy who bedded every woman in his path, and graduated with a 4.0 in business management without even trying. A man who believed in fun and frolic before work, owned a wicked sense of humor, and was the sexiest male specimen she'd ever laid her eyes on.

Yeah. She despised him.

He'd literally tortured her throughout college. Stuck sharing a dormitory, with her room a short distance down the hall from his, she spent those years watching him go through every last woman on campus and party his ass off. While she worked and studied nonstop, he gained his A's easily. He never went to the library, never turned a paper in on time, and was the leader in every social activity at Cornell. He was revered by teachers and students, walked on water like the Golden Boy he was, and made it his goal to annoy the hell out of her every step of the way.

Yet . . .

Every verbal battle emphasized a strange connection between them. The sparks when they fought literally whizzed in the air, and he had a way of defusing her ironclad rules with a sense of humor that sometimes even had her struggling to remain serious. They were picture-perfect opposites—doomed to be anything but enemies with a tad of grudging respect mixed in.

Until the kiss.

Riley scowled as the memory hit her hard. She refused to think about that short, weak moment. She'd completely forgotten it anyway. Kind of.

"Hey, darlin'. Long time, no see."

Her temper rose. His Texas drawl may have been hot shit at Cornell, but she knew the truth. He used it on purpose to score, and called every female darlin'. Like they were special. He also knew she despised the lame term with its chauvinistic facets. So, it was to be war from the beginning, huh?

Bring it.

"What are you doing here? Where have you taken me?" she demanded.

That sulky lip curled halfway up. "Your car slid into the ditch. I caught it on the security camera, pulled you out, and now you're in my house."

"Your house?" She studied the room again, remembering the spooky massive mansion rising above the mountaintop. "You live here? In the creepy house?"

A touch of annoyance lit his gaze. "It happens to be historic, and I had the place refurbished. What I find more creepy is you sneaking around my place during a blizzard. Miss me, darlin'?"

Riley managed not to bare her teeth and hiss. "Hardly. I was meeting a date at the skating rink. I have no idea how I got here, I must've taken the wrong way at the fork in the road. My car slid when I reached the top."

"Rinker's Park is the left."

"Great, my fifty-fifty shot failed again. Would be nice if there was a sign."

"You probably missed it in the storm. Must be some date to risk your life for a bit of ice-skating."

She glowered. "I didn't realize it would be this bad. The report said a dusting."

"At 7 a.m. They changed it later this morning. Why didn't your date cancel?"

No way was she letting him know the truth. Blind dates were humiliating to begin with, let alone admitting she had to use a matchmaking agency because she was so hard up. Never. "It's a long story. Listen, thank you for playing the prince on horseback role, but I need to get home. Where's my cell?"

He shrugged. "Probably in the car."

Riley gasped. "My purse? Did you get that?"

"No, I was more focused on pulling your body from a vehicle that could burst into flames. Sorry I didn't check for personal belongings."

His sarcastic wit hit home. How was he able to make her mad at the same time she wanted to laugh? He continuously kept her off balance throughout school until she erected a barrier to keep him at a distance. Usually she figured out exactly what made a man tick, what he wanted, and his strengths and weaknesses. She knew it was a talent that served her well in the business world. With Dylan, she was still clueless.

Okay, plan B. She lifted her hand and touched her scalp. Nothing felt tender. She had gotten lucky.

"How are you feeling?"

She scooped her hair away from her face. "Fine, I just got shook up."

He nodded. "Do you remember everything? You know, where you live, what you do, et cetera."

She rolled her eyes. "We're not in one of those awful chick flicks where I get amnesia and you help me rediscover the beauty of life. Of course I remember everything."

"Good to see you remembered your charming disposition."

Riley was tempted to stick out her tongue but it would be too undignified. Better to focus on getting off this mountain and away from him. "If I can use your phone, I'll take my disposition out of here. I'm sure there are some tow services that come out in the storm."

"Doubt it. Besides, there's no cell service. The telephone lines are coated with ice and the mountain is a death zone. Supposed to get a foot overnight. No one's getting in or out of here till tomorrow."

Worry nipped her nerves. "What about the facility? The employees should know how to contact emergency services. This is a huge skating complex."

He hadn't lost the easy confidence that made students part the hallway to let him through. As if he owned not just the campus, but every room he walked into and claimed. He cocked his head, then offered a faint smile. "Everything's shut down. We closed early and sent all the workers home. There's no one here but you and me, Riley."

No. Way. She stared at his amused look and clenched her fists in frustration. "How do you know so much about the park anyway? You're trapped in an empty building from *The Shining* and completely isolated! I bet if I hiked over there I'd find someone to help me."

She waited for him to sputter out excuses, but he kept staring at her with those kaleidoscope eyes that did very bad things to the sensitive spot between her thighs. He seemed to savor the moment of charged silence.

"Because I not only own this house. I own Rinker's Park." She stiffened, watching as he slowly came toward her and closed the distance. His presence radiated shocking heat and a purpose she didn't want to examine too closely. "I suggest you get comfortable, because you're not going anywhere."

chapter 4

. . . .

$\mathcal{D}$ylan watched her eyes widen. Her face reflected a dozen emotions as she sought to process and organize, probably already planning two forms of attack.

The woman never surrendered easily.

"Let's recap. I'm trapped here alone with you over-night in a spook house. Why are you here anyway? You're supposed to be in some trendy Manhattan condo making your billions."

He smothered a laugh. "Maybe you don't know me as well as you thought. If I give you a tour you'd see the benefits of living here. I have privacy, beautiful scenery, and complete access to the park whenever I'd like. I can also commute easily into the city."

She rose from the sofa and swiped her hands over her black knit pants. The fabric fit snugly over the line of her thigh and curve of her rear. A cheerful red sweater emphasized the same impressive cleavage she had back in college. Dylan used to wonder how her breasts would fit in his hands, then be so freaked by the thought he'd go get drunk. Sequined black fur boots encased her feet. She looked like a sleek snow bunny who needed a tumble. He always wondered if Riley Fox lost all that well-earned control in bed.

An interesting idea to toy with.

She straightened up and propped her hands on her hips. "I have a better idea. You show me where a spare room is, and I'll see you in the morning. Haven't gone to bed early in a while. Extra sleep will be good for me."

His lips twitched. "Sorry, you may have a concussion and I'm not taking any chances. You stay with me."

She waved a manicured hand in the air. "No worries, I'm fine. I can take care of myself."

"I don't care. You're still not leaving my sight."

"You're kidnapping me?" she demanded.

Dylan arched a brow. "Dramatic, much?"

She let out an annoyed breath. He was positive not many people argued with her, or even managed to change her direction. She was bullheaded and determined to do things her way. A spark of challenge lit within. She'd never be an easy woman to live with, but she'd never be boring. "Fine. But I'm drinking. Please tell me you have wine somewhere."

"I happen to have an excellent wine cellar. White or red?"

"Red, please."

He walked over to the elaborate scrolled-iron wine

rack climbing up the corner. He usually took a few bottles out to be handy, so he grabbed a nice French vintage and popped the cork. "Now that we have the whole night, why don't you tell me about this date of yours?"

He felt rather than saw her tense. Hmm. What was she hiding? And why was she on his mountain in a blizzard? Dylan poured two glasses and walked over. Their fingers brushed when she took her glass, and once again, the current of electricity tingled. Her hand jerked a bit but she managed to speak coolly.

"Nothing to tell. We got our signals crossed."

"First date?" he asked.

She hesitated, then shook her head. "No, we've been out a few times. He's quite charming."

She stuck her nose in the glass to breathe in the aroma, then slowly took a sip. He enjoyed the way her lips curved in pleasure, and her eyes half closed. The unexpected sensuality of her reaction made his gut clench and his dick stir. He remembered those moments in college. Living in the dormitory, sometimes she'd come strolling out in the common area with her hair up in a messy ponytail, faded T-shirt, and flannel pants. Face scrubbed free of makeup. She'd sit cross-legged on the rug, joining in the conversation. Dylan was fascinated with her natural beauty, open laugh, and quick wit. She'd meet his gaze with her usual cheekiness, but something else stirred beneath the surface. Most of the time she was removed from the crowd, set apart by her own personal drive for success. But that night he remembered she told dirty jokes, drank a few beers, and relaxed. He was fascinated by the different sides to her personality, and longed for more. But the next time he saw her, she was back to her usual conservative demeanor, refusing to acknowledge they actually had fun the night before. She drove him nuts.

Dylan pushed the memory away. "What's charming's name?"

"Ryan."

Warning bells clanged. Ryan? The enormity of the situation overtook him as he finally processed the truth. Kate had told him she wouldn't provide a last name for his blind date. He never would've agreed to such an insane proposal, but he'd been a client of Kinnections for a long time and Kate had earned his trust. Her ridiculous spouting of being open to the impossible by not letting himself prepare or make assumptions before meeting this mystery woman seemed like a bunch of female fantasies he didn't believe in.

He sifted through his conversation with Kate. His mystery woman would meet him at 7 p.m. at the gate of Rinker's Park. Tall, with long dark hair. That was all he got.

Holy shit.

Riley Fox was his blind date.

"Why are you looking at me funny?" she asked.

The truth almost made him laugh out loud. Oh, this was too much fun. And one thing he remembered well was Riley's inability to lie. Fortunately for him, he was great at it. Dylan frowned and cocked his head. "How odd. I know a Ryan who's quite familiar with the rink. What's his last name?"

She averted her gaze. "Ugh, I forgot. I'm sure you don't know him."

"I think I do. What does he look like?"

She scrunched up her face in her usual revealing way, as if trying desperately to come up with a plausible story. "Brown hair. Blue eyes. Very handsome." She turned her back on him and pretended to inspect the various trinkets by the fireplace.

"Interesting. And you've been seeing him for how long?"

"A few dates."

"What does he do?"

"Do?" She gulped a few more sips of wine. "He's a teacher."

"Sounds like a great guy. What does he teach?"

"Why are you so interested?" A touch of annoyance threaded through her voice.

Dylan tried to keep the glee from showing on his face. "Just am. What does he teach?"

"History."

"Nice. Where'd you guys meet?" Oh yeah, she was stumped on that one. She glared back at him, obviously searching for an answer. "Don't you remember?"

"Of course I remember! A—a café. We both ordered the same coffee."

"Very romantic." He pressed his lips together. "Must not be the same Ryan."

"I told you."

"See, the Ryan I know signed up for his date at Kinnections. But obviously you didn't meet him at a matchmaking agency."

Score.

Her mouth dropped open. She sucked in a breath and stared at him in stunned silence. "Did you say Kinnections?"

"Yep. You know them?"

Her mouth closed with a snap. Suspicion carved out the lines of her face. "Wait a minute. How do you know about Kinnections?"

Dylan rocked back on his heels and grinned. "Because I'm your date."

She blinked. Spent a few moments analyzing the situation in the clinical way that had made her business such a success. "Impossible," she declared. "My date's name is Ryan."

"I know. My full name is Ryan Dylan McCray. Have you forgotten I go by my middle name? I was supposed to meet a woman with long dark hair at the park gate at exactly 7 p.m. Sound familiar?"

Her brows knitted together and her breath accelerated. "N-no. You can't be my date. You'd never belong to a matchmaking agency!"

Dylan shrugged. "Why not? You are. Though you'd deny it to the end. You've always been a terrible liar."

Her cheeks tinged with temper. Excitement heated his veins and roared in his blood. What was it about this woman that made arguing so much damn fun? It was better than going to the gym or closing a big deal. "Because it was none of your business!" She moaned and paced the floor. "This is terrible. A nightmare. I trusted Kate to find me my husband, not some man candy to fool around with."

He laughed with delight. "I'm man candy, huh? Guess I'll take it as a compliment."

"How could they have possibly matched us? This proves their computer system is completely inaccurate. All that time I spent on my questionnaire is wasted. You have none of the qualities I listed. You probably signed up to get laid!"

His reputation in college preceded him, but it had been a decade of change. Somehow, knowing Riley still believed he was the same person bothered him. "I'm looking for my soul mate just like everyone else is. Using a well-known, statistically proven agency to help me find her is a smart business move. I don't like to waste time." He studied her face and the slight flush to her cheeks. "Why are you using them? Thought you'd have dating all figured out now. Shouldn't you be settled with a husband making six figures, two kids, eco-friendly house, and a hypoallergenic dog?"

That got her. She treated him to a withering look, as if he was a bug beneath her feet, and they were off to the races.

God, it felt good.

"Your asinine theory is exactly what I would expect from a man who has Peter Pan syndrome and never looked beyond a double-D cup to amuse himself."

"Darlin', I never discriminate," he drawled. "B's and C's are just fine."

"I'm not your darlin'." She mocked his fake drawl with a syrupy sarcasm he adored. The woman didn't give him an inch. He loved it.

"Okay, sweetheart."

She let out an aggravated breath. "I get it. Kate does the hard work trying to find you an actual intelligent woman to be your life partner, while you continue screwing around with your little playboy bunnies. Quite ingenious. You were always good at pawning off the labor to others."

He clucked his tongue against the roof of his mouth. "Are you still steaming over the A I received in Marketing 101? A B is perfectly acceptable, Riley. Get over it."

She shimmered with rage, clenching her fists. Dylan bet she was barely holding back a stomp of her feet. "Everyone knows you got Tyler to do that for you! He had a bad case of hero worship and would've done anything you asked. You cheated, I know you did."

"No, I didn't. Besides, you were such a teacher's pet and up their ass all the time, it's no big secret why the class resented you. Wrecking the curves, volunteering for extra projects—who does that?"

"Not you, that's for sure! But of course, I had to work for a living. You didn't give a crap, because you were able to step into your father's conglomerate with a starting salary of a million frikkin' dollars because of your last name."

Ouch. The hit hurt, but he didn't blame her. That was the way it looked to everyone, and very few knew how hard he had to work for his father's respect and to eventually get to a top level of decision making. He started at the bottom of McCray Technologies and took years to learn the business and build his reputation. "You're wrong. I didn't start making a million. Not until my six-week probation was over."

The air caught and sparked between them, like a live wire plunged underwater. She literally trembled. With the need to hit him? Or something else? How much fun would it be to put all those delicious emotions to better use?

Like slamming her against the wall and fucking her so thoroughly she had nothing left to say.

There wasn't a woman alive he couldn't charm or finagle a favor from. Except Riley Fox. Four years in Cornell and she'd busted his balls every chance she got, as if his very presence on campus irritated her. He never realized how much fun it was to needle her until graduation came and she was out of his life.

He still thought about the kiss.

Dylan was surprised at how the memory would surface late at night, right before he slid into sleep.

It started as a joke. He'd gotten an A on his organization theory presentation along with a standing ovation. She got an A-minus and seemed ready to murder him, especially since he'd admitted he wrote his speech that morning. She began razzing him about his whore-like tendencies, which he denied. He, in turn, needled her about her control-freak ways in and out of the bedroom, which she denied. And suddenly, in that empty corner hallway, he got a crazy-ass impulse.

Steal a kiss and prove his point.

So he had. He pushed her against the wall and kissed her. And yeah, it had done the job all right. Besides shutting her up, the woman lit up like a ball of fire. His tongue sank into pure heaven, and when they finally pulled apart, they both realized something had changed. Even then, he remembered the raw desire, and the horrifying fear of wanting a woman who drove him apeshit. She seemed to echo his thoughts.

The solution?

They ignored it.

Over the years, he'd caught news of her epic rise in business, and the opening of her publishing firm. He'd seen the cover of *Fortune* magazine and felt sheer pride at her achievement. Many times, he even wondered about contacting her, before he shook off the urge and got back to his life.

But here she was a decade later. He was a different person, and she'd been delivered to him in a blizzard for one reason. This was no coincidence. The whole situation screamed kismet and all that other bullshit.

Because Dylan realized in that moment he wanted her.

She turned up her nose and looked down like a queen to her peasant. "I despise you."

He waved his hand in the air in dismissal. "Don't be silly, you've always been secretly attracted to me. You're probably cranky because you're hungry. Let's go into the kitchen and eat. I have leftover turkey sandwiches."

Riley glared, probably caught between hunger and her need to win the argument. After a few moments, she drained her glass and held it up. "Only if there's more wine. If I'm going to get through an entire evening without hurting you, I need more alcohol."

"I can manage that."

"Good. Let's go."

She walked out of the living room and down the hallway like she owned the place.

Dylan grabbed the bottle of wine and followed, shaking his head.

This was going to be a hell of a night.

❄ ❄ ❄

Riley stalked down the carpeted hallway that seemed longer than the Appalachian Trail, trying not to shudder at the huge portraits canvassing the walls. No way. She'd been to the Haunted Mansion at Disney and she refused to catch the eyes moving. She'd never sleep again.

He followed her, probably waiting to laugh when she walked into some gigantic closet or something, but Riley refused to give him the satisfaction by asking where the kitchen was. She'd eventually find it.

She came into a huge foyer, with a curving staircase and stained-glass windows. How did one person possibly live here? Four arched openings were available. She did the eeny meeny miney mo again, knowing she screwed up the first time, and chose the second doorway.

Nope. The library. Wow, the floor-to-ceiling mahogany bookcases and burgundy Oriental rugs seemed familiar. Hmm, where had she seen something like this before? The room had massive arched windows, and there were leather recliners with afghans draped over the arms and drink tables spaced throughout. And . . . there was another fireplace. Wow.

Dylan's dry voice echoed behind. "We can eat tomorrow if you want to go through all the rooms. Or you can give up and just ask me where the kitchen is."

She hated it, but was afraid she'd never find it on her own. And damn, she was hungry. Riley pursed her lips like she sucked on a lemon. "Fine. Where's the kitchen?"

He treated her to his famous badass grin that always made her stomach do the weird flip-flop thing. "Follow me."

Back to the foyer, and toward the left. She'd never play eeney meeney miney moe again. She sucked.

"Are you some kind of perverted hermit who wants to hole up in this dusty old place and guard his fortune? Because this is a little weird, dude. Are there servants?"

"Yes. And Mrs. Potts would be devastated to hear you call the place dusty."

"That's it!" she screeched. "This place reminds me of *Beauty and the Beast*!"

He laughed. "Still addicted to Disney movies, huh? I was only teasing. I have a maid and a cook, but you won't find a withering rose in the east wing."

She sniffed. "I'll believe it when I don't see it. And I'm not addicted to children's stuff. That one was up for an Academy Award."

"Sure. That's why I always caught you watching those movies on your portable, huh?"

"At least I wasn't watching porno."

"Wonder who was more satisfied."

She stuck her tongue out. His broad shoulders shook

as if he knew. Why did she revert to juvenile gestures around him? She was always so calm and in control of a situation. Even in college, he was the only person who'd cause her to lose it. Sometimes mentally. Sometimes physically. Sharing the common area bathroom and seeing him half naked all the time never helped. How many times had she interrupted one of his make-out sessions? She'd make gagging noises until Dylan would grab the girl's hand and pull her into his room, giving her the smoldering look he believed worked on everyone.

Riley hated the way her body flamed to life. Begged to be the woman in his arms. She'd been able to fight through it until that awful, horrible, wonderful moment between them.

The kiss.

This time, the memory wouldn't be denied.

Senior year. They'd been doing their usual. Arguing about something; hell, she couldn't even remember what it was. One minute they were engaged in a lively argument, the next he pushed her against the wall and kissed her. She never even paused or thought to deny him. Riley kissed him back like she was starving.

She still remembered every sensation, from the scent of cinnamon on his breath, the warmth of his lips skating over hers, the hot, wet thrust of his tongue as it breached her barriers and sunk deep inside. She had no time to think or plan. Instead, her body roared forward and overtook, falling into the kiss full steam, savoring his taste and his hunger, the feel of his hands gripping her waist, holding her still for his pleasure. God how she loved it, the feeling of being out of control yet safe, and for those rocketing moments, nothing existed but Dylan McCray.

Afterward, they didn't even speak. He pulled away, gazed into her eyes, and turned on his heel to walk away. They never discussed the kiss, and sometimes Riley wondered if it had just been a dream. Except she remembered every scorching detail, even ten years later.

She'd lost her virginity with her high school boyfriend, had three affairs, and nothing compared to those few minutes of passion in his arms.

Of course, he'd never remember.

Of course, he'd never know her true feelings about the strength of that kiss.

Riley slammed into his back. He spun around and caught her by the shoulders. "You okay?"

So stupid. No more daydreaming about a ridiculous kiss from college. "Sorry. I'm fine. Just hungry."

"Then let's get you fed."

He walked into the kitchen and she almost had an orgasm. Almost.

She loved to cook. Found it a respite from stress, and adored a good plate of food. Her home was small, but she'd created a haven for her baking hobby, even though most of the times she ate by herself.

But Dylan's kitchen was a gourmet fantasy come true.

Stainless steel everywhere. A Sub-Zero refrigerator. A Wolf oven. A brick oven for pizzas, cappuccino makers, high-grade food processors, with actual copper pots dangling from some crazy gadget over the kitchen island. Endless granite counters, three sinks, and a four-tier spice rack. The room was done in pure black and white with pops of red.

Riley moaned and squeezed her thighs together. Oh, God, the appliances were beautiful. The things she could do here . . .

He was staring at her with fascination and something more. Hunger lit those amazing eyes, darkening the colors to a stormy blue and brown-black. "You like?" he murmured.

She swallowed as her body lit up like a damn pinball machine. She pulled herself together. "I have a thing for stainless steel."

Those full lips twisted in a half smile. "So it's my kitchen you're lusting after? Pity."

Riley rolled her eyes but turned away so he couldn't spot the truth. "Get over yourself. Wasn't nailing my roommate enough? She left the next semester and I got stuck with Smelly Sally for the rest of the year."

Dylan refilled her wineglass and began pulling out ingredients from the refrigerator. She perched on one of the red stools by the island. "Pris knew the deal. Come on, we dated like twice and she said she was in love with me. I never led her on."

Riley snorted. "So that makes it right? You broke her heart and she left to go to another dorm. I told her not to go out with you!"

He lined up the post-Thanksgiving meal with freshly cut turkey, large slices of rye bread, and an assortment of condiments. She watched his graceful fingers put together the sandwiches and tried not to think of the other talented things they could do. He was dressed simply in jeans, boots, and a white cable-knit sweater. The material highlighted the blond in his hair, and made him look like some mythical Thor from above. His sexiness made her crankier. No one should look like that. It tipped the favor to the male species.

She drank more wine.

"You were always a bit obsessed with my dating life," he commented, pulling down two plates. "Or was it my sex life?"

"Just trying to protect the innocent from an expert man whore."

He chuckled and grabbed a jar of pickles. "First time I heard women need protecting from orgasms."

She tilted her head. "Cocky, huh?"

He grinned. "No. Just honest."

Riley refused to let her girly parts go all aquiver. "Or delusional," she muttered.

His eyes lit with amusement. The man was infuriating. "So, tell me what really drove you to Kinnections?"

The wine loosened her tongue. Why hide the truth? She wasn't ashamed. "I want to get married."

His brow shot up. "We didn't even have our blind date yet."

"Not you. Kate was supposed to find me my perfect match. I have a detailed list of requirements, and I'm ready to settle down." She prepped herself for his teasing, but he seemed to be thinking over her statement.

"Why now?"

"It's time," she said simply. "I spent the first half of my life focused on my goals and career and I don't regret it. I gave up things, some opportunities that may have led to marriage and a family. I refuse to have regrets but my priorities shifted. I want a husband. Children."

Dylan nodded. "I can understand that. You launched a successful business, but it takes everything you have. If you had settled too soon, things may not have worked out because you weren't ready to commit completely."

"Yes, exactly. But now I'm focused and know what I want."

He added two pickles to the plates. "Give me the list."

"So you can make fun of me? No way."

"I won't, promise. What's the requirements?"

A nice hazy glow enveloped the stainless-steel kitchen. Why not? She didn't care what he thought. "He has to have a secure job. I want to have a strong friendship first before we go into sex. He needs to want children, be trustworthy, dependable, intelligent, even tempered."

"Even tempered?"

She glared. "Yes."

Dylan cleared his throat. "You'll eat him for breakfast and spit him out for dinner. Darlin', you're a hellcat. You need someone to stand up to you or you'll get bored."

She stabbed a finger at him. "I am not a hellcat! I never lose my temper with anyone but you. I need a companion, father, friend, and general helper to make a successful marriage."

"What about sex?"

"That's not important."

He stared at her in astonishment. "It's the basis of a relationship. Sex bonds two people together."

"Sex doesn't have to fit in the box."

He frowned. "What box?"

She sipped more wine. "You know, the box. When you're ready to settle down with someone and make a life together, it's best to create a sort of mental box where that person can fit comfortably. The box needs to conform with your lifestyle so you're both compatible. For instance, sex is nice but it doesn't have to fit in the box. It's pleasurable, but not necessary."

Dylan reached for the wine and refilled his glass. "Now I need alcohol. You've managed to stump me with this one. Why didn't I know about this box?"

"Because it's my own creation," she said stiffly. "Marriage isn't easy. I don't want to give up my business. I intend to hire more staff, work from home, and be more flexible. But my husband is going to also have to sacrifice, and it's not always passion and games and romance. It's brutal, hard work. And I want that. I want to be exhausted and happy with someone and wake up in the morning and do it all over again, knowing we wouldn't choose differently. Now do you get it?"

"Sex has to be in the box."

She glared. "It's my damn box and I say sex isn't in it. Sex can be in your box."

"What if we have the same box?"

She almost choked on her wine. "We can never have the same box. We're complete opposites."

"Funny, I think we have a lot more in common than you think."

"Yeah? Name one."

"We both signed up with Kinnections for the same reason." He cut the sandwiches in half, looked up, and grinned. "Let's eat in the dining room."

Still reeling from his remark, she grabbed her wine and slid off the stool. "You want to seriously get married?" She trotted after him. "I don't believe you. You're a billionaire, used to parties on yachts and impromptu vacations. You live in the land of the beautiful and fantastical. Domestic boredom and routine would freak you out and you'd run for the hills."

"A complete illusion. You're basing these assumptions on the boy I was ten years ago. Do you think you're the same person from Cornell?"

"Well, no."

"Neither am I. I come from a strong family background. My parents have been married for thirty-four years. I have two sisters, tons of aunts, uncles, and cousins, and it was always a rotating door of people visiting. My grandmother lived with us. When I got home from school, she'd make coffee and I'd sit in the kitchen with her and talk. She told me about my parents when they were young. They grew up together as friends, turned enemies as teens, and married in their early twenties. I know marriage isn't easy because I see what they go through every day. I have no illusions. They run a successful empire so Dad has to travel. Mom gets lonely a lot. And my sister had a drug problem that almost tore us apart. But they love each other."

Riley followed him into the dining room, fascinated by his story. He placed the plates down, turned, and met her gaze head-on. "They're in it for the long haul, and by God, if that's not romance and passion, I don't know what it is. They have friendship, respect, and trust. But sex still needs to be in the box."

Her head whirled. She opened her mouth to say something, then got struck by the magnificence of the dining room. "Holy crap. You do live in the Beast's castle."

The formalized area held a solid marble table over ten feet long—enough to fit King Arthur and all his knights. The runner gleamed gold and silver and spread the entire length. High-backed cushioned chairs spread around the table, and a vase filled with exotic blooms was set in the center. The dark wood floors were bare and held a polished shine. The walls were a soft dove gray and displayed an array of tapestries. A French door lined with burgundy velvet drapes led onto some type of balcony area.

Once again, there was a fireplace. Two candelabras of bronzed gold rested on the mantel. The scent of damp logs drifted in the air, along with the sound of crackling wood.

"Umm, Dylan? How many fireplaces does this place have?"

He tilted his head in thought. "About ten."

"Riiiight." She picked up her plate and placed herself at the head of the table. Why not? She felt like she'd slipped into a fairy tale anyway. Might as well play the part of Belle. His words still echoed in her head, making her heart beat wildly. To imagine Dylan settled down with a wife and family filled her with a sweet longing she didn't understand. It couldn't be true. Maybe he thought he wanted to settle down, but if so, why hadn't he found his wife yet?

"How long have you been a client of Kinnections?" she asked.

He walked over to the fireplace and grabbed the candelabras. "Awhile."

Aha. Now she'd prove the truth of his inability to hold down a long relationship. "But you still haven't found who you're looking for? Doesn't that show you're not ready to settle down?"

Dylan opened the china cabinet drawer and slid out a book of matches. "No. It proves I haven't met her yet."

"But you still trust Kate to find her?"

He swiped the match and struck a flame. Then began lighting the candles. "Yes. I've met many incredible women and enjoyed the dates. All owned traits I want, but none had the spark I'm looking for."

She leaned forward, intrigued. "What spark?"

"The spark of connection. That unknown quality that screams in your gut when something's wrong and something's right. I can usually tell from the first date, so I don't waste their time."

Riley shook her head in amazement. "No. Way. Dating services hook you up by determining similar interests that fit. You're telling me the most important thing to you for picking your life mate is an unknown, mystical, magical spark?"

Dylan replaced the vase of flowers with the candles. He took the chair on the opposite end of the table and picked up his sandwich. "Correct."

Annoyance surged. He couldn't do that. It was a ridiculous way to decide on marrying somebody and made no sense. Of course, Dylan McCray never made sense. Why should she expect anything else?

But a strange longing curled in her belly and bloomed heat beyond. What was wrong with her? Yes, he was hot as Hades and oozed sex like a weapon. Yes, he was funny and witty and intelligent. But he would never fit in her box.

Ever.

"Why are you lighting candles like we're about to welcome more guests? A bit much, don't you think?"

"Let's just say we'll probably need it."

She sighed and dug into the turkey. The moistness of the meat on thick rye bread held the perfect texture and taste. He'd used just enough salt to create a nice bite. So good. Eating turkey sandwiches in such a formal room, with the fire crackling, snow falling, and flickering candlelight *was* kind of cool. Romantic, even. She bet the woman Dylan picked would have a life full of surprises, sharp turns, and excitement. Exactly what she *didn't* want.

Exactly.

As if he heard her thoughts, he spoke up. "Why do you think we're so different?"

Riley snorted and rolled her eyes for double effect. "Duh. Don't you remember Cornell? We drove each other nuts. I'm a planner. I'd be early to class, you were late. I did all my homework, you got people to do it for you."

"I object."

"Overruled. You partied. I studied. You messed up the dorm and made it disgusting. I cleaned it up. Opposites."

As usual, the air charged and energy surged between them. It reminded her of a hurricane wind: warm, seductive, but insanely brutal and strong.

"I think we're the same but approach our goals differently," Dylan said. "You're more of a take-charge, steam-ahead type. You use fact gathering, drive, and sheer will to race ahead of the pack and stay there. Contrary to your low opinion of me, I never inherited McCray Tech. My father told me straight out I wouldn't get a piece of the company just because I had his name. To do that, I needed to carry my weight. That's why I enrolled in Cornell. At graduation, I started from the bottom and worked my way up, which took many years. Only recently have I been officially put on as a legal partner."

Another assumption blown to crap. How was this possible? "But you never studied in college! You never cared about impressing teachers, or acing exams. Partying was your real major. I saw you!"

"Did you?" He dropped his voice. "Maybe you weren't looking too hard."

"I never had to look, Dylan. You made it obvious to the entire campus you weren't interested in academics."

"Yet I got the same GPA as you."

She clenched her wineglass and took another slug. The fact always pissed her off. "I never understood how you managed that."

"I intended to enjoy myself at Cornell, because I knew once I stepped into the business the real partying was over. But I was as serious about my grades as you. I just hid it better."

"How?" she demanded.

His lips twitched. "I don't need much sleep—never have. Four hours is my maximum, I'm just built that way. I studied at night. I also have a photographic memory, so remembering facts and figures is easy. Lucky, I know, but I used it to my advantage."

She wanted to challenge him but he told the truth. She could tell. He'd always been smart, but had she really thought he'd be able to pull off a 4.0 by doing nothing? From one executive to another, she grudgingly had to admit he built his success on his own. Would his father really let him inherit his company if he didn't trust Dylan to run it? Probably not. And she bet he deserved it by working his ass off.

Just like her.

Ah, crap. She'd been kind of a bitch. Riley placed her glass down and met his gaze. "I'm sorry, Dylan. I never knew. You hid it so well."

She waited for his sarcastic retort, but instead he dipped his head, as if bestowing his forgiveness. A stray white-blond strand fell over his brow. His lips curved in a smile. "Apology accepted. I did love my man whore, party animal reputation."

She smiled back. Warmth traveled from between her thighs, up her belly, and flushed her neck. Damn, the fire was getting hot. How was the man able to steal the oxygen in a room just by his sexiness?

They stared at one another for a few moments until finally, he bit into his pickle with straight white teeth. She imagined those teeth nibbling on parts of her body, so she had to down more wine.

"Now that we solved that issue, what other things don't we have in common?" he asked.

She shrugged. "We fight, of course. Fighting is definitely not in my box. I want my spouse to respect my opinions, be calm in all situations, and have patience to think things through a logical sequence before making a decision." She was quite proud of her speech, so when he burst into laughter she wanted to climb over the table and hit him.

"Couples fight, Riley. Life would be pretty dull and boring if no one stood up for their opinions, or completely succumbed to their partner."

"Oh, please. Have you ever been trapped at dinner with a couple who fights? They pick at everything the other does, and you're so uncomfortable you want to die. Last time that happened I had to skip dessert, and I *never* skip dessert. I don't want that type of tension in my marriage."

"We're talking about a different type of fighting. Take us, for example."

"What about us? We fight all the time."

He reached for his wine and swirled it around, as if contemplating the burgundy liquid gave him all the answers. "It's different," he said again. "You challenged me in school. Forced me to defend my beliefs. Made me reach deeper to really examine things, whether it be a business solution or an ethical issue or an opinion. You also pushed me to do better. I have respect for you. I enjoy the fighting, because there's something going on beneath it. Make sense?"

Wow. The words brought a warm glow, but she shook her head. "I disagree. Can you imagine if we were to-gether and had a difference of opinion on everything? That's exhausting and detrimental to a healthy relation-ship."

"After one of our fights, did you ever feel damaged by my words? Disrespected? Undermined?"

"No. Just majorly pissed off."

He grinned. "Me, too. I'm just saying there's different levels of fighting, and ours is more of a part of commu-nicating. Sure, we each got in a jibe now and then, but I never wanted to hurt you."

Riley went over the endless incidents, battles, and ar-guments that made up her years at Cornell. Funny, she never really thought of it like that. But when she stormed off, she was more aggravated he wouldn't do what she wanted. He never took potshots, or bullied, or ever made her cry. Huh. Weird. In a way, it was almost like . . .

Foreplay.

Her eyes widened.

She couldn't stop looking at those lips, wondering if they'd feel the same or she'd be in for a huge disappointment. After all, it was a decade ago, and she'd changed. So had he. Innocence and illusions were gone. The kiss had probably been blown up in her memory as something untouchable. Right?

"Do you believe me, Riley?" His voice caressed her name in a low, deep rumble. Her breath hitched, and suddenly she was burning up in her chair, desperate to touch him.

"Yes."

"Good." Those beastly erotic eyes burned across the table and held her captive. "You know a lot of fighting is well documented to be an indicator of repressed sexual attraction."

Usually she'd treat him to a withering remark, or a derisive snort. Instead, her tongue remained glued to the roof of her mouth. She sat helplessly still in her chair, unable to move.

Because he was right.

There was some type of attraction between them. Maybe lust. He may not be suited to be her husband, or fit in her box, but Dylan McCray made her want. Bad things. Dirty things.

They were stuck together overnight, while a blizzard raged outside. She was a bit tipsy from the wine. They dined in a gorgeous room with a cozy fire. All the pieces slid together, and in that one blinding instant, she wanted to give herself this one night. If she offered, would he take her up on it? Was every step of banter up to now leading to this?

One night of reckless passion and abandonment. Her skin tingled from the thought. Did she dare? Her mind spun with the possibilities, caught on the precipice of impulse and reasoning, and then the final, irrevocable element locked in her decision.

The lights went out.

chapter 5

· · · · · · · · · · · · ·

*S*omething was happening.

The lights snuffed out and Dylan was left in the dark, sporting a mental fog and a massive erection. She completely entranced him with her quick-witted dialogue, more intoxicating than whiskey and more of a turn-on than a *Sports Illustrated* cover model.

The memory of her as a young girl was a faint shimmer of the woman she'd become. Magnificent. How many dates had he been on and been disappointed? Too many to count. Always needing more . . . wanting more . . . yet not able to figure out what the elusive element was.

Until now.

Riley was spit and vinegar, smart and sassy, and he wanted her. Under him. Over him. In his house, and his bed.

Tonight.

Dylan finally managed to speak. "Guess those candles were a good idea after all."

Her husky laugh stroked his ears and other places. Shadows fell on the wall and played. Her silhouette from the fire and candlelight illuminated her in a fiery glow. The thoughts of what he wanted to do with her, to her, made his gut clench and his dick stretch uncomfortably against his jeans. Now he just had to convince her to play.

Dylan rose, taking one of the candelabras to the other end of the table. "Are you okay?"

She tilted her head. God, she was beautiful. The burgundy in her hair, the soft violet of her eyes, the redness of her lips. The deep V neck of her sweater tempted him to taste the tender flesh there, pull down her sweater to bare her breasts. Suck and bite her nipples until she grabbed his shoulders and cried out his name.

She seemed to catch the vibe in the air and trembled. So close. Her barriers were shifting, opening, allowing just a tiny access point where he intended to jump right in. Timing was everything.

Yes, she was just as aware of him as he was of her. They'd always had a strange physical chemistry that battled with their verbal and mental clashes. Maybe that's what made it so damn hot.

"For being trapped in spook mansion with no lights in a blizzard? I'm peachy."

"I have a backup generator. Need to go put it on."

She stretched out her legs with a languorous air and propped one elbow on the table. "I don't know. It sets the mood."

Dylan stiffened. Was she flirting? He'd planned on trying to seduce her, but Riley Fox always seemed to switch things up. He got off on trying to anticipate her next move. "Mood, huh? We spoke about everything else. Maybe it's time we talked about the kiss."

Ah, he'd managed to surprise her. His skin tingled with anticipation. They'd been dancing around each other all night, and it was finally time to get honest. The tension tightened a notch. Her scent enveloped him in a mix of exotic musk and a touch of jasmine—kick-ass and powerful—and not the least bit subtle. Just how he liked it.

He wanted her. There was a reason she was trapped in his house on the night of a blizzard. Kinnections had matched them. It was a sign, and he'd spent most of his life listening to his gut to balance the logic in his head. Too much logic and control caused mistakes. Too much impulse and freedom caused sloppiness.

Balance equaled success.

Riley had it all along or she'd never been able to build her business. Somewhere on her journey, she trusted her gut to make bold decisions that didn't make sense on paper. He knew well the ugliness out in the world when dealing with money and power, and no one came away without disillusions. She'd taken hers and made herself stronger. Every part of her fascinated him, and he intended to plumb the depths tonight.

She tapped a finger against her glass. "Surprised you remembered."

"What if I told you I still dream about that kiss?"

"I'd say I barely put a blip on your radar. You were always happy to move on to the next pretty face and good set of boobs."

"You're right. I was too young, raw, and ambitious. I wanted to savor every flavor life threw at me, suck the nectar dry, and have no regrets. And I don't, Riley. Except for one."

"What?"

Without breaking her gaze, he dropped in front of her, his hand resting lightly on her knee. Slowly, he parted her legs and knelt between them. Her harsh indrawn breath drifted to his ears in a symphony. Dylan reached out and grabbed a tendril of hair, sliding it between his fingers from root to tip, enjoying the feel of raw silk wrapping itself around him in a tight bind. The thought of her gorgeous hair wrapping around his dick as she pleasured him made a low groan rumble from his throat.

"You," he said simply.

Shock mingled with an arousal she couldn't hide, evident in her wide eyes, the tightening of her nipples, the way she squeezed her thighs together mercilessly, as if desperate to keep him from scenting the truth. Dylan bet if he slipped his hand beneath her panties he'd find her wet and willing to do whatever he wanted. The key was getting her mind on board with her very delectable, sensual body.

He sunk both hands into her hair, holding her firmly at the nape of her neck. "That kiss haunted me. Do you know how many times I jerked off to just the memory of your lips over mine, your taste against my tongue? How badly I ached to lay you naked on my bed and take everything you'd give me? Bring you so much pleasure you'd scream and beg me to stop? To continue? To fuck you so thoroughly there's not another man on the planet you'd be able to touch without thinking of me?"

A shudder wracked her body. He waited for her reaction. Would it be retreat? A scathing remark meant to barb and push? A flirtatious, frustrating cat-and-mouse game?

Instead of retreat, she leaned in, so her breath struck softly against his lips. The heat between them pulled and tantalized. Dylan clawed for control, when all he wanted was to take her mouth, strip her naked, and see how many orgasms it would take to finally get her to surrender. He hoped a lot. He planned on it.

"What makes you so sure I remember it?" she drawled against his mouth.

His dick wept for mercy. The primitive male in him roared to take her and show her the truth. Instead, with an inch between their lips, he smiled real slow.

"I'm betting you thought about that kiss, too. Late at night. Under the covers. Wet and aching for me. Let's finish what we started. Let me take you to my bed."

In his wettest, wildest imagination, Dylan never would've believed the woman could raise the stakes so high and so fast. Yet, in typical fashion, she managed to blow him away.

Her voice was a husky whisper of smoke and temptation. "Why? I see a perfectly good table in front of you." His hands tightened brutally in her hair. "Do you have the guts to use it?"

Dylan waited a full beat. Two.

Then slammed his mouth over hers.

❄   ❄   ❄

The world tumbled in slow motion, then stopped for a brief moment. Her blood rushed in her veins, wetness seeped between her thighs, her pulse pounded with a mad glee, and then he kissed her and it was all over.

She was lost.

A low moan ripped from her throat at contact and his tongue plunged deep. Completely raw, with little finesse and all dark hunger, he invaded her mouth.

The past and present blurred together, but this time, there was no retreat. Meeting him halfway, their tongues tangled and fought in a sensual dual she was happy to lose. He claimed and plundered, pressing her back over the chair until she was stretched out and he loomed over her. His other hand cupped her breast, flicking the tight bud of her nipple. She gripped his shoulders and arched against him, asking for more, and without breaking the kiss, his hand slipped underneath the V neck, under the lace of her bra, and hit bare skin.

Oh, God. It felt so good, his fingers tweaking, causing a lightning bolt to hit straight to her clit, which was so full and desperate for pressure. Never had her body lit up so fast, with just a kiss and simple touch. Usually it took awhile for foreplay to get her going, but holy crap, she was going to come right now if she could just lift her hips a bit and rub—

"Don't think so, my little hellcat." He murmured the words against her lips, pausing to bite, then suck. "I waited ten years to have you. I'm not letting you get off on a quick rub in the chair."

She should be completely embarrassed, but Riley was beyond caring how she got there. She wasn't into casual sex or one-night stands—she was on the hunt for a husband. But right now, tonight, the need in her body hurt too much. Her hunger reached beyond any type of rationality. Riley craved the hard fall of the unknown, living the fantasy of becoming his lover for one night. Plenty of time to restock and get her plan back in order tomorrow. She tugged harder, trying to lift her ass higher. "You win. I want you."

He chuckled low and dirty. "Oh, baby, you're still gonna pay."

Shivers raced down her spine. He teased her nipple, flicking it back and forth, until it was so taut and swollen she knew one swipe of his tongue could take care of the agony. "I didn't do anything."

He broke the kiss and looked deep in her eyes. "You did everything. You just don't know it yet."

The words made no sense, but he gave her no time to ponder. He lifted her up and pressed her down on the dining room table. With deft motions, he moved the empty plates and her wineglass. Her legs dangled over the side, her back supported by the marble. Riley waited for the frantic pull of clothes, the feel of skin on skin, the mad rush toward orgasm that usually accompanied a passionate encounter. Instead, he towered over her at the edge. With his exotic, simmering gaze trained on hers, Dylan smiled, telling her immediately he was in no rush.

Oh, God, he was going to kill her.

He toed off his shoes and pulled off his sweater with one easy motion. His skin gleamed in the firelight, a beautiful golden brown, with well-defined pecs and biceps. A line of light hair traveled down washboard abs and disappeared into his jeans. Her fingers fisted to unsnap, rip them off, and feast. Riley was just about to jump him when he moved out of reach.

"Stay there. Don't move."

He grabbed one of the candles and disappeared, coming back with a few wrapped packages he placed beside him. Oh yeah. Condoms. Thank God he remembered, because her mind had become putty, just like her body.

Without a word, he pulled off each of her boots, rubbing her foot through the stockings in a slow massage. As he pressed into her instep, she swallowed a moan and kicked her leg a bit so he'd get on with the more important parts. Her body throbbed for relief, but he took his time with each foot, then gently let them sway back, dangling in midair.

"Dylan?"

"Yes, darlin'?"

"Umm, we started at a good pace there, but things have slowed."

A glint of white teeth flashed. "Ever hear the motto 'it's all in the journey and not the destination'?"

"Yeah. I always thought that was bullshit." She scooted an inch down and wiggled her hips. "Getting to goal is a good thing." The thought of a mind-blowing orgasm with her secret fantasy had all her circuits firing. She enjoyed sex, but found her mind was way too involved, so she did best with a quick, intense session that got her to climax. Riley had accepted her limitations and issues a long time ago, and though many times she wished to be less complicated, she also realized it was easier to accept and move on than try and fight her natural inclinations.

"What if I told you I intend to change your mind?" He played with her ankle, slipping his fingers under her pants and rubbing her calf. Damn, the man could've been a massage therapist and made a million. Her muscles flexed while he kneaded, then caressed the back of her knee. Bolts of pleasure streaked through her. "What if I told you I don't intend to let you get to goal until you're begging me?"

Uh, yeah. Good try. But she was so hot right now, as soon as he got close for any friction she'd take care of herself. Besides, he didn't know about her issues of nonstop mental chatter. Still, she smiled. "I'd say good luck."

His grin was very smug and very male. A shiver of warning trickled down her spine. She'd never begged for anything in her life, especially for a man to satisfy her. She didn't intend to start now.

Dylan leaned over and skated both hands higher, pausing right underneath her thighs. He squeezed hard, and her hips lifted unconsciously. "I'm going to love every moment of this." With one deft movement, he gripped the material of her pants and pulled them off her. The white lace of her panties was already past damp, but when she tried to close her legs an inch, he lifted her legs high and placed them on the edge of the table. Far apart.

Riley sucked in a breath, feeling exposed everywhere. His hot gaze took in every inch of her skin, lingering on her most private parts, until a secret thrill began to build. Something dark and dirty stirred to life. A man never took the time to study her body with such razor intent, as if dying to ravish, taste, mate. She trembled, not knowing what to do with the crazy feelings beginning to surge.

"So pretty," he murmured, tracing one index finger over the elastic, skimming over the front so she struggled to remain still. "So wet. But not enough. Not yet."

His talk shocked her. Men didn't talk . . . like that. Did they? And why did she like it? Dylan leaned over, and she released a sigh, waiting for the final barrier to be off and feel him inside her.

Instead, he lowered his mouth and pressed kisses over her thighs with a leisurely intent that told her he was in no rush. His tongue lashed out at her, tasting the sensitive skin of her inner thigh, knee, calves, and slowly back up. Her mind spun and grabbed for purchase, but there was no logic. She tried to grab his head and urge him upward, but he ignored her. A nibble here, a lick there; his hands consistently roved, pushing up her sweater and dipping into her belly button, squeezing her hips, playing with the damn elastic of her panties until a whimper broke from her lips.

Finally, he inched his way back up. The heat of his skin burned into hers, and with the same easy pace, he pushed up the sweater, propped her up, and guided it over her head.

"You taste like I imagined. Exotic. Sweet."

Her voice sounded like sandpaper. "Orange blossom body lotion."

"And jasmine."

"Yes, that's in there, too. Dylan, what are you doing?" Her eyes begged him to give her the orgasm and stop the torture, but the wicked grin that tugged at his lips told her he had other plans.

"Everything. By the time I taste your pussy, you'll beg me to let you come against my tongue. And I'll demand it, Riley. Every last bit of it is mine."

Filthy. Words like this had never been spoken to her, but she grew wetter, and her skin itched with such sensitivity she rolled back and forth in an effort to soothe. He laughed, cupping her breasts through the sheer white lace that matched her panties. Her nipples were already hard and aching, desperate to be released from their prison, but he just dipped his head and began licking her through the material, scraping his teeth over the sensitive nub again and again until a low scream built at the back of her throat. His erection behind his jeans seemed massive, pressed against her swollen core, and she half lifted to press against him. His teeth nipped sharply against her nipple and she cried out. The pain lashed and turned to excruciating pleasure, forcing her head to thrash back and forth. Too much. It was all too much.

"I can't do this," she moaned. "It's taking too long."

Dylan unsnapped her bra and cupped her bare breasts, lifting them up to his mouth. "It's never enough. Not for you. Don't know what dickheads you've been with, but 'wham bam thank you ma'am' is not your style."

"Yes! It is!"

His lips closed around her nipple and he sucked. She held on to him in a fierce grip, arched upward, burning alive to satisfy the ache between her legs and the need for this man to take all of her, any way he wanted, over and over and over.

"Open your mouth for me, Riley." His eyes seethed with demand and lust. "Now."

His tongue surged between her lips and she almost wept with the pleasure. He plundered every last secret, then softened the pressure so he could play. The dual effects of hard and soft, rough and gentle, slow and fast, broke down her mental barriers and left her with nothing.

Just freedom.

By the time he broke the kiss and moved his way back down her body, Riley was ready to surrender. "Oh, please," she whispered. "Please."

"Better. You're almost there." He tugged off her panties and laid her bare for his gaze. "Do you know how long I fantasized about tasting you here?" He dragged a finger over her dripping slit, lightly playing on her clit, and Riley writhed with a dark need to let him do anything. "Is that what you want?"

"Yes!"

"Ask me, Riley. Beg me."

"P-p-please kiss me there."

"Where?"

Shame burned within but she was past caring. "Please kiss my pussy. Please lick me."

"Beautiful. You're so beautiful, you were made for this. For me." He cupped her ass and lifted her up for his mouth. The first wet swipe of his tongue caused a long wail to escape her lips. He avoided her clit, once again taking his time, murmuring terrible, dirty words about her pussy, curling two fingers and plunging inside her at the same time he licked her clit, so lightly and gently Riley felt the last of her sanity shred.

"Dylan, please! I need—I'm begging!"

Without hesitation, he increased the pressure and pounded three fingers into her weeping channel.

She came apart.

The climax tore through her, stole her breath, and ripped her to pieces. She screamed and bucked beneath him, but he never stopped, dragging the pleasure on and on until she was a shivering, trembling mass of exposed nerves.

Riley collapsed, boneless. The hiss of a zipper cut to her ears. The rip of a wrapper. And then he was dragging her down the length of the table, her legs spread wide, feet propped high on his shoulders, completely open to anything he wanted to do.

His cock paused at her entrance. Pushed in an inch. Another. Slowly, he filled her completely, taking everything she had without apology. She stretched to accommodate him, relishing the tightness, and when he was buried deep within her, he interweaved his fingers with hers.

His voice broke. "It's you. Why didn't I realize? It's always been you."

She had no time to process the words or their meaning. He withdrew all the way, then slammed himself fully back, sheathing his throbbing dick to the hilt. Again. Again. Again.

The ride was wild, long, choppy, thrilling. The second climax shimmered just out of reach, the feeling of him taking over her body, his hips working in a primitive dance, sweat drenching their skin, over and over until—

Riley broke apart, dimly noting him following her over the edge. She gripped his hands as her only anchor, his weight pressing her against the table, until they collapsed.

She closed her eyes.

Her mind was completely and blissfully empty.

chapter 6

· · · · · · · · · · · · ·

*H*ad he died? Nope, his body ached a bit. He was getting older and he couldn't remember the last time he'd had sex on a table. Of course, he'd never be able to eat here again without thinking of her.

Her voice drifted to his ears. "That may have been worth the ten-year wait."

Dylan chuckled and nibbled on her neck. So sweet. She was still shaking slightly from the string of orgasms, making him want to do the whole thing over again. And again. "Brat. Is sex back in the box?" He eased off of her and disposed of the condom.

"No. I told you it can't be."

"Foreplay? Oral?"

She gave him that adorable glare that always turned him on. "That's included with sex."

He turned to go stoke the fire. Curious, he wondered what else she thought she had to have in a husband. So far, her list was way off. She'd destroy a mild-mannered accountant who did anything she said. Dylan shuddered just at the thought. She bored without a challenge, and to him, love and marriage and kids was the ultimate goal to conquer.

"Tell me what else you see happening in this fictitious perfect future of yours?" he asked.

She eased to a sitting position, her naked body a gorgeous silhouette. "So you can make fun of me? Hell no."

He threw up a hand in a Boy Scout gesture. "Promise not to make fun."

Her lower lip jutted out in a hint of a sulk. He walked back over and kissed it off her, until her hands gripped his shoulders and her nails dug in hard. Damned if she wasn't making him hard again.

"Fine. I'm going to sew all my children's clothes. And knit. I'll make the afghans and do little booties for the boy and two girls I'll have."

He stared at her and waited for the punch line. Never got one. A wild laugh scratched at his chest, dying to escape, but he battled it back. Barely. "You told me you flunked home economics in high school. You hated it, Riley. You'd go apeshit if you tried to sew."

She gasped and pointed her finger at him. "See! I told you! I'm going to like it this time. Crochet is in my box. And my husband is going to do all the maintenance around the house. Mow the lawn, fix the plumbing, maybe help build an addition."

He pressed his lips together. His eyes began to tear. "Don't you make a crap load of money?"

Her brows knitted in a frown. "So?"

"Why the hell does he have to do that shit if you can hire out? Aren't you going to be running Chic Publishing? You gonna take up yoga next?"

Her stony silence was answer enough.

No. Fucking. Way. With her temper? She used to tell him that sitting still with her own thoughts for too long made her want to jump off a cliff. Riley had boundless energy, was a classic multitasker, and craved multiple goals and projects going on simultaneously. This time he couldn't help it. He burst into laughter. "You're nuts. I'll pay to see you try and sit cross-legged and be quiet for five minutes. Hell, one minute and you'll be opening your mouth to speak."

She jumped off the table and pushed him. "Yoga is in my box! I want to bring a measured, balanced energy into my life, and yoga is the key."

Dylan wiped at his eyes. "Sure, darlin'. I just think it would be easier if you recognize your true personality and find someone who will fit, rather than try to change. Like me. I bet I'd fit in your box. That's the reason Kinnections matched us."

She sucked in her breath. "Not possible. Especially if you're not on board with knitting, yoga, and friendship before sex."

He couldn't help it. She was so damn cute when she got riled up. He grabbed her hair and kissed her hard and deep and long, until she grew quiet and malleable. His blood sung and roared in victory. He was the only one able to tame Riley Fox. Now he had to prove it to her before the morning came.

"I'm going to turn on the generator so we can get the lights back on. Stay here. And don't put on clothes."

With one last kiss, he grabbed a candle and went out to the hallway. He took the staircase down to the control room, then after a few minutes got the generator running. The lights flicked on and he came back upstairs, ready to go for round two and three with the woman who had exploded back into his life.

She was wrapped in the dining room runner.

The gold and silver covering made her look like a yummy Christmas gift ready to open. Seeing her in full light—the rich texture of her hair spilling over her shoulders, the soft, flawless skin, the plump, swollen lips—took his breath away.

"God, you're gorgeous," he murmured. A slight flush traveled over her cheeks and upper chest. "Why are you wearing a tablecloth?"

Those extraordinary eyes narrowed and sparked. She spoke with pure haughtiness. "Because I don't do naked."

He gave a wolfish grin. "Covering you up should be a crime. I'll have to convince you."

He came forward but she jumped back, her hands clasping the edge of the runner. "No! I mean it, Dylan, I refuse to be so uncivilized."

Amusement cut through him. She was so much fun. "Is this also in the box? Civilization and covering up what I just touched and tasted?"

Her composure never faltered. "Correct. I should've never told you about my box."

"Suit yourself, darlin'. Come on, I want to show you something." He stalked over to French doors and pulled back the heavy curtain. He felt her glare at his bare back, but also knew she was staring at his ass and enjoying the view.

"What about you?" she practically squealed. "You need clothes."

He arched a brow. "I'm comfortable being naked. Do you have a problem with that?"

He noted the high flush of her cheeks and the hungry stare. Oh yeah, he had her good. "Yes, I do," she said primly. "I can't concentrate."

Dylan winked. "I don't want you to concentrate. Now get your gorgeous behind over here."

"Fine." She huffed out an annoyed breath and stomped over in her bare feet. The elegant cloth trailed behind her like a queen's robe. Dylan unlocked and pulled open the French doors. He tucked her into his chest, then she leaned forward and peered out over the balcony.

Then gasped.

It was sheer magic. A winter wonderland children dreamed of. His home sat on top of the mountain with the perfect view overlooking Rinker's Park. Pine and evergreen trees flanked the entire skating rink and edged the park, encrusted with thick layers of ice. Fat flakes fell down slow upon the scene. The skating rink could be seen in the distance, safely covered by the roof, and the painted horses in the elaborate carousel looked frozen in time. White icicle lights wrapped around the park and twisted through the trees.

This was the reason he'd bought the park. Besides the privacy he desperately needed, and his love for living in a natural isolation, there was something about the place that brought back an elemental piece of innocence left behind. It made Dylan remember what was important, what he wanted from life, and the constant struggle for balance. For a little while, overlooking the scene with the snow and fire behind him, with Riley held in his arms, he reached perfection.

"It's so beautiful," she whispered, as if not wanting to break the spell. "And this is all yours?"

"Yes." Pride rang through his voice. "It's mine."

She shivered in the wind, but he felt nothing but the burning heat of her skin against his. The surge of possession rose through him like a tsunami and crashed. He practically shook with need for her again. To claim, push, torment, pleasure. Half dazed with want, he turned toward her and lowered his mouth to hers.

❄   ❄   ❄

Damn the man.

How could she enjoy the view or think about anything except how good he looked naked? His body was spectacular, from the dusting of golden hair, toasty skin, lithe muscles, and the hard, taut muscles of his ass flexing as he walked. He wore his nakedness like his clothes, confident, comfortable, and a screw-you attitude if you didn't like it.

There wasn't a woman in the world who wouldn't like it.

Need overcame her. She shuddered with raw emotion, feeling as if she wanted to climb inside him and experience everything he had to give. When he kissed her, she surrendered. Sliding her arms up around his shoulders, he pulled her in for more, gently sipping from her lips and then pushing his tongue inside to deepen the kiss. Riley floated, anchored to Earth by only him, and wondered if this night would ruin her forever.

He broke away, breathing hard. His eyes flashed with hunger. "I need you again."

Riley didn't answer. Just held on tight when he scooped her up and strode up the stairs and into his bedroom. She caught the barest glimpse of a huge sleigh bed, dark wood, thick carpet, and another fireplace before he stripped the tablecloth off her and pulled her in tight. They were gloriously naked, breast to chest, hip to thigh, mouth to mouth.

They feasted on each other, hands exploring, tongues tangling, until his very breath and taste and scent was imprinted not only on her body but on her soul. When she sank to her knees in front of him, taking him fully in her mouth, he groaned with an animal wildness that spoke to that hidden place in her. Crazed with the need to make him lose all control, she cupped him, stroking his steely length, running her teeth gently down the front of his cock. Dylan chanted her name, hands fisted in her hair, and when he finally released, she took all of him, milking out his orgasm until he shuddered under her, completely surrendering.

Riley waited for a normal recovery time, but he pushed her to all fours on the bed, fit himself with a condom, and began gently rocking his partial erection against her wet core. Riley groaned, pushing back, but he was back under control. Teasing her with his cock, he played with her breasts, pinching her nipples until they were hard and swollen. Sinking in a few inches deeper, he moved his hands lower, stroking her belly, clit, labia, giving her a little bit more of him at a slow, steady pace.

The relentless pressure of her oncoming orgasm made her his slave. She begged, rocked her hips, desperate for him to claim her completely, and as if he realized what she needed, he grasped her hips hard and slammed into her.

Riley cried out at the exquisite fullness. Keeping a brutal, fast pace, he took her with a savagery that engulfed her, as if desperate to mark her again as his, and she reveled in the knowledge that their lovemaking wasn't close to being pretty, or elegant, or surface, but a give and take of basic, primal needs and wants that ripped away all civility.

Her skin bruised under his grip; her fingers ached as they twisted into the mattress; her muscles screamed with use. None of it mattered in the drive for release, and when his fingers finally slipped over her clit to pinch hard and release, she went over the edge.

A sob caught in her throat as everything inside of her emptied out and shattered. He was there to hold her when she collapsed, murmuring tender, nonsensical words in her ear as she came down from the wicked heights of pleasure, and for that one instant she knew she was safe.

Time had no meaning. Was it seconds? Hours? Finally, he rolled over, kissing her temple, pushing back her hair, and whispered in her ear.

"Are you ready?"

She groaned. No way. Riley couldn't have another orgasm—she'd die. She shook her head. "No."

"I'm taking you anyway."

"I need a nap. A rest." She pushed weakly against his chest.

"Such a dirty mind. I'm taking you somewhere else."

"Where?"

His grin was wolfish and wicked and sexy as hell.

"Skating."

chapter 7

· · · · · · · · · · · · ·

$\mathcal{H}$e loved the way she blinked with a heavy languor and stretched out, her glorious body free from covers and open to his gaze. She practically purred with satisfaction, and the fact he gave it to her made him feel like Rocky fucking Balboa.

"I don't understand."

His lips twitched. "I'm taking you ice-skating. Come on, I have another set of snow pants and ski jacket."

Those swollen lips pursed in a pout. "Outside? There's a blizzard in case you've forgotten." The ping of ice pellets against the windows tinkled in the air. Dylan pressed a kiss to her forehead and got up.

"Good, that's the best time to see it."

She shook her head, all that dark messy hair swinging over her bare shoulders. "I don't know. Doesn't seem very reasonable." She tried to crawl back under the blanket. "I already saw the rink from the balcony."

He laughed and reached over her, sliding out the bureau drawer. "I think you need a bit of motivation."

"That type of motivation will keep me from walking normal tomorrow."

"Hmm, you really do have a filthy mind. As much as I'd love to take up the challenge, I was thinking more of sugar."

Riley peeked from under the sheets. "Sugar?"

He slid out a king-size, bittersweet dark chocolate bar and peeled back the foil. Then broke off a square. "Open up." A shudder wracked her body. Her lips parted and he placed the chocolate on her tongue. He watched as she moaned and half closed her eyes in pleasure. Damn, the woman was so sensual. "Good?"

"Heaven. I shouldn't be surprised you keep chocolate in the bureau. You used to hoard those snack-size Hershey's bars. I still remember cleaning up endless wrappers in the dorm."

He shrugged and popped a square into his mouth. "Never know when you'll need a lift. Worked for us. Do you still eat buckets of Lucky Charms when you're stressed?"

She stared at him with surprise. "You remember that?"

"Of course. I'd find those little bags filled with cereal around finals. You always ate the marshmallows first."

"They're the best part."

They finished eating in satisfying silence. When she was done, he carefully rewrapped the bar and stuck it back in the drawer. A tiny smear of melted chocolate stuck to her lip. Dylan leaned over and kissed her, swiping the last of the sweetness on his tongue. She felt so soft and warm and willing in his arms, as if she'd always belonged there. He pulled away with regret. "Now we're ready." He ignored her groan, walked to the closet, and began pulling out items. "I promise it will be worth it."

She grumbled under her breath, but he caught her half smile.

He threw a few items onto the bed and donned a pair of snow pants and a thermal shirt. "Make sure you put on the socks to keep your feet warm. Be right back."

Feeling like a kid on Christmas, he went downstairs to the basement and took the tunnel to the mechanics room. He spent a few minutes turning on the switches and setting things up. After carefully checking all circuits, he headed back to the main house and his bedroom.

She was dressed and ready to go. Those violet eyes brimmed with curiosity, but she crossed her arms in front of the overly large jacket. "I feel like a stuffed sausage. Have I told you I'm not crazy about surprises or impulsive decisions?"

"Another item that should be in the box. You need a man to challenge you. Push boundaries. Urge you to try new things."

"I don't think I like skating," she grumbled.

Damn, she looked cute. His clothes swallowed her up, but she'd be warm and dry, which was the goal. "You will. Let's go."

She clomped behind him in too-heavy boots, and

he led her downstairs, through the darkened hallways in the secret tunnel, his gloved hand firmly enclosing hers. "Dude, if I didn't trust you this whole thing would reek of a B horror movie set."

"Nothing to worry about. I already ripped your clothes off and ravished you."

"Oh yeah, cool."

The door opened. Massive machinery hummed and buzzed, but Dylan didn't pause. Finally, they stepped outside onto a large open terrace that was barely lit.

The whip of the wind scratched like icy fingernails against his cheeks. They ducked their heads and he increased the pace. "Just a little more."

"It's cold! There must be a foot already out here and it's still not stopping. Dylan, maybe we could dump this plan and drink some hot cocoa without our clothes again because this is a bit— Oh my God."

She stopped short. He took in the scene before him with full satisfaction. Yes. This was the reason he'd bought the park. This was what he needed to show her.

The bare trees lined the view of the hills and set off the large circular skating rink as if cradled between mother nature's hands. Endless white lights twinkled in a vision of blinding light, twisted in the branches. A large Christmas tree gaily decorated stood in the center, a miniature version of Rockefeller Center. Christmas carols streamed from the speakers. Soft, pure white blanketed every spare inch of ground, and crusted ice threw out a thousand rays of light, like a diamond showing off in all its glory. An elaborate roof covered the main rink and gates around it, protecting the precious ice from any type of weather conditions and allowing patrons to use it during inclement weather. Sure, it cost a bundle, but Dylan believed it was worth it. He saved so much on maintenance by not needing twenty-four-hour crews keeping the rink cleaned during storms or regular snowfall.

She squeezed his fingers and her voice came out in a husky whisper. "I feel like I'm in *Frozen*."

"Hmm. Not that you watch children's movies."

"It also won an Academy Award. Now be quiet or I'll punish you by singing *Let It Go*."

"Let's not be hasty." He smiled. "This is why I bought Rinker's Park. When you visit, you believe in something bigger, something beautiful. Don't we all need that?"

When she turned to look at him, a shift occurred. He held his breath, recognizing the crumbling of a barrier between them; recognizing the naked emotion in her eyes as confirmation. Dylan leaned over and pressed a soft kiss to her trembling lips. Then smiled.

"Let's skate."

They needed to hike through mounds of snow to get to the gallery where he housed the skates and equipment. She fell a few times, muttering under her breath about his crazy-ass ideas, and hung on to his hand as he dragged her through thigh-high powder. Dylan quickly fitted them with skates and led her onto the rink.

He tamped down the laughter for the first twenty minutes. Besides grabbing on to the rail and refusing to let go until she was ready, Riley frowned, muttered, and looked generally pissed off at his ability to skate perfect figure eights, backward and forward, while a few tentative tries landed her on that gorgeous backside.

Dylan enjoyed the transformation, though, when her usual stubbornness drove her forward into the middle of the ice in a sink-or-swim approach. Like most things the woman did in her life, she took the gamble.

And she swam.

He glided by her, grabbed her hand, and they hit stride. Watching fat chunks of snow surround them and ice sparkling added to the dreamy atmosphere. Dylan sunk into the moment, not needing conversation, just the presence of the woman he'd fallen in love with in an evening.

"My dad wanted a boy," she said.

Dylan didn't answer. A gut instinct told him to be quiet, because something bigger was happening underneath the surface and he didn't want to jinx it. After a moment, Riley continued.

"When I was born, he was disappointed. Of course, I didn't realize this until much later, after the tragedy. Sure, I knew he treated me with a distance, and seemed uninterested in anything purely female. But I had my mom, so that was okay. Dad's world revolved around my brother. He was three years younger. His name was Rick."

Dylan swallowed. He noted the terms she used, and knew the story was a rough one. But he kept skating, because he knew if he paused or said a word, she'd stop talking.

"I couldn't be too jealous because I adored him, too. Dad was always pushing him, in sports, grades, social status. Had dreams of Rick doing something really successful, and always talked about him being the head of some super conglomerate or running his own company. Rick would roll his eyes and crack jokes—he had this great sense of humor that just made everyone love him. He made things easy for me. Mom rarely gave me crap, happy that I was happy, and Dad concentrated all his efforts on making sure Rick would excel at everything he did."

Over the sound system, "Jingle Bells" turned to "We Wish You a Merry Christmas." They did a few more laps and she was able to continue.

"Rick and my mother were killed in an auto accident. June 11, 1998. I was sixteen. He was thirteen. Guy fell asleep at the wheel and hit them head-on. No one survived.

"After that, it all changed. Dad walked around like a ghost. So did I. I felt so guilty. I was obsessed with my social status at school, crushing on this guy in my biology class, and hoping he'd ask me out. I felt so stupid, worried about ridiculous things when my brother had been working so hard to give Dad what he wanted. Excellence. Success."

She lapsed into silence. "What did you do?" Dylan asked.

"I changed. I had to. I stopped worrying about friends and boys, and studied all the time. I decided to give Dad what we were all missing, and try to honor Rick's memory. In a way, it wasn't even hard. I learned to focus. I think I had the skills needed all the time, but I'd never been pushed before. I began enjoying the control and discipline it took to reach goals and depend on yourself. Much easier than maneuvering through social conventions, relationships, and teenage angst. Suddenly, my life was . . . cleaner."

Dylan fought the need to take her in his arms and comfort her. All his questions about her drive and talent were answered. Of course she'd take her brother's place. Of course she'd dedicate her life to making her father proud. It was probably always within her, but never had the opportunity to flourish with her brother being in the spotlight. His heart hurt for the family they were, the girl she'd once been, and the sacrifices she made. But he sensed she'd locked up this story for a long time, and it had festered, like an abscess. In order for her wound to heal, it needed to be lanced. Shared. Purged.

"Did your dad notice?"

A tiny sigh escaped her. "No. But I don't blame him. I know he loves me. I know he's proud of me and what I've accomplished with Chic Publishing. He framed the cover of *Fortune* magazine and hung it in the living room. But Rick and Mom left a hole that couldn't be filled, no matter how good I was. And maybe that's okay. Maybe that's the way it should be."

He stopped. Tipped her chin up. Tenderness coursed through his body, his heart, his soul. She blinked furiously, her face a picture of confusion and sadness and longing. "I bet your mom and brother look over you every day, so damn proud of who you've become. Others would have sunk and given up. Whined and bitched and given excuses. You're a hell of a woman, Riley Fox. A hell of a daughter. And a hell of a sister."

She nodded. Accepting his comfort. Listening to the words and taking them deep to find a place where they could fit. He broke then, needing to touch her, protect her, make her happy.

The kiss was pure giving and comfort, but she turned it fast, grabbing on to him as if needing more. Dylan groaned and held her tight, his tongue plunging into her mouth and savoring her taste. The spark caught and exploded. He pushed her against the railing, ripping at the bulky clothes loaded with zippers and buttons, desperate to hit skin and give her the connection they both needed. She whimpered, and he swallowed it whole, managing to get the jacket open, sweater hiked up, and his fingers down her pants.

Holy crap, she was dripping wet and hot as his fingers hooked under the panties and sunk deep into her pussy. She bit down hard on his lower lip, but he didn't break contact, moving his fingers and dragging them across her clit, pushing her higher even as she bucked and bit and moaned underneath him.

"Give it to me, Riley. Now. Give it all to me," he demanded, twisting his fingers and slamming deep against her G-spot. And then she was coming, flooding his hand, while his mouth crushed her screams, never releasing the pressure they both craved. He kept his fingers inside her for a while, kissing away the one tear skidding down her cheek, murmuring inane nonsense in her ear while she settled. He kissed her, held her, and she relaxed completely in his arms.

"I need you," he said. "In my bed. Naked. Open."

"Yes," she whispered. "I need that, too."

Dylan tried not to shake as he fixed her clothes, took her hand, and led her out of the rink.

❄ ❄ ❄

He moved over her, surged inside, and began the rhythm to break her apart so he could put her back together. Riley lived her life on her terms, but tonight there was nothing she couldn't give him. A distant fantasy and memory of a man whose image never left her now claimed her completely. She knew it wasn't real. Couldn't be. But for these last few hours, Riley didn't care.

She opened herself wide and met each thrust. Her lips opened to his tongue, her nails scraped down the muscled ridge of his back, drawing blood, making her own mark so tonight could be remembered. When her climax came, he commanded her to open her eyes. He was witness to it all—both brutal pleasure and the completion of the fall she'd started ten years ago at the first touch of his lips on hers.

She fell in love with Dylan McCray. Owned it. Relished it. Reveled in it.

She called his name over and over while her heart screamed out the words she refused to utter.

I love you. I love you. I love you.

❄ ❄ ❄

The mingling scent of sex and musk and sweat rose to his nostrils in the sweetest perfume in the world. Dylan stroked her shoulder as she rested, staring at the woman naked in his arms, in his bed. How many times had he wondered what it would be like if they met again, yet recognizing they may never be able to transition the connection between them into the real world.

When he joined Kinnections, he'd been so hopeful. He was ready to settle down and find his forever. The team was incredible, noting every one of his points, and even digging under the surface until they found needs he didn't realize he had. Most of his dates impressed him. Made him laugh. Engaged him in stimulating conversation. Many even caused a physical reaction that would've led directly to sex, or at least a lot of foreplay.

Usually after the first date, he realized the truth.

None of the women were meant for him.

Frustration beat in his blood, and he had trouble convincing Kate he wasn't screwing around, wasting their time. How do you explain the search for something that many didn't believe existed? The magic of a connection, a deeper knowledge you met the one meant for only you? Especially coming from a male, he'd be laughed out of Kinnections and by anyone who heard the ridiculous story. So, he made half-assed excuses and kept his mouth shut.

About a year ago, Dylan began to believe that kind of relationship didn't exist. The depression he felt realizing he'd have to settle haunted him, but he promised to give the search a bit more time before he accepted the fact he'd never have what his parents have. How could he even understand what he was looking for when he'd never experienced it personally?

Tonight, the shattering conclusion of his journey shocked him to his core. Riley Fox was the one. The one he'd been searching for. The moment he buried himself deep into her body, clasped her hands, looked into her eyes, a low hum vibrated in his gut and spread throughout every inch of him, refusing to be denied.

It was as if he'd found his other half. His mind settled, his heart ripped open, and he gave himself to her with each stroke, binding her body to his in the most primeval way possible for a man to claim his mate. He craved to protect her, push her, fuck her, comfort her.

Love her.

Holy shit.

"You okay?"

He blinked as the sound of her voice broke his short-term panic attack. No way could he tell her that. Not so soon, after a few hours in her company. Somehow, knowing Riley's sense of control and order, he figured his big news would have her launching herself naked out the window into a pile of snow.

He'd need to ease her into the same realization. Failure wasn't an option, because this time Dylan wasn't letting her go.

He pushed the hair out of her eyes and tucked it gently behind her ear. Her skin glowed, her lips were slightly bruised, and her eyes shone like a woman who was well satisfied. Dylan fought the urge to beat on his chest like a primate. "I'm better than okay." He propped an elbow on the pillow and leaned his head on his palm, studying her. "How's your head?"

She gave a low chuckle and stretched her leg. "Not my head I'm worried about right now. Other parts are taking up my attention."

"Just what I like to hear," he growled. "Can I tell you the fantasy wasn't half as good as the reality? And trust me, I can spin a very dirty fantasy."

"I bet you can." She smiled, her face open and relaxed as she gazed at him. "I never knew it could—it could be like that."

He pressed a thumb against her bottom lip, dragging it over the tender flesh. "Me, either."

She wasn't ready to hear the words, but he could show her in other ways.

Dylan spent the rest of the night showing her over and over again.

chapter 8

. . . .

*R*iley opened her eyes.

The bedroom was half lit, a lazy breaking sun shining through the windows. Her muscles ached like a bitch, she was sore between her thighs, and she smelled of sex.

She couldn't remember a time when she felt this satisfied.

The deep rumble of a snore drifted to her ears. She turned her head and studied the angelic profile of his face. God, he was perfection. A blinding beauty mixed with the carnality of a sexual animal. Waves of white-blond hair fell over his forehead, and a rough stubble coated his jaw. The lean muscles of his face were relaxed in sleep, gentling the curves to blend in fluid symmetry. The sheet was tangled around his hips, baring his impressive back to her gaze, making her fingers itch to touch him, though she hadn't had her hands off of him for over twelve hours.

What was she going to do?

In the cold light of morning, panic edged her nerves. What had she done? In one evening, she'd shared secrets of her past, stripped naked, let him make love to her in a variety of ways, and begged for more. But this couldn't be real. Normal people didn't begin relationships jumping into bed in the middle of a snowstorm. The evening seemed like a hazy dream of blurred images and feelings that could never survive. She didn't need a mind-blowing sexual affair doomed to fail. She wanted something solid and real, reasonable in everyday routine.

Dylan McCray was larger than life. Bigger than a boring domestic schedule no matter what he said about his parents or his true goals. If she believed him, Riley knew she'd throw away her ridiculous list and go for it. She'd follow him anywhere, do anything, and live in a fantasy world that would eventually crash. And once it did, could she ever settle for something less?

No. At least this way she had a beautiful memory to warm her nights. She had more than she had before. It would have to be enough.

Swallowing past a lump in her throat, Riley carefully climbed out of bed. Grabbing her clothes, she tiptoed out the door, dressing quickly. She headed to the kitchen and peeked out the window.

The snow had finally stopped but there was definitely two feet out there. The walkways and paths were covered, and God knows there'd be no way to get down the mountain until some crews came out to clear the roads. Her heart beat faster and she fought back panic. She had to get out of here. Her instincts screamed the quicker the better to avoid a confrontation she dreaded. Should she—

"Morning."

She whipped around. He stood in the doorway, feet apart, hip cocked. He'd put on a pair of sweats and was naked from the waist up. The sexy morning-after stubble made her ache to cross the room and rub it against her tender lips, slip her fingers around his rock-hard length, stroke, suck— Oh, God, what was she doing?

"Morning."

"I'll put on some coffee." He motioned toward the window. "How bad is it?"

"Snow stopped but it's a mess. I'm hoping the phone lines are back up. I need to get my cell phone from the car. Umm, any idea how I can get out of here?"

He filled the pot with water and took out the grinder. "Figured we'd spend the day together. I'll have my staff get you towed. Plow guy should be here in a few hours."

"Oh. Well, that sounds good, but I really need to leave as soon as possible." She gave a nervous laugh. "I'm way behind on— work."

He finished grinding the beans, filled the filter, and flipped on the brew switch. Then turned to her. "Got the spooks, Riley?"

She stiffened. Cooled her voice. "I don't know what you're talking about. I have a ton of work, messages to return, and can't afford to be trapped on a mountain all day."

He nodded, seemingly calm, but a dangerous aura pulsed around him. "I see. Are we going to at least talk about last night?"

She blew out a breath. "Sounds like an old eighties movie. I didn't think we needed to, Dylan. Last night was amazing. But now it's daytime, and we need to get on with our lives."

"How neat and tidy. Sorry my answer won't be."

"What answer?"

"Fuck that."

She jerked. Anger flooded her, pure and hot and mean. "Look, I don't know what you think last night was, but I refuse to be spoken to that way."

"Didn't mind it last night when I was buried deep inside you. Seemed to like anything I said then."

Her face turned warm. Damn, she hated blushing. "That was then. This is now."

"Why don't you tell me what last night was about, then?" Dylan rested his fists on his hips, challenging her with a gaze that dared her to lie.

Why was he doing this? Wasn't he the man in the relationship? He was supposed to be stumbling over himself in an effort to get her quickly out of his house and praying they wouldn't be talking about feelings or expectations. Screw this. She refused to cower under his overbearing high-handedness.

"Fine. You want me to be truthful, I will. Last night was wonderful. It was hot, and a fantasy, and a memory I'll never forget. But I think we both realize we were trapped in a snowstorm, had some leftover feelings from our time together at college, and needed to get it out of our system. Now I need to go back to my real life. You wouldn't fit, Dylan, and you know it. Let's do the right thing by admitting our time together was special, and deciding to move on. Maybe even be friends?" She choked on the word but managed to forge ahead. "How does that sound?"

He moved so fast she never saw him coming. Suddenly he loomed over her, his hands gripping her shoulders, fury transforming him into the rebel archangel bent on getting what he wanted. "I think your plan sucks," Dylan stated coldly. "I think you're so scared of how deep things got the only way to feel safe again is to pretend it didn't mean anything. I may not blame you, but I gotta admit, Riley, it's pissing me off. I thought you were braver than that."

She gasped. "How dare you! We spent one night together and that doesn't give you a right to pretend to know me! All we have together is great sex. It's not enough to base a relationship on."

"I disagree," he growled. "The sex is the best I've ever had, but it's about connection. We get each other. It's not rational or good on paper, but there it is. We fit. And walking away from it because you think I'm suddenly gonna spook, or some bullshit about me not owning nine out of the ten qualities on your ridiculous list is a cop-out."

"It's not ridiculous, it's real! Don't you get it? The sex is too good. We're too—intense." Her voice broke, making her even madder, but his grip gentled and he pressed his forehead to hers.

"I know it was intense, darlin'. I know it's a lot to take in, and it was only one night, but here's the truth. I'm giving it all to you in one shot. My whole life I've been searching for something incredible. My other half, a woman who made me feel whole. From the moment I found you in that car and carried you in, my senses have been in overdrive. And when I finally drove inside your body, felt your heat around me, I knew. I just knew.

"It's you. I've been searching for you."

Her body shook like it was in the grip of a fever. Fireworks went off in her brain, short-circuiting, and she tore apart in two. Half of her sobbed in relief and surrendered. The other half cringed in bone-gripping fear of the unknown and unrealistic.

Marriage and relationships were about compromise. Communication. Likability. Not this crazy hormonal ride, and soul-ripping, raw need. It couldn't be.

So Riley stood in his arms, frozen, not able to say a word. His hands stroked her cheek, the truth shattering them both, and then he kissed her.

Pure. Oh, his kiss gave everything she'd always wanted, sweet and gentle and humbling. She kissed him back, savoring every last moment, and when he pulled away she knew what she had to do.

"It'll never work," she whispered. She closed her eyes, trembling with the force of her need, and the iron-will control she had to stay strong. "You and I together will never . . . fit."

"That fucking box again." He stepped back, releasing her. He quickly turned, but she already caught the agony on his face, making a moan emit from her throat. He fisted his hands, cursing viciously under his breath. Finally, he spoke, but kept his back turned.

"I guess you've made your decision. I can't force you to take a chance. I can't force you to have feelings you may not. And I'm sorry, too."

He moved toward the door. "I'll call the tow truck to get you out of here and give you a lift home. Help yourself to coffee."

He left. Riley shuddered, slumping down to rest in the chair and catch her shaking legs. She knew he had done more than left her in the kitchen. He'd respected her very rational, logical decision and let her go completely.

Too bad the win suddenly felt like the biggest loss in her life.

chapter 9

. . . .

*T*wo weeks later, Riley slumped in her office chair. Usually, her work schedule energized her, revving her up. Goals and deadlines were her happy place. But since she left Dylan, everything seemed . . . flat. Uninspired. Even the chocolate chips she'd put in her bran muffins didn't make her happy.

Now, that was just plain scary.

Holding back a sigh, she tapped the pen against her blotter and tried to think. She'd told Kate to schedule her as many dates as possible with partners who complemented her list. She'd gone on four dates. A lawyer, accountant, teacher, and doctor. They'd been intelligent, low key, and respectable. They wanted children. She had a good time. But God, they were so dull.

Dylan had ruined her.

She'd reached for the phone to call him a hundred

times during the past two weeks. He'd probably hang up on her. Riley ached that she'd been the one to hurt him, when all he had done was be brave and confess his true feelings. The same exact feelings she had for him, but was too chickenshit to follow. What a mess.

The unstoppable truth haunted her night after night. Dylan McCray was the man she was meant for. He may not be the type she imagined, but he completed her. Got her. He didn't allow for her bullshit, respected her career, knew her past, ravished her body and soul with a hunger never matched. Life may be calmer without him. More reasonable. But it would be empty and lonely and dark.

What was she going to do?

How could she get him back?

The red light flashed on her phone. "Ms. Fox, you have a visitor. He's not on your schedule but insisted you'd see him. Dylan McCray."

Her mouth fell open. After trying to talk several times, she finally managed a squeak. "Yes, thanks, Cindy, you can send him in."

She scrambled to neaten her desk, stood up, sat back down, then stood up again. Sweat dampened her palms. What did he want? Was he still angry? Would he try to get her back? What if he laughed and said her leaving was the best thing that ever happened to him? He strolled through the door thirty seconds later in a navy blue pin-striped suit, red tie, and leather loafers. He was the symbol of the gorgeous, successful American man, pow-erful and commanding with every move, the sharp fabric creased perfectly and a tangy aftershave floating from his skin that made her want to keep sucking in air.

"Dylan." Her voice ripped from her throat. "I'm surprised to see you."

"Riley." He nodded, but his eyes gleamed with a mysterious intent. "I'm surprised I'm here myself. But after the two weeks I had, I realized I had no choice."

She stumbled forward. The space between them yawned with emptiness. His body heat hummed from across the room. "Do—do you want to sit?"

"No, thank you. This shouldn't take long."

Riley fought a shudder and tried to look calm. She shifted on her high heels, glad she'd worn her smart pink plaid Jones suit. She needed all the confidence possible. "Why are you here?"

He grinned. Shot his cuffs. His casual pose reminded her of a jungle cat lazing in the woods for a nap before hunting its prey. "I'm tired of waiting. I was a good boy, deciding to give you the time you need. But watching you go out with other men has been pissing me off, and I've lost patience. Who's in the box, Riley?"

Her heart hammered in her chest. Excitement slithered in her veins and she was thrust from dreary Kansas to Oz in seconds. She took a step forward. "You."

Those eyes burned hot and demanding. Her muscles softened in surrender. Finally, the truth released her and joy burst through her body. She blinked away the mad sting of tears.

Dylan nodded. "Damn right. About time, too. Now there's just one last thing you need to do."

She'd do it. She'd do anything for him. Because Riley knew in that moment she belonged to him as wholly as he did to her. They were a team, and she'd never doubt it again. "What?"

He gave a slow grin. "Prove it."

❄   ❄   ❄

"This is ridiculous. It's the middle of the day. People just don't do these things in the afternoon, Dylan. It's too . . . decadent."

He tried not to laugh at her whispered horror, because he knew she frikkin' loved every second of it. Hands firmly clasped together, he led her around the circle of the rink while the lights twinkled, and the scent of popcorn and candy filled the air. The carousel sang merrily, the painted horses bobbing up and down as children laughed with delight. Still dressed in her work clothes, heels swapped out for skates, they glided in perfect coordination, and Dylan realized he'd never been so completely and utterly content.

He'd finally found her.

"You love it," he said. "Maybe we'll get married here."

She stumbled and he caught her. "You always were arrogant, egotistical, and assuming," she declared.

"I'm also right."

"Funny, before the marriage part comes another element I haven't heard yet."

He laughed, spun her around, and pressed her back against the gate. Her nose was red, her cheeks flushed, and her eyes sparkled. Dylan lowered his head. "I love you, Riley Fox. I probably always have. It was you I was searching for all along."

"Damn right." She lifted her arms and buried her fingers in his hair. "And I love you."

"About time. I have a wonderful plan already for the honeymoon."

"Oh yeah? Someplace warm and tropical?" she teased.

He nibbled on her lower lip. "No. I intend to fill an entire room with stainless-steel appliances and fuck you thoroughly on every last one of them."

Her body shuddered and a low moan vibrated from her throat. Crap, he loved this woman. Body, mind, heart, and soul. He couldn't wait to see what the next fifty years would bring.

"But for now, I just want to skate with the woman I love."

She smiled and pressed her lips softly to his.

And they skated.

It's a Wonderful
Tangled Christmas Carol

. . . .

EMMA CHASE

chapter 1

. . . .

Deck the halls with boughs of holly,
Fa la la la la, la la la la.
'Tis the season to be jolly,
Fa la la la la, la la la la.

*U*rban legends. We've all heard of them—eating pop rocks and soda will make your stomach explode; the tourist who gets his kidney stolen in a faraway land; alligators living in the sewers. By the time you reach adulthood, you realize they're all crocks of shit. Stories that get passed on from generation to generation to scare the hell out of us and keep us on the straight and narrow.

Well . . . except for the alligator one—I've lived in New York City my whole life and that's completely possible.

But the others, yeah, all lies.

In the latter part of the last century, new urban legends sprung up that society's all too willing to fall for: action stars who die on movie sets doing stunts; rain-forest plants that cure obesity; and Justin Bieber actually having a set of balls.

Sometime in the late 1970s, after the city's crime rate began to drop and New York became more tourist friendly, another urban legend was started—one that annually throws a fucking wrench into the otherwise smoothly operating machine that is my life.

That would be the myth that New York City is a prime place to go Christmas shopping.

I don't know what moron started the rumor, but I will gladly stick my foot up his ass if I ever find out. Because now, scores of people from Pennsylvania, New Jersey, Connecticut, and upstate clog our bridges, tunnels, and streets from Black Friday to Christmas Eve, scurrying to make their holiday purchases like rats going after a gourmet piece of cheese. To get little Timmy a train set from FAO Schwarz and grandma a brooch from Tiffany.

Sure, they've heard of the Internet. Of course they know it'd be easier—and less expensive—to order online and have packages delivered right to their front door.

But for them, it's not about what's easier. Christmas shopping in the city is now—say it with me—*tradition*.

They want to see the big tree, the lights. They want to stand in an endless line to skate in Rockefeller Center and take a picture with Santa at Macy's in Herald Square. They want to watch the fucking Rockettes and eat a family dinner at a restaurant whose menu has been price-gouged to the gills.

You can forget about getting a cab—they're all taken. And even walking down the sidewalk is an exercise in frustration, because every few feet a stroller-pushing, shopping-bag-carrying tourist will come to a complete frigging stop right in front of you to take a picture of the red-and-green-lit Empire State Building.

You think I sound pissed off? How very perceptive of you. The Christmas spirit and me? We're not friends. Ebenezer Scrooge had the right idea: bah fucking humbug.

The reason for my current antiholiday rant is because I'm in line—the same line I've been in for forty-five minutes—trying to buy a last-minute gift for my perfect wife.

Please, take my money and just let me fucking *leave*.

When it comes to gifts, I'm usually way ahead; eleventh-hour purchases aren't my style. But walking past Saks Fifth Avenue, I saw a pair of Valentino crystal and silk heels that would look amazing on Kate. She'll enjoy wearing them, and I will definitely enjoy watching her wear them—especially naked—so it's a win-win.

Except for the line.

I'm not used to waiting in lines. I'm used to personal shoppers and commission-seeking salespeople vying for my attention with phrases like, "Can I hold that for you, Mr. Evans?" "We have that in four other colors, Mr. Evans." "Would you like that wrapped, Mr. Evans?"

But this is Christmas Eve. Which means stores don't give a crap about the quality of the shopping experience. It's all about quantity—getting as many shoppers through their doors as possible before closing time. Which brings me to my next point:

Most people in the world today are fucking idiots.

Don't laugh—you may be one of the walking stupid and just not know it. But it's true. Say what you want about income inequality or the inferior public school system—the harsh truth is, the majority of the population is simply *not* intelligent. And even more suck at their job. They don't give a rat's ass about doing it well or longevity; they're only interested in performing the minimum required to get a check.

And there's no better example of that than the temporary holiday employee.

Companies don't hire them because of their skill or what they may contribute to the work force. They're hired because they have a pulse. Spare bodies, decked out in holiday ensembles, whose main purpose is to corral consumers the same way a fence encages cattle. And they're equally as helpful.

The twentysomething blonde behind the register is one such employee. You can tell by the slow, cautious way she pecks at the keys and her confused expression if someone—God forbid—asks her where an item can be found. She's the reason for the sick amount of time I've wasted waiting to buy these shoes.

The good news is, I'm about to cross the finish line. I step up, with only one more customer left in front of me—a tall, regal-looking older lady in a pricey red coat and genuine pearl earrings. I take out my wallet so I can pay as quickly as possible and get the hell out of here.

See the blazing yule before us,
Fa la la la la la, la la la la.

Strike the harp and join the chorus,
Fa la la la la, la la la la

But my hope of an imminent escape is crushed when the blond temp rings up the purple Burberry of London tie and tells the old lady, "That will be one hundred and ninety-five dollars and thirty cents."

Pearl Earrings looks offended. "That can't be correct. This tie is on sale for one hundred and fifty dollars—not one eighty."

A panicked expression swamps the blonde's face. She taps a few buttons on the register and swipes the tie's bar code with the red laser beam. "It's ringing up at one hundred and eighty. Plus tax."

I push a hand through my dark hair and listen for the predictable old woman response.

"That's false advertising! I refuse to pay a penny over one fifty."

The hopeless temp looks around for assistance, but there's none to be found. So, like the knight in shining armor I am, I come to her rescue.

"Why don't you do a manual override?"

Her eyes gaze at me without a clue. "A what?"

I gesture to the register. "It's a computer—it has to do what you tell it to. Override the price and put it in as one fifty."

She gulps. "I . . . I don't know how to do that."

Of course she doesn't.

"I'm going to have to find my manager."

No. No way I'm gonna stand here twiddling my

thumbs for another twenty frigging minutes. And I refuse to walk out, either—too much of my precious time is already invested in these shoes.

Despite the frustration churning in my gut, I shift my attention to the pearl-wearing red coat and turn on the charm that—even with a ring on my finger—women of all ages are still helpless to resist. "Last-minute Christmas shopping?"

She nods. "That's right, for my husband."

"You have excellent taste. I'm a connoisseur of ties myself, and that one is superb."

It's working—she smiles. "Thank you, young man."

"Tell you what, how about we save some time and I'll front the extra thirty dollars so you can purchase this tie for your lucky husband, at not a penny over one hundred and fifty dollars?"

Her brow wrinkles. It was already wrinkled with age—but now it wrinkles more.

"It's not about the cost, it's the principle of the matter. They should stand by the price advertised."

"I couldn't agree more. Principles are important—which is exactly why I'm making my offer. Here it is, Christmas Eve, and I've been too busy to show any goodwill toward my fellow man—or woman. This gesture will make me really feel the Christmas spirit. You'd be doing me a favor, miss."

The "miss" was just the right touch. Because her eyes sparkle, and she grins warmly. "Well, when you put it that way, how can I say no?"

I wink. "I guess you can't."

I smack thirty dollars on the counter and the old lady hands over her black card. While the very relieved temp places the boxed tie in a shopping bag with a ridiculous amount of useless tissue paper, Pearl Earrings glances at my left hand. Then she pulls a business card out of her purse, slides it toward me, and whispers low, "My husband and I host parties every month. Parties for . . . adventurous . . . couples."

Oh boy.

"You'd certainly be doing *me* a favor if you attend." She winks. "I would thoroughly enjoy having you. Think about it."

I wait until she walks away before I chuckle. Just goes to show you—don't judge a freak by their cover. The wild ones come in all shapes, sizes . . . and ages.

The holiday-hire hands me my prized shoes, and I'm finally able to head home to my wife and our terribly wonderful son.

Follow me in merry measure,
Fa la la, la la la, lu la la.
While I tell of Yuletide treasure,
Fa la la la la, la la la la

❄ ❄ ❄

I shut the door to our apartment and toss the mail down on the front hall table—mostly last-minute Christmas cards. Nothing says "you were an afterthought" like getting a Christmas card on Christmas Eve. I hang up my black wool coat and slide the shopping bag with Kate's new shoes under the table, to be wrapped later.

Unlike me, Kate is good about waiting. She likes to be surprised, so I don't have to put in the extra effort of hiding her gifts to keep her from sneaking a peek.

I walk into the living room—and stop dead in my tracks. I was planning on going home only for a few minutes, to let Kate know I'd be at the office the rest of the evening. But those plans get tossed out the window.

Because reclining in the chaise longue is a gift that beats the hell out of anything I've ever seen sitting under a tree.

My wife, Kate Brooks-Evans.

Kate Brooks-Evans in lingerie.

Kate Brooks-Evans in see-through, Christmas-themed lingerie.

Her smooth legs are crossed at the ankle, bare except for the spiky heeled, shiny black boots that end below her knees. A sheer red nightie, trimmed in fluffy white fur, covers tiny red panties—held together by two silk bows tied at her hips. A shiny black belt cinches her flat stomach, and more white fur embellishes the strapless neckline, bringing my attention to her perfect breasts and pink nipples pressing against the gauzy fabric. Kate's luscious dark hair falls over her shoulders, curled at the ends, and a fleecy red-and-white Santa hat sits on top of her head.

She smiles mischievously. "Welcome home, Santa."

"Mrs. Claus," I smirk, "you've changed."

"It was time for a makeover."

I start unbuttoning my shirt. "Want to sit on my lap . . . or my face . . . and tell me if you've been a nice girl this year?"

Kate chuckles. Then she tucks her legs under her, rises onto all fours, and crawls down the chaise toward me.

It's so damn sexy my cock stiffens so hard that you could hang an ornament from it.

"Well, I've tried to be nice, but every time I look at you, the naughty just takes over."

Kate bites her lip—'cause she knows it drives me crazy—and watches my every move as I toss my shirt on the floor. Her eyes caress my arms, chest, and abs, then focus on my fingers as I slowly unbutton my jeans and lower the zipper.

I shrug. "I've always thought 'nice' was way fucking overrated."

With my typical lack of shyness, I push my pants down and step out of them. My dick juts out proudly, eye level with Kate, straining for her attention. But before she touches me, I remember James—our five-year-old.

"Where's the evil elf, by the way?"

"I dropped him off at your sister's. He's decorating gingerbread cookies with Mackenzie and Thomas."

"And biting their heads off?"

"Of course."

Here's an interesting fact: how you eat a gingerbread man says a lot about your personality. Head-first eaters are ambitious, independent, and magnetic. Feet-first are the more artistic, creative types, and those who start with the hands are kind and nurturing. Same rules apply for chocolate Easter bunnies.

Maybe you're wondering how I came to know this information?

I looked it up. Because James is a head-first eater.

And Kate and I were . . . unsettled . . . by all the headless chocolate bunnies lying around last Easter.

But—good news—he's not a serial killer in the making, he just has the same driven, bound-to-be-a-success temperament as his parents.

During my research, I also discovered that sociopaths and CEOs share a lot of character traits—but we'll talk about that another time.

There are other, more crucial matters at hand.

"So, we have the whole apartment to ourselves?" I ask.

Kate licks her lips happily. "Yep."

My dick gets even harder, thinking of the possibilities. "That means we can fuck in the living room? The hallway? The kitchen?"

A center island is the perfect height to comfortably eat a woman out while she's perched on the counter.

Coincidence?

I think not.

Kind of makes you rethink the meaning of "eat-in kitchen," doesn't it?

Kate replies, "Yes. Yes. And definitely yes. I've missed kitchen sex."

I've missed bending her over the arm of the sofa and pounding her from behind.

Oh—and sleeping naked. I haven't slept naked for a

year and a half. Not since my son crawled into our bed in the middle of the night and asked why I wasn't wearing pajamas. Telling him the truth—that it's liberating and makes it more convenient to screw his mother—was out of the question. So I just said I forgot.

He thought that was funny. And I've slept in boxers almost every night since.

When people tell you having kids changes things—they're not screwing around.

But all thoughts of our child fly out of my head as Kate envelops my dick in her warm, wet mouth. My head lolls back, relishing the sensation of her stroking tongue. But after a few seconds, I have to look and take in the sensual sight of Kate's head bobbing up and down, doing what she does so very well.

My hand skims her spine. I lift the sheer red fabric, exposing her firm ass, scarcely covered by the red silk panties. My stomach contracts in hot pleasure as she sucks me harder. I pull on the red ribbons tied at her hips and the panties fall away. Then I knead the soft flesh of her ass before sliding my fingers between her open legs—into her warm pussy. She's already slick for me; her muscles tighten around my fingers as I pump them slowly.

I pull my hips back and I slide out of Kate's awesome mouth. I cradle her face with my hands and bring her up to meet my lips. We kiss playfully, my teeth scraping along her jaw to her neck, licking and sucking—both of us moaning. I wrap an arm around her waist and lift her to her feet, dragging us to the couch.

Without a word, Kate assumes my favorite position—

bent at the waist, her stomach draped over the arm, feet apart, her delectable ass high and waiting. Her hands brace against the cushions and my hand rests on her shoulder. My other hand grasps my dick and makes two teasing passes across the opening of her sweet cunt. She wriggles back against me, reaches out her hand, and pushes behind my thigh—trying to maneuver me where she needs me to be.

Always so eager.

Although our sex life is fantastically frequent, we can't be as . . . vocal . . . as we once were. Not with a kid in the house. So I plan on taking advantage of this opportunity to hear Kate's voice in all its hedonistically desperate beauty.

I cover her—my chest flush with her back—nudge her silken hair with my nose, and bring my lips to her ear. "Do you want me to fuck you, baby?"

"Mmm," she groans. "Yessss."

I nip her earlobe. "Tell me."

"Fuck me," she whispers.

Yeah. She's gonna have to do better than that.

I straighten up, smiling, and tease her again with the head of my dick. "I'm sorry, I didn't quite get that."

Her hips squirm with frustration, and she yells, "I want you to fuck me, Drew!"

Almost.

"God, *now* . . . do it . . . *please*. Fuck . . ."

Beautiful.

I push inside her with a moan and her back arches.

I rest my hand on her hip, holding her in place as I rear back. Then thrust in long and slow and deep.

"Yes," she keens loudly. "Just like that."

I look down where I move in and out of her—disappearing into her gorgeous, welcoming body. It's a view that never gets old.

"Christ, you feel good, Kate. Always so goddamn good."

It's true. And it's got nothing to do with the fact that Kate's is the only pussy I've ever been inside without a rubber.

It's her. The life we've made together—the way she matches me in every way—her desire, her humor, her mind.

Her soul.

I used to think that stuff about soul mates was bullshit. The idea that out of the billions of people on Earth, there was only one that you're supposed to be with. That you belong to. Sounded like a fairy tale, a stupid chick flick, or a terrible romance novel that my sister would read.

But now . . .

Now I believe there's something to it. Maybe not for everyone—but definitely for us. Because I just can't fathom having this profound, intense love that borders on obsession—the good kind—with anyone except her.

It's crazy. Like . . . a miracle.

The rhythm of my hips speeds up, 'cause it feels too fucking amazing not to. And Kate drives back against me, meeting me thrust for thrust and moan for moan.

But then I find the strength to grasp her waist with both hands.

And still our movements.

I pull out and Kate groans, "Don't stop."

I spin her around, cup her ass, and press her against me with a squeeze. She stands on her toes to trail hot kisses across my throat.

"I want you on top," I explain with a grin. "I want you to ride me."

Kate wiggles her eyebrows. "So you can watch my 'bells' jingle."

I laugh. "Exactly."

She pushes my shoulders, backing me up to the couch. I sit down heavily and she wastes no time climbing aboard. I surge up into her—deeper from this angle—and once again thank God for the wonderfully tight grip of Kate's snatch.

She closes her eyes and rocks against me. I yank the strapless nightie down, freeing her breasts, and they jiggle as she rotates her hips in tantalizing circles. I palm them in my hand, so soft and full. Kate gasps as I pinch her already puckered nipples. And she groans when I replace my fingers with my lips. Suckling greedily, I rub my tongue against the pointy peak, savoring the exquisite taste of her skin. Kate rises and falls on me quicker—bucking harder.

When I grasp her nipple between my teeth, she holds the back of my head—pressing me against her—pulling my hair. I moan around her flesh and lave at her breast.

And then Kate stiffens, and the sound of her screaming my name echoes around the room as her inner walls clamp down. My fingers dig into her hips as I thrust up once, twice more, then I'm pulsing inside her, grunting and cursing against her chest.

For a few moments we stay right there—catching our breath. Until Kate leans back and gently brushes my black hair from my forehead. "Were you surprised?"

"Very pleasantly, yes."

Her smile is joyful. "Good. It's nice to finally give you a present that you didn't already know was coming."

I kiss her soft lips. Then glance down the hall toward the kitchen. "Speaking of coming . . ."

❄ ❄ ❄

Later, after some quality countertop time, Kate and I lay bare ass on the chaise longue, under a downy red throw blanket—recuperating.

I check my watch. *Shit.* I have to go, though a big part of me—the large lower part—wants nothing more than to stay right in this spot with my wife. But I kiss Kate's forehead and force myself to stand. I grab my discarded shirt from the floor, slipping my arms into it.

Kate rests back on her elbows. "What are you doing?"

I can't find my underwear, so I slide on my jeans without them—being ever so careful with the zipper. "I'm going to head into the office for a few hours."

"But . . ." Kate stutters. ". . . but it's Christmas Eve."

"I know. But Media Solutions is finally ready to have a sit-down with Hawaii. We're going to video conference at nine our time. That only gives me three hours to prep."

Media Solutions is a conglomerate I've been courting for weeks, and I've finally got them right where I want them on a deal that'll revolutionize social media. Think Twitter, reality TV, and YouTube combined—posting broadcasts from and on your television, the star of your own channel.

Narcissistic techies will bow down like it's the second coming of Steve Jobs.

I give Kate a wink. "But your holiday seduction was definitely worth the lost work time. That Mrs. Claus outfit is going straight to the top of the spank-bank pile."

She blinks and sits up straight. The blanket falls down, exposing one creamy breast . . . and suddenly three hours seems like a whole lot of extra time.

I can make do with two.

"I'm not worried about your lost work time, Drew. Why are you working at all?" Her enunciation sharpens— the way you'd talk to an old person who's hard of hearing. "It's Christmas Eve."

Kate Brooks-Evans is many things—a loving wife, an amazing mother, a brilliant *businesswoman*. It's that last one that has me expecting her to understand my rationale.

"If I don't do this tonight, I lose the deal."

"Then you should have told them it's their loss, not yours."

"And you think that's what you would've done if you were in my position?"

"Absolutely."

I button my shirt. And call bullshit. "Easy to say when the deal isn't actually on your desk, Kate."

She doesn't confirm or deny my observation, which means I'm on right on the money. She stands and wraps the blanket snugly around her body. Kate hiding her assets from my appreciative gaze is never a good sign. "We're supposed to be at your sister's in an hour for dinner. They're expecting us."

Her mouth is pursed, her cheeks are flushed, and there's a fire in her eyes that . . . well . . . that gives me a renewed boner. Always has, always will.

My dick likes to argue. Sue him.

"Go without me. You can represent. Drink eggnog with my mother, pretend to listen to my old man talk about holidays past."

Her voice rises. "I don't want to represent! I want to spend the evening with my husband! There's a time for work and a time for family, and tonight is supposed to be about family."

"It *is* about family!" I counter, my voice doing a little raising of its own. "In the next several hours I'm going to make a shitload of money for *our* family."

She shakes her head. "Oh, please. This has nothing to do with the money, Drew. Not for you." Then a new thought occurs to her. "And what about James's gifts? For weeks we've been pushing off putting his big presents together—the bike, the trampoline . . ."

Damn it. I forgot about those.

"I'll see if Matthew can come over later and help you

out. Until he does, after James is asleep, start to do it on your own."

"If I'd known I was going to be alone, I would've gone home to see my mother."

I step closer. "First of all, *this* is your home. Second, we talked about this—I'm not dragging James out to Bumfuck, Ohio, for Christmas. We'd be in line at airport security longer than we'd actually be at your mother's!"

"We spent last Christmas with your side—"

"And if your side wanted to see us that badly, she could've hauled her ass to New York. She's one person— our three beats her one. Majority rules, sweetheart."

"Screw your 'sweetheart'—I am so angry at you right now!"

I roll my eyes. "And we both know you'll get over it."

Kate's mouth widens in a gasp. And a black boot comes hurtling at my head. She has the aim of a major-league closer, but in the last few years I've become a master ducker.

Smash.

Another lamp bites the dust.

"You're an asshole!"

"A fact you were well aware of before you married me." I shrug. "No take-backs."

Kate growls.

So hot.

Then she stomps down the hall into our bedroom and slams the door behind her, rattling the picture frames on the walls.

And they say men are the violent ones.

I sigh. I just don't have time to deal with this right now. Don't look at me like that—I'm not trying to be a prick. I love Kate; I hate that she's mad. But give me a break—it's *one* day. Why does she—why do women everywhere—have to make such a big fucking deal over *one* day?

I put my shoes on, then walk down the hall and brace my hands on the frame of the bedroom door. And talk through it.

"Okay . . . so, I'm gonna head out."

I wait. I listen.

Nothing.

"So that's how you're gonna play this? Not speaking to me? Real nice, Kate—very mature."

Still nothing.

I admit—her cold shoulder bothers me. Not enough to change my plans, but enough for me to try to talk her out of the silent sulk one last time.

"You're not even gonna kiss me good-bye? What if I get pushed in front of a subway train by a deranged homeless person? It could happen. And if it does, you're going to feel awful."

That does the trick. The bedroom door is yanked open.

Kate stands there, with one hand on her hip and a sugary sweet smile on her face. "And we both know I'll get over it."

Then she slams the door in my face.

chapter 2

· · · · · · · · · · · · ·

$\mathcal{A}$lthough I don't believe I have any actual firsthand knowledge, it's colder than a witch's tit outside. Wind cuts through the city streets and the sky is a gloomy gray, hinting at a coming snowstorm.

On the corner, a block from my building, a scraggily faced man in layered, shabby clothes shouts about the apocalypse—the end of days—and how we all need to turn our lives around before time runs out. It's not an uncommon occurrence; guys like him litter the city. But today it seems weirdly . . . foreboding.

I open the door to the building and am greeted by Sam, a security guard in his early twenties who typically helms the night shift.

"Merry Christmas, Mr. Evans."

"Same to you, Sam." He swipes my ID badge and I ask, "They put you on Christmas Eve?"

He shrugs. "I volunteered. Hard to argue with time and a half. Plus it gives the fellas with families time to spend at home."

Guilt pokes at me like the spring of worn-out couch. But I ignore it. "You don't have any family?"

"Not yet. My girlfriend and I are going to my mother's for dinner tomorrow. She's out in Yonkers."

I slide my badge into my pocket and pull a fifty out of it. "I'll be here pretty late tonight. In case I don't catch you on the way out, have a happy holiday." We shake hands and I slip him the fifty. Because I subscribe to my father's line of thought: an employee who feels appreciated—and well compensated—is a productive employee. And if I want anyone to be productive, it's the guy responsible for keeping the building safe.

He smiles gratefully. "Thanks a lot, Mr. Evans."

I nod and head up the elevator to the fortieth floor.

The offices are dark, the only light coming from the full-size Christmas tree in the corner and the illuminated electric menorah on the table beside it. The whole floor is quiet and still.

Not a creature is stirring, not even a mouse.

I flick the lights on in my office and sit down at my desk to get to work. While my laptop boots up, I look at the phone.

And consider calling Kate.

I don't like it when she's pissed at me. It feels . . . wrong. Off-kilter. And it's distracting. Tonight I need to be focused—on top of my game.

I don't pick up the phone.

Because calling her to say I'm sorry, but I'm staying at the frigging office anyway, won't go over well. Besides, she's never been able to stay mad at me for long. By the time I get home, I bet she'll be over it, just like I said.

❅ ❅ ❅

An hour later, I'm staring at my computer screen, reviewing the proposal I'm gonna pitch to Media Solutions. I yawn deeply and my vision blurs. The scorching rechristening of our living room and kitchen must've worn me out more than I thought. I stretch my arms and crack my neck, trying to wake myself up.

But after five minutes, as I read paragraph seventeen, my eyelids become heavy. Until they droop and drag to a close.

❅ ❅ ❅

I bolt awake at my desk—disoriented and slightly panicked. The way my grandfather used to snore away in his recliner, before jerking up and claiming he was just "resting my eyes."

Glancing at my watch, I'm relieved to see it's only been a few minutes since I dozed off. "Wake the fuck up, Evans. No time for a nap."

I head over to the conference room and make myself a quick cup of coffee. I sip the hot beverage of the gods and step back into my office.

And there, sitting on my suede couch—the same suede couch that played such a prominent role in my early Kate Brooks fantasies—is a woman.

Do you see her, too?

She's strikingly beautiful. A pert nose, full lips, bright green eyes, and aristocratic cheekbones. Her hair is honey blond and long with a slight curl. She's wearing a conservative white dress, blazer, and heels—something Kate would wear to the office. A string of pearls adorns her long neck and matching earrings decorate her lobes.

"Hello," she greets me in a warm voice.

My eyes dart from her to the door. Security always calls before letting a client up.

"Hi," I return. "Can I . . . help you?"

"Actually, I'm here to help *you*, Drew."

Huh. She knows my name.

Has she crawled from the sea of my former one-night stands? It wouldn't be the first time one tracked me down at my place of business. But with me riding the monogamy bandwagon these last eight years, it hasn't happened for a long time.

"Have we met somewhere before?" I ask—but I really mean *Have we fucked somewhere before?*

She laughs, though I don't know why. It's a pleasant, alluring sound. "Always so clever. I've been watching you for a long time, Drew. You never fail to entertain. "

I set my coffee on the desk and face her head-on. "You've been watching me for a long time? Yeah, 'cause there's nothing weird about that."

"Well, it's my job to watch you. I'm your guardian angel, after all."

There's a lot of crazy walking around New York City. And I don't just mean the obvious vagrants mumbling around Penn Station or the naked cowgirl in Times Square. Professional dog walkers, bicyclists, and most employees of the sanitation department have several fucking screws loose, too.

You have to be careful with insane people. Getting them worked up isn't a good idea. So I just nod and try to keep her calm.

"Interesting. You don't look like an angel."

"How do you imagine I should look?"

"Wings, halo, blinding heavenly light."

She winks. "I only bring the halo out for formal events. As for my wings . . . I'm still working on earning them."

I snap my fingers. "That sounds familiar. To earn your wings, you have to, like, stop me from offing myself, right?"

Her jade eyes round with surprise. "Oh, nothing as drastic as that. If things became that desperate I wouldn't be doing a very good job. I'm here because you're starting down the wrong path, Drew. We need to nip your behavior in the bud; get you back to where you should be."

With a chuckle, I sit down in my chair and roll closer to the phone.

Her head tilts to the side, regarding me. "You don't believe anything I'm telling you, do you?"

"I'm sorry, but no, I don't."

She's unperturbed. "That's all right. No one believes at first."

You're probably wondering why I'm not getting the hell out of here. I'm a fantastic judge of character, and in this case, I'm just not feeling the psycho vibe. In fact, despite the words that are coming out of her mouth, she seems completely harmless. So I play along.

"For argument's sake, let's suspend reality for a second and say that you *are* my guardian angel. I think I should fire you. You've done a shitty job. Where were you when I thought Kate was cheating on me, and I pulled that stupid stunt with the stripper? That would've been a good time to show up, kick me in the shin, and say, 'Hey asshole, it's not what you think.'"

She nods sympathetically. "It was difficult to watch you go through that. But I couldn't intervene. It was a lesson you could only learn by living through it. Kate, as well."

"But you're here now?"

"That's right."

"Because I'm about to commit some grievous sin?"

"Because you already have."

I brace my elbows on the chair, clasp my hands, and rest my fingers against my lips. "You've got your wings crossed, honey. I haven't done anything. I work hard every single day to be a good father and a devoted, thoughtful husband."

She raises a doubtful eyebrow, reminding me of Kate.

"Thoughtful? Really? Were you being thoughtful when you came to work on Christmas Eve, even though Kate asked you not to?"

I roll my eyes. "This is a onetime thing. It's not a big deal."

"It's never a big deal, Drew. Until it is. Do you think

the Grand Canyon was created in a day? No. It happened in increments—one small grain of soil at a time. Tonight is how it starts. Then you're missing birthdays, basketball games, anniversaries, simple but crucial quiet moments. You mean to make it up to them later, but later never comes."

I put up my hand. "Hold up—that's . . . that's not gonna happen. I would *never* do that."

"Just like you would never leave Kate to put together your son's gifts all alone on Christmas Eve?"

Bull's-eye.

She has a point. A completely impossible, unrealistic point—that makes me feel like dog shit all the same.

"The first step downhill is the hardest, Drew. After that . . . sliding is easy. Taking our loved ones for granted works the same way. "

I stare at her for a moment. And she looks so sincere, I almost believe it . . .

Until I come to my fucking senses.

I laugh. "Did Kate put you up to this? Are you a friend of Dee-Dee's? An actress?"

She sighs. "Tonight, you will be visited by three spirits."

"Wow, a foursome. Will they all look like you?"

That makes her chuckle. "No."

I pick up the phone from my desk. "While this has been memorable—and totally bizarre—I have work to get done."

"They will come to you one by one—the spirits of Christmas past, present, and future—to show you what you will never again forget."

"Since it's Christmas Eve and all, it seems only fair to warn you—I'm calling security."

"Good luck, Drew. It was a pleasure meeting you, at last."

I look down at the phone and punch in the extension for the security desk, then glance back at the couch. But—you guessed it—she's gone.

What. The. Fuck?

I stand up and look out the door. No trace.

"Can I help you, Mr. Evans?" Sam asks through the receiver.

"Did you see . . ." I clear my throat. "Have you let anyone up to our floor tonight? A woman?"

"No, sir. It's been quiet down here."

I knew he was going to say that.

"Well, if anyone comes by, make sure you call before letting them up. Okay, Sam?"

"Sure thing, Mr. Evans."

I put the phone in its cradle and stand there, brow furrowed. What the hell was *that*?

My cell phone chimes with an incoming email. It's Media Solutions' lead attorney, confirming our conference in . . . *damn it*, in two hours.

I brush off the uncomfortable, eerie feelings left from the crazy woman's little visit, and sit down at my desk to focus on what's really important. What I came here to do—pissed off my wife to do.

Close this major fucking deal.

chapter 3

· · · · · · · · · · · · ·

*H*ere's where shit gets weird.

Weirder.

Ten minutes later, while I'm detailing the projected profit margin in my proposal, I hear a giggle from the hallway.

A feminine, familiar giggle.

And a second later, my niece Mackenzie comes breezing through my office door.

She's twelve years old now, with her mother's build—tall and lithe. Her blond hair is pulled back in a long ponytail, and she's wearing a red coatdress with pearl buttons, black leggings, and flat black boots.

I have no frigging idea how she got here or why, but you can bet your ass I'm going to find out.

She talks into a glitter-covered cell phone. "Tell them if we don't have those numbers by tomorrow, their balls are going to be sitting in a glass case on my desk, god-damn it."

It's safe to say the whole bad-word jar thing didn't work out like my sister had hoped.

"Mackenzie?"

She ends her call and flops down into the chair across from my desk. "Hi, Uncle Drew."

"Did you come here by yourself? Do your parents know where you are? What are you doing here?"

"Oh, come on—you know why I'm here." Mischief dances in her big green eyes.

Which is frigging strange, because Mackenzie's eyes are blue.

I don't have time to comment, because in a flurry of red fabric, she's on her feet holding her hand out to me. "Let's get going. Places to go, people to see. Time is money."

I take her hand and we walk out of my office, down the hall to my father's closed office door. Mackenzie opens the door and we step over the threshold.

And I feel the color drain from my face.

Because this isn't my father's office. Not even close.

I stumble backward, making contact with the yellow living room wall.

"What the fuck . . ." I whisper. Confused. A little horrified.

"You don't look so good, Uncle Drew," Mackenzie comments.

Losing your mind will do that to you.

I turn in a circle, taking in beige couches and an oak

entertainment center housing a television that is definitely not a flat screen. *Miracle on 34th Street* is on, and the air smells like fresh baked cookies. A modest Christmas tree sits decorated in the corner and dark red poinsettias are scattered between multiple framed family photos on the shelves. Family photos of my parents, my sister, and me—until I'm about five years old.

And then I finally fucking realize what's going on.

"This is a dream," I say, in a voice that can't decide if it's a question or a declaration. "I fell asleep at my desk and I'm dreaming right now."

Funny. Usually my dreams are the more X-rated variety. Involving me and Kate in multiple porn-toned scenarios. Sometimes I'm a Roman emperor and she's my toga-less slave girl who feeds me grapes and happily caters to my every whim. Sometimes I'm Han Solo and she's Princess Leia, screwing our way across the galaxy. Other times she's the powerful, ambitious businesswoman who lands a major client with me, then we fuck on the conference table until neither of us can walk.

Oh, wait—that last one actually happened.

The point is—out of all the dreams I remember having, my sweet niece sure as shit hasn't featured in any of them. And not a single one took place in this place—an apartment I barely remember living in.

Mackenzie shrugs. "If it keeps you from wussing out on me, we'll call it a dream. Do you know where we are?"

"This is the apartment we lived in when I was a kid, before we moved uptown."

"That's right. Do you know why we're here?"

I try really hard. "Um . . . the sushi I ate for lunch was bad and the toxins have spread to my brain, causing some strange-ass hallucinations?"

Giggling, Mackenzie drags me forward. "Come on."

We enter the kitchen. Sitting at a small round table is the preteen version of my sister, Alexandra. Around this time, she hadn't yet grown into her nickname, "The Bitch," but the early signs were there. She's chewing gum and flipping through a *Tiger Beat* magazine with the New Kids on the Block on the cover. And her hair—Jesus Christ, she must've used a whole can of hair spray, because her bangs form a poof on top of her head, stiff and unnaturally high.

Sitting beside her, looking dapper in a long-sleeved *Back to the Future* T-shirt, is me. Five-year-old me. I'm kind of small for my age; the growth spurt won't hit for another few years. But with my thick black hair brushed to the side, my deep blue eyes shining with youthful exuberance, I'm nothing short of fucking adorable.

There's a plate of cookies in the middle of the table, with still-warm gooey chocolate chips. My mom's home-made cookies. They're indescribably awesome. But when young Drew reaches for one, Alexandra smacks his hand. "No more cookies, Drew. You're going to give yourself a stomachache."

"But they're so good," I whine. And I give her the puppy dog eyes. "Just one more? Please?"

At first Lexi's expression is stern. But under the power of young Drew's cuteness, she melts. "Okay. One more."

Are you feeling the foreshadowing here?

He smiles his thanks and talks with a mouthful of cookie. "You're the best sister ever, Lexi."

She ruffles his hair.

I chuckle and tell Mackenzie, "How irresistible am I? Didn't even have to work at it."

Mackenzie laughs. "You were really cute. Watch—this part is important."

My mother breezes into the kitchen, smooth skinned, blond, and beautiful—despite the atrocious Christmas tree sweater she's sporting. In her hand she holds a cordless telephone.

A heavy, square cordless phone. With an antenna.

"Drew, guess who's on the phone?" she asks.

"Is it Daddy?" he asks hopefully.

"No, darling—it's Santa Claus! He took time out of his busy day-before-Christmas-Eve schedule just to talk to you." She taps five-year-old Drew on the nose.

He flies off the chair, knocking it over behind him. Lexi, who by this time was old enough to know the truth, smiles at his excitement.

Young Drew brings the phone to his ear. "Hello?"

"Ho, ho, ho! Merry Christmas!"

And it all comes back to me. Like a door opening to a dark room, finally letting the light in, I remember this.

"How do I know this is the *real* Santa?" My five-year-old self asks skeptically. Because even as a kid, I was damn sharp.

My father answers in a deep, bellowing, disguised

voice, "Well, I've got the Christmas list you mailed to me here in my hand."

Young Drew braces the phone on his shoulder and walks out to the living room. Mackenzie and I follow. "Okay, let's hear it."

Santa clears his throat. "A BMX bicycle, the new Sega system, GI Joe action figures, a Walkman."

That's right, a Walkman. Because this is the eighties, kiddies.

"Holy crap, it really is you!" five-year-old Drew yells.

"It really is. Now tell me, young man, have you been a good boy this year?"

His face scrunches up as he attempts to be honest. "I try. It's hard to be good."

Santa chuckles. "Do you do what your mother tells you?"

He nods. "Yes, sir."

"And do you listen to your sister?"

He frowns. "Lexi's bossy."

"Yes, she is bossy. But she's your big sister, Drew—she wants what's best for you. You should always listen to her."

Reluctantly, he nods. "Yes, sir."

"Well, young man," my father exclaims. "I'm getting my sleigh all ready for the big night! I should be at your house tomorrow, on Christmas Eve, with lots of presents for you."

Five-year-old Drew looks behind him—making sure the coast is clear. Then he speaks hesitantly into the phone. "Hey, Santa, can I ask you something?"

"You can ask me anything, Drew."

"Would it be okay to add something to my list?"

I hear worry in the old man's voice when he responds, "Add something? I'm not certain we could—"

"Or, I could trade. You can keep my other presents— I think I really only want one thing."

"What do you want, Drew?"

"I want you to bring my daddy home for Christmas."

There's silence on the other end of the phone.

My younger self explains, "He had to go away for work, and Mom says she doesn't think he'll be home on Christmas Eve. And . . . she's sad about it. We all are. It's not as fun. I miss him." He sighs. "So, if you can make sure he's home tomorrow—you can keep the other stuff."

I grin. Because I know what's coming next.

Wait for it.

"Well . . . maybe not *all* the other stuff," he amends. "You could still drop off the Sega. But you can keep all Lexi's gifts—she won't mind."

Santa's voice turns rough with emotion and conviction as he promises, "Your daddy will be home for Christmas Eve, Drew. I promise."

Young Drew smiles with so much enthusiasm. Delight. Innocence.

It makes me think of my son. The sound of his laughter. The warmth of his embrace. The way he bounces on the bed—even when Kate tells him not to—and he jumps into my arms, with total abandon. Complete faith and trust. Because he knows I'll catch him. That I'd never let him fall.

•

That I'd never let him down.

"Thanks, Santa," my younger self whispers earnestly.

Mackenzie looks up into my eyes. "Did Pop make it home in time?"

My voice takes on a faraway tone, because I remember what happened the next day—and I remember exactly how it felt.

"We went to the Fishers' for Christmas Eve dinner. We were all there—me, Matthew, Steven. At seven years old, your dad was already following your mom around, wanting to hang out with her. I kept watching the door. Waiting for my dad to walk through it. Hoping."

A smile comes to my lips. "And then he did. Laughing and loud and bigger than life. I ran to him and—even before he hugged my mother—he scooped me up and spun me around. Carried me on his shoulder like Tiny fucking Tim. And it felt . . . magical. Like real Christmas magic. And I was so . . . proud of myself. Because I thought my wish brought him home."

I blink, snapping out of my reverie. And I gaze down at Mackenzie. "Out of all the Christmases I enjoyed as a kid . . . that one . . . that one was the best."

"But you forgot about it?"

That's how it happens, right? You grow up, and the wonder of the holidays fades. It becomes more of a burden—places to go, traffic, gifts that have to be found and bought. And you forget the little things, the simple moments that are supposed to make a regular day—more.

"Yeah. I guess I did."

It's only when I glance up from Mackenzie's face that I realize we're not in that small apartment anymore. We're back in my office. My head swims a little—like vertigo. I sit down on the suede couch until it passes. I glance at my watch, and it's the same time as before Mackenzie walked through my door. Still two hours to go before my conference.

"Do you know why I showed you this particular memory tonight?" Mackenzie asks me.

I snort. "To demonstrate I'm obviously more like my father than I ever realized?"

She shakes her head. "No. I showed you this because moments matter. You may not have remembered it, but it still played a part in who you grew up to be. And how you felt about Christmas, your dad, and in some ways, yourself. It's the little things, all added together, that make us who we are. So now that you remember, what are you going to do, Uncle Drew?"

I rub the back of my neck. "I'll . . . I'll find a way to make it up to James after Christmas. Maybe take him to a basketball game for some quality time. Just the two of us."

Mackenzie sighs. And she seems disappointed. It's similar to how Kate looks at me when she comes home from the salon and I'm not excited by the fact that she trimmed off a whole quarter of an inch.

Like . . . I'm missing something.

"Well," she laments, "it's time for me to go."

Even though I'm still *sure* this is a dream—I'm not

taking any chances. "Hold on, sweetheart. I can't leave yet. Hang out here with me and I'll get you home when I'm done."

She sits down on the couch. "Okay, Uncle Drew. Whatever you say."

I head back around my desk, sit, and refocus all my attention on my presentation.

chapter 4

· · · · · · · · · · · · · ·

$\mathcal{M}$ackenzie plays quietly on her phone while I work. She's mature and considerate like that. After a half hour I glance at the couch to thank her—and see that she's fucking gone.

I shoot to my feet. "Mackenzie?" When there's no answer, I rush for the door. Flinging it open I call, "Mack—"

I actually said her full name, but you couldn't hear it.

Because the blaring of "Angels We Have Heard on High" drowned out my voice. And if that wasn't loud enough, there's the echo of bells jingling in the background, the hum of a dozen audio-animatronic elves, reindeer and headless gingerbread men scattered around—and let's not forget the crunch and whistle of falling snow.

Yes, actual snow—inside my goddamn office building.

The main floor outside the offices has been transformed into a winter wonderland.

I just stand there. Stunned.

But I have to say, this beats the shit out of anything the mall has ever come up with.

Then my sister, Alexandra, comes walking around the corner. She's decked out in elegant holiday finery—a red, strapless satin dress, black heels, her hair piled high on her head, with a pearl tiara nestled in the blond curls.

She surveys the room. "God, I'm good."

I cross my arms and lean back against a snow-covered desk. "A little overdone, don't you think?"

Alexandra raises her shoulder. "If you can't overdo Christmas, what can you overdo?" Then she regards me with bright green eyes.

And I deduce, "You're not here to pick up your daughter, are you?"

"No, my daughter is safe and sound. Why do you *think* I'm here, little brother?"

"I'm starting to think it's because every member of my family has been body snatched by green-eyed aliens hell-bent on keeping me from getting any fucking work done."

She shakes her head. "Even your alien invasion theories are egomaniacal."

I push off from the desk. "All right, let's go. The sooner we do this, the sooner I can get back to my desk." And I can't keep the sarcasm out of my voice. "Show me your vision, Christmas ghost. Teach me the error of my ways."

Alexandra scowls. And checks out her manicure. "Now I'm not in the mood."

I grit my teeth. "Alexandra . . ."

"I don't like to be rushed, Drew. You have to invest the time—smell the holly bush, get the full experience. I'm not some wham-bam-thank-you-ma'am."

My face contorts. "I certainly hope not. That's fucking gross."

"The heavens have chosen to intercede on your behalf!" She stomps her foot. "To *help* you. A little gratitude would be nice."

I pinch my nose, breathe deep, and compose myself. Because the spirit bitch is obviously in a tormenting mood, like a cat toying with a mouse before it's devoured. Trying to wriggle out from under her paw will only prolong it. My best option is to just give in. Play dead.

Submit.

"I apologize for being flippant, Alexandra. Thank you for taking the time tonight to educate me. I'm truly fortunate to have a sister and heavenly angel who care so much for my emotional well-being."

Her head bobs side to side, weighing my sincerity. "And do you like the decorations?" she asks petulantly.

I smile. "The decorations are lovely."

Alexandra's expression slides toward appeasement. "And the music?"

"One of my favorite songs—a classic."

She grins teasingly. "I worked *really* hard on the snow."

Submission isn't my forte.

"Goddamn it, Lex!"

She holds her hands up. "Okay, okay." She straightens and clasps my hand. "Come with me."

Together we walk to Steven's office. Instinctively, I close my eyes as we step through the doorway. Then I open them.

"This is . . . this is your apartment," I state.

My sister's condo has the typical regal appointments of an exclusive and ultraexpensive New York City living space. Panoramic views, high ceilings, detailed dark wood moldings, shiny, pristine marble floors. But there's a warmth to it—earth-toned walls, comfy couches, colorful throw pillows, children's framed artwork—that makes it a family friendly home.

"Brilliant observation, as always," she returns.

"When is this?" I ask.

Alexandra's eyes turn sympathetic. "This is tonight. At this very moment. These are the memories you won't be a part of."

We go into the family room, where all the familiar faces are congregated. There's my father, in a black suit and red tie, with a ridiculous Santa hat on his head, talking to Frank Fisher—my father's lifelong friend and business partner—at the wet bar. He pours apple cider into a shot glass for Mackenzie, who's perched on a stool between the two men. A small smile comes to my lips as I gaze at my mom, who looks a couple of decades older than her earlier incarnation, but every bit as beautiful—this time in a simple red dress and black pumps. She's chatting with my sister on the couch. On the far side of the room is my brother-in-law, Steven, his blue eyes sparkling with pride behind his dark-rimmed glasses as he bends his head to hear what his son, Thomas, tells him. They stand in front of the Ping-Pong table—our latest family get-together pastime. They're getting ready to play my best friend, Matthew Fisher, and his five-year-old son, Michael, as they stand on the other side of the table, looking a little like twins with their short light brown hair and similar button-down green shirts.

Adjacent to the table is a love seat, where Matthew's wife and Kate's best friend, Delores "Dee-Dee" Warren, is seated, surprisingly wearing one of her lower-key outfits—a short red leather skirt, a snug white striped sweater, and glowing, dangly Santa Claus earrings.

Next to Dee is Kate, and I can't take my eyes off of her.

An elegant long-sleeved black velvet dress hugs her in all the right places, her dark, shiny hair falls over her shoulder in waves, and open-toe green heels encase her feet. Three-carat diamond earrings—earrings I gave her for our second wedding anniversary—glitter on her ears. She's flawless. And so gorgeous I actually feel my chest tighten with a mixture of pride and ever present desire.

It's the perfect family gathering. Evergreens and bows add a holiday flair to the decor, Christmas music plays cheerfully in the background, and dozens of delicious-smelling dishes rest on a buffet table, waiting to be uncovered. It's a modernized version of an idyllic Norman Rockwell image—the entire room is alive with laughter and joyful chatter. Everyone's happy to be there, everyone's having a good time.

Everyone except my son, James.

He's unusually quiet, sitting on the recliner next to the love seat. His dark brown eyes alternate between watching the Ping-Pong match and glancing down the hall toward the front door.

Steven, who's always been attuned to how others are feeling, nudges James with his elbow. "What do you say, buddy? You want to be on Thomas's and my team? We could use another man."

My five-year-old son smiles genuinely and glances down at the two Ping-Pong paddles in his hands. "That's okay, Uncle Steven—I'm gonna wait for my daddy. I'll be on his team."

And doesn't *that* just make me feel like two cents' worth of shit. Because he's completely unaware that I have no intention of showing up.

James's words immediately grab Kate's attention, and she crouches down in front of him. "Honey, remember I told you Daddy had to work tonight? He didn't want to, but he had to. I don't think he's going to be here to play Ping-Pong."

James smiles at her reassuringly. "Yeah, I remember, but he'll come after he's done working. I know he will. He'll make it in time."

Kate's eyes cloud with worry, because she doesn't want our little boy disappointed. Not on Christmas Eve. And sure as hell not because of his father.

"Can I play with you?" she offers. "I play a mean game of Ping-Pong."

James giggles. "Thanks, Mommy, but I want to wait for Daddy."

Kate tries again. "But what if he can't come, honey?"

James gazes back at her calmly, confidently, because he believes every word he's saying. "Daddy told me that 'can't' isn't a real word. That anything someone wants to do badly enough—they'll do. He said 'can't just means they won't,' or that they don't want to. So that's how I know he's coming. Because it's Christmas Eve, and there's nowhere Daddy wants to be more than here with us. So he'll be here."

Guilty pain lances my heart, and I cover it with my hand. I think I might actually fucking cry.

"Ouch," my spirit sister says beside me. "That's gotta hurt. And you thought the mother guilt was bad."

I shake my head. "I'm such a dick. How can I be such a giant asshole and not know it?"

Christmas Alexandra takes pity on me. She pats my shoulder. "You're not really that bad. You're just a little self-absorbed sometimes. You don't see things from others' perspectives—how your actions may affect them."

Back in the apartment, Kate brushes back the locks of James's hair that have fallen over his forehead. "You are the smartest, sweetest little boy ever, you know that?"

He grins. "Yeah, you're pretty lucky."

My wife laughs. Then she kisses his forehead and moves back to the love seat, next to her best friend. She glances worriedly down the hall toward the front door, and there's sharp anger in her tone when she whispers to

Delores, "If James gets hurt tonight because of Drew, he and I are going to have a *major* problem."

Delores nods. But then—maybe Christmas really *is* magic, because she defends me. Kind of. "Don't give up hope, Katie. Dipshit may actually pull his head out of his ass long enough to realize where he should be. He's come through before when I didn't think he would. So . . . keep the faith. You never know."

Kate sips her wine, looking distinctly uncomforted.

Then the Ping-Pong participants shout loudly as Michael gets the ball past his uncle—scoring the winning point. His father gives him a high five and a hug.

"Well played, sir," Steven congratulates.

"Nice shot," my son calls sincerely.

Then he sighs. And goes back to watching the door.

Though I know he can't hear me, I start to move toward him so I can explain how crucial tonight's conference call is. So he'll understand. But even in my head, the justifications sound pretty fucking hollow.

And I don't get the chance to, anyway. My sister's hand on my shoulder stops me. "Come along—we still have another stop to make."

"So I can feel even worse than I do right now?" I give a sarcastic two-thumbs-up. "Yay."

She takes my hand and I reluctantly follow her out the front door.

❄   ❄   ❄

And we step seamlessly into my apartment.

There's a fire burning in the living room fireplace

but the lights are turned down low. And it's quiet—the only sound to be heard is Kate's singing voice floating softly down the hall from James's bedroom. She does that sometimes—sings him to sleep. At the moment, she's doing a fucktastic rendition of "Have Yourself a Merry Little Christmas." I imagine her running her fingers through his soft hair as his eyes grow heavy. Then, when he's finally out—she'll kiss his forehead and smell the still-child-sweet scent of his skin.

"This is later tonight," my sister informs me. "While you're at the office on your video business meeting."

A few seconds later, the song ends and Kate comes walking down the hall. Her hair is pulled up and she's wearing a dark green silk nightshirt that accentuates the green flecks in her eyes. With white socks, because hardwood floors are freaking freezing in the winter.

In her hands, Kate holds a bottle of wine and a single glass. She uncorks it on the coffee table and pours a double serving into the glass. Then she opens the hall closet and sticks her head inside. As she rummages around, pulling out baseball bats and ski jackets that I astutely used to camouflage the presents inside, the back of her nightgown starts to ride up, and the "Ho, ho, ho" written across the ass of her red panties peeks out.

I tilt my head for a better angle of the luscious sight.

Addiction is an illness. But there are times—like this one—that it's an enjoyable one. I can't help myself, and if I'm being honest, I don't really want to.

Alexandra frowns at me. "Focus, please."

I clear my throat and nod.

Eventually, Kate succeeds in dragging out two boxes that are longer than she is.

She opens them, lays out all the pieces neatly, and settles herself among them on the floor. She takes a sip of her wine, opens the instruction manual, and gives herself a pep talk.

"If Drew wants to work, he can work. I got this covered. How hard could it be?"

We should pause here briefly and think about that statement. How hard can putting a child's toy together really be?

Past experience tells me—pretty fucking hard. If you have kids, you know exactly what I'm talking about.

I don't get it. Clear illustrations, simple direct steps—is that really too goddamn much to ask for? And don't get me started on the packaging. I realize that shoplifting is a drain on stores, but is it necessary to wrap *every single* fucking component in plastic, wire, and industrial-strength tape? The only people that deters are the parents trying to put it together.

I've wondered who makes that call at the toy companies. Who decides which pieces get tied down and at what potency. Whoever it is—I bet he was bullied in high school. Or maybe he was poor and didn't get to play with any toys when he was a kid. So now—every day—he takes his sick, twisted revenge by making it as difficult as humanly possible for anyone to put together a toy that should be a piece of fucking cake.

I feel better now that I got that off my chest. Thanks. So, back to Kate: fifteen minutes after getting started, she's got all of three pieces put together on James's bicycle.

She picks up the instructions and turns them sideways. Then she holds them upright and tries turning her head sideways.

"Are you kidding me?" she yells at the paper, flinging it to the ground. Then she speaks threateningly to the bike parts as she tries to force them to connect. "Just. Go. In. You. Bastard!"

When that doesn't work, she takes a breath and a sip of wine. She brushes the wisps of hair that've escaped her bun away from her face. Then she picks up a blue metal rod. "You are component A. You need to be inserted into component B's hole. Work with me, here."

And now she's back to shoving.

I squat down next to her. "It looks like rod A is too well endowed for B's hole. Maybe they need some lube."

If she could hear me, Kate would chuckle. And she'd look at me like I was the cleverest man in the world.

But she can't. So she just continues to grit her teeth and struggle with the metal bars.

Until her hand slips.

And her finger gets pinched between two pieces of steel.

With a curse, Kate drops the bike pieces and flaps her hand, trying to shake the pain away. Then she puts her finger in her mouth.

It's something I would've done if I were here. Sucked her finger until it was all better. Then I would've gotten her a Band-Aid or ice.

Once her finger is probably just a dull throb, Kate rubs her forehead. She looks tired.

And sad.

And for the first time tonight, I wish I'd chosen differently. It's not only because I feel guilty—though I do. But if I could go back, I'd be here with her right now. And it would be a shitload more enjoyable for both of us.

Kate picks up her glass of wine, eyes the red liquid, then holds it up unhappily. "Merry Christmas, Kate."

And I'm done.

I don't want to watch this anymore. I don't want to know that my actions have hurt the feelings of the two people who mean the most to me.

Because I'm a guy. And to the great annoyance of women everywhere—guys are doers. We don't just listen to you babble about your problems; we tell you how to fix them.

And we never understand why you get pissed off about that. Why you just want us to be a "sounding board" or a "good listener." What the fuck is the point of sounding off if you're not going to *do* anything about it?

So I'm going back to my office, and then I'm going to haul ass home to help Kate assemble James's presents. And I'm going to wake up my son and tell him I'm sorry. That I'll play Ping-Pong with him every damn day if it makes him happy.

I stand up and look into the eyes of my big sister. Almost like she can read my mind, she says, "Okay. Let's go, then."

Alexandra holds my hand and we walk to the elevators outside my apartment door. We step inside and they close behind us. When they reopen, we're on the fortieth floor of my office building. And all the decorations—the music, the snow—are gone now.

Outside my closed office door, I turn toward my sister.

"Thank you, Alexandra. Really, this time."

She smiles. "Do you know what life is, Drew?"

"A cosmic joke?"

She snorts. "No. Life is a memory. Sure, we enjoy the moments as they come, but for many, time goes by too fast to truly appreciate those moments as they happen. It's only later, when we remember them, that they become precious to us. A life well lived is one where the good memories outweigh the bad."

I rub the back of my neck. "That's kind of depressing."

"It doesn't have to be." She shakes her head softly. "Never pass up the opportunity to make a beautiful memory, Drew."

Then she kisses my cheek and disappears.

chapter 5

. . . .

After Alexandra is gone, I wait.

My guardian angel said there'd be three spirits visiting me, and I have a feeling I'm not going to wake up from this dream until bachelorette number three gets her turn.

When nothing happens, I try to help things along. "Hello? Anybody here? You win—I feel really fucking guilty. I'm going to cancel my conference and go home now. Happy?"

The only answer I receive is silence.

I take one last glance around, then open my office door and step inside.

And I'm blinded by flashing green and red lights. A pounding electric guitar version of "Jingle Bells" pierces my eardrums, while a white foggy mist clouds my vision of the room. Out from behind my desk steps a tall creature whose face is obscured by a flowing red satin hooded robe.

Suddenly, the flashing lights disappear and the music cuts off.

I wouldn't say I'm scared . . . but intimidated fits nicely. "Are you . . . are you the spirit of Christmas future?"

I don't expect an answer. In the movie, the last, most frightening spirit never talks. If it pulls the hood back, I suppose it'll have a black hole where its face should be—maybe a skeleton head. I brace myself as hands with long red nails reach for the hood and reveal the countenance beneath it.

Did I think this was a dream? Nope. It's a nightmare.

Because standing before me, grinning evilly, is none other than Delores Warren, the ever-present pain in my ass.

"That's me," she proclaims. "The biggest, baddest Christmas spirit there ever was."

I hold out my hand to shield my view. "Can you put the hood back up?"

She glares. "Ha-ha, asswipe. I wouldn't be making jokes if I were you, seeing as how you've screwed up. *Again*."

I cross my arms. "I guess that means you're taking me to the future. Show me my grave, and how no one gives a shit that I'm dead because of my selfish ways?"

She scrunches her nose and shakes her head. "That's Ebenezer's gig—he's always been an emo-bastard." Delores fingers the pearl brooch at the neck of her robe as she asks, "Have you ever wondered how your life would've turned out if you and Kate had never met?"

"Not really."

I was never big on philosophy. Waste of time, as far

as I'm concerned. Besides, Kate and I did meet, so the *would've, could've, should've* doesn't apply.

"Well, I have," she says. "I always suspected Katie would've been better off without you. So we're not going to the future. I'm going to show you this night as it would be if Kate had never come to New York, and never fell victim to your man-whore charms."

Is that something you want to see?

Because I'm not interested. Because . . . if Delores is right, and Kate really is better off without me? That knowledge would break my fucking heart like nothing else ever could.

I shake my head. "No, thanks. I'll sit this one out."

Her green eyes gleam. Almost menacingly. "Lucky for me, you don't have a choice in the matter."

With that, she spins toward me, the red cloak billowing around us. I feel her hand on my arm and the whole world shifts—falls—then comes to a jerking stop, like the end of a roller-coaster ride.

I look around. We've landed back in the outer hallway of my sister's condo. The door is open and a version of me stands in the doorway, saying good-bye to his family inside. He seems a little more worn around the edges—but still one hell of a good-looking guy.

"So this me made it to Christmas Eve dinner?" I ask.

"Without a wife and kid taking up your time, you were able to get the conference with Hawaii done earlier." Then Delores points at the other me. "Notice the crow's-feet. Since he didn't settle down with Kate, there's a few more years of hard partying under his belt—and his eyes. But, sorry to say, no one's kicking you out of her bed yet."

I wave my hand, quieting her annoying commentary so I can hear the conversation going on at the door.

"You're sure you don't want to stay the night?" Alexandra asks. "You could wake up with us, open presents—nothing makes Christmas feel more like Christmas than kids getting up at the crack of dawn."

Kateless Drew hugs Mackenzie and Thomas, then kisses Alexandra on the cheek. "Sounds tempting, but I'm good."

His mother clicks her tongue disapprovingly. "I hate the idea of you being all alone."

He smirks. "Then you have nothing to worry about, Mom. I hardly ever spend the entire night alone."

Steven chuckles and taps Drew's fist.

His mom rolls her eyes. "It's Christmas Eve, don't be vulgar."

Drew shakes his father's hand. "See you guys tomorrow."

With that, he leaves. But he doesn't go home.

He walks a few blocks until he comes to the most dependable pickup spot in any city. The place responsible for more sexual encounters than a highway rest stop bathroom.

A hotel bar.

While he stands at the entry, scanning for prospects, I do the same. It's been awhile for me, but spotting the easy pickings is like riding a bike—a skill you never really forget.

Our eyes settle on a forty-something redhead in phenomenal shape, sitting alone at a corner table. Drew orders two drinks from the bartender—a Jack and Coke for himself, and whatever the lady is having.

Then he makes his move.

"Mind if I join you?" he asks her with a smile.

After her eyes shamelessly undress him, she nods. "Please." He sets her drink in front of her and she thanks him.

He assumes she's at the hotel because she doesn't actually live in New York. So he asks, "Are you visiting the city for business or pleasure?"

She sips her drink and licks her lip provocatively. "Originally, business—I'm in real estate. But now it seems I'll be multitasking."

Drew winks. "I'm an excellent multitasker. I'm able to give my attention to many different areas at once. I'd love to demonstrate that talent for you sometime."

Redhead smiles wider. Then she says, "Mistletoe."

"Pardon?"

She points above them. "My hotel room has mistletoe printed on the sheets, in honor of the holiday season. How would you feel about kissing me under it?"

Drew chuckles. "I believe that's a holiday tradition that should always be observed." They finish their drinks, then stand. Ever the gentleman, Drew motions with his hand. "After you."

And together they head upstairs.

❄   ❄   ❄

The redhead's room is actually a suite. Delores and I sit on the couch in the common area while the other version of myself and the redhead get busy in the bedroom.

From what I can hear—which is a lot—Redhead is quite flexible.

"Uh . . . fuck."

"Oh . . . oh . . . oh."

"Shit . . . yes!"

"Oh . . . yeah."

"That's it . . . yes . . . more . . . make me your bitch."

"Jesus . . ."

And on it goes.

For an hour.

Then two.

From the couch, I stare at the ceiling. And think about repainting the home office.

Delores glares at me. "You're enjoying this, aren't you?"

I squint as I consider her question. "Not as much as I thought I would. I mean, it's not really me, so I have nothing to feel guilty about. But still . . ."

Hearing any version of myself banging the hell out of a woman who isn't Kate is just . . . bizarre. In a disturbing kind of way. Not a turn-on.

After a high-pitched scream and a roaring grunt, the noise from the bedroom quiets down. Until . . .

"Mmm . . ."

"Oh . . ."

"Uh . . . uh . . . uh . . ."

Delores throws up her hands. "Now this is just fucking ridiculous."

I shrug unapologetically. "Picasso had his clay, Rembrandt had his brushes—I have my cock. Every true artist has a favorite tool. And you can't rush fine art."

"*Yes, yes, yes . . .*"

"*Oh fuck . . .*"

She rolls her eyes. "I'm fast-forwarding."

"Thank Christ. Why didn't you think of that sooner?"

I follow her out of the hotel room door. And we step into the living room of my apartment. My *old* apartment, before Kate and I lived together. The ultimate bachelor pad—black, stainless steel, and big-boy toys, remember?

We stand in the living room as Kateless Drew comes strolling through the door—his shirt half buttoned, whistling a merry tune. He takes a quick shower, then, clad only in boxers, pours himself a bowl of cereal. He sits back on the couch, puts his feet on the coffee table, and flicks on the television.

With a mouthful of cereal, he smiles. "*A Christmas Story.* Cool." And he settles in to watch.

"I don't understand," I say.

"'Cause you're a moron," Delores answers flatly.

"Instead of insulting me, can you explain what the hell I'm supposed to be getting from this? I thought the point of showing me my life without Kate was to demonstrate how miserable I'd be without her." I gesture to my other self on the couch. "He's fine. He loves his life. What's the lesson here?"

With restrained impatience, Dee explains. "Of course he loves his life—being a raging man-slut was one of your favorite things. You always enjoyed your work, your life before Kate. But if you can't see the lesson, then you're not looking hard enough, Drew."

I push a frustrated hand through my hair and look again. The other me chuckles at the TV and puts his empty bowl on the table. Then I gaze around the apartment. The pristine neatness, the monotone furniture, the valuable abstract art on the walls.

And for the very first time, it feels . . . cold. Flat.

Empty.

I think of my apartment with Kate and James—our home. It's light and vibrant and messy in the best frigging way. There's pencil marks on the wall showing how James has grown and a few scratches on the hardwood floors. There are mementos from vacations and pictures all over of our wedding and every significant moment in James's life. There are toys and work papers, coats and shoes. It's not messy, but—lived in. Busy.

Full.

"He's happy," I realize. "Because he has no idea what he's missing."

Delores nods. "That's right. He doesn't know what he's missing."

A cold shiver runs through me. Because this easily could've been me. It could've turned out so differently, and I never would've known.

"I want to go back," I tell her firmly. "Right now. I want to see Kate and James. Take me back, Dee."

She looks at me with an unfamiliar sympathetic expression. "Almost, Drew. One more stop to make."

She laces her arm in mine and we're off.

❅ ❅ ❅

We stand inside a corner office on an impressively high floor of a city high-rise. Beige granite and polished glass accent the desk, while unwelcoming white couches face off with a glass table between them. Before I can ask Delores where we are, the door opens and in strides Katherine Brooks.

Her hair is pulled back in a low bun; she's wearing just a touch of makeup, an immaculate white-and-black skirt with a coordinating jacket, and high heels. She's stunning, perfectly professional and cock-stiffening sexy all in one petite package.

In long confident steps, she makes her way behind the desk while talking into a headset microphone. "I'm sorry, that's not a stipulation we're willing to budge on. Take it or leave it."

I glance at Delores. "Is this . . . is it still Christmas Eve?"

Her lips purse with curiosity. "Yes it is."

I point my finger. "Ha! I was right—I *knew* Kate would work on Christmas Eve if the shoe was on the other foot."

I can't wait to tell her I was right.

Again, Dee's eyes roll. "That's the first thing you want clarification on?"

I shrug. "I was right. It's a big deal."

"We're in Chicago."

"Why Chicago?"

"Because in this reality, this is where Kate and Billy

moved after she got her MBA." She pauses. "And after they got married."

My head snaps to her. "What? She actually fucking *married* Douche Bag? Are you shitting me?"

For those who need a little backstory, here you go: Billy "Douche Bag" Warren is Delores's cousin and Kate's high school sweetheart. He was her fiancé when we first met. Not too long after, he became her ex-fiancé, clearing the way for her and me to enjoy a stupendous fuck-fest of a weekend. It still ranks as one of the best weekends of my life. And it was during that very weekend that I came to the shocking realization that I was utterly and pussy-whippedly in love with Kate Brooks.

Because Kate and Billy had grown up together, had so much history together, they stayed close friends—much to my dismay—after their breakup, after she and I got together, and after we were married.

Which all explains why I'm feeling frustration, disgust, jealousy, anger. Pick a negative emotion, and I'm feeling it at this moment.

"Why would she do that?" I demand.

Dee lifts a shoulder casually. "Because they were engaged. Because they thought they loved each other . . . enough. Because they settled. And also because she never met you—so she never realized what genuine passion and love are supposed to feel like."

"I can't believe she married him." Again, my hand covers my heart.

Because it aches.

"If it makes you feel any better, they got divorced."

I perk right up. "You should have started with that. It makes me feel hugely fucking better, by the way."

Under her breath, she hisses, "Ass." Then she explains. "Billy and Katie stuck it out for three years, then called it quits. He went out to LA and she threw herself into her work like never before. They don't speak at all. When a marriage goes sour, it always leaves a bitter taste."

My attention turns back to Kate as she speaks into the headset again. "Stop busting my balls, Saul. You and I both know the glory days of your technology division are behind you."

I take a seat on the stiff couch and watch her. I could look at Kate all day and never get bored, but watching her work? Seeing her in her element?

It's fascinating. A thing of true beauty.

She braces her hands on the desk, tapping her toe on the floor. "You're quickly becoming a small fish in a very large ocean. Before long, a big bad shark is going to come along and chomp you into little pieces. But if you do the smart thing, sign with me and let me make this deal for you—I'll be your own personal harpoon. And we'll feast on shark fin soup together. What's it gonna be, Mr. Anderson?"

Fucking Christ almighty.

Saul Anderson.

There's a blast from the past.

The first client Kate and I tried to close. The one who basically sexually harassed her, and who I told to go screw a pooch. And now Kate has him on the ropes.

Even though this is some weird, fucked-up alternate reality, I'm so damn proud of her.

I don't hear Anderson's answer, but I don't have to. The adorable hand-flapping, hip-shaking dance of joy she does around her desk says it all.

Though she's smiling wide enough to pull a cheek muscle, she composes her voice. "That sounds perfect. I'll have the papers overnighted to you. Excellent. Yes, to you as well—I think this will be a very happy New Year."

She ends the call, and her dancing turns to jumping. Laughing.

And I laugh with her.

She picks up the phone and dials a new number. "Hi, Christopher. Oh . . . yes, Merry Christmas to you, too. It sounds like you're having quite the party there."

She pauses as *Christopher* responds.

I ask Dee sharply, "Who's Christopher?"

"Relax, Hulk—he's her boss. Nothing more. In fact, she has a less-than-zero social life."

I consider that for a moment. "She doesn't date? No boyfriend? No random hookups, no no-strings-attached fuck-buddy waiting in the wings?"

Delores shakes her head. "Kate was never a one-night-stand kind of girl. After Billy, she gave up on relationships altogether. Too much effort, very little payoff."

I smile.

And Dee inquires, "That makes you happy, doesn't it?"

I cannot tell a lie. "Yeah, it really does."

She throws a pillow at my head.

Kate's voice brings my eyes back to her. "I wanted to let you know that I just signed Saul Anderson. That's right! Merry Christmas indeed."

Christopher responds, and a look of pure pride and joy washes over her face. "I'm thrilled to accept the vice president position. Yes. Absolutely—you can count on me, Chris. Okay, I will. Have a pleasant evening, as well."

She hangs up and more dancing commences. Her boobs bounce in time with her hips, and the only thing that would make this show better is popcorn.

Well . . . and if her clothes spontaneously fell off.

Kate picks up the phone and tells her mother all about the big promotion. They only talk for a few minutes—Kate promises to come home soon to visit. Then she hangs up.

She takes a bottle of champagne out of her minifridge and pours a single glass. Then she kicks off her shoes and walks to the window, gazing out over the lights of the city.

I stand up so my view is unobstructed.

As Kate stands there, her joyous expression slowly falters. Turns . . . sad . . . awash with yearning. Lonely.

I think about all the different faces of Kate that I've seen. Passionate, hot and horny, sweet and tender, silly and smart-assy . . . nurturing, loving . . . motherly.

She's a perfect wife. And she's the most amazing mother.

But here, now, she didn't get to be any of those things.

And that's so fucking wrong.

Kate glances at her glass of champagne and whispers, "Merry Christmas, Kate." Then she takes a sip.

"Hey, Dee?"

"Yeah?"

"Remember when I said I was happy that Kate wasn't involved with anyone?"

"Yes."

"I'm not happy about it anymore."

Delores walks to me and takes my arm. "Then it's time to go."

❉   ❉   ❉

We're back in my office—my *real* office. The family portrait of me, Kate, and James sitting on my desk proves that this is *my* time, *my* reality—where Kate and I met, fell in love, spawned, and married.

And I sigh with blessed fucking relief.

I'm at my desk while Delores sits cross-legged in one of the chairs across from me.

"You were thinking about soul mates before. Remember? The truth is, soul mates are real: halves of the same coin. They can live without each other, go on to have successful, content existences. But they'll never be as perfectly happy as they would've been, and could be, if they find their other half. That's what you and Kate are like."

I smile. "That sounds just about right to me." I rub a hand down my face. "I want to go home, Dee. I want to hug my kid and kiss my wife and just . . . be with them. I want to look back and remember having this awesome night—with them."

Delores grins and she almost looks proud of me. "First you have to wake up, Drew."

And she snaps her fingers.

chapter 6

. . . .

I jolt violently awake at my desk, nailing my shin on the drawer in the process. "Goddamn it!"

I rub my leg and check the time. Seven thirty. Though it feels like a lot longer, only an hour and a half has passed since I arrived at the office.

I still have time.

I rattle off a quick email, canceling my conference with Media Solutions and attaching a PDF of my proposal. I tell them, in a professional sounding way, that they can take it or leave it, and if they leave it—it's their loss.

Then I grab my stuff and sprint through the city.

I walk through my sister's apartment door twenty minutes later, brushing snowflakes off my shoulders from the storm that just started. I head right for the family room—and see everyone there, just like I knew they would be.

A dark-haired little blur runs toward me. "Daddy!"

Laughing, I scoop him up and hug James until he squeaks. He leans back and gifts me with a faultless smile. "I knew you'd come."

A lump clogs my throat.

I push past it to tell him, "And I'm so happy that you knew that. I love you, buddy. More than anything else in the whole world."

He giggles. "I know."

I keep him in my arms as Alexandra comes to greet me. "It's about time."

"Sorry I'm late." And I hug her just a little longer than usual. "I don't think I've told you lately, but you're the best sister ever, Lexi."

She ruffles my hair. "How sweet are you?"

From across the room, Mackenzie raises her shot glass of apple cider. "Glad you could make it, Uncle Drew."

"Glad to be here, sweetheart! You and I need to talk—I owe you. I'll explain later."

My sister insists, "No ponies, or farm animals of any kind!"

And the whole room laughs.

I pass Delores and shock the shit out of her by kissing her on the cheek. "Merry Christmas, Dee."

She looks at me like I've lost my mind. "Are you drunk?"

I chuckle. "Kind of feels like it."

Then I spot Kate. And every fiber of my being hums with devotion and relief.

She eyes me warily. Stiffly. Still annoyed.

I set James on his feet. "You want to kick Uncle Matthew's and Uncle Steven's asses in Ping-Pong?"

"Definitely!"

I jerk my head to the table. "Go set it up. I'm going to talk to your mom a sec."

I walk up to Kate and guide her to a corner of the room, out of the others' earshot.

"Did your meeting finish up early?" she asks in a steely voice.

Can't really blame her.

"I canceled the meeting."

Her big, gorgeous brown eyes look surprised. And hopeful. "Why?"

"Because being here with you is more important than any deal. I never should've scheduled work on Christmas Eve. I never should've left the apartment when you were upset about it. I won't do it again. I'm sorry."

Kate gazes into my eyes, reading my sincerity. Then she smiles. With so much love, it makes my knees tremble.

"I forgive you."

I pull her to me and kiss her deeply. Tenderly. Stroking her cheek with my thumb.

Then Kate looks up into my face. "Are you okay? You seem different."

"I had this really screwed-up dream. I'll tell you about it later." Then I think of something else. "Hey—what do you think of going to Bumfuck, Ohio, for New Year's Eve?"

She smiles even brighter. "I would love that."

I wink. "Then so will I."

❊ ❊ ❊

Later, after we tuck James into bed and he's out cold, Kate and I spend two hours putting together a shiny blue bicycle and an eight-foot-wide kid's trampoline with enclosure that will take up residence in the formal dining room.

At least that room will finally have a frigging purpose.

When we're finished, just after midnight, we sit back on the couch and gaze at the fruits of our labor. The twinkling lights of the tree reflect magically off the big red bows and the green reindeer wrapping paper. Behind the tree, outside the large picture window, delicate snowflakes cascade down from the dark sky—it's a picture straight out of a goddamn Hallmark holiday special.

Kate's eyes settle on me. Adoringly. "We make a pretty good team."

I rub her shoulder. "We really do."

It's something I'll never forget again.

I get up and head to the kitchen. When I come back, there's two wineglasses and a bottle of Chateau Petrus 2002 in my hands. I uncork the bottle, letting it breathe for less time than I should, and pour a generous glass for each of us.

Kate takes the wine with a smile, and I raise my glass. "Merry Christmas, Kate."

She taps my glass with a clink. "Merry Christmas, Drew."

We sip, then I lean in for a wine-flavored kiss.
Delicious.

Next, I stand up and mess with the stereo. The sound of Michael Bublé singing "Have Yourself a Merry Little Christmas" fills the room, low enough not to wake James. I take her glass and set it on the table.

Then I hold out my hand to my amazing wife. "May I have this dance, Mrs. Evans?"

Her warm hand slides into mine. "There's nothing I'd rather do, Mr. Evans." Then—because Kate is the perfect woman—she adds, "Well, maybe there's one thing—but I'm sure we'll get to that later."

I chuckle deeply. My arms wrap around her, holding her against me, her head resting against my chest. And in the light of the Christmas tree, we sway in time to the music.

Was it all just a dream?

Honestly? I don't fucking know. But I'm grateful it happened. Because even someone as brilliant as me needs a refresher once in a while about what's really important. The moments that matter. And the people we can't and don't want to imagine living without.

As I dance with the love of my life on Christmas Eve, I swear I hear the soft ring of a bell. And if you believe what that legend says, then somewhere, an angel has gotten her wings.

Saving Grace

A Love Under the Big Sky Novella

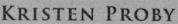

KRISTEN PROBY

chapter 1

. . . .

~ Grace ~

You have to come with us," Cara Donovan exclaims over her third glass of Moscato. "Seriously, Gracie, it's going to be so fun."

"I'm not a skier," I remind her dryly.

"There will be a lodge and hot ski instructors and a spa," Jill Sullivan reminds me.

"I plan to take advantage of that spa," Lauren Cunningham agrees.

"To spas and hot ski instructors!" Jenna Hull raises her wineglass in a toast.

I sit back in my seat and stare at my four friends assembled in Jill's living room. They're all beautiful, fun, wonderful women.

"Seriously, a bachelorette weekend in Aspen?" I ask with a frown. "Couldn't you choose somewhere tropical? I probably won't drown from a chaise longue by the pool."

Jill tips her head back, her dark hair falling down her back in waves. "Cara likes the snow."

"This is Montana. We live in the snow," I reply stubbornly. "Didn't you have a say?" I ask Lauren.

Both Cara and Lauren were recently engaged, and to celebrate, the five of us are going to take a weekend trip away. I was all in when I had visions of palm trees and cabana boys, but now . . .

"I think it sounds fun," Lauren replies with a grin. "We chartered a plane and everything."

My jaw drops and my gaze travels from Lo to Cara in disbelief.

"You chartered a freaking *plane*?" Jenna replies with a squeak. Jenna is stunning. Classically beautiful, reminding me of Grace Kelly with her perfectly coifed blond hair and startling blue eyes. Not to mention her perfect figure.

If she wasn't so incredibly sweet, we might all hate her.

"Hey, this is a celebration," Lo reminds us and sips her wine, tucking a strand of her auburn hair behind her ear. The ring on her finger winks in the candlelight.

"Guys, you know I'm totally on board for celebrating your engagements. I couldn't be happier for you." I swallow the last sip of wine in my glass and bite my lip. "But we all know what a colossal klutz I am. I won't survive the trip."

Jill refills my glass as Cara shakes her head.

"We have a surprise for you," she says.

"A sumo wrestler suit I can wear while skiing so I don't break every bone in my body?"

"No," Lo replies with a laugh. "A night on Whitetail Mountain."

I frown, not understanding. "The ski resort, Whitetail Mountain?"

"The same," Jenna replies smugly. "Grace, it's time you learned to ski."

"I've lived at the base of this mountain for six years," I remind them as my stomach sinks. "I've never been on a pair of skis for a reason."

"Don't be silly." Jill waves me off and pushes an envelope at me. "We've booked you for Friday night. It's a half day at school for you, so you can make your two o'clock lesson time."

"You'll stay the night at Snow Ghost Lodge, have another two-hour lesson Saturday morning, and then a massage at the lodge's spa, just in case."

"I don't think it's safe to massage broken legs," I mutter.

"Grace, Aspen won't be the same without you." Cara bats those big hazel eyes at me and I know I'll cave. She's one of my closest friends. How can I say no?

"Okay," I agree softly and swig my wine. "I'll go learn to ski."

"You're going to love it," Jenna assures me. "And my place is nearby, so if you need me, just call."

"Why don't I just stay at your bed-and-breakfast?" I ask. "We could have a sleepover."

"I'm booked for the season," she replies with a wide grin. "Business is good."

"Good for you!" Lo exclaims and holds her fist out for a bump.

"So you get a minivacation twenty minutes from home." Cara grins and clinks her glass with mine. "May you find many hot ski instructors."

"They're probably all college kids, Cara. I'm a bit too old for them."

"You look like a college kid yourself," Jill says with a wink. "You have the cutest pixie cut I've ever seen, by the way. Is it easy to take care of?"

"I love it," I reply and push my fingers through my short blond hair. "It's super easy, but don't you dare even think about cutting off your hair."

The conversation segues to hairstylists and shampoo and I listen with half an ear, dreading this coming weekend. I am the world's biggest klutz. I fall every day. I'm lucky I'm small because if I were a bigger girl, I'd be in constant pain.

As it is, I keep a bottle of Advil on me at all times.

Ah well, what's a few broken bones when your friend's happiness is on the line, right?

"Right, Grace?"

"I'm sorry, what?"

"Kyle at work has been acting really weird," Cara repeats.

"I think his wife is sick," I reply softly, my heart immediately hurting for our boss and friend.

"Kyle Reardon?" Jill confirms.

"Yeah, I heard that Lily has cancer."

"That's so sad," Lo whispers and sips her wine.

"They have four children," Jenna adds with a shake of her head. "That's horrible."

"I'll have to go see him tomorrow, see if they need anything." Cara pulls out her phone to make a note.

"So, back to your mini ski-cation," Jill says with a glint in her eye. "You're going to have so much fun."

"I heard the lodge sold recently," Lo adds. "I wonder who bought it?"

"Some billionaire," Jill answers.

"Did you sell it to him?" I ask her. Jill is a real estate agent, and a damn good one.

"No, my boss got that deal." She sighs and sticks her lower lip out in a pout. "But I hear Mr. Billionaire is hot."

"I've seen him," Jenna replies with a shrug. "He's pretty hot. Seems nice."

"When did you see him?" Cara asks. "You've been holding out!"

"I went up there for dinner one night and he was having dinner at the same time. His staff seems to like him. Especially the women." She wiggles her eyebrows with a laugh.

"I'm sure I won't run into him." I take one last swallow of wine and decide to call it a night while I can still walk down the block to the house I share with my roommate, Hannah.

I hope I can walk that far.

"Well, if you do run into him, maybe you can have a nice weekend affair with him," Jill says nonchalantly.

"Right, 'cause I just have weekend affairs on a regular basis." I roll my eyes and then giggle at the ludicrous thought.

"If you can't bang the billionaire, bang a hot ski instructor," Lo says.

"I'm not banging anyone!"

"Why not?" Jenna asks. "You're hot. You should bang someone."

Dear God, the girls are all drunk.

"Maybe you'll find a hot ski instructor to bang in Aspen," I say to Jenna who cracks a wide, drunk smile and raises her glass.

"From your lips to God's ears, my friend."

❆ ❆ ❆

This is a mistake.

The road up Whitetail Mountain is well paved and sanded, but still treacherous. It's narrow, and the switchbacks are tight, making me nervous with the fresh snow and cold weather.

I should have taken the commuter bus that runs up and down the mountain during ski season.

I pass Jenna's B&B, The Hideout, grinning as I think of my pretty friend. I'm so proud of her for making a success of her business. I honk and wave, just in case she can see me, then turn around one more switchback and climb another quarter of a mile before driving into a quaint, beautiful snow village. Ski lifts climb up to the summit of the mountain, forging a path in the evergreens, moving slowly with people sitting in the seats, their skis dangling from their feet.

A condo complex sits on the left, the balconies full of bicycles and hanging plants that died months ago.

Up ahead is a wide parking lot before a grand, beautiful, rustic lodge. The Snow Ghost Lodge, to be exact. It sits right at the base of the ski lifts, convenient for those who want to step outside, fasten their skis, and set off for a day in the powder.

People of all shapes, sizes, and ages are milling about, in ski pants and coats, hats, and gloves, carrying skis on their shoulders. Kids throw snowballs at each other and their parents yell at them to keep it to the hill.

It's absolutely stunning.

The tall evergreen trees are covered in white powder, and I'm reminded how blessed I am to live in such an amazing place.

So far away from the desert of Arizona.

I park in the valet area of the lodge and climb out of my SUV just as a parking attendant comes to help me with my bags.

I slam my door shut and move to walk away, but am pulled up short.

I've slammed my coat in the door.

I sigh and close my eyes, then tilt my head back and look up at the sky.

"Really? Already? You couldn't wait until I've at least put skis on my feet?"

I open the door and rescue my coat, then turn to find the valet and several others watching me curiously.

Great.

I simply smile and nod and take my bag from the young valet, tip him, and walk into the beautiful lodge.

Immediately to my left is a large river-rock fireplace, complete with a roaring fire. There are clusters of soft couches and chairs arranged to sit in and warm up, or just wait for your loved ones to ski while you read a book and sip a hot toddy.

I think I'll need a few of those hot toddies.

I approach the desk and am greeted by a smiling, gray-haired woman.

"Hello, I'm Grace Douglas. I have a reservation for this evening."

"Welcome to the Snow Ghost Lodge. Where are you visiting from?" She slides a paper across the desk for me to fill out as she checks me in.

"Cunningham Falls," I reply with a grin. "I'm just up for some ski lessons."

"Oh, great! I'm Jeanette. Feel free to call down for anything you might need." She consults her computer and makes me a key for my room. "Looks like your first lesson is in about thirty minutes. That should give you time to settle in. We have cookies and warm cider over there." She gestures to her left, opposite of the monster fireplace. "Take a look around. Your instructor will have all the equipment you need."

"Thank you," I reply, eyeing the oatmeal raisin cookies.

"You're welcome."

I snag a cookie and nibble on it on my way up to my room. The girls went all out. This place isn't cheap. My room is on the fifth floor, and the window looks out onto the ski hill. It'll be beautiful at night.

After a quick glance about the room, I grab my new ski pants and coat, my scarf and gloves, and set out to get this first lesson over with. It should be two hours of pure hell followed by either an ambulance ride or a few hours sitting by the fire.

I'll pray for the latter.

I approach Jeanette at the desk again with a smile.

"I'm sorry, I forgot to ask for my instructor's name, and where am I supposed to meet him?"

"Oh, I should have said," she replies and flicks her fingers over the keys. "It looks like he's right over there." She points to two men standing by the front entrance. I thank her with a nod and approach both men. One is young; he has to still be in high school. Maybe college. He's all gangly arms and long legs and doesn't look like he's ever shaved a day in his life.

He must be the student before me.

The other man is tall, much taller than my five foot four. He has golden blond hair that is long, just touching his collar, and begs for a woman's fingers to dive into it.

Jesus, down girl.

He's wearing black ski pants, but he's taken off his jacket, revealing a dark blue North Face fleece that molds around strong arms crossed over his impressive chest.

Hello, hot ski instructor.

"Hi." I stop next to Mr. Hottie and hold my hand out to him. "I'm Grace, your next victim."

Bold, green eyes turn down to mine and he grins slowly, closing his large hand around mine.

"I'm just going to apologize now," I continue, my mouth rambling. I'm completely unable to control it.

He's so damn hot. Why can't I be one of those women

who loses her words when confronted with a delicious man?

"This could very well be the worst two days of your life."

The kid next to him starts to speak, but Mr. Hottie holds up a hand, stopping him. He nods and the kid leaves us alone.

"Why do you say that, darling?"

Holy Jesus on a stick, the man has a British accent.

And cue the wet panties.

"I'm a bit of a klutz." I cringe and pull my hand out of his grasp. "But my friends are making me learn to ski. I'm your two o'clock."

"It's nice to meet you, Grace. I'm Bax."

"*Bax?*" I ask with a frown. "Did your mother not like you or something?"

Bax laughs, showing off a gorgeous smile, with one tooth just barely crooked in the front. His chin is covered in stubble, and I have to ball my hands into fists to keep from reaching up and plunging my fingers in that thick blond hair that I can now see has flecks of gold and copper running through it.

"It's short for Baxter, which is my last name."

"Well, that's nice, but we're not sixteen. What's your first name?"

He cocks a brow and tilts his head, watching me closely and then says softly, "Jacob."

"Much better," I reply with a smile. "I hope you don't mind if I call you Jacob while we work together?"

"No, darling, I don't mind."

If he keeps calling me "darling" in that accent, I might jump him in the snow.

"Okay, well, I'm ready when you are."

"You look like you're walking out before the firing squad," he laughs as he shrugs into his coat.

"I feel like it."

"Don't worry, love, I won't let you get hurt."

He opens the door and ushers me out ahead of him.

"First, we need to walk over to the rental shop to get you some boots, skis, and poles."

"I'm glad I get poles," I say with a laugh. "Balance isn't my strong suit."

He chuckles, and as I look up at him, my foot slips on a patch of ice and down I go, *whoomp,* flat on my ass.

chapter 2

. . . .

*A*nd so it begins.

Jacob squats next to me and takes my hand in his, helping me to my feet.

"I warned you." I laugh. "You might want to just go ahead and put the paramedics on standby. My ass likes the ground more than my feet."

He whispers something under his breath about my ass, but before I can ask him to repeat it, he says, "I've never met someone yet whom I couldn't teach to ski." He winks and keeps my hand tightly in his as he guides me into the rental shop. "Once you get the hang of it, you'll love it."

"I'll take your word for it," I reply with a smile. Jacob motions to the clerk behind the counter.

"Hey, Bax! What can I getcha?"

"What size shoe do you wear, love?"

"Eight," I reply.

"She needs boots, skis, and poles, Evan," Jacob tells him. "I'll be her instructor today and tomorrow."

Evan grins.

"Is that right?"

"Should I ask for a different instructor?" I ask and nudge Jacob's arm with mine, teasing him.

"Nah, Bax's as good as it gets." Evan slides boots over and Jacob lifts them easily.

"Can you grab my stuff for me from the back?" Jacob asks Evan.

"Sure thing."

When Evan leaves to fetch Jacob's gear, Jacob leads me to a bench where he helps me wriggle my way into the boots and fastens them.

"They're going to feel tight, but that's okay. We don't want you slipping around in there. That's how ankles get broken."

"Thank God for protecting my ankles."

Jacob chuckles and supports my calf in his hand as he guides the other foot into the boot. His grasp is firm, warm, and sends electricity through me.

I wonder what it would feel like if he touched my bare skin?

Hmm . . . a naked Jacob. It's not a bad thought in the least.

I lick my bottom lip, watching his mouth move as he tells me about bindings and wax and things that I just don't understand or, frankly, give two shits about.

"Understand?"

"Sure."

"Did you even hear what I was saying?"

"Sure," I say again.

"What did I say?"

I frown and watch his deep green eyes as they smile down at me.

"You said something about bondage and hot wax." I bite my lips to keep from grinning as he tosses his head back and lets out a full belly laugh.

"Not exactly."

"My apologies." My voice doesn't sound apologetic in the least. I haven't flirted this openly in a long, long time, and it's damn fun. Jacob is a hottie, and there's no ring on his finger, so why not?

Maybe a fling with a ski instructor isn't such a bad idea after all.

"Come on, Grace, let's get you on the snow."

"This is the part that scares me." Suddenly, the flirty is gone and is replaced by gargantuan butterflies and dread.

"Hey," he says and cups my chin in his hand, making me meet his gaze. The zing from his touch travels down my breasts, my spine, and directly to my core, and I suck in a breath and feel my eyes go wide. "I promise. I'll take care of you, darling."

"Okay," I whisper and discreetly fan myself as he stands and turns his back to me, slipping his feet into his own boots, but I notice they aren't ski boots.

"Why do I feel like I have a storm trooper's boots on?" I ask as I follow him out of the rental shop and into the snow. Jacob has my skis balanced on his shoulder. I have a pole in each hand, stabbing the snow and ice as I walk beside him. "These poles are great. I should walk with them everywhere."

"I can't believe you're that clumsy, Grace."

"Oh, I am. Always have been. It's not a big deal." I shrug and take a deep breath of cold, fresh mountain air. "I think my parents named me Grace as a cruel joke. God, it's beautiful up here."

"Where are you from?"

"Cunningham Falls."

His head whips around to stare down at me and his eyes narrow with renewed interest. "Seriously?"

"Yeah, my friends bought me these lessons as a gift."

"Why would they buy you ski lessons if you have no interest in skiing?"

"Because we're all taking a ski trip to Aspen in a few weeks for a girls' weekend away, and they think I need a head start so I can flirt properly with the hot Aspen ski instructors without needing medical attention."

"So you're all going to hit on ski bums?"

"No." I wave him off and laugh. "Cara and Lauren just got engaged, so it's really a bachelorette weekend. I probably won't actually hit on anyone."

"Why not?"

"Why aren't you wearing ski boots?" I ask instead of answering him.

"Answer the question."

"You answer mine." I stop walking and throw him a mock glare, making him grin.

"I can't be on skis if you're on skis and need me to help you. I'll be on skis with you tomorrow."

"How long have you been doing this?" And really, how well can this pay? Jacob looks to be in his thirties. Is this his career?

"You answer my question first."

"I don't even remember what we were talking about," I reply and begin to stomp away when he crowds me and tilts my chin back with his free hand.

"Don't lie to me, love. That's one thing I won't have. There's no need of it."

"I'm not a good flirter," I whisper and watch his breath come in and out in soft puffs.

"Could have fooled me," he replies with a grin. He leans down and kisses my forehead, then quickly resumes walking to a wide, clear area.

"Where are we going?" I pick up the pace, my short legs in the heavy boots trying with all their might to keep up with his long strides.

"Over here."

"The ski lifts are over there."

"You're not getting on a lift yet. Maybe a little later."

"Well, this is boring."

He sets my skis on the snow and motions for me to step into them. "Keep your balance with your poles and click your boots into the bindings. Good girl. See? You're a natural already."

"And you're full of the blarney," I reply in a horrible Irish accent.

"That's Ireland, darling. I'm from London. Okay, first thing's first."

"You never answered my question," I interrupt him.

"Which one is that?"

"How long have you been doing this?"

He props his hands on his hips and squints his eyes in thought. "I've been skiing since I was four, but teaching since I was sixteen, so I guess almost twenty years."

"They have a ski hill in London?"

"There are many ski resorts in Europe, darling."

I shrug and watch as he walks away from me, his ass looking spectacular in those black ski pants. God, what he must do to a pair of jeans.

Did I just growl? Shit, I hope not.

"Okay, first we're going to start with the snowplow."

"The plow hasn't been through here?" I glance around, looking for a big tractor. "If you plow the snow away, what will we ski on?"

"No, darling," he laughs, pinching his nose between his thumb and finger. "The snowplow is how you're going to slow down or stop when you need to."

"Oh, okay." I keep a death grip on my poles, determined not to fall. "How do I do it?"

"You're going to point your toes in." He demonstrates and I follow suit.

"This will make me stop?" I ask with doubt lacing my voice.

"It will."

"What next?"

"Put your poles up."

"No, they're helping me stay standing."

"Grace, put your poles in front of you so I can pull you and you can snowplow for real."

"I'm good where I am."

"Grace." His voice is firm but tender. "You won't fall."

I raise the poles and watch my feet.

"Head up. You have to watch where you're going."

"I'm not going anywhere right now."

Jacob moves to me and tilts my head up. "You have to watch what's around you when you ski. Your feet are fine. They'll go where your toes are pointed."

"Okay."

He moves directly in front of me and grips the poles.

"Keep your skis parallel for now and in a moment, move into the snowplow to slow down."

He walks backward, pulling me. My eyes widen and I let out a squeak, but amazingly, I stay upright.

"Beautiful, Grace." He grins and watches my form. "Okay, point your toes."

I follow his direction, and just like he said I would, I stop.

"It worked!"

"Of course it did. Okay, now we're going to go over here where there's a bit of a slope and you can try it for real."

I nod and firm my chin. I can do this.

"After you loosen up," he says. "You're too stiff. If you do fall, you'll get hurt. This is fun, darling. Keep your hips and arms loose."

I take a deep breath and shake my arms and hips, and

suddenly, my skis slip and I feel myself start to fall, but strong arms wrap around me, holding me up.

"Maybe not that loose, now," he says with a laugh.

And for the next hour, he shows me how to walk sideways, stop, take the skis on and off, and all of the other simple things I'll need to know.

"Okay, I think I've mastered this." I sniff, my nose drippy from the cold air. "I love the cold."

"Do you?"

"Yeah, it feels good to have cold cheeks and to breathe in the chilly air. I love living here."

"Well, then, this sport is perfect for you."

"You're a good teacher, you know."

He takes a glove off and pushes his hand through his hair and I suddenly ache to be the one to do that for him. The man has seriously touchable hair. "Of course, it takes one to know one."

"You're a teacher, are you?"

"Aye, I am," I reply in a horrible Scottish brogue.

"I'm not from Scotland, love." His green eyes dance with laughter as he shakes his head at me. "What do you teach?"

"I've taught fourth grade for close to six years."

"Did you skip school today to hang out with me?" He helps me snap off the skis and leads me to the chairlift.

"No, I had meetings this morning, and the rest of the day off. Are we going up the chairlift now?"

"Yes, but just the bunny hill today, I'm afraid."

"I'm okay with the bunny hill. I work with ten-year-olds every day, so I'll be among my people." He helps me get situated on the lift. "How did you choose this for a career?"

He frowns, and looks like he's about to admit something to me, but he shakes his head and says, "I have always loved the snow. My family took many winter holidays and those were always my favorites."

I nod and watch the trees pass beneath us.

"I love your enthusiasm," Jacob murmurs. "You're a beautiful woman, Grace."

"Thank you," I whisper, unsure what else to say.

"Have dinner with me tonight."

"Oh, I shouldn't," I immediately respond.

"Are you driving back down to town when we're done today?"

"No, I have a room at the lodge."

"Perfect."

"I'm going to fall off this lift. I'm warning you." I'm watching people hop off the chairlift as it nears the top, but the chairs don't stop completely. You have to be quick.

"No, you won't." He takes my glove-covered hand in his and squeezes. "Have a little more faith in yourself, love."

chapter 3

· · · · · · · · · · · · ·

~ JACOB ~

*H*ave I ever been this captivated by a woman in my life? Not that I can recall. This little pixie is a spitfire, full of energy and quick to learn. Her sense of humor is damn hilarious and I'm dying to know what secrets she has hidden beneath all those layers of heavy snow gear.

I could easily spend days with her and not tire of her. That itself is a novelty.

I can feel her tense up as we near the top of the lift. She laughs off her awkward clumsiness, but I can see the unease that it causes, making my heart go out to her. I've never known what it is to not feel comfortable in your body. Athletics always came easy to me.

"You'll be fine, darling," I murmur, and help her off the chair, keeping a hand on her arm and leading her away as I wave at the ski lift operator.

"Hey, Bax," he calls with a smile.

"You're popular around here," she says with a grin. "I guess I can see why."

"And why is that?"

"Well, you're friendly. And handsome. And you seem to know what you're doing."

"I'd better know what I'm about, love. I can't have anyone getting hurt, now can I?"

"No, we can't have that."

I lead her over to an area that has a gentle slope and is perfect for beginners. It shouldn't scare her. Though I've skied places on this mountain that made me break out into a cold sweat.

She'll never see those places.

"So you think I'm handsome?"

"You know you're handsome." She laughs and brushes some snow off her pants. It's begun snowing. Large, fluffy flakes are lazily making their way to the ground.

"Handsome enough to have dinner with tonight?"

She bites her lip and I know she wants to say yes. I want her to say yes. I want to do much more than have dinner with her, but I'm willing to take it slow.

For the first time in a long time, I'm enjoying a woman's company when she's fully clothed.

Good grief.

"Well, you *are* rather handsome," she replies, trying to copy my accent and failing miserably.

Fuck me, she's adorable.

"Your accent needs work," I reply, and brush my finger over her nose.

"I'm just trying to blend in. I'm a chameleon." Her

face is perfectly sober, but her hazel eyes are full of laughter. Her golden blond hair is cut short, shorter than I normally prefer, but it's perfect on her. It frames her delicate face, setting off those witching eyes.

"Dinner, Grace," I remind her.

"If you insist."

Oh, I think I'll be insisting on quite a few delicious things, darling.

I smile softly to myself and lead her through more snowplow moves, how to turn, and damn if she isn't learning quickly. She's a natural.

"You're doing great, Grace."

"I am?" She smiles widely as I help her out of her skis.

"Absolutely. You'll be flying down this mountain in no time."

"How are we getting down to the lodge?" she asks nervously.

"We're riding the chair, love."

"I'm sorry, this can't be very much fun for you."

"Actually, I'm having a lovely day." I help her back onto the chair and hop on next to her. "I'm grateful that your friends are getting married and talked you into Aspen."

"Me, too." She smiles up at me and I want to kiss her more than I've ever wanted anything in my life. I pull my glove off and pull my knuckles down her cold cheek, glide my thumb over her plump lower lip.

"Grace, I'm going to kiss you here on this chairlift."

Her tongue pokes out of her mouth, wetting her lower lip and brushing my thumb and my cock tightens. I lean in and rest my lips on hers, waiting for her to push me away, but she plunges her fingers into my hair and holds on and I sink into her. I rub my lips back and forth over her soft skin before licking her lower lip and slipping my tongue inside, over her tongue and exploring her mouth. She moans softly, opening readily and I sink in farther, caught up in her clean scent and the smell of the snow around us.

I pull back to find her eyes wide and glassy. The pulse in her throat throbs quickly, matching my own.

Bloody hell, I want her.

I glance around to find that we're almost to the bottom of the lift. I lean in and place my lips beside her ear, press a soft kiss, and then whisper, "I owe you dinner."

"I'll collect," she immediately replies as a shiver moves through her, making me grin.

Sweet, strong girl.

We hop off the chair without incident. She seemed to grow more confident as she became more sure on the skis, and it's showing now. She's less hesitant as we move away from the lift toward the rental shop.

"I'll be glad to get rid of these boots," she says with a wrinkled nose. "They're heavy."

"It's a workout, indeed."

"Indeed," she mimics.

"You enjoy teasing me about my accent, love."

"I don't mean to be offensive," she rushes to assure me. "It's my stupid sense of humor. You can tell me to shut up."

I pull her to a stop and drop my face close to hers. "I

think you're charming and delightful, and I don't want you to shut up. I was teasing you in return."

"Okay."

"I told you before, I'm enjoying your company very much."

"Thank you."

"You're welcome. Now, let's ditch this gear and get you warmed up."

"I wonder if I can order a hot chocolate in the lobby and sit by the fire."

"I'm quite sure you can order whatever you like," I reply. *You can have anything you want.*

I've known the woman for a matter of hours and I'm ready to offer her the world.

Jesus Christ, grow a pair, Bax.

We turn in her equipment and walk back to the lodge, avoiding the icy patch that she slipped on earlier.

Watching her fall had my heart in my throat.

"Jeanette," I call as we walk through the lobby to the fireplace. "Would you please order us two hot chocolates?"

"Of course, Bax," she replies with a knowing smile. She's such a mother hen. Always trying to set me up with someone.

Maybe this will shut her up.

"Have a seat, love." I lead her to a plush love seat, but instead of sitting next to her, I sit on the ottoman across from her and take her boot off of her left foot, pull it up into my lap, and begin to rub it vigorously over her wool sock.

"You do *not* have to touch my sweaty foot!" She tries to pull away but I hold strong.

"I'm warming you up, Grace."

"The fire will do that for me."

I raise a brow and watch her quietly as I continue to rub her slender foot. She finally relaxes and sinks back into the cushions of the couch.

"God, you're good at that."

"We can't have your toes fall off from frostbite."

"I don't think I was quite there yet," she replies with a laugh. "But thanks for having my back."

"What did you think of your lesson?" I ask and turn my attention to her right foot. I want to strip her naked and explore every inch of her tiny body, lose myself in her for hours on end.

Once I started, I don't know if I could ever let her go.

And where in the bloody hell are these thoughts coming from?

"I had fun," she replies with a soft sigh. "I didn't fall once, thanks to you."

"I told you I wouldn't let you fall."

"You might have to come with me to Aspen. Who needs poles when they have Jacob to keep them upright?"

She laughs, and I smile at her, but my insides still. The thought of her in Aspen, with another ski instructor paying her the same attention I am, pisses me the fuck off.

And that's absolutely ridiculous.

"Jacob?"

"Yes, darling."

"Where did you go? You zoned out there for a minute."

I shake my head and join her on the couch as our drinks are delivered.

"Here you go, Bax." The young room service attendant places the tray holding the hot chocolate and freshly baked cookies on the ottoman before us. I slip my hand into my pocket, pull out some money, and hand him his tip.

"Thank you, Michael."

"Anytime."

"Your coworkers are very respectful to each other," Grace observes, and nibbles a cookie.

Now is the time to tell her. It shouldn't be all that difficult to mention that I'm not merely an employee, but the owner of the place. However, the thought of her anger and embarrassment is like a punch to the gut.

I'm just a normal bloke, having a conversation with a woman. Not the playboy billionaire from London.

I rather like the way this feels.

"Thank you," I reply instead, and take a sip of the warm chocolate. "It's a nice place to work."

"Hmm," she agrees. She's leaning back in the seat, her eyes growing heavy as she sips her drink, lost in her thoughts. I watch her for a while, wondering what she's thinking, but not wanting to ruin this quiet moment.

"We'd best get back to our rooms so we can change out of these clothes for dinner." I stand and hold my hand out to her, pulling her to her feet beside me.

"I'm on the fifth floor," she says. "Where do you stay?"

"I have a place here in the lodge." I don't mention that my living quarters are a three-bedroom suite that I've commandeered. "I'll walk you to your room."

"You don't have to."

"A gentleman always walks his lady home." I ignore the looks that the staff sends us as I lead her to the elevator, and once we reach her floor, she leads me to her door. She's in one of the standard king rooms. They're top of the line, comfortable, and perfectly fine. But I also know in this moment that regardless of how many nights she's reserved to stay in this room, and I intend to find out, she'll spend only one night in this room.

"Thanks for walking me *home*." She grins.

"My pleasure." I wait for her to unlock the door, and before she can escape inside, I pin her against the doorjamb and kiss her passionately, deeply. Hungrily.

Her fingers find their way into my hair again, and I long to feel them there as I bury my face in her pussy, making her come over and over again.

Yes, this is just the beginning for Grace and me.

I pull away from her mouth, drag my nose along her jawline to her ear.

"I'll be back to pick you up in an hour."

She swallows hard as I pull away from her.

"Okay, I'll be ready."

Grace smiles and turns to walk into her room.

"Grace . . ."

She turns at the sound of my voice, but I'm too late, and she runs smack into the doorjamb.

"Ow!"

"Oh, love, I'm so sorry."

She giggles and rubs her temple where she hit the hardest.

"At least I'm not standing on ice. I'd be a goner." She shrugs and waves before closing the door behind her.

chapter 4

. . . .

~ *Grace* ~

Well, that was elegant. Way to run into the door, like in some slapstick movie, as the hottest man you've ever seen in your life looks on with lust-filled eyes after kissing you unlike you've ever been kissed before.

I wonder if all the British kiss like that?

Because seriously, the man knows how to use his lips.

He never makes me feel clumsy or stupid. When I fall or walk into a wall, he doesn't look at me like I'm a moron. He laughs *with* me instead of at me.

And let's face it, the sexy factor is through the roof.

His hair is as thick and soft as it looks. I never wanted to let go.

So what do I do? Have a weekend affair like the girls suggested? Why not?

Perhaps I'm jumping ahead of myself here. The man asked me to dinner, not to jump into his bed.

Get a grip!

I strip out of my clothes and turn on the shower, then struggle with what to wear. I didn't bring anything dressy because I didn't plan to go out on a date. I wonder what he's wearing?

I don't even have his phone number.

Shit.

Suddenly my phone buzzes on the bathroom vanity with a number I don't recognize.

This is Jacob. Dinner will be casual. See you soon.

How did he do that? Would Jeanette have given him my phone number? Probably, but that seems rather unprofessional.

I shrug and type back a response: *Sounds good!*

I take a long hot shower. My muscles are already moaning from the activity today. Tomorrow will be horrible.

Thank God I'm scheduled for a massage!

In a moment of optimism, I shave my legs and bikini line, then wash my hair and step out of the shower.

Thankfully, my short hair has trimmed a good ten minutes off my time. It blows dry quickly, and with a few brushes with my fingers and a little hair gel, I'm good to go. I keep the makeup simple and casual, then dress in my jeans and red cami with a black shrug over the top. I slide my feet into black Toms and take a spin in front of the mirror. My breasts are pushed up, thanks to the

...rged on, and my ass looks great in

...l as it gets with my limited wardrobe

...oth some gloss on my lips, there's a light knock on the door.

"'Ello, govna!" I exclaim as I open the door, and then I lose all control of my tongue. I think it fell out.

I hope I'm not flapping my mouth about like a guppy.

Jacob is delicious in faded blue jeans and a well-worn white T-shirt with a blue plaid button-down open over it. The sleeves are rolled up to his elbows.

His hair is still damp from a shower, but he didn't shave that scruff off his chin.

Thank God.

"You are beautiful," he murmurs. He leans his shoulder against the doorframe and watches me watch him with hot, green eyes. "Are you ready?"

"Hold on, I'm not done," I reply.

"Done with what?" he asks with a half smile.

"Looking," I whisper.

The smile disappears from his face, replaced by pure, unadulterated lust.

"Keep looking at me like that, and I'll push my way into your room, uninvited as it stands right now mind you, and take you up against that wall."

I blink at him, tempted to take him up on the offer, when my stomach growls.

"I think I'm hungry."

"As am I. Let's feed you, love." He holds his [...]
for mine and leads me down the hall to the elevato[...]

"You smell great." God, I have got to learn to use [...]
filter when I speak to this man! Shit just pops right out.

"Thank you," he murmurs with a smile. "I hope you're
content with the restaurant here in the hotel."

"Sure, I've heard good things," I reply truthfully. "I've
never been up to check it out, but my friends love it."

"I'm happy to hear that."

The hostess smiles widely at Jacob as we approach,
but the light in her eyes dims a bit when she sees me.

*That's right, he's with me. At least for a few hours,
anyway.*

"Hello, Riley."

"Hi, Mr. Baxter. Your usual table?"

"That will be fine, thank you."

I frown up at him. *A ski instructor has a usual table?*

She leads us through the restaurant to the back of the
room, tucked in a corner with wide windows that look
out over the ski hill.

He seats me in the corner and sits with his back to the
room, facing me.

"I didn't think men liked to sit with their backs to
the room," I say. *There's no way in hell he's a fucking ski
instructor.*

"A gentleman always seats the lady so she can look
out to the room," he replies matter-of-factly, perusing
his menu.

"I like that." I clear my throat without opening the
menu. "Who are you, exactly?"

His eyes whip up to mine in surprise. "I've told you who I am, darling."

"You lied," I reply, without emotion in my voice. "Let me guess. You own the joint."

"Hey, Mr. Baxter, what can I get you both to drink?" a waitress with the name Babs pinned to her shirt asks as she approaches the table, interrupting us.

"We'll need a moment, please." His eyes never leave mine as Babs walks away.

"I own this lodge, yes," he replies, and holds my gaze steadily.

"So that whole, 'Don't lie to me, love. That's one thing I won't have. There's no need of it,' was just, what? A line?"

"That's fair, Grace, and no, it wasn't a line." He snaps his menu shut and scratches his fingers through his hair.

"So you played me. Good job."

"No." He grabs my wrist to keep me in place as I move to leave and clenches his jaw shut. His grip isn't hard or biting, but just enough to let me know that he wants me to stay. "Please let me explain."

"I feel foolish," I whisper. *Way to go, you clumsy idiot. Just another way to make a fool of yourself.*

"No, love." He shakes his head and clears his throat. "If anyone should feel foolish, it's me. I didn't mean to mislead you."

"You *mistakenly* failed to mention that you own this damn lodge all day long?" I ask incredulously. "Do you think I'm stupid as well as clumsy?"

"You're neither stupid nor clumsy, Grace. When you

approached me this afternoon, I was speaking with the boy who was supposed to be your instructor for the day."

"You employ toddlers?"

Jacob's lips twitch with humor. "He's a very young-looking nineteen and an excellent skier. You were mistaken when you assumed I was to be your instructor today."

"My mistake. I apologize."

"I apologize, Grace. I just instantly liked you. With your immediate apology for your clumsiness and your sense of humor and your gorgeous hazel eyes, I just . . ." He blows out a breath and searches for his next words. "I just wanted to spend the day with you."

"Look, Bax," I begin.

"Jacob," he corrects me softly. "I like the way Jacob rolls off your spectacular tongue."

Oh, God, he's good.

"I don't know what you want me to say. I'm here under false pretenses."

"Everything else I told you today is true. Everything. I just didn't mention that I owned the lodge. I was a ski instructor at sixteen, in Switzerland during winter holiday with my family. I've been skiing since I was four. I didn't lie."

I sit back and watch him carefully as Babs returns to the table.

"Are you ready to place your drink order, boss?"

Again, his eyes stay on mine. "Stay. Have dinner with me."

"Why didn't you correct me right away?" I ask bluntly.

"Because I didn't want you to treat me differently when you found out about my status here." His face is sober and honest, and I feel just a little pity for him. It can't be easy to have the money he has, to always wonder if someone is interested in you as a person, or you as a *wealthy* person.

"I'll stay," I reply after a long silent moment.

"Thank you." His smile is wide and genuine as he cocks a brow. "Now, what would you like to drink? I, for one, could use a glass of wine."

"I'll join you in that," I reply, with a nod. "Pinot Noir?"

"Excellent." He rattles off the name of an Oregon wine I recognize and then pulls my hand to his lips, nibbles my knuckles, sending shivers up my arm. "Thank you."

"For?"

"The second chance." We settle into a companionable silence as we browse the menu. Should I have let him off the hook so easily? Am I so desperate to get laid—if that's even where this is going—that I'm willing to forgive his lie by omission and have dinner with him? I glance up to watch him read the menu, and realize that it doesn't have much to do with wanting a quick fuck and everything to do with this weird attraction I feel toward *him*, the whole package.

But that doesn't mean that I have to bare my soul to him. He didn't see fit to come clean with me, and perhaps I should keep the same attitude, keeping most of my own secrets closely guarded.

"I want a big hunk of meat for dinner." I rub my flat stomach as I return to the menu. "Steak. Potatoes. Oh, God, you have huckleberry cheesecake. That's going to be in my belly before this night is out."

"You are the most beautiful woman I've ever seen," he murmurs quietly. I'm stunned speechless as I gaze over my menu at him.

"Excuse me?"

"Don't ever lose your enthusiasm for life, Grace. Your excitement over a dessert is one of the sexiest things I've ever witnessed."

"You've led a sheltered life, then," I reply, and lay my menu over my plate.

"Quite the opposite, love. I'm very happy that you mistook me for your instructor today. It's perhaps the best thing that's happened to me in a long while."

"There's that blarney again," I reply with a laugh. "But thank you. And back at you. What made you come to Montana?"

"I was here on holiday years ago," he says, and sips his wine. "It's beautiful here."

"Very different from Europe."

"Indeed. But it's become home." He takes my hand in his again and threads our fingers together. "How long have you lived here? Are you native?"

"No." I take a sip of my wine and think about how much I want to confide in this sexy, sweet man. "I've been here since I started teaching. About six years."

"Where are you from?"

"Arizona."

He nods and watches me, waiting for more.

"I don't have any siblings."

"I had a younger brother," he says softly. "He drowned when he was nine."

I tighten my hand on his. "I'm sorry."

"It destroyed my parents. They've never been the same." He tilts his head. "Your parents?"

"I don't speak to them." I firm my lips, determined not to tell him any more.

His jaw ticks at my response, but he doesn't push. He just nods and smiles at Babs when she returns to take our orders.

"The lady will have the rib eye with a baked potato. Would you like salad, love?"

"Yes, please. With ranch. Medium on the steak."

"And for you, Bax?"

"I'll have the same."

Babs nods and takes our menus. "Oh, Bax, Jerry asked me to tell you that he wants a word with you before you leave."

"He'll have to wait. I am with a guest. Tell him I'll have a word with him tomorrow morning."

"You're the boss." She winks and saunters away, leaving us alone.

"Maybe Jerry's issue can't wait."

"Jerry always has an issue, and trust me, it can wait." Jacob grins and drags his knuckles down my cheek. "I'm in the middle of a very important meeting."

"So I'm a business meeting now?" I ask with a cocked brow. "I'm flattered."

Jacob laughs and shakes his head. "You were telling me how you ended up in Montana."

"I went to college with someone from here. I joined her one weekend when she came home to see her parents, fell in love with the town, and decided to move here when college was done."

"I'm glad you did."

"Me, too. I love snow." Babs sets our salads in front of us. "The cold doesn't bother me."

We eat in relative quiet, making small talk about the unusually dry winter, the days getting shorter, and what we studied in college. The meal is as delicious as the conversation.

"Oh, God," I moan, and lean back in my chair. "There's no way I can eat the cheesecake. I'm stuffed."

"We could share it," he offers.

"You're far too tempting, Jacob Baxter."

"I hope so, Grace."

"Okay, fine. I'll eat half."

Jacob hails Babs and orders our dessert. "What are your plans for the rest of the evening?" he asks.

"Yoga pants and a Lifetime movie," I reply.

"Can I talk you into doing those things in my suite?"

His face is hopeful and sexy and I'm so fucking tempted to say *hell yes!* But I've known him less than a day. And he wasn't honest with me.

"I take your silence as a no," he says ruefully.

"Jacob, you are an intriguing man. The chemistry between us is . . . impressive. I'm interested. But I just met you today."

"I understand, darling. Completely."

Babs sets our dessert, two spoons, and two black coffees on the table, winks at Jacob, and walks away. We dig in with gusto, and when Jacob wraps his lips around that spoon and moans in appreciation of the sugar and sweet fruit hitting his tongue, I almost change my mind about his offer and beg him to take me to bed *right now*.

But instead I laugh at him, eat my half, and keep quiet.

Finally, he walks me down the hall to my room. He pushes my back against the wall beside my door, braces his hand on the wall next to my face, and leans in. Almost unbearably slowly, he drags his nose down my own and nibbles the corner of my mouth.

"Good night, sweet Grace." He kisses me softly, but with no less passion, leaving me a quivering mess.

"G'day, mate," I whisper. He laughs, and leans his forehead on mine.

"God, Grace, you're so damn funny. I can't wait to spend tomorrow with you."

"Back at you, mate."

"I'm not your mate, love." He nuzzles my nose once more before backing away. "I'm going to be much more than that."

chapter 5

· · · · · · · · · · · · ·

$\mathscr{I}$ close the door behind me and lean against the wood, panting, aching, wanting with all my heart to call him back here.

I've never done an impulsive thing in my life.

It's about time to change that.

I yank the door open and stick my head out into the hallway, just in time to see Jacob press the call button for the elevator.

"Jacob, wait."

He stills and whips his head toward me.

"Don't go."

He marches back to me and gazes down into my face with bright green eyes. "What's wrong, darling?"

"I don't want you to leave," I whisper, and watch his lips as he licks them.

"What do you want?"

I find his gaze with mine and simply say, "You."

"Invite me in, please."

"Another one of those gentlemanly things?" I ask softly.

"Grace, I'm on a very precarious ledge right now."

"Won't you come in?" I step back and open the door wide. He swoops in, pushes me deeper into the room, cups my face in his hands, and devours me with his mouth. The door slams shut behind him and I can only cling to him as he kisses me almost desperately, as though I'm a mirage that will disappear.

He pulls my shrug off my shoulders, letting it fall to the floor, and reaches for the button of my jeans next, deftly unfastening them with one hand. He pushes his hands inside them, glides them down my ass, and lowers my jeans down my legs until they're pooled around my ankles.

"I told myself that once I finally had you like this, I'd take my time and explore every inch of your gorgeous little body . . ."

I whip my cami over my head just as he reaches behind me to unclasp my bra and am now pinned against the wall in my plain pink panties.

". . . but I feel like I'm going to die if I don't taste you."

He kneels before me, yanks my panties down, pulls my leg up onto his shoulder, and with reverent hands, touches the insides of my thighs gently.

"Jacob, I'm going to fall."

"I won't let you fall."

"Trust me on this one," I reply and gasp when his fingers spread my lips, opening me up to his hot gaze and warm breath.

"I just need one taste." He leans in and places his lips over mine and sucks gently. I plant my hands in his hair and hold on as an urgent wave of pure lust consumes me. I whimper, and my breath comes in shallow, short pants.

"I can't, babe." Dear God, I'm losing my balance.

He growls, guides my leg over his shoulder, and lifts me off the fucking floor, his face still buried in my pussy. With his other hand braced on my back to keep me from falling, he carries me the short distance to the bed, lays me gently in the center, and continues to feast on me, never missing a beat.

"Holy shit!"

I feel him grin against me, then he licks up to my clit and circles it with the tip of his tongue.

"You. Are. So. Sweet." Each word is separated with a kiss planted to my lips. "You're so swollen and pink. So fucking wet."

Those naughty words spilling from his mouth in that sexy-as-hell accent have me writhing beneath him, never wanting this moment to end.

I whimper and bite my lip as he tilts my pelvis up and licks the crease of my thigh, around my mound to the other side, avoiding the sensitive spot I want him to concentrate on.

His hand glides up my belly to my breast. His fingertips dance over my nipple, barely grazing it, sending goose bumps over my entire body.

"You like that, love?" I nod and he chuckles against me, sinks a finger inside me, and wraps his lips around my clit, sucking gently.

"Oh, God," I whisper, as the base of my spine tingles, my legs begin to shake, and I feel the orgasm work up and through me. I clench his hair in my hands as I pant and tremble, grinding my pussy against his magical mouth.

Jacob kisses my inner thighs and slowly pulls his thick finger out of me, then sticks it in his mouth and licks it clean.

Holy fucking shit.

He kisses his way up my body, exploring my navel, my ribs, and each breast before dragging his nose up my neck and kissing me softly, thoroughly.

He cups my head in his hands and massages my scalp firmly with his strong fingertips. Dear God, if he'll just keep doing that for about three months I'll be his sex slave for life.

"You are so beautiful, Grace," he whispers against my lips. He's still fully dressed, his hips are pressed to mine, and I can feel his erection pressed against me.

"You're wearing too many clothes," I reply, and push his shirt off his shoulders. He grins and stands at the side of the bed, shucks out of his clothes, leaving his Calvin Klein boxer-briefs on. He lifts me effortlessly off the bed, pulls the covers back, and settles us both inside the bed, my back to his front.

And now I'm completely fucking confused.

What the hell?

My head is lying on his bicep. He has his arm curled

up so he can brush his fingers through my hair sooth-ingly, and his free hand is on my belly, his fingertips thrumming up and down my stomach, my ribs, grazing my breast, but he never goes near *the goods*.

His erection is pressing against the small of my back, for fuck's sake. I know he's turned on.

Deciding to take matters in my own hands, so to speak, I lay my hand over his and guide him farther south. His middle finger barely grazes over my clit and his breath hitches in my ear at the contact.

"Grace, you're making it very difficult for me to be a gentleman."

I wiggle my ass against his cock and bite my lip when his finger again grazes my sweet spot.

"I thought I made it quite clear that I didn't want you to be a gentleman."

He lets out a low growl and I'm suddenly under him, my legs hitched up around his hips and his cock, still cov-ered in his Calvin Kleins, nestled against my core.

"I need you to be very sure, love."

"I'm so sure, babe." I let my fingers glide down his back to his ass and back up again, then sink them in his soft hair. He rests his forehead against mine and takes a long deep breath.

I drag one hand around his waist and between our bodies, caressing his pecs, his amazingly defined abs, and just as I'm making the journey down that trail of hair that leads to *his* goods, he grasps my wrist and pulls it to his mouth, plants a kiss on my palm before pinning it over my head.

"If you touch me right now, I will explode, my darling." He kisses me once, twice, then drags his lips down my jaw to my neck and bites me there before kissing it soothingly. "Your body is amazing. The way it trembles at my touch. The way you taste."

I roll my hips at his words and pull in a long breath as he continues whispering in my ear.

"Your body flushes when you come, from your cheeks to your thighs and everywhere in between. Your pink nipples pucker." He tweaks one with his thumb and smiles against my neck when I moan softly.

"Those sexy whispers and loud exhales make my cock throb." His hand travels south, pushes between my thighs, and he sinks one—two?—fingers inside me, stretching me deliciously.

"Jacob," I whisper and wrap my arms around his shoulders, keeping him close to me. I love the way his big body covers me so completely, enveloping me in his warmth.

"Ah, look how sweet you are, Gracie." I grin at the nickname. I don't allow many to call me that, certainly never a lover, but it's so sweet coming from his sexy mouth I soak it up like a sponge.

I feel him moving, reaching, sliding his shorts down, and then the sound of a wrapper—thank God!

"I'm going to sink home now, sweet Grace," he murmurs as he guides himself to my entrance. "If you don't want this, you have to tell me."

"I want you," I whisper, and hold his face in my hands as I feel the tip of him press against me. Damn, he's big.

"You're so damn wet, so ready." He doesn't push farther. Instead he waits, allowing my body to adjust to him. "Since the moment I saw you I've wanted to be here with you, like this."

"I held out for a whole eight hours," I whisper. He leans back and pulls his knuckles down my cheek, watching me soberly.

"Moving fast doesn't make it insignificant." He pushes farther, making me gasp.

"You're big."

"You'll make room for me, love."

He kisses me softly, nibbles my lips as he pushes farther still, at a slow, steady pace until he's seated fully inside me.

"Your body is so small, but look how perfectly you fit me." I open my eyes to see him gazing down at me in wonder. I'm panting softly, more turned on than I've ever been in my life.

I circle my hips again, but he shakes his head and clenches his eyes.

"I can't move yet, love. I don't want to come."

"I need . . ."

"What do you need?"

"Fuck," I whisper. I can't find my words.

"I love hearing those dirty words come from your gorgeous mouth." He pulls back, pauses, and then thrusts home again. "Ah, bloody fucking hell, I won't last long. You're incredible."

I wrap my arms around him and hold him tight as he begins to move in earnest, rocking in and out of me, panting. I reach between us and circle my clit with my finger and his eyes dilate further.

"Yes, fucking touch yourself. Just like that. Ah, God, that looks amazing."

He watches as I reach down farther and press my fingertips to the base of his cock, rubbing it as it moves in and out of me.

"Oh fuck, Gracie." I tremble and clench around him at the sound of my name. "God, look at you. You're going to come again. Your body is flushing again." He leans in and presses his lips to mine then whispers. "Let go with me, love."

I grip him hard and shiver as the orgasm rips through me. He groans as he follows me over, rocking his hips against mine, riding out his own release until finally he collapses, but manages to roll us, reversing our positions.

"Holy shit," he whispers and presses his lips to my temple. "You are simply brilliant."

"I am simply spent," I reply with a chuckle. "You wore me out today."

"Tomorrow is going to be more of the same, so get some sleep." He hugs me to him and buries his nose in my hair, breathing me in. "Thank you."

"For?"

"This amazing gift. You are a rare woman, Grace." He kisses my head and glides his hand down my back to my ass. "Sleep now, love."

chapter 6

. . . .

~ JACOB ~

The world is still dark as I slowly drift awake and feel Grace's warm body snuggled close to my side. Her leg is draped over my thigh, her arm over my belly, and her head rests on my chest.

I can't remember the last time I woke with a woman in my arms. I never spend the night. It suggests an intimacy that I've just never felt.

Until Grace.

I kiss her forehead and roll her onto her back, gently untangle myself from her, and pull on my clothes. Just as I step into my shoes, Grace stirs and frowns up at me.

"Making a hasty retreat?" She yawns and searches for the clock.

"No, darling." I crawl back onto the bed and pull her into my lap, hugging her close. "I have some things to see to this morning. I didn't want to wake you."

"It's okay." She buries her face in my neck and sighs, and if I didn't know better, I'd say she's about to fall right back to sleep.

"Go back to bed, love. I'll have breakfast sent up in about an hour."

"Will you be joining me?" Her voice is soft, maybe a bit hesitant. I hug her more tightly and tip her face back with my finger.

"No, but I'll see you at our lesson at ten."

"Oh, you don't have to keep teaching me, I'll be fine with a real instructor."

"I *am* a real instructor, and I'll be in charge of your lessons." I kiss her chastely and my groin stirs at the feel of her small body pressed against me. "I can't wait to spend the day with you."

"Okay, have a good morning."

Her eyes are drifting closed again, making me grin. She's clearly not a morning person.

I lower her back to the bed, tuck her in, and leave her.

I do have things to handle this morning, but I also need a couple of hours to clear my head. To think. And the best place for that is on the hill.

I return to my room and change into ski gear, grab my equipment, and head out. The lift operator is just settling into his position and waves as I approach.

"Good timing," he calls out.

"So it seems," I reply with a nod, and hop onto a chair as he starts the lift. I ride all the way to the summit of the mountain, watching in awe as the world comes to life.

It's overcast, but not snowing yet, and the rising sun casts everything in a gray glow.

There is fresh powder on the earth, covering the trees. The snow ghosts that my lodge is named for cover the ground, the trees are so blanketed in the snow that the green no longer peeks through, hence the name.

It never fails to take my breath away.

As the lift approaches the top, I jump off, secure my goggles, and take in the view. The valley stretches before me, and the clouds are up high enough that I can see Cunningham Falls below, the lake, and to my left, the peaks of Glacier National Park.

There is a serenity up here in the stillness that I've never found anywhere else, no matter what mountain I was on in Europe. When I came up here for the first time, took in this view, I knew this was where I was meant to be.

And now it has brought me to Grace.

The quiet surrounds me. The only sound is my own breath as I point my skis down and begin the smooth ride to the bottom. The groomers have already been out this morning, and conditions are perfect.

As I gently slide down the mountain, my thoughts turn to the amazing woman I held in my arms all night long. I woke several times just to feel her skin against me, to breathe her in, to listen to her soft breaths. Not once did I get the urge to flee.

For fuck's sake, what is it about this woman that has me all tied up in knots? She's beautiful, yes, but I've known plenty of beautiful women in my life.

And fucked a good portion of them.

And yet I can't remember the face of a single one. All that fills my mind is Grace's soft sighs, her whimpers, the way her body reacts to mine. Her cheeks flush beautifully just as she's about to come, and she's not a screamer, not in the least. Instead, her body clenches and tightens, and she trembles, her breath comes in soft pants, and it's the most brilliant thing I've ever witnessed.

But if I'm honest, it's much more than the sex. In the few hours that I've known her, she's made me laugh like I haven't in years. Her clumsiness is endearing rather than frustrating, most likely because of the way she reacts to it, like it's just a natural thing and is what it is.

She's unapologetic about who she is. She eats what she wants to, works at a job she enjoys, and has a zeal for life that encourages those around her to join her in it.

She's bloody incredible.

And I do believe she has me under that charming spell of hers. I want to explore this chemistry between us. That she lives in Cunningham Falls is a blessing. I can court her properly, and see her regularly.

I approach the bottom of the run and immediately return to the lift and ride it to the top. Then I point my skis downhill and take a different run this time, a bit more challenging, and lose myself in the snow.

❄ ❄ ❄

"So, Bax, how are things going with a certain beautiful blonde?" Jeanette grins behind the reception desk. Paul, Grace's original instructor is chatting with her.

"Yeah, man? What's up with that? You stole her out from under me. She's hot. I thought I might score with her."

Jeanette's jaw drops and she watches me warily as my eyes narrow on the young man.

"Don't mistake my easygoing demeanor, Paul. It seems you've forgotten to whom you're speaking. If I ever hear you disrespect any guest that way, you'll never set foot on this hill again. Am I clear?"

"I'm sorry, Bax."

"As you should be."

Paul scampers away, his proverbial tail between his legs.

"Boys that age are all horny little bastards," Jeanette mutters.

"Most men are," I agree, and chuckle down at her. "But a lady should never hear of it. I'm not his mate, I'm his boss, and I didn't hire him so he could attempt to lose his virginity."

Jeanette laughs and pats my arm. "I like you, Bax. How *are* things with Grace?"

"That, my darling Jeanette, is none of your business." I wink down at her just as Jerry rushes out from the restaurant.

"There you are!" His hands are clasping and unclasping at his chest in agitation, his cheeks are red with frustration, and I already know it's going to be a chore calming the bloke.

I silently thank the heavens that ten o'clock is just a few minutes away as I turn to the brilliant chef.

"How can I help you, Jerry?"

"I sent Babs out for you last night, but you ignored me." He sniffs and pushes his nose in the air. If he wasn't such a talented chef, I'd boot him out on his ass. Instead I tread lightly, because finding someone to replace him in this small town is impossible.

"I was with a guest, Jerry. What is the problem?"

"The butcher sent *choice* cuts of meat instead of *prime* for the second time this month. How am I supposed to work with that? And don't even get me started on that twit of a sous chef you hired."

"Let's discuss this later this afternoon. I have an appointment at ten."

"But I need to resolve this now."

I stop short and watch the man quietly for a moment. Have I been wrong to let my staff address me as Bax? Am I too laid back with them?

"We will resolve it when I have the time to speak with you, Jerry."

His cheeks redden further, but I hold my hand up, stopping any words that he was about to spew at me.

"Watch yourself. You're a talented chef, but not irreplaceable. I will see you this afternoon."

I nod at Jeanette and walk toward my suite to change before meeting with Grace.

chapter 7
. . . .

~ Grace ~

"I only fell on my ass five times!" I cry, and launch myself into Jacob's embrace, wrapping my arms and legs around him and planting my lips on his for a quick kiss. "That's got to be a record."

"You are incredible, love." His smile is wide and happy as he holds me effortlessly against him. "You've caught on so well."

"I can probably ski as good as you now, govna."

"Let's not get carried away." He chuckles and nuzzles my nose with his. "But you can move on from the bunny hill to something a bit more challenging."

"Blimey, I'm good."

"Clever girl," he mutters as he sets me on my feet. "Let's grab something hot to drink."

"It's a date." He wraps his arm around my shoulders and walks me to the rental shop to turn in my gear, then leads me to a nearby coffeehouse. He finds us an empty table in a corner. "This is a cute little place," I say as I glance around the small but welcoming café.

"I had it built a few months ago," he replies, and helps me out of my coat. "The space was for lease, and I thought a coffee shop would do well here."

"And is it?"

"It is," he confirms with a grin. "What will you have, darling?"

"Vanilla latte, extra hot, please."

"Pastry?"

"No, thanks. I have a massage in a little while and I don't like to have much in my stomach."

He nods and crosses to the barista to put in our order. He's in black ski pants and a long-sleeved, blue T-shirt that molds his muscular shoulders and arms. I suddenly remember the way those muscles flex when he's hovering over me, the way they flex as he comes, and I have to shift in my seat, trying to alleviate the sudden throb between my legs.

"What are you thinking about, love?" he says, as he sits and passes me my coffee.

"Nothing."

"That flush on your cheeks isn't nothing."

I feel myself blush harder and look down at my cup.

Jacob leans toward me and brushes his fingers through my short hair behind my ear. "It's okay, love. I can't stop thinking about it, either. Spill it."

I glance about the small space, satisfied that no one is close enough to hear our intimate conversation.

I lean in and press my lips to his ear. "I was thinking about how spectacular you look when you're above me, how I love the way your muscles flex, and how completely you fill me." I brush my fingers through his soft, thick hair and his breath catches. His green eyes are on fire as I pull away and smile up at him innocently.

I clear my throat and take a sip of coffee. "I have to check out of the lodge and stow my things in my car before my massage."

He frowns and takes my hand in his. "I'm not ready for you to leave yet."

"I only had the room for the one night."

"I'd love to have your things moved to my suite while you get your massage. You can come directly to my rooms when you're finished."

I bite my lip and then smile. "I'd like that. But I don't want you to feel obligated . . ."

"One thing you'll learn about me, darling, is that I never do what I don't want to do. I want you with me tonight."

His words warm me and intensify the ache in my core. "Okay, then, I'd like that. Thank you."

"The pleasure is all mine, Grace." He smiles and drains the rest of his coffee, then consults his watch. "Unfortunately, I have to work for a bit this afternoon. I'll leave a key to my suite with Jeanette for you. Just pick it up when you're finished with your massage. I'll handle having your things moved."

"I feel very pampered, Mr. Baxter."

He glances at me and his body softens as he leans

toward me. "You deserve to be pampered. And that's Sir Baxter to you, missy."

"*Sir* Baxter? You've been knighted?"

"I have." He nods and then chuckles. "But don't tell anyone."

"I do believe this is the first time I've seen you get bashful." I cup his face in my hand. "Don't worry, your secret is safe with me. As long as you arrange for me to have tea with Kate and the baby."

He raises a brow and then breaks out into a laugh. "I'll see what I can do, silly girl." He checks his watch again.

"Go ahead. I'm going to be lazy here for a few minutes, call Cara, and then mosey on down to the spa. It's a rough life. The suffering is immense, but I'll be brave."

"Enjoy it, my brave girl." He kisses me long and hard, not giving a shit about who may be watching, then stands and shrugs into his coat. "I'll do my best to meet you in my room when you're finished."

"No worries. Have a good day, dear."

He winks and strides out of the café, turning heads as he goes.

Christ on a crutch, the man is a walking mass of sex appeal.

I pull my phone out of my pocket and dial Cara's number.

"Hey, how were the ski lessons?"

"I'm in the hospital."

"Oh my God!"

"I'm kidding. The lessons have been great. I didn't fall nearly as much as I thought I would."

"We told you you'd love it! You can tell us all about it tonight at girls' night out."

"That's why I'm calling. I won't be able to make it."

"Why?"

"Well, I might be having an affair with my ski instructor. Except he's not an instructor, he's the billionaire hottie that bought the joint." I bite my lip as silence descends on the call. "Cara?"

"Are you fucking kidding me?" she shrieks. "This is awesome! I want details!"

"Take it down a notch there, sister." I laugh and shift in my seat. "Yes, it's awesome. He's hot as hell, Cara. Like, movie star hot. And he's British so his accent is crazy sexy."

"I'm so jealous right now."

"You have your own hottie."

"I know, but I can still be jealous." She laughs and I can hear her jumping up and down. "I'm so excited for you!"

"So, he wants me to stay one more night, and I accepted. Am I being stupid?"

"Does the sex suck?"

"Hell no."

"Is he a douche bag?"

"No even a little bit."

"Then no, you're not being stupid. Enjoy him, honey."

"Okay." I grin and check the time. "Oh shit, I have to get to my massage. Thank you for this weekend, Cara. Seriously, I needed it."

"I know, and you're welcome. I'll want every naughty detail when you get home."

"Deal."

❄   ❄   ❄

"That massage was amazing. Thank you." I smile at the therapist and turn to leave, but she stops me.

"Wait. You're scheduled for a facial and pedicure as well."

I frown and shake my head. "You must be mistaken. My friends just bought me the massage."

She consults her computer again and nods. "It says right here you're scheduled for a facial and a pedicure, courtesy of Mr. Baxter."

My jaw drops. The man is seriously over the top. But I am not going to refuse it. That would be rude, right?

"Wow, okay."

I am buffed and polished from head to toe by the time I leave the spa. Every muscle in my body had been whimpering earlier, from the skiing and the bout of energetic sex last night, but now they're sighing contentedly.

What a lovely way to spend an afternoon. It's much later than I anticipated when I approach Jeanette at the registration counter.

"Do you work 24/7?"

"No, I'm about to leave in just a few minutes. Bax left this for you." She slides an envelope to me. "He's a good man."

I nod slowly. "Yes, he is."

"Have a good night." She gives me directions to his

suite, then winks and turns away. His room is on the top floor of the lodge, tucked in the back of the building that faces the valley. I can't wait to see the view from his windows.

I knock, but when there's no answer, I unlock the door and push inside. I flip on the lights and see a note sitting on the table.

> *Grace,*
> *I had to go handle another one of Jerry's*
> *"issues." I'll be back as soon as I can. Make yourself*
> *at home, love.*
>
> *Jacob*

I flip the switch for the gas fireplace and watch it come to life, then open the blinds and stare out at the valley below.

Holy million-dollar view.

Cunningham Falls and the lake are spread before me. Dusk is descending, and lights twinkle in the town. I walk through the living area that has a full kitchen and dining area attached, down a hallway. There are two small bedrooms, a bathroom, and finally the master bedroom with a huge four-poster dominating the room. The linens are white, crisp, and clean. My bag is on the floor of the walk-in closet and my clothes have been hung.

I walk into the bathroom to find my toiletries mingled with Jacob's.

It feels weird to see my things with his. I've never shared space with a man before.

I suddenly hear the front door open and I hurry out to meet him.

He's pushing a room service cart. His hair is a bit messy from his fingers combing through it. He's changed into a green V-neck sweater and jeans and is just pure deliciousness.

"G'day, mate! Did you bring me some Vegemite?"

"That's Australia, darling." He laughs and catches me up in a hug. "And I don't recommend the Vegemite. It's an acquired taste." He wrinkles his nose and shudders. "But I did bring dinner, because now that I have you here, we won't be leaving again, and I don't want any interruptions."

"Do all of the single female customers get this kind of attention?" I ask with a smile.

"As a matter of fact," he replies, while setting out our dinner, "I don't remember the last night I spent with a woman. They tend to get too attached, make assumptions, and it's just best all around if we don't make a night of it."

I inwardly cringe. *Don't ask a question you don't want the answer to, Grace.* I put on a brave smile and change the subject.

"You spoiled me today," I say softly. "Thank you."

"Did you enjoy it?"

"Oh yes. I'm all buffed and polished and soft now."

He grins wickedly. "I can't wait to see that for myself. But first . . ." He uncovers the plates and transfers them to the table. "I ordered us both pasta with Alfredo sauce and salads. I hope that's okay."

"Sounds great. I'm starved." I sit and dig in with gusto, moaning when the Alfredo sauce hits my tongue. "Dear sweet Jesus, that's good."

"Keep making those sounds, love, and I'll carry you to my bed straightaway."

I giggle and roll my eyes. "You'd think you've never seen a girl enjoy her food before."

"I love watching you enjoy everything. It's a sight to behold."

"Blarney." I shake my head and then drip sauce down the front of my shirt. "I'll just save that for later."

"You'll be out of that shirt soon enough, so it won't matter. But I can have it cleaned for you if you like."

"No, it's no biggie. I'll wash it when I get home tomorrow."

He nods and takes another large bite of pasta. "So tell me more about yourself."

I frown and shrug. "I'm not terribly interesting. I think I already told you the highlights."

"You're fascinating," he disagrees and takes a sip of water. "Why don't you speak to your parents?"

I lower my fork to my plate and wipe my mouth with my napkin. Do I talk about this with him? I rarely talk about it with anyone.

"This is a sordid story for another time," I reply.

"There's no time like the present," he replies, catching my gaze. "Talk to me."

I watch him for a long moment and then shrug. " I don't speak to my parents because they're both alcoholic assholes who enable each other and were always more interested in being in an liquor-induced coma than paying attention to their only child. I don't respect them. I worked my ass off in high school so I'd have scholarships to go to any school I chose and left the day I graduated."

I wait for the change. The disgust. The pity. But he just takes another bite of food and watches me thoughtfully.

"Those sound like good reasons."

I nod and look down at my plate, my appetite suddenly gone.

"My parents weren't alcoholics," Jacob says quietly. "But after my brother died, they lost themselves in their grief. They divorced. Father lives in Paris. Mother stayed in London. I was mostly raised by housekeepers. I was too old for a nanny."

My eyes meet his, and in this moment I've never felt this kind of connection to another human being. There is no pity or disgust.

Just understanding.

"Are you about ready for dessert?" He smiles gently and I know that I could easily fall in love with this man.

"Ready when you are."

chapter 8

$\mathcal{H}$e stands, pulls a freshly corked bottle of champagne from a bucket of ice, and uncovers a bowl of strawberries. "Follow me."

"No glasses?"

"We don't need them." He leads me into one of the spare bedrooms and sets the bubbly and berries on a bedside table before turning to me. "I will make love to you in my bed tonight, but first we're going to make a mess and I won't have you sleeping in that."

"Good plan."

"Remove your clothes, Grace." There's no *please* at the end of the sentence, as it's not a request. It's a command, one I'm perfectly content to obey. I slip my sweater over my head, then shimmy out of my jeans and stand before him in just my bra and panties. He cocks a brow. "You're not fully undressed."

"You could help with these."

"No."

Now it's my turn to cock a brow and turn my back to him. I unclasp my bra and let it fall to the floor. All he can see is my naked back, and I hear him chuckle at my stubbornness as well as his own clothing rustling. Next I hook my thumbs in my panties, slowly working them over my hips and down my legs to step out of them.

"Turn around."

I do and about swallow my tongue when I see his magnificent naked body standing before me. His erection is thick and heavy. His body is golden and firm, with little hair, and in the soft glow of the lamp beside the bed he reminds me of a Norse god.

"You are beautiful," I whisper. His eyes flare and he reaches for me, lifts me into his arms and kisses me silly as I wrap my legs around his waist, his cock nestled against my core.

"I'm going to tease you in the most delicious of ways," he murmurs softly as he pulls the covers back on the queen-size bed and lays me down gently. He plucks a strawberry out of the bowl and bites into it, then offers me the other half while it's still propped in his teeth. I take a bite and as the juices flow down my chin, he kisses me, lapping at the sweet juice.

"Mmm . . . Grace and strawberries. Delicious."

I grin and watch as he reaches for the champagne. "This is going to be cold," he warns softly as he tips it over me and drizzles just a light stream of the cold, bubbly wine down my torso, between my breasts to my navel, then leans in and licks it up, nibbling and tugging on my skin.

"Jacob," I breathe, and writhe beneath him.

"You're right, that was rude." He chuckles and tips the bottle, pouring just a sip into my mouth. "Another strawberry?"

He repeats the process from before, enjoying the red fruit with me, kissing me as we chew it, then pouring more wine on my belly.

"You're fucking delicious," he growls before pouring a small splash onto my pussy, sending my hips bucking into the air from the cold and the sensation of the liquid against my clit. He sets the bottle on the floor and dives in, lapping at my lips, gently tugging them with his teeth and sucking them again. He licks up to my clit and pushes two fingers inside me, finding my sweet spot.

"Oh fucking hell," I whisper, lost to him and the delicious things he's doing to me.

"That's right, love. God, you're bloody sexy." I love how his accent thickens when he's turned on. "Look at how pink your pussy is. How swollen."

"My turn," I whimper. God, I want to drive him as crazy as he's making me.

"Your turn?"

"Fuck yes, I want to torture you for a while, Sir Baxter."

He chuckles as he kisses up my body, settles in to suck, nibble, and generally torture my nipples, then kisses up my neck to my mouth.

"I think you're stuck to me now," I whisper against his lips. The champagne has turned sticky. He slowly peels himself off me and then flops onto his back and I reach for the strawberries.

I nibble the end off, then trace the fruit over Jacob's nipples and navel. The juice runs down his sides but I don't make a move to lick it up. Not yet.

"I like making a mess," I murmur with a wicked grin.

"So I see," he replies. "Are you going to clean it up?"

"Eventually." I grab the champagne and tip it over his torso, drizzling it gently over his nipples and down to his navel. I lean in and lick around his navel, drink the champagne, and then nibble my way up to his nipples, sucking them gently. I reach down, grab his hard cock in my hand and give it two firm pumps, then brush my thumb over the tip and feel a bead of wetness.

"You like this."

"I fucking love it, darling." His green eyes are on fire as he stares down at me, watching me devour and explore his body. I move onto my knees at his side and push my ass in the air as my lips travel down the trail of hair to his cock. His hand cups my ass and rubs it softly, then slaps it firmly before caressing it again. "Your ass is brilliant."

"I'm going to suck your cock, Jacob."

With a growl, he pushes me back, and before I know it, he's lifted me in his arms and is stalking through the suite to his master bathroom.

"Hey, I was having fun!"

"I need to get you into the shower, wash you off, and bury my cock inside you, love."

His words thrill me, but he's not off the hook. I want to suck his cock, and by God, I will.

He sets me on the counter, braces his hands on either side of my hips, and kisses me like a man starved. I grip his hips and hold on, riding the waves of lust that pour off of him.

Finally, he backs away, gasping, and rests his forehead against mine. "I'm going to turn on the shower. Don't move."

"I don't think I can move."

He grins wickedly, then turns away to start the water in the large glass-enclosed shower. The tile is green, the same color as his eyes.

When he's satisfied with the temperature, he lifts me off the counter and carries me to the shower.

"I'm capable of walking. I can't guarantee that I won't fall on my ass, but I can walk."

"I like carrying you," he whispers, and presses his face to my neck before setting me on my feet. "You're a tiny thing."

"It's a good thing, or it would hurt like a bitch when I fall." I grin up at him, but sober when I see the intense look on his face. "What's wrong?"

He shakes his head and reaches for a washcloth and soap. "Nothing at all. You're just stunning in my shower. The green makes your eyes glow."

He washes the champagne and strawberries off of my body, paying close attention to my breasts and pussy, and just when he's about to wash himself, I shake my head and take the cloth from his hands.

"Oh no. My turn, handsome."

He watches me quietly as I soap the cloth back up and run it over his chest, down his belly, and finally to his cock.

"Grace," he warns me, but I sink to my knees and rinse him clean, then circle the tip with my tongue.

"Lean your hands on the tile and enjoy, Jacob." He follows my direction and swears under his breath as I pump his cock slowly, steadily, and finally press my tongue to the base at the underside and lick along his thick vein to the tip. I pull him inside my mouth and sink down until I can feel him at the back of my throat, then move up and down, my lips firmly gripping him, milking him with every push and pull.

"Ah, fuck, love," he whispers in awe. I look up into his eyes, so full of lust and affection, and I feel him harden even more in my mouth. I begin to jack him with my hand, and just when I feel his muscles quiver, he pulls away and yanks me to my feet. "I will not come in your mouth tonight, Gracie." He kisses me hard, shuts off the water, and reaches for a towel. He dries me quickly, then runs the same towel over his body, tosses it aside, and lifts me back into his arms, cradling me against his chest.

"More dessert?" I ask with a smile.

"Fuck no. I need to be inside you."

"Thank God."

He laughs as he climbs onto his wide bed with me still in his arms and covers me with his large body. "You know, I wasn't done sucking you."

"Is that right?" He gets a new gleam in his eyes and suddenly reverses our position, turning me around so I'm facing his feet. He pulls my hips back until I'm hovering over his face. "Well, I won't be left out."

I circle his cock in my hand and lean down to take

him in my mouth just as he laps at my core and we both moan in delight.

"Ah, God," I whisper and sit up for just a moment, grinding my pussy on his face. "I've never done this before."

He growls and gently pushes me back down, his hand planted on the center of my back, and I continue sucking him with a vengeance, pumping him with my hand and working him with my mouth. He inserts a finger inside me and I simply can't take it anymore. I come hard, whimpering and panting. I reach over to his nightstand and pluck up one of the condoms he has set out, rip it open with my teeth, and sheathe him in it before crawling down his torso, and with my back still to him, sink down over him.

"That's right, love. Ride me. God, look at your ass." He cups my hips in his hands and guides me up and down. "You're bloody beautiful, Grace."

I brace my hands on his thighs and ride him hard, as though I'm chasing something that's just out of my reach. Finally, I circle my clit with my fingertip and feel the tremors move through me as I bear down and clench him hard.

"Yes, come, Grace. Oh fuck!" He pushes hard up into me, lifting me up off my knees as he succumbs to his own release. I brace my hands on the bed between his legs and try to catch my breath, then shake my head and laugh.

"Holy shit." Jacob lifts me off of him, and rolls me to the side so he can tuck me against him. He kisses my cheek, my neck and settles his lips against my ear.

"I'll be right back."

He moves from the bed and I can hear him in the bathroom, water running, toilet flushing. When he returns he scoops me back into his embrace and tucks me close to him. "Take a nap, darling. It's going to be a long night."

❋   ❋   ❋

And a long night it was. I can't believe I'm awake. Jacob fell back asleep about an hour ago after our last bout of vigorous sex. That man is a machine. I've lost count of how many times he woke me up, with either his tongue or his cock pressed to my core.

Not a bad way to wake up.

I'm leaving him today, going back to the real world. I know that I live only twenty minutes away, but it may as well be a world away. He's a billionaire who owns a freaking ski resort. I'm a schoolteacher.

I'm not foolish enough to think that those two worlds can blend.

I manage to slide out of his embrace, pack my bag, and use the bathroom without waking him. I stand at the side of the bed and take him in, his gorgeous, messy blond hair with coppery streaks, his square jaw with that amazing stubble that feels great on the inside of my thighs. And his muscular body, naked from the waist up, the sheet covering his lower body.

I wish I could hear him call me *darling* or *love* one more time, or tease him by spewing out a bad imitation of an accent, but it's better if I just go and avoid the whole awkward good-bye thing.

I tiptoe to the dining room and find a piece of paper and a pen and jot a quick note, dropping my purse to the floor with a loud *clunk*. I still and listen, my lip clenched to my teeth, praying I didn't wake him.

I'm so fucking clumsy! Not hearing any rustling noises from the bedroom, I turn to the pen and paper and try to think about what I'm going to say.

> *Jacob,*
>> *Thank you for everything this weekend. It's been an experience I'll never forget. I can now cross have a hot affair with a sexy ski instructor off my bucket list.*
>
>> *Best wishes,*
>> *Grace*

"What are you doing?" I whirl at the sound of his voice and cringe inwardly.

"I was just going to leave."

He cocks a sleepy brow and shuffles to me, takes the note out of my fingers and reads it, his eyes hardening as he raises them back to me.

"Is that what it was, Grace? A hot affair to cross off your bucket list?" His voice is soft and raspy from sleep, but his eyes are narrowed on mine.

No! That's not all it is! I want to yell those words at him, launch myself in his arms and ask him if I can stay another night, or if we can continue seeing each other after this weekend, but I know that's ridiculous.

"I had a lovely time," I reply, and lift my chin. "But I really should get home and start preparing for my classes tomorrow. I have work to do."

"Of course." He pushes his hand through his hair in agitation. *God, just leave, Grace!* Why did he have to wake up and make it so damn uncomfortable?

"Can I talk you into breakfast at least?" He's polite again, and is careful not to touch me, and I feel more foolish by the minute.

"Oh, no, thank you. You've been more than generous." I hope the smile I give him looks more genuine than it feels as I stand on my toes and kiss his cheek. "Take care, Jacob."

He brushes his knuckles down my face and smiles softly. "You, as well, Grace."

I grab my bags and hurry out of his room and down to the lobby, praying that I'm able to keep the tears at bay until I'm on my way back home.

The valet is quick to fetch my car, as there aren't many customers at barely six o'clock in the morning, and I make my way down the mountain, wondering if I did the right thing. Should I have stayed for breakfast?

No, that would have just been awkward. I can't have him thinking I'm getting attached and making assumptions. It was just a weekend fling, after all. There were certainly no promises made from either of us that we'd continue seeing each other after last night.

So why does it feel like my heart is being torn out of my chest?

chapter 9

· · · · · · · · · · · ·

~ JACOB ~

*T*hree fucking days. She's been gone for three days and I'm moping around like a lost puppy.

It's bloody horrifying.

I take a sip of cold tea and motion for Babs to send over a fresh cup. I'm sitting in the restaurant, my laptop open in front of me, and I can't bloody focus.

I can't stop thinking about Grace.

"Here you go, boss." Babs winks and replaces my cold tea with a fresh cup of hot water and Earl Grey on the side.

"Thank you, Babs."

"Need anything else?"

I shake my head and wave her off. She shrugs and walks away and I stare out the window at the people skiing down the hill, others riding up the lift. It's late afternoon and I've been sitting here since this morning.

I'm supposed to be looking over reports from my financial adviser, but I gave up long ago.

When I first read the note Grace left me that morning, her standing there all rumpled from a long night of sex, I was tempted to shake some sense into her and convince her that I wanted to keep seeing her.

But her note, her words, her body language were clear. It was a weekend fling for her, and nothing more, and as much as it bruises my ego—and my heart—it's something I just have to learn to live with.

But fuck me, I miss her like mad.

A single woman is seated across the room from me. Her eyes survey the room and stop when she sees me. She looks me up and down and then offers me a cocked brow and a half smile. My gut rolls.

A week ago I would have charmed my way into the beautiful woman's bed. Now, after Grace, the thought repulses me.

It all comes back to her. Her scent in my sheets, making it impossible for me to sleep at night, yet I've forbade housekeeping from changing them. The reminder of how she looked on her knees in my shower every time I step inside it. Grace, making me laugh my ass off as I taught her to ski on my hill.

Fuck, I need her like I need to breathe.

My decision made, I snap my laptop shut and shove it into my briefcase, grab my coat, and stride into the lobby and straight to Jeanette.

"I need Grace's address, please."

She tilts her head and says, "You know that's a violation of privacy law."

I slap my hand on the counter and lean over it menacingly, baring my teeth. "I'll bail you out of jail, Jeanette. Give me the bloody address."

She shrugs and pulls up the information on the computer, writes it down, and passes it to me. "Hold on."

She disappears into her office and then returns with a scarf. "Grace left this here. You might as well return it to her."

"Why didn't you tell me this sooner?"

"It was yours to figure out, Bax. But I'm glad you finally did, because you've been prowling around here, snapping at anyone who dares look at you sideways all week." She laughs and shakes her head. "Love is wasted on the young."

"I never said love . . ."

"Call it what you want." She waves me off and returns to her computer. "Just go get your girl."

I hop onto the desk and lean over to lay a smacking kiss on Jeanette's cheek, then jog out to the valet. "I'll need the SUV, please."

"Sure thing." The attendant leaves to fetch my car and I check my watch. It's after four. She should be home from school by now, shouldn't she?

My car arrives and I make my way carefully down the narrow mountain road. If I fall over the embankment, I'll never get to Grace.

I finally pull up to her small house in a quiet, well-kept neighborhood and cut my engine, watching the house.

I've turned into a bloody stalker.

I shake my head as I climb out of the car and make my way up the sidewalk to her front porch. I ring the bell and wait. The house seems to be still. Maybe she's not home yet? I ring the bell again and hear footsteps in the house, then an angry meow and a loud thud.

"Motherfucker!"

chapter 10

· · · · · · · · · · · · · ·

~ *Grace* ~

*T*his has been the day from hell. I really need to climb into bed and stay there before I break a bone or knock myself out.

I gently touch my cheek and wince as the pain shoots through my head. I pull into my driveway and frown when I see Hannah's car also sitting in the drive. She's never usually home at this time on a weekday. As Cunningham Falls' newest OB/GYN physician, she works long hours.

Sometimes I forget I even have a roommate.

I trudge through the snow up to my porch and trip on the top step, sending me headlong into the door. I barely catch myself with my hand, but still manage to scrape my palm.

"Fucking A, this day sucks," I mutter between clenched teeth, and push my way inside.

"Grace?"

"Yeah, it's me." I toss my keys onto a table by the door and toe my boots off before walking into the living room. "What are you doing home so early?"

"I just ran home to change my clothes," she replies as she smooths her red hair into a ponytail. "I had a messy delivery."

"Gross, I don't want to know." I shake my head and drop onto the couch.

"What happened to your cheek?"

I shrug one shoulder and don't answer her.

"Grace, let me look at that."

"It's just a bruise."

"No, it's not. There's a cut there, too. Come here."

"If I move I'll probably end up flat on my ass for the fourth time today, and I just don't have the energy to get back up."

"Come on, friend." Hannah helps me to my feet and leads me to her small bathroom. "I'm just going to clean it up a bit. It doesn't need a bandage."

"It hurts like a bitch."

"I'm sure it does. How did it happen?" She dampens some cotton balls with peroxide and dabs the cut. I suck my breath in through my teeth. "Sorry," she murmurs.

"It doesn't matter how it happened."

"Wow, you've been a bitch to live with all week, Grace. Wanna talk about it?"

I hang my head in my hands and sigh deeply. "I'm sorry, Han. I don't mean to take my mood out on you. Just kick me and tell me to stop being a bitch."

"I'd rather talk with you about what's wrong. This is so unlike you."

"I can't always be Miss Roses and Sunshine," I snap and then slap my hand over my mouth in horror. "Jesus, I'm sorry!"

"See? Bitch."

"I kind of miss Jacob."

"He's right at the top of that mountain," she reminds me, and points toward Whitetail Mountain.

"I know."

"So go up there."

"No, it was just a weekend fling."

"Right." She shakes her head and puts the peroxide back under the sink. "I think you should try dating him, but I don't have the best track record when it comes to men, so you can take that advice or leave it. I do know this: do what makes you happy because, girl, you're miserable. And you don't deserve that."

I wrap my arms around the pretty redhead and hug her close. "Thank you for being the best roomie ever."

"You're welcome. I'd suggest a nap, but that blow to the head looks like it could have resulted in a concussion." She narrows her eyes and peers deeply into my own eyes. "Look up at the light." I comply and sit patiently as she looks me over.

"There are benefits to living with a doctor."

"I'll send you a bill," Hannah murmurs with a grin. "Nope, no concussion. You should take a nap."

"Good idea. You headed back to work?"

"Yes. I have one other woman laboring and a few more appointments this afternoon."

"Ugh, I don't know how you can work around all of those bodily fluids." I shiver and follow her out of the bathroom. "See you later."

"Bye!"

Meow. Slater, Hannah's old cat, winds his way between my legs, purring and begging to be picked up.

"You're going to trip me one of these days, you little terrorist." I pick him up and nuzzle his head and carry him into my bedroom with me. I quickly pull on an oversize T-shirt and climb into bed. Slater joins me, purring happily as I drift off to sleep.

Dingdong!

I wake up and look about the room groggily. There are two kinds of naps, the kind where you wake up refreshed and rested, and the kind where you wake up with dry mouth, drool on your cheek, and not entirely sure what year you're in.

This nap was the latter.

The ringing persists, so I throw the covers back and stomp out of the bedroom, not even bothering to pull on some yoga pants.

I'm not going to actually open the door. It's probably a salesman. We definitely need to buy a No Soliciting sign.

Just as I'm crossing the living room to look out the peephole, Slater runs right into my legs, tripping me, and I fall flat on my ass.

Again.

I pound the floor with my fists and scream out, "Motherfucker!"

My ass hurts, my head hurts, and my heart hurts, goddamn it!

I hang my head in my hands and battle the tears that want to come. I'm so frustrated. Why can't I be graceful? Why am I such a damn klutz?

The door opens and I feel the rush of cold air on my bare legs, before it closes and I'm suddenly lifted off the floor by strong arms.

"What happened, love? Are you okay?"

I look up into worried bright green eyes and am mortified to feel a tear slip down my cheek.

"No, I'm not okay," I whisper. Jacob sits on my couch and keeps me cradled in his lap.

"Did someone hit you?" His voice is suddenly hard as steel as his eyes roam over my face. He raises a hand to touch my cheek but I flinch back. "I'll kill whoever did this to you."

"I ran into a door," I reply with embarrassment. "No need to become homicidal."

"Talk to me, darling. What's wrong?"

"Why are you here?"

"In a minute." He pulls his knuckles down my uninjured cheek. "First, tell me what's happened."

"It was a horrible day. The kids were loud and crabby. They didn't want to listen. One of them dumped my potted plant onto the floor in a temper tantrum. I walked into a door and did this." I point to my cheek. "My car's battery was dead when I got in it to come home, so I had to wait for roadside assistance to come help because most everyone had already left for the day, and I freaking miss you like crazy, and I probably just scared the shit out of you because everyone knows it's relationship suicide to say something like that when you're not even *in* a relationship."

"Take a breath, my love." His lips twitch as he soothingly rubs my back and my bare legs. "Do I need to remind you that *I* came to *you*, not the other way around? So I guess we can say that I missed you, as well."

"You did?"

He nods. "That is a bugger of a day that you've had."

"Aye, 'tis."

He chuckles softly. "I'm not a Scotsman, darling."

I shrug and smile softly. "So, why are you here?"

"You left your scarf at the lodge," he replies, and pulls my scarf out of his coat pocket, handing it to me, and I'm instantly mortified.

"Oh, thank you." I turn to move out of his lap, but he holds me firm.

"And, more important, I wanted to talk to you about the other morning."

"You did?"

He nods and watches me with sad eyes. *Sad?*

"Did you really only want a weekend fling, Grace? Is that all it was to you?"

I look down at my lap, but he tilts my chin back to meet my gaze. "No," I whisper.

"Then why did you say that? Why didn't you wake me and talk about where to take this next?"

"Because we didn't make any promises to each other, Jacob, and we'd just barely met."

"Yet I feel like you know me better than anyone else in my life." His voice is calm and sure and unapologetic.

"You're a British knight who owns half of that mountain, and I'm just a schoolteacher."

"Say that about yourself again and I'll take you over my knee, love. You're not *just* anything."

I gape at him and then frown in confusion. "I just don't see how it can work."

"Let's look at it this way." He kisses my fingers and instantly ignites sparks in my belly. I bite my lip and watch his eyes soften. "I've been quite miserable without you these past few days. I miss your laughter, your quick wit, and I miss sleeping next to you, sweet Grace. I don't make a habit of spending the night with women, and I don't want to spend the night with any woman but you."

"I've missed you, too," I admit softly. "I can't concentrate, which is probably why I've been extra clumsy." I comb my fingers through his hair. "I like you very much."

"Well then, it seems to me that there's no reason for us to not see each other. You can come to me on the weekends and I can come down here during the week when you're in school."

"You'd do that?"

"Until I talk you into moving in with me, absolutely."

He winks and then sobers. "We can take our time learning each other, darling. I'm looking forward to it."

"Hmm . . . learning each other, you say." I take his face in my hands and nuzzle his nose with mine. "What did you have in mind?"

"You want a demonstration?"

"Absolutely. Studies show that it's easier to learn by doing than by telling. And I know from firsthand experience that you're an excellent teacher."

He grins wolfishly and lays me back on the couch.

"You're wearing nothing but knickers under that shirt."

"Indeed," I reply with my best British accent imitation. "I am wearing knickers under this shirt. Should I be wearing *trousers*?"

"I love your smart mouth, darling." He chuckles and pulls my panties down my hips, off my legs, and throws them onto the floor. "What's under here?" He lifts my shirt to find me braless. "Were you in bed, my love?"

"I was napping."

"Mmm . . ." He pulls a nipple into his mouth and gently sucks while tweaking the other between his fingers. My back arches up off the couch. "I'm sorry I woke you."

"I'm not."

He kisses up my neck as I feel him shifting, pulling something out of his wallet, and then tossing his wallet onto the floor.

"You're wearing entirely too many clothes."

"Maybe you should take them off for me."

I tug the hem of his T-shirt up over his head and drop

it over the edge of the couch before gliding my hands over every inch of smooth skin and hard muscle. "I love your body."

He groans and buries his face in my neck, kissing and biting up to my ear.

"Take my *trousers* off, darling."

I grin and pop the button on his jeans, slide my hands into his underwear, cup his ass in my hands, and push his pants down around his thighs. His cock springs free.

"Oh, someone's happy to see me."

"I'm bloody ecstatic to see you, love."

I take the condom out of his hand and sheathe him myself, then take his heavy fullness into my hand and guide him to my opening.

"This has to be slow, Grace. You're so fucking small. I couldn't stand it if I hurt you."

"You won't hurt me, babe."

He kisses me hard as he slowly pushes inside me. When he's seated fully, he braces himself on his elbows at either side of my head, his hands bracing my head. He's panting, doing his best not to move quite yet.

"You feel amazing, Grace."

"God, so do you." He begins to move, slowly at first, but before long his thrusts speed up. He hooks one of my legs over his shoulder, opening me up farther so he can go deeper, and we both sigh in pure bliss.

I feel myself contract around him as the energy makes its way through me. I tighten my grip on his shoulders and bite my lip as I come apart beneath him, rocking my hips quickly, insistently.

"Ah, Grace, you're taking me with you, love. Fucking hell, I'm coming." With a growl, he rests his forehead on mine and clenches his eyes shut as he finds his own release.

"I'm so happy that you came to find me, Jacob."

"Always, darling." He kisses my cheek and smiles down at me. "Shall we continue our lesson in the bedroom?"

"Aye, we shall."

epilogue

. . . .

Seven months later . . .

*H*ow was your last day of class, darling?" Jacob meets me outside of the lodge and hugs me as soon as I climb out of my new car. He said that I needed a new one, and surprised me with it last month.

I kept insisting the one I had was fine, but when the battery died for the fourth time, he insisted.

And I must admit, it's not bad driving a Lexus. It's quite nice, actually.

"It was . . . long." I laugh and hug him back as he lifts me up off my feet and kisses me soundly. "I'm ready for summer."

"Excellent. You can move in with me now."

I shake my head and prop my hands on my hips, but he pretends he doesn't see it and leads me through the lobby of the lodge, past a waving Jeanette, to his suite.

"We've talked about this, Jacob. I'm not ready to move in together. It's only been seven months."

"That's plenty of time for me to know that I love you and want to spend the rest of my life with you. I want you to live up here with me."

My heart stills and then picks up double time as it always does when he tells me he loves me. It never fails to surprise me.

"I love you, too, you know that."

"Brilliant. I'll arrange for the movers."

"You'll do no such thing!"

"Jesus, Gracie, just bloody marry me so we can move past this ridiculous argument and we can stop hopping from one house to the other every fucking night!"

I stand and stare at him and then laugh myself silly. "And I thought I was the klutz."

"What is that supposed to mean?"

"That was the clumsiest marriage proposal I've ever heard!"

He swears under his breath, props his hands on his hips, and hangs his head before looking up at me. "You're a stubborn woman."

"How can you be so sure?" I ask softly.

"Sure about what?" He takes my hand and guides me into the living room, sits in a brown leather overstuffed chair, and tugs me into his lap. "Talk to me, Gracie."

"How do you know for sure that I'm the one you want?"

"I'm not going to get angry about that statement because I know that your parents did a number on you and I love you so much it makes me ache. But I'll not have you ever repeat that again, love. Do you think this happens to me every day?"

"I think that women—"

"Fuck the women, Grace. I haven't looked at another woman since the day you fell at my feet and charmed me off of mine. I don't give two shits about any other woman. It's only you. And I'm telling you, I'm promising you, it will only ever be you."

My eyes fill with tears at the fierce determination in his face, in the way he's holding me so tightly against him, as if I might jump up and run away.

"I love you so much that the thought of ever losing you brings me to my knees," I whisper. "It scares me."

"Ah, darling." He kisses my temple and rests his forehead against my own. "You're not going to lose me. I'm yours until my last breath, I promise you that." He pushes his hand into his pocket and pulls out a ring, not in a box, just an amazing round solitaire the size of my fist. "I was going to do this in a more romantic setting, but it seems this is our moment. Please, Grace Elaine Douglas, will you do me the great honor of becoming my wife?"

He wipes the tears from my cheeks with his thumbs and waits patiently for my answer.

"Of course."

"Thank Christ." He slips the ring on my finger and lifts me off the chair, walking swiftly toward the bedroom.

"Where are you taking me?"

"I'm in the mood to demonstrate how much I love my new fiancée." He grins down at me as he lays me on the bed.

"Jolly good!" I cry and laugh with him as he covers my body with his.

"You'll get it eventually, love."

Safe in His Arms

....

MELODY ANNE

prologue

· · · · · · · · · · · · ·

Can you believe that Edna took off like that?"

"What do you expect, Bethel? Her grandbaby needed her," Eileen replied.

"I know. I know. But the Christmas pageant is coming and it just won't be the same without her," Bethel said.

"Yes, of course, but don't you see the opportunity this presents?"

Both women turned to look at their friend Maggie, whose grin ran from ear to ear. The three women were thought to be in their sixties, but no one knew for sure—they guarded their age more securely than Fort Knox guarded its gold.

"What do you mean?" they asked in unison.

"We don't get too many new people here in town," Maggie told them. "Hawk's been single for long enough.

Now that my boy Bryson has gotten married and settled down, I'm more than ready to see the same happen for Hawk."

"Ooh, I like your thinking, Maggie," Bethel said, her eyes twinkling with understanding.

"So, we just need to find an . . . *appropriate* teacher," Eileen said with a giggle.

"Yes, yes, yes," Bethel burbled. "I'm so glad to be on the school board, so we have the task of finding Edna's replacement."

"Did they include photographs with the résumés?" Maggie asked.

"Sure did!" Eileen told them as she flipped open her laptop.

"Shouldn't we bring Martin in on this?" Eileen asked quietly, and a slight blush tinged her cheeks.

Bethel and Maggie knew that something was happening between their friend and town businessman Martin Whitman, but they weren't about to call Eileen out on it.

"We will . . . eventually," Bethel said. "But not right now. This girl needs to be for Hawk. Martin would try to steal her away for one of his four boys."

"Well, we need to find some women for those ornery sons of his, too," Maggie chimed in.

"Let's just focus on one kid at a time," said Bethel, always the logical one. "Besides, I already have plans brewing for my granddaughter Sage and one of the Whitman boys. As soon as she's done with medical school . . ."

Maggie's eyes widened. "Oh, do tell."

"Now's not the time." Bethel said, clicking through the résumés. "Girls, I think we have a winner!"

The other two women leaned over, and then all three of them smiled as they read about Natalie Duncan, who was seeking work as an elementary-school teacher.

"I think you might just be right," Maggie said.

Poor Natalie had no idea what she was about to step into . . .

chapter 1

· · · · · · · · · · · · ·

*H*er heels clicking on the hard tile floor of the airport, Natalie Duncan smiled and popped a Hershey's Kiss into her mouth. Her first teaching job! It was a dream come true. Four years of college, thousands of study hours, even more volunteer hours, a teaching internship at a beautiful elementary school in sunny LA, and she had finally received the call she'd been waiting for.

Sure, it was November, and sure, she'd been called only because another teacher was going through some sort of family emergency and had to leave the state suddenly, but Natalie was still stoked. She'd been the one the school had called. She was the one who would be stepping into her very own classroom come Monday morning.

The small town of Sterling, Montana, wasn't exactly where she'd wanted to begin her career, but it was a job teaching what she loved. This was only a stepping-stone.

Wholly unaware of the masculine eyes that were following her in her sharp blue pencil skirt and four-inch heels, Natalie pressed forward. With her slim five-foot-three-inch frame and her fiery red hair, green eyes, and full lips, she was made to turn heads. The thing was, Natalie wasn't looking for male attention. She had plans. She had goals. And men were far down on her list of priorities. After all, she was only twenty-three. Work first. Marriage and family later.

A smile flitted across her lips as she thought about her life fifteen years down the road. She'd have a white picket fence and one girl and one boy running through the sprinkler on a nice, hot day while she sat next to her husband and enjoyed the successes of her life.

Wrapped up in her fantasy future, Natalie stepped through the airport doors buzzing with excitement and a huge smile plastered on her face, which vanished in an instant when the biting Montana wind slapped her in the face.

"What the hell?"

Her voice came out choked as she struggled to regain the breath that had been sucked from her.

She'd been born and raised in Southern California, and was in no way ready for this sort of weather. She'd been so excited over receiving the job she hadn't even thought to research what climate she was stepping into. Stupid, stupid, stupid. Running back inside she gulped warm air into her frozen lungs.

"Okay. You can do this," she told herself as she looked

down scathingly at her completely inefficient shoes. "Heels? What was I thinking?" Heels and sexy lingerie were her concessions to blatant femininity. Otherwise she wore beige and dark colors, and downplayed what she'd been blessed with.

Raising her head, she studied the people passing her by. None of them were wearing heels and a skirt. No. They were clad in warm boots, thick coats, and trousers. She threw her suitcases a disgusted look as it dawned on her that she'd have little choice but to spend some of her precious savings on warmer clothing.

Reaching into her carry-on bag, she pulled out her warmest jacket, which wasn't going to do much, but it was better than nothing. She was wishing she'd done a lot more research on the weather in Montana before her arrival. Making her way back to the doors, Natalie glared at them as if they were the gates to hell, and took a deep breath before moving forward again.

As she stepped outside, tears sprang instantly to her eyes, and her entire body shook, but she forced herself to trudge to the curb. Thankfully, there was a cab waiting. Fearing she'd never feel warmth fully return to her body again, she huddled in the backseat after giving the driver the address for the little furnished house the school district had set up for her.

The people of Sterling had been unbelievably kind. One woman—her name was Bethel—had even sold Natalie a small Toyota sedan, dirt cheap. That was one less thing she had to worry about. The vehicle should be parked in her driveway already.

First she'd get settled in, and then she'd drive around town. She hoped they kept the roads plowed, because her little car wasn't going to make her feel particularly safe, and she couldn't fork out the money needed for a truck or SUV. Her mind drifted as the miles passed and she gazed out absently at an endless expanse of white.

"Looks like Hawk's here to show you the place."

Startled, Natalie looked up to see the cabbie peering at her through the rearview mirror. "What?"

One of Natalie's worst faults, or at least what she felt was one of her worst faults, was that she'd get so lost in her own head she'd tune out the rest of the world.

A vivid imagination was great when you were teaching young children, but not so great when trying to hold normal conversations with other adults. How pathetic. Her life was so dull that she spent most of her time in a fantasy world.

That was going to change, though. She was a teacher now. A *professional*. Pulling a little notebook out of her purse, she turned to the list of goals she'd written out in clear, even handwriting. With pure delight, she checked off *Get first teaching job*. Of course, not everything on that list would be crossed off so easily.

"Hey, Mickey. How was the drive?" asked a husky male voice.

Whoa. When Natalie looked up and saw the man leaning against the side of the cab, she felt frozen to her seat. And it had nothing to do with the cold air drifting through the now open window. A pair of linebacker shoulders completely swallowed up the open space. He was wearing a thick coat, sporting dark and slightly unruly hair, with piercing brown eyes with lashes that seemed to go on forever.

And those lips. They were full and turned up in an electrifying smile as he bantered with the cabbie. Natalie had no idea what the two men were saying, because the deep timbre of this man's voice enveloped her. It seemed to be sending all sorts of wrong signals to her stomach, which was fluttering.

Suddenly, her side door flung open and the man stood there with his hand out while saying something to her, but all she could hear was buzzing in her ears.

Nonsense!

This was total and utter nonsense. She didn't believe in love at first sight, or even lust at first sight. So to be looking at this man as if he were a piece of her favorite chocolate was freaking ridiculous.

She was a professional woman who'd just had a weak moment. He was holding out a hand to help her from the taxi. That was all. She could do this. She'd reach out casually, take his hand, say a polite thank-you, and make her way into the house. Easy-peasy.

But when she did reach out, the sensation of his gloved fingers gripping her bare ones sent tingles through her body. She somehow managed to climb gracefully from the vehicle. But as their eyes met for the first time, she felt as if she were being sucked into another dimension.

"Hawk Winchester."

It took her a moment to realize he was introducing

himself. It took her another moment to notice the narrowing of his eyes, the slight pursing of his lips. His smile had vanished, and it seemed she wasn't the only one confused by this instant attraction.

Never before had she felt any sort of zing with a stranger. Never before had she stood in front of someone and wanted to tear off her clothes without any preliminaries, civilized or not. She was Natalie Duncan, innocent and repressed schoolteacher. She'd been the one in the library while her peers were out partying. She'd never had lustful thoughts about *any* man, any man at all.

Yes, she'd fumbled through sex during college, but that was just going through the motions. She'd never before experienced the intensity she was feeling at this moment, looking at Hawk. As this stranger held her gaze, she couldn't seem to shake the irrational vision of the two of them entwined together in reckless passion. Oh, this was bad. So very bad.

It didn't have to be. The man was just being neighborly. Helping her into her new house. After this moment passed, she wouldn't see him again. Out of sight, out of mind, right?

Right.

"Natalie Duncan."

She'd finally found her voice. Pulling her hand away, she began walking up the cleared path to the front steps. Let the men handle her bags. There was no possible way she'd be able to get her fingers to quit shaking long enough to actually lift one of those suitcases.

Suddenly the heels she was wearing didn't make firm contact with the slick path, and she felt herself slipping slightly.

"Wait!" Hawk's low voice called.

Too late. Her heel caught in a gap between the front porch boards. Her hands flew up, imitating a windmill, and she felt herself falling backward.

Closing her eyes, she prepared for a nasty fall into that wretched snow, but instead she landed in solid arms and against an even more solid chest. Afraid to open her eyes, she peeked up from under her thick lashes.

She should have kept her eyes closed, because the smoldering fire burning in Hawk's eyes was enough to make her feel faint. He didn't move, just looked at her as if she were the main course for dinner. Yeah, she'd have to avoid this man at all cost! Because she found herself wanting desperately to close the minuscule gap between them, and that just wasn't in her plans.

She just had to think of her list. Her life was mapped out—school, check; career, check; ten years of hard work, not checked. Nowhere on that map was the gorgeous man now holding her in his arms.

"Well, Natalie, I always do enjoy it when a beautiful woman falls right into my arms," he said, his eyes bright, his lips set in a smoldering, confident grin.

Womanizer! That's what this man was. He figured he was cute enough that he could say a few words and she'd simply invite him in. Natalie hadn't fallen under a man's spell before, and she certainly wasn't going to do it while she was frozen, grumpy, and more than irritated to be caught in such a vulnerable position.

"I'm grateful you didn't let me hit the ground, but you can wipe that look off your face and let me go." Her voice stern, her eyes anything but receptive, she was satisfied when his expression changed to one of confusion.

But he quickly regained his composure. "Hmm, not the usual reaction I get when I have a beautiful woman in my arms."

"I'm not a usual woman."

Just as quickly as he'd caught her, he let her go, nearly making Natalie tumble backward again. Barely catching herself, she grabbed the ice-covered rail and climbed the couple of steps just as the cabdriver set her bags by the front door.

Thanking the man, she paid him, then turned back to Hawk, who for some reason was holding her house key in his hand.

"As I said, Hawk Winchester," he said smoothly. "Local fire chief, and . . . your landlord."

Crap.

Putting away her anxiety, she held out her hand, hoping like hell he would just drop the key into it without any further physical contact. Of course, that wasn't going to happen. He gripped her fingers and wrapped them around the key, his eyes once again smoldering as he captured her gaze. "I'll be seeing you again real soon," he said, and then turned away, leaving her shivering by the front door.

She watched him leave, his stride smooth, his movements confident. Before he reached the sidewalk, she shook her head and turned back to her door, her fingers shaking so hard it took a few tries before she was able to unlock it. Natalie had a feeling her time in Montana wasn't going to be quite as easy-peasy as she'd thought it would be.

chapter 2

S omething was wrong. As she started to come out of a deep slumber, Natalie realized her nose was frozen. After pulling the covers over her head with one hand, she let the other hand crawl up her body until it reached her face. Dammit. Her nose felt like a Popsicle. What was the matter with this place?

No way could she crawl from this stupid bed. Even beneath five blankets, she was fighting not to shiver. What was wrong? The old furnace had been working when she went to sleep.

And how long had she slept, anyway? Groping the nightstand for her watch, she was shocked to discover it was already nearly eleven o'clock. She'd been exhausted, true, but she had too much to do to lie here any longer.

Deciding to test the temperature again, she slid the blankets down. Sheesh. Frigid air assailed her body and made every hair stand on end atop giant goose bumps. Yanking the covers back into place, she curled into a ball and fought tears.

Unfortunately, her bladder was screaming at her.

It took her another five minutes, but she finally talked herself into making a run for the bathroom. Throwing off the covers, she leapt from the bed and sprinted through the small house to its lone bathroom. She cranked up the shower to the hottest setting to try to build up steam, and dashed through her morning routine despite the shivers wracking her body. When the water in the shower finally reached a reasonable temperature, she jumped beneath the spray.

It took a full two minutes before she felt heat return to her beleaguered limbs. And when she stepped out of the shower, she gloried in the steam that filled the small bathroom. Mostly dry, she gazed at the door leading to the rest of the house.

"It's like I know there are a thousand snakes on the other side of it, yet I have no choice but to go out there," she muttered before laughing at herself. "This is ridiculous!"

Wrapped in a towel, Natalie took a deep breath for courage and opened the door. Yep. It was as bad as she'd expected. She darted back to the bedroom and made a beeline for the dresser. After yanking her undergarments on, which wasn't easy—she was shaking more violently than a single leaf in an autumn breeze—she found her warmest pair of wool pants.

Next, she piled on four shirts, a sweater, and a coat that didn't want to fit over the bulk of her cleverly "layered" clothes. The only shoes she'd brought were not going to cut it, and she was kicking herself for that now. Her toes were going to turn black and fall off with frostbite before this Montana adventure was over.

Once she'd clothed herself as best as she could, she moved over to the blasted furnace, which was really just a glorified space heater. Not knowing what else to do, she slammed it hard with palm of her hand and stood there shaking as she waited for a miracle.

Nothing happened.

"All right. Time to go shopping."

She'd never thought she'd be the type of woman to wear hopelessly unattractive long underwear, but if she was going to survive a Montana winter, she'd dang well better get used to the things. She didn't even care what color they were, just as long as they kept her warm.

Rushing outside, she gazed at her "new" car, a small blue Toyota probably from the Pleistocene era. It had most certainly seen better days, but it was hers and the heater worked, and nothing at the moment was more beautiful than the thought of a burst of warm air blasting from the vents. It took the old metal heap about five minutes before the heat actually began flowing, but once the warmth hit her, she smiled in delight.

"Not so bad," she muttered. It occurred to her that maybe she was talking to herself just a little too much. "Oh well."

Driving into the almost comically small town, Natalie was surprised by the lack of traffic. No one seemed to be around. What was going on? These people had to be used to driving in the snow. But all she'd seen on the roads were big plows clearing the streets.

She reached a stop sign and tapped on her brakes, and in the blink of an eye everything began to go wrong. Though her taps were growing urgent—hell, they were stomps now—the car wasn't responding, and in front of her was a gigantic black truck.

"No. No. No!"

Nope. That didn't work. Her car kept on going, and she crashed into the back of the behemoth. And even though she was going less than fifteen miles per hour, her tiny Toyota had no chance of surviving.

Her car went beneath the truck's bumper. Her hood crinkled, and steam flew up into the air as her radiator was impaled. The impact jolted her head forward, but the small car's air bags didn't deploy for some reason and she felt the sting of her forehead connecting with the steering wheel.

Dammit! She hadn't even insured the car yet! Now what in the heck was she going to do? Tears sprang to her eyes, but with a will borne of hard times, she blinked them away and stepped out of what was once a running car. At least she hadn't suffered more than a couple of bruises and a huge dent to her pride. She really hoped the bulk of the physical damage was only to her car and not the other vehicle.

"What in the hell are you doing out on the road if you can't even do as simple a task as stopping at a big red sign? Did you decide that today would be a great day to plow into a complete stranger?"

Instant fury filled her. Natalie's eyes burned as she watched Hawk Winchester stalk toward her, his face a mask of irritation.

"Yeah. I just learned how to drive. I thought, what the hell—I'll go screaming through this incredibly small town, and then I'll blow through a stop sign and kill my car on the back of some idiot's butt-ugly truck!"

Sure, she might regret her quick temper later, but right now, she was ready to throw a kicking, screaming, and gleefully adolescent temper tantrum. Too much had happened in the last fifteen hours, and this was just the icing on a very frozen cake. At least her fury was masking the fact that she was still freezing. There was nothing like an exploding temper to heat the blood.

"Why would you be driving a car without snow chains in this weather?"

"I just moved in last night, as you well know, and I haven't had time to buy chains, not that it's any of your business!"

"Well, maybe you should have walked. Of course, that's another disaster waiting to happen in those absurd shoes you're wearing."

Natalie had been mad enough before, but his disdainful look made her want to smack the crap out of the man. She had never, *ever* had the urge to close her fingers into a fist and slug anyone, but at this moment her mind was urging her to do just that.

Too bad her fingers were freezing and incapable of forming a fist.

"You are the most pompous, self-absorbed man I have

ever met in my life." She'd thought of him as gorgeous the night before, but now he counted as monstrous, like his truck. "Just bill me for the damage." She spun around and did her best to storm off. Not easy in heels and all that snow, *and* without a working car. But she was so done with this conversation, done with speaking to this man, and done with a ridiculous town that didn't even have an open store on a freaking Thursday, for goodness' sake.

"You can't just go off like that. We haven't even exchanged insurance information yet!" he yelled, but she wasn't listening.

"Call the cops on me, then!"

She was feeling pretty damn good about her exit until her feet decided they weren't going to cooperate. She didn't even have a chance to stop the fall.

"Natalie!"

He couldn't catch her this time. One minute she was walking away. The next, everything went black . . .

chapter 3

. . . .

$\mathcal{H}$awk reached Natalie just in time to see her head slam into the ground and her eyes roll back in her head. Damn! Possible concussion. He lifted her in his arms and raced back to his truck, where the heater was still running. "Come on, Natalie. Open your eyes," he commanded.

She began to stir. "What happened?" Her eyes fluttered open, then widened when she saw him only a few inches from her face.

"You fell down and hit your head," he said, and then he ran his hands over her ankles and wrists.

"Ouch!"

"That's what I thought. You bruised your wrist, too."

Dammit! It was Thanksgiving and he was already running late. His mother was going to kill him.

"I'll take you to the doc. Give me a minute to move your car out of the road."

Leaving her on the front seat of his truck, he jogged back to her car. She'd crushed her radiator, and there was no chance that the heap of metal would start now. After he put the car in neutral, it took him a few tries for his feet to gain traction on the ground, but he managed to roll the car to the curb before jogging back to his truck. He found Natalie there huddled in a ball, her entire body shivering.

"It's okay. Don't worry about the car," he told her. "But the doc should look at you." He knew he didn't sound very reassuring. Normally, it was his job to reassure people who'd been in accidents, as he was a damn fine paramedic as well as being fire chief. So why was he so tongue-tied all of a sudden?

"I'm fine. If you can just drop me off at my house . . ." she said, her voice alarmingly quiet.

"Not gonna happen."

He didn't say anything else. He threw his truck into drive and headed out of town. The doc didn't live far from his parents. Maybe he'd even get a piece of the doc's wife's sweet apple pie. That woman had the best pie in the county—hell, maybe the country—though he'd never say such a thing to his mother, or he'd be banned from her table.

Hawk's gaze strayed repeatedly over to Natalie as he cruised the snow-covered country roads. Forcing his eyes forward, his thoughts strayed to the conversation he'd had with the town meddlers.

We have a perfect tenant for your house. That should have been Hawk's first clue that the women had been up to no good. When he'd received a phone call from his mother demanding that he make the new teacher feel welcome in their little town, he'd been suspicious, but apparently not enough to say no to letting her use his rental house.

What in the hell did his mother and her best friend, Bethel, think? That he was going to make Natalie some blueberry muffins and show up on her front porch carrying a basket? Hawk didn't do that. And he certainly didn't mingle with fiery-tempered red-haired schoolteachers. Not ever.

Hawk liked women. That's *women*, plural. He never dated anyone like the schoolteacher, who was *really* rubbing him the wrong way right now. She was the sort of woman who would want commitment—he could see that clearly from the moment he'd met her in her uptight clothing.

Hawk dated a woman for only one night. Okay, he wasn't rigid about it. If she was truly spectacular, then he'd make it two or three nights. Third time, however, was the charm. It would only go downhill from there, so he chose to avoid any further contact after that.

This was a prime reason he never, *ever* dated women from Sterling. It was too small a town and he couldn't run and hide from them. He'd had several false fire calls from eligible women *and* their mothers, just to get him to their house. He'd been forced to get a little stern once or twice to stop all that from happening again.

The last such call that had come in had been from a

mother who'd purposely set her trash can on fire. He'd lectured her for an hour about the danger she'd put her home, family, and pets in. As he'd walked out the door, the woman had still had the gall to slip her daughter's phone number into his pocket.

Women! He just couldn't figure them out.

Arriving at Dr. Holo's house, throwing the truck in park, and rushing around to Natalie's side of the vehicle, he lifted her into his arms before running up the walkway to the front door.

"Hawk, what are you doing out on Thanksgiving? And with such a pretty young woman?"

"Hi, Maybelle. This is the new schoolteacher, Natalie Duncan. We had a slight fender bender, and then she fell and hit her head. Wrist seems bruised, as well."

"Oh, darling," Maybelle gasped. "That's not a very good welcome to our town." Ushering them both inside, Hawk set Natalie on her feet and then Maybelle wrapped an arm around her shoulders. "Alfred just finished his Thanksgiving dinner and was getting ready for dessert, but he'll certainly take care of you first. Hawk, you just sit on down and I'll dish you up a piece of pie," she added, and then led Natalie away.

Hawk felt much better when a juicy slice of pie was put before him, and he began devouring it.

His grumpiness had almost completely dissipated. A smile even appeared on his lips as he sat back and waited for Natalie. That smile vanished when the doc came back into the room with the new schoolteacher and Hawk heard the tail end of their conversation.

"I'm so sorry about ruining your holiday, Doctor. I didn't even realize it was Thanksgiving."

Hawk was baffled. How could she not have known it was Thanksgiving? It was Turkey Day. Well, turkey and his favorite, pie. And family, and of course football. How could anyone forget about this particular day? Didn't she have a mother to call? A family to go home to?

Of course, she *had* just arrived for her new job, so she didn't know anyone here yet. But why wouldn't she have come on Friday or Saturday instead, so she could spend Thanksgiving with her family?

Hawk caught himself worrying about her, but he didn't want to know about this woman. He certainly didn't want to be *concerned* about her. He *wasn't* going to be interested in her. That was for damn sure!

"She has a slight concussion. Nothing too serious, but I don't want her alone for a straight twenty-four hours," Doc said, looking meaningfully at Hawk.

Dammit!

"Of course not."

"I'm fine, really," Natalie said, shifting from foot to foot. "I just need a ride home."

Because she refused to meet Hawk's eyes, she didn't see the withering look he sent her before he turned back to the doctor. "I'll take her with me to my parents' place for dinner and then make sure she's not alone."

Finally looking up, Natalie gaped at him, but he just turned back to Maybelle instead.

"Thanks for the pie. It really is the best in the county," Hawk said, kissing her cheek.

"You come back anytime. I always have a fresh pie for visitors," she said, a rosy glow where he'd kissed her.

"You know that you're both more than welcome to come on over and eat at my mom's," Hawk said. His parents always had a few extra people at their table. They couldn't stand the thought of anyone being alone on a holiday.

"I'm going to turn the game on in a few minutes and focus on digesting," Doc said with a laugh. "Serious work. You just take care of my patient and I'll rest easy."

"I can assure you that she'll be well looked after," Hawk told them as he ushered Natalie toward the front door.

"That's a good boy," Doc said, and Hawk felt as if he should bend down so the doctor could pat him on the head the way the man used to do years back. Instead, Hawk said good-bye and led Natalie outside.

When they got back inside the truck, Natalie turned toward Hawk with nervous eyes. "It's really okay for you to leave me at my place. I promise to not go to sleep right away." She spoke bravely, but she was almost shaking.

Hawk was now even more curious. Why was she so determined to get away from him? Sure, they'd been less than pleasant to each other after the wreck—they'd both lost their tempers—but he wasn't a monster. It hadn't gotten out of hand. Besides, he wasn't used to women trying to avoid him. Women running after him, yes. Women giving him their number, also a big yes. Women who would rather suffer from a concussion alone than be with him? That was a new one.

"I said I'd take care of you, and that's what I'm going to do." As far as Hawk was concerned the subject was closed. "I hope you're hungry, because my mother's made a feast."

"No. I can't intrude on your family," she gasped.

"What's your problem?" When she flinched, he felt a twinge of guilt about the way the words had come out, and he was careful to speak more gently now. "Sorry. It's just a meal, though. You don't need to get so worked up."

"I'd just rather be at home," she mumbled, her arms folded across her chest.

"Well, tough." So, his vow to be gentler had lasted ten seconds. It was the thought that counted, right? With no more conversation, he headed toward his parents' sprawling raised ranch house. Half the county's pastureland surrounded it.

His mom was so going to read this the wrong way. Hawk had never brought a woman home before, not even for a brief visit, and definitely not for a holiday. His heart pounded as he pulled down the long drive.

It was time to get his game face on. His mouth had better be faster than his mother's brain, because if she saw a matchmaking opportunity, he was screwed.

chapter 4

· · · · · · · · · · · · ·

Natalie could barely hold herself together. Her entire body was shaking as she sat huddled by the door of Hawk's huge truck. She couldn't do this, couldn't go into his parents' house and act as if this was normal for her.

This was so far from normal she didn't know where normal began. It had always been just her and her mom. Her father had left them both before Natalie was even born, and her mother had never remarried.

They'd struggled throughout Natalie's childhood, never having money, never having much time together. Her mom worked two jobs just to keep a roof over their heads and food on the table. Then, the time they were together had been . . . she couldn't exactly describe it in words.

Her mother had led a difficult life and she'd had the right to be bitter, to be angry over the cards that had been dealt to her. She'd warned Natalie not to fall in love, that it only led to heartache, and *certainly* not to end up getting pregnant.

Natalie didn't hold any ill will toward her mother, choosing to focus only on the good memories, though they'd been few and far between. And Natalie had promised her mother that she wouldn't settle, wouldn't accept less than the best for her life.

When Natalie had lost her mother during her freshman year in college, she'd wanted desperately to quit, to just give up, but because she'd loved her mom in spite of it all, she'd pushed through the grief. She'd tried that much harder.

As they arrived at Hawk's parents', she felt as if she was betraying her mother. Her mom had never gotten to celebrate a holiday, had never been welcomed into somebody's home with open arms.

"I really can't do this."

Hawk turned and his intense gaze held hers. It was unnerving—she felt as if he could actually see what she was thinking.

"You can, Natalie. My family doesn't bite." His voice was soft, almost a caress.

"I'm sure they won't appreciate an uninvited guest," she pointed out. Surely he'd see reason.

When he laughed, that really got her hackles up. She didn't like to be laughed at.

"I'm sorry," Hawk told her when he saw her veiled outrage. "I'm not laughing at you, but as soon as you meet my mother, you'll realize how untrue that is. The more people, the better—that's her motto."

Unless Natalie wanted to create a scene, she was stuck. She found herself being helped from the truck just as the door to the large house in front of her opened. She turned and lost her balance and of course, fell right into Hawk's arms.

"You seem to have trouble staying on your feet," Hawk said with a smile as his arms tightened. Before she could respond, a female voice rang out.

"Well, I guess you're forgiven for your monumental rudeness in being so late."

"You can . . . um . . . let me go now," she said, her voice little more than a squeak.

"Oddly enough, I don't want to," he blurted out. His words made her head snap up in surprise. Nothing he seemed to say or do was consistent from one moment to the next.

"Dang, Hawk. Would you quit groping the girl and introduce us?" Natalie peered nervously upward, looking for the speaker. About ten people were looking down at her. How could she climb the steps onto the wraparound front porch without disgracing herself again?

Hawk slowly—reluctantly? She couldn't be sure—released his hold on Natalie, only to place his arm behind her back. She refused to read anything into the gesture. It had to be his way of ensuring he wouldn't have to catch her again if she tripped.

If she didn't get some good boots, and soon, her ass would be grass. Correction. Her ass would be snowbound.

"Sorry I'm late, Mom. We had a little accident in

town. This is Natalie Duncan, the new third-grade teacher. Natalie, my family. There are too many names for you to even try to remember them all," Hawk said with a wink.

"As much as I love my son, I know his failings. Ignore him, dear," a tiny woman said as she took Natalie from her son's arms and rushed her inside. "What in the world are you wearing, my child?"

That was the question of the hour. Or maybe the last day and a half. "I . . . um . . . wasn't prepared for the cold here."

"I'm Maggie, Hawk's mom, and I'll get you introduced to the rest of the gang real soon. For now, we need to find you some better clothes. You must have ripped your pants in the accident, and those shoes just won't do." Maggie was talking so quickly that Natalie was having a hell of a time keeping up.

"I didn't realize it was Thanksgiving, so I went looking for a place that sold boots . . ."

Maggie just stared at her as Natalie trailed off in embarrassment. *Damn.*

"Oh, darling," Maggie exclaimed. "No one should forget Thanksgiving. You look about the same size as my daughter, Taylor. Let's go raid her closet." She took Natalie's hand and dragged her up an extrawide staircase to a room with a large sign on it that said, ironically enough, Do Not Enter.

"What size shoe do you wear?"

"I'm a seven, but really, I can wait until tomorrow and go buy some appropriate apparel."

Natalie's protests were clearly falling on deaf ears—Maggie was already digging around in the closet.

"Aha! I knew you were about the same size. Here's a brand-new pair of UGG boots, size seven," she said triumphantly. "I bought them for her two years ago, but Taylor disdains any article of clothing without a Fox label on it. She races dirt bikes."

Natalie's mouth dropped wide open. "Your daughter races?"

"Yes, and she's very good at it. This is the first Thanksgiving in years that she hasn't been home. She made it to the finals. It breaks my heart, but I understand." Maggie's sudden sniffles belied her final words.

"Doesn't that scare you?" Natalie asked.

"Oh, it can if I let it," Maggie said, "but I'm very proud of my daughter. Her two brothers, on the other hand, are constantly preaching to her about how unsafe racing is. They don't realize that the danger makes her that much more competitive. Someday they'll learn, but I fear it won't be anytime soon." The woman kept pulling out clothing.

As the pile grew higher and higher on the bed, Natalie shifted on her feet. "I really shouldn't just borrow her clothes without her permission."

"Nonsense, darling. Taylor would want you to have them. You can wear what you want now, and then we'll bag the rest of the things up for you before you leave." And apparently the woman was just like her son, because she didn't listen to any further protests, but instead just walked from the bedroom and shut the door behind her.

Natalie's knees suddenly turned weak and she found herself sinking down onto the neatly made bed. She was so exhausted. But she couldn't help looking around Taylor's room. Pictures of dirt bikes and Fox racing gear lined the walls, and there was a floor-to-ceiling shelf with so many trophies on it that Natalie couldn't count them all. Taylor was apparently really, *really* good at racing.

Knowing that if she went back downstairs without changing, there was a very good chance that Maggie would march her back up and dress Natalie herself, she picked out a nice pair of jeans and a thick sweatshirt.

When she slipped on the fur-lined boots, she had to admit her toes wiggled in warm appreciation. Okay, maybe the boots were worth the slight guilt she was suffering from taking clothes from a stranger's closet. And they probably made up a little for the torture of feeling out of place, of knowing that she'd essentially barged in on this nice family.

Although she wasn't happy about facing the crowd again, she couldn't hide in this bedroom all night. So she took a deep breath and moved to the door.

She opened it, and then fell backward with a squeak. Hawk was standing right in front of her, and the smoldering embers leaping from his eyes sent a shiver of anticipation deep into her core.

Heat invaded her system, and she found herself wanting to find out exactly why that was.

chapter 5

. . . .

*H*awk stood in the doorway staring at Natalie and couldn't move. At least she was now far more decently dressed for the cold Montana weather, but she might as well have been naked by the way he was gaping at her. He didn't understand the hold this virtual stranger had over him.

This woman was messing with his head and causing him to feel emotions he couldn't fathom—emotions more suited to a teenager than a grown man. He'd been with his share of females, and there had been nothing to elicit any real feeling at all beyond the simple exchange of physical pleasure. Not that there was anything wrong with that . . .

"You look better." His curt tone made him shudder, but he couldn't seem to do anything to stop it. She took a startled step backward, and he felt like a complete tool.

"Um . . . thank you," she finally murmured, casting her eyes to the floor.

No. That wouldn't do. He needed to look into her eyes, and he needed for her not to hide from him, though he didn't know why. So he stepped forward and, placing a gentle finger under her chin, tilted her head up.

"Sorry. That came out wrong. I meant you look warmer," he said, purposely making his voice softer. "We've really gotten off on the wrong foot. I'm not a bad guy. I'm just a bit . . . gruff sometimes."

Her eyes widened at his words, but she quickly looked past him. Yeah, he wasn't making the situation any better. He should take his hand away. And he would . . . in just a minute.

"All right," he told her. "Let's just scratch everything that's happened from the moment we laid eyes on each other." He finally removed his hand and took a step back so he could think properly. "My mother is an incredible cook. Let's go have some dinner," he said, offering his arm and waiting, afraid he might spook her if he moved any closer.

"That sounds nice," she finally said, reluctantly accepting his arm.

As they descended the stairs, Hawk looked out to find every last person staring up at them, some of them with knowing grins on their faces.

"Ah, you look wonderful, Natalie," Maggie said as she came up to them holding his niece close to her heart. "I hope you have a healthy appetite, because I've been cooking for two days straight. Well, okay, to be honest, I've been mostly directing this year as I can't seem to put my granddaughter down."

Natalie didn't even get a chance to reply to Maggie because suddenly she was surrounded, everyone attending Thanksgiving dinner wanting to speak with her. That's how his family and friends were. There was no such thing as strangers; everyone was simply a friend they hadn't met yet.

When he sat down, Hawk found himself directly across from Natalie. "Where did you move here from?"

"I grew up in Southern California," she answered after a beat.

"I guess it's just a bit warmer there," he said, giving her his most trustworthy smile. He knew he should just back off, but what his brain was telling him and what he was doing were two entirely different things.

"Yeah. It's not like I'm stupid. It's just that I wasn't expecting quite this much . . . cold," she said with a nervous laugh as she accepted the large bowl of potatoes passed to her and took a small scoop.

"I've done a lot of traveling, or I used to, at least. I've always enjoyed the beaches in California." See, he could be friendly, have a normal conversation with this woman. He'd have patted himself on the back if he were able.

"I always thought it would be fun to travel. Maybe someday," she said with a soft sigh that almost wasn't noticeable.

"Where would be the first place you'd go?" He could

see that she'd rather be left alone, but Hawk didn't feel like doing that, so he just looked at her and waited as other conversations went on around them.

"I guess Europe. I'd love to go to Venice, but that's stupid, really."

"Why would that be stupid? It's beautiful."

"Because it's not practical," she replied.

"We don't always do things because they're practical, Natalie. We have to also live our lives and have some fun."

"Some people have that privilege."

The sudden sadness in her eyes made him want to know her story. And Hawk was determined to get that story despite the dangers it posed to his peace of mind.

His dad interrupted before he could ask Natalie anything else, and when he turned back to draw her into the conversation, Hawk found Natalie speaking with his brother. When Bryson made her laugh, Hawk felt a bizarre pang of jealousy. If he hadn't known how much Bryson loved his wife, Hawk might have suffered a little more from the green-eyed monster.

But even as the thought crossed Hawk's mind, his brother shifted in his chair and leaned into his wife to steal a kiss before turning back to Natalie. It was sweet. It was also a bit disgusting. Bryson, his own freaking brother, had changed so much since meeting Misty.

"Are you excited about the Christmas pageant, Natalie?"

Hawk saw the way Bethel was grinning. And the way Natalie blanched before her smile disappeared.

"What pageant?" she asked.

"You do know that you will be in charge of the school Christmas pageant? It's a wonderful tradition here," Bethel said matter-of-factly before taking a bite of her gravy-covered mashed potatoes.

"No one said anything about a pageant," Natalie almost gasped, her fork clattering against her plate.

Eileen jumped in. "It's so well organized that you won't have any trouble at all."

"I've never done anything like that before," Natalie replied.

"Don't worry, darling," Maggie said, a reassuring smile on her face. "You'll have Hawk to help you. He volunteers his time every year."

Hawk's eyes narrowed. These women were getting out of hand.

"I . . . uh . . . guess I'll talk to the principal about it on Monday. She'd be much better off having one of the other teachers do it, one who's been here longer than a day," Natalie said with a nervous giggle.

"Nonsense, darling. You'll do just fine."

And just like that, the problem was solved, at least in the minds of the meddlers. Natalie sat there bewildered as the conversation turned to another topic. Hawk wasn't content with the way things were going, and he watched Natalie squirm in her seat.

And then his mother glanced over at him with a sly smile. No, no, no, he wasn't at all happy. Yes, he was attracted to this woman, but if the people of this town thought they could rope him into a relationship, they'd be sorely disappointed. But then his eyes wandered back over to Natalie, and suddenly the room disappeared as she looked up and their gazes collided.

Heat. Steam. Sex. *No!*

He reined his thoughts back in and focused on the good food before him. But as the night went on and his eyes continued to stray toward Natalie, he knew he was in trouble. Wary as he was, especially with the strong suspicion that his mother and her friends were up to no good, his body and a good part of his mind didn't seem to be listening to him. He couldn't turn away from this woman.

The school pageant—working closely with Natalie over the next month—wasn't a good idea. Not a good idea at all . . .

chapter 6

. . . .

$\mathcal{N}$atalie twisted a strand of her hair in trembling fingers. She could do this. True, the school was surprisingly large for such a small town. But it was just an elementary school. Just a place filled with young kids. They weren't judging her. They weren't hoping she would fail.

Who was she kidding? They were *all* hoping she would trip in the doorway and fall flat on her freaking face. They would take immeasurable joy in laughing and pointing as she picked herself up off the floor and endured the utter humiliation.

No. She couldn't think like that. They were only *children,* for goodness' sake. But she, too, had once been a child and she'd written the book on mischief, at least in her early years. And now she was teaching children who were in those early years.

All she knew for sure was that she must be strong. If they sensed weakness, they'd strike faster than a nest of irate wasps, and chaos would reign in her classroom forever.

Practicing her breathing techniques, she made her way to the main office suite and stepped through the doors. Because of the holiday and the swiftness with which she'd had to be hired, she hadn't gone through the standard orientation. She was early today, as she knew she had to get her classroom ready before the doors of the school opened up to all and a flood of kids came pouring in.

"Hello, Natalie. It's great to meet you."

Natalie looked up, startled. An older woman was smiling at her, and a quick downward glance revealed a nameplate that said Dorothy Simms, Secretary.

"Good morning, Ms. Simms. I'm here to meet with Carol O'Connor." Excellent. Her voice was calm, self-assured. These people would never know that she was actually shaking in her borrowed boots.

"Yes, she's been waiting for you. Go right on in. And it's a real pleasure to have you here with us."

"Thank you. I already feel welcome," Natalie replied, surprised that she did feel welcome. With as much confidence as she could muster, Natalie walked over to the principal's door, knocked timidly, and went inside. She found a petite blond woman sitting behind a desk, reading on her laptop.

When the principal finally looked up, a big grin split Carol's face, and she stood up. "You must be Natalie. It's so good to finally meet you in person," she said as she stepped around her desk. "I hope you're settling in nicely at your house."

"Yes. The furnace was broken, but maintenance fixed it almost immediately."

A shudder passed through Natalie at that thought. After Thanksgiving dinner, she'd been told there was no way she could go home alone for the next twenty-four hours, and Maggie had insisted she stay the night. At some point the topic of her furnace had come up, and as soon as she said there was a problem, Hawk had jumped up and left his parents' house.

The next day, when he came to pick her up and he drove her home, she'd been more nervous in his presence than ever before. But then the two of them walked into her place, and she couldn't suppress the bounce in her step when she felt the heat.

It seemed that when Hawk decided to do something, he did it fast. And the proof was in the fact that in only a weekend, this man had managed to wedge his way permanently into her brain. And that's where he seemed to be staying.

It would be good to get to work, because she needed something to focus on other than a very sexy fire chief who always seemed to be around. She'd run into him at least four times over the weekend. At the small clothing store. In the post office. At the diner. He just seemed to be everywhere.

"Well, you can't have a broken furnace in this weather," Carol said with a laugh. "You're in Hawk's old house, right?"

That quickly snapped Natalie back to the present. "Yes, it's a lovely home."

"Hawk's a good man. A little rough around the edges, but there's nothing that man won't do for the people he cares about, which happens to be just about everyone in our close-knit community. He has a heart of gold. If only I were twenty years younger," she said with a sigh before turning to Natalie again. "Oh, and if I didn't already have a husband," she added with a laugh.

Natalie didn't know why, but she found herself blushing. Could everyone please talk about something other than Hawk Winchester? She really didn't know what to say to that statement—it was far from *professional* as she understood the word. But everything here was just different, so she'd have to learn to go with the flow or she'd never fit in. Still, she was tongue-tied and more than grateful when Carol started speaking again.

"I know this is your first job as a teacher, Natalie, and if you have any questions, please don't hesitate to ask me or any of the other teachers. Dorothy is a godsend for this school, and she's your best source of information. She knows everything, and I do mean *everything*!"

"Thank you. I do have one question. I was told I would be in charge of the pageant? I'm not complaining—not in the least—but as I'm so new, it might be better to have someone else in charge."

There. That had come out professionally. She didn't sound as if she was whining. Or at least she really hoped she didn't.

"Nonsense. You'll be just fine." And that was the end

of that as far as Carol was concerned. Everything suddenly moved at warp speed.

Carol moved to her door, and she continued speaking as she led Natalie down the hallway to one of the classrooms. Natalie gulped when she walked through the doorway and found a giant *Welcome* on her chalkboard with little messages from all the other teachers.

When Carol left her and she was alone in her first real classroom, she read those sweet and hospitable notes. Natalie really hadn't wanted to come to this small town; she'd always dreamed of working in a prestigious private school where she could feel she was molding future presidents and high-level businessmen and -women.

But as she stared at the chalkboard, she was so overcome with emotion that she was struggling to fight off the tears. This wasn't the sort of place where she'd feel intimidated, where parents would try to bribe her to give their kid a better grade.

No, this was the type of school where she would find young children eager to learn, and parents who asked to see their homework. Taking out her cell phone, she snapped a few photos so she could always remember this moment, and then she picked up the eraser and cleared the board. It was time to be practical. Cool, calm, collected. Time to get her lesson plan up, and time to jump into her first day of being a real teacher.

Just as she finished writing on the board, the bell rang and the sweet music of children's voices filled the halls. Laughter preceded the kids into the classroom. With a shaky smile, Natalie turned to face her class—thirty pairs of young eyes looking back at her, trying to decide whether she made the cut or not.

"Good morning, class." The noise didn't die down as the kids all settled into their chairs, so Natalie tried again, this time louder. "Good morning, class!"

The voices quieted; heads turned and eager eyes looked back at her. "Good morning, Ms. Duncan."

Natalie beamed at the little blond girl sitting in the first row.

"Thank you for answering," Natalie said as she pulled out a piece of candy and tossed it to the now-excited little girl. "Each time you answer a question today, or respond to a statement, you get a small treat.

"Since this is my first day here, I thought we'd start off by you each introducing yourselves to me, and then I'll do the same," she said, and a burst of confidence blazed through her as thirty hands shot up. Nothing like having a bag of candy to get them to listen.

The day passed in a blur of activity, and when the final bell rang, Natalie dropped into her chair. When she was sure no one was looking, she scooted backward, kicked off from the floor, and set her chair to spinning, then hugged her knees to her chest as she whirled around and around.

She'd survived. Not only had she survived, but she'd had a wonderful day, one full of great kids who were eager to learn. She felt on top of the world. A happy giggle flew from her lips as she continued spinning. She didn't stop until her head was light and she knew if she continued she'd make herself sick.

"It appears that you like your new job."

Natalie froze, but her chair spun one more time before her feet touched the ground and she could focus her eyes on the doorway. Leaning against the doorjamb, and looking far too good, was Hawk, sporting a sexy-as-hell smile and those made-for-dreams smoldering eyes.

Oh, this was going to be a very, *very* long month if she had to work with the man every day. As the wattage on his smile kicked up a notch, her stomach shook.

Yes. A *very* long month . . .

chapter 7

. . . .

Slow and painful torture would be better than this!"
Hawk's stomach dipped when his hand brushed against
Natalie's for the tenth time this day alone. His muscles
tight, his mind anywhere but where it should be, he
moved quickly to the other side of the gym, feeling her
gaze follow him.

"What's your problem?"

Turning, Hawk found his best friend, Colt, walking up.

"None of your damn business," Hawk grumbled.

"Ha! Obviously it's woman trouble."

"How would you know about woman trouble, Colt?"

"That's a hoot, Hawk! Weren't you mocking me this
past year while Brielle put me through the ringer?"

"Well, that was *you*. It was much more fun to watch."
Hawk had definitely enjoyed how uncomfortable Brielle
Storm had made his friend.

"Yeah. Well, payback's a bitch," Colt said with an evil grin.

"We're in a school, Colt," Hawk reminded him. He looked around and was grateful not to see any kids listening in. "And what are you doing here anyway?"

"I had to drop off the green paint I picked up."

"Well, you did. Now leave," Hawk said, not in a mood for visiting.

"If I promise to be good, will you tell me about your troubles?"

What the hell. "The entire situation is ridiculous, Colt. I barely know this woman, but suddenly I can't seem to think of anything else but her." Blowing out his breath, he waited for Colt to mock him.

"Maybe you should just take her out, see where things could go," Colt told him as they both turned to stare at the woman in question while she moved through the gym hanging decorations.

"Nah. Women are great and all, especially for one thing. However, they're also pretty much interchangeable, and most important, they're *always* temporary. Natalie lives in this town, so she's automatically out. I don't sleep with women here, you know that."

"Yeah, I remember that rule. That was until I met Brielle . . ." Colt said with a knowing laugh.

"You're not being any help at all, Colt. This woman is just too damn complicated. Too messy. Too . . ."

"Too what?" Hawk's eyes narrowed. Was his best friend mocking him?

"Hell, this is insane. I just need to get over myself, quit acting like a damn teenager."

"All I can say is, good luck, buddy," Colt said before laughing and walking away.

"Thanks a lot!" Hawk replied, but all he got back was a chuckle from his engaged and far too happy friend. "They all fall sometime," he muttered, and tried to focus on what needed to be done for the pageant to be a success.

Thirty minutes later, when he took a step back and knocked into Natalie, nearly tripping over her as she leaned over a chair, he was barely able to stop the groan that seemed hell-bent on escaping from his dry throat.

Her ass should have Warning: Lethal pasted right on it, because for a woman who had shown up in town in such uptight clothing, she'd sure found her own casually hot style during the last week. The jeans were enough to give him a heart attack, and the tight sweaters she'd decided to wear with those jeans didn't leave much to his imagination.

Conversation. That's what they needed. Then he'd discover she wasn't so appealing after all. He'd grow bored and the fact that she had a great body wouldn't matter, because he couldn't stand a woman who didn't know how to hold her own while talking.

He cornered her by the gym wall. "We never finished the discussion we began at Thanksgiving, Natalie."

"We've talked plenty of times, Hawk," she said with a nervous laugh.

"Not about anything important. It's usually just you telling me what to do."

"Isn't that what women are supposed to do?"

Her sass had him smiling. "That's what my mama says, anyway."

"Ah. I like a man who knows that he's supposed to listen to women," she said, making his stomach clench.

"So you like me, huh?"

This was where he expected her to blush and run away. That was her usual reaction when he flirted with her. This time, she must have had a bowl of Wheaties for breakfast, because she took his breath away when she winked at him.

"Nah. I think you're a pain in the butt, Hawk, but you do make a great worker bee." She turned.

"No way," he said, stopping her easily and trapping her against the wall with a hand on either side of her head. "You don't get to make a statement like that and then just walk away."

Her breathing hitched, making his groin tighten, and he leaned just a bit closer. Conversation certainly wasn't helping him get over his fascination with Natalie Duncan.

"Hawk, I get to say whatever I want and then walk away because it's my prerogative." She looked a bit jittery, but not nearly as spooked as she'd been a week ago.

"Then you'll have to learn that if you play with fire . . ."

"If I play with fire, what?"

Amazing. She wasn't backing down.

"Then the fire chief has to come put out the flames," he said. Their bodies were practically touching now; Hawk had forgotten they weren't the only two people in the gym.

"Well . . ." she said, making his heart thunder. "In that case, I'll have to . . ." He waited with bated breath, and she looked deep into his eyes. ". . . stop playing with fire."

It took several heartbeats for the words to process in his muddled brain. When he realized she was through with this little dance, he pulled his hands from the wall, releasing her.

After watching the sway of her hips as she walked away, Hawk leaned against the wall for several agonizing moments, unwilling to turn and show everyone in the gym just what effect Natalie Duncan had on him.

When he knew it was finally safe to turn, he looked out and saw Natalie going about her business as if nothing had just happened. That irritated him more than anything else. How could she play so hot one minute and then so cold the next? What was her problem?

As things were wrapping up for the night, Hawk watched Natalie climb up a ladder, those jeans hugging her ass to perfection and putting far too many images in his head while he was in a room full of giggling children.

He had to wonder again what in the hell was wrong with him. Again, he thought about calling in a crime report on the town's three meddling women, who were currently up on the stage, paintbrushes in hand, heads bent close as they planned something else that was sinister, he was sure.

Hawk looked on nervously as Natalie stepped close to the top of the ladder, stretching her body as far as it would go to hang a star from the ceiling. His stomach flipped over when he saw the bottom of the ladder wobble. She was going to fall and crack her head wide open!

Rushing away from the wall he'd seemingly been holding up, he grabbed on to the bottom of the ladder to steady it, and got a far too close glimpse of the soft white inch of skin showing on her stomach as she stretched out her arms.

Just when he began getting a good handle on himself and his lustful thoughts, he heard an *oof* and felt the ladder wobble dangerously. He looked back up just in time to see Natalie slip from the rung she'd been barely holding on to. Letting go of the ladder, he held out his arms, then groaned as she landed safely against his chest, her arms automatically reaching up around his neck.

"Oh my gosh!" Her eyes were wide, her mouth open, and her cheeks flushed.

Hawk didn't even think, didn't hesitate. He simply closed what little gap there was between them. He might regret this later. Hell, he *would* regret this later. But right now, oh yes, he had to taste those lips. Feeling almost as if he were in a trance, he ran his fingers through her long and beautiful hair and pulled her head closer to his.

Hawk tried to rein himself in, but he gave up when his lips brushed hers and he felt her breathing change.

His first taste of her was like an explosion of flavor, cherries and mint and heat. A whole hell of a lot of heat.

He held on to her tightly as his mouth demanded her full attention. There was no struggle, no awkwardness. It was as if they were made to fit together. He could go on kissing her all night long.

After a few more seconds, he realized he was on the verge of losing control, and only then did he pull back. As her eyes fluttered open, Hawk knew the truth. He *would* have sex with this woman. And it *would* be out-of-this-world incredible. He could fight it all he wanted, but it was going to happen. And it was going to happen soon. His raging hormones demanded it.

"Excuse me," he said as he set her down on her feet, slowly. Without another word, he turned and walked away, not looking back once. If he had turned around, he'd have noticed the panic flare in Natalie's eyes. He would have noticed how she immediately closed herself off.

Sure, he felt the eyes of all the adults in the room on him. Screw it! He didn't care. It was time to drink an ice-cold beer, and then maybe he'd kick his own ass for acting like such a damn fool.

chapter 8

· · · · · · · · · · · · ·

$\mathcal{N}$atalie snuck away from the gym. Parents were beginning to arrive to pick up their children, and she couldn't face them right now. She had to get away from here, had to get away from the eyes that she knew were upon her.

Not once in her life had she shared a kiss with a man in a public place—not that she'd shared many kisses in her twenty-three years, but she had shared a few. But those had been nothing to prepare her for the feelings assailing her body from the simple touch of Hawk's lips on hers.

Although almost in a daze, she made it to her class room. She put on her new thick coat and slipped on her boots. The walk home took only about ten minutes, but it would be enough to clear the cobwebs from her head.

Once outside, she cringed when she saw Maggie approaching her. The woman made eye contact and there was no possible way to get out of this mess. So, with her heart pounding, and snow falling down upon her, Natalie waited for Hawk's mother to approach. She could only hope the woman hadn't witnessed the kiss. But her luck was never that good.

"Are you leaving already, Natalie?" Maggie's smile was sweet and inscrutable.

"Yes. I have to get my lesson plan ready for tomorrow." Natalie answered Maggie's smile by pasting on the most convincing one she could manage.

"I bet you're so overwhelmed right now. A new teaching job, and then thrown into doing this pageant at the same time. You poor thing."

Natalie's shoulders relaxed. Maggie might not have seen the kiss. Thank goodness! "Yes, it's a bit overwhelming, but it's always much nicer to be busy than to have too much time on my hands."

"That's always been how I feel. How long will the lesson plan take?"

It was an innocent question, one that didn't raise any suspicions for Natalie, so she answered honestly. "Only about an hour or so, but I really need to go to the grocery store, too. I tend to forget to shop until I'm out of just about everything, and a person can only live on ramen noodles and microwave mac and cheese for so long." She didn't add that her other staples were frozen pizza and corn dogs. Maggie was the type of woman to be horrified by that sad fact.

"Oh, darling. You can't eat like that. I insist you come to my place for dinner tonight," Maggie told her.

Natalie's anxiety instantly reappeared. "I promise you I wasn't fishing for a dinner invitation."

"Of course not, dear. But I won't take no for an answer. I'd be hurt if you refused."

"But . . ." Natalie tried to think quickly. Yes! She had it! "I don't have a car," she nearly shouted.

"That's no problem at all," Maggie said as she took out her cell phone. "Hawk, darling. Where did you disappear to?" Maggie was silent for a moment as she listened to her son. "Perfect. I need you to stop by Natalie's house in one hour and pick her up. She's coming over for dinner and doesn't have transportation." Silence again and then, "Thank you, son. I'll see you in a little while."

Maggie hung up and gave Natalie a big grin. "It's all settled, then. Hawk will pick you up. We're having a nice big pot roast. See you tonight."

Maggie headed away, leaving Natalie standing there with her mouth gaping. The one person she'd wanted to avoid for the next century was now going to be showing up on her front porch in an hour. Tears threatened, but Natalie wouldn't cave in to them.

This was just another bump in the road. No big deal. After all, it was only a little kiss. From what she'd heard about Hawk from the other teachers, he was quite the playboy, and kissing was almost a pastime for him.

He'd probably forgotten all about it by now. That's what kept her going as she trudged home and slipped inside. No lesson plan was made as she sat on her couch and watched the clock, the hands seeming to move so much quicker than normal.

When the doorbell rang exactly on time, her heart gave a little lurch, and she was still no closer to figuring out what she was going to say to Hawk. *Keep it light.* She could do this.

Of course, that all flew out the window the second she opened her door and found Hawk leaning against her rail, his cheeks slightly flushed from the cold, his dark eyes carrying a sparkle in them, and his lips instantly turning up when she caught his eye. Before she could utter a single word, he opened his mouth.

"I decided I liked that kiss a whole hell of a lot. I've also decided I'm not going to fight the attraction I feel for you. If I thought you didn't feel the same way, I'd back off, but that small hitch in your breath and that look in your eyes tell me there's something between us, something strong. And I want to explore it further."

The way he spoke was casual, as if they were discussing nothing more significant than what was for dinner. But the look he shot her was anything but casual. Hunger burned inside her, and Natalie knew she was in serious trouble.

"I think this is a very bad idea, Hawk," she whispered.

He took a step closer, and for the life of her, she couldn't back away like she needed to.

"You know, all the best things in life happen because of bad ideas," he said, his words a promise that sent a shudder right through her.

"We don't know each other."

"No one knows each other at first. Finding out all of the things that make you tick—that's where the fun comes in." He reached out a hand and cupped her cheek.

"The teachers here love to gossip, Hawk. Really love to gossip."

"Aw, heck, Natalie. Don't you want to know me for yourself?" he countered.

"It's just that you're a popular topic around the school. Every eligible woman in Sterling would love to be the one to wear your wedding ring." Then a slight smile tilted her lips. "Well, to be fair, you're neck and neck with the Whitman men."

"Oh, honey, I'm much better than any of the Whitman *boys*," he said with a laugh.

"You and the Whitmans were described to me as royalty in this small town. There's been a lot said about none of you settling down, but even more said about your character and how you love your family and neighbors. I think this could be too complicated. I'm not interested in settling down."

"Good. Because I'm not ready to settle down, either. But there's nothing wrong with taking a beautiful woman out. There don't have to be any expectations."

"Well, I also heard you don't date women in your hometown." She was trying desperately to stand firm, but failing epically.

"You're not from here, so we're okay."

"I think we're far from okay, Hawk.

But he wrapped an arm around her and tugged her close.

"I have the remedy for that," he told her, as he bent forward and kissed her for the second time. Natalie didn't even try to pretend she didn't want it. Maybe it would be for the best if she just held on and enjoyed the ride.

chapter 9

· · · · · · · · · · · · ·

*N*atalie had ended up playing Othello with Hawk until about midnight. Then he'd taken her home, given her a scorching kiss on her front porch, and gone away with only a wave. She hadn't heard from him for the next two days. Was this his idea of keeping it casual?

She hated that she felt unsure about herself, hated that she was even thinking about Hawk as much as she was, and hated that her plans seemed to be coming unraveled. It was too soon. Entering into a serious relationship was way down on her checklist, and she couldn't stray from that list. Not that Hawk wanted to get serious. He'd even said that. So she was worrying for nothing, right? Right!

Peeking around a corner, Natalie watched the gym buzz with activity. The pageant was coming together, and decorations covered the walls in brilliant blues and silvers. Everyone, adult and child, sported a major smile.

The next moment, she noticed something strange. Concealed by a wall, she watched as Hawk peeked through a doorway—not unlike what she was doing!— with a large box in his hand. When he saw that nobody was paying any attention to him, he set the box down and casually walked over to his mother and her two friends, who were painting a giant board to look like a snow-covered mountain.

After a few moments, he strolled over to a small group of children and sat on the floor with them, and soon their voices rang out as they practiced one of the musical numbers.

With her curiosity overriding her need to hide from the man, Natalie walked swiftly into the gym. Almost as if Hawk had built-in GPS on where she was, he turned his head and their eyes collided.

"Ignore it," she told herself, but it was so difficult. She felt quite accomplished when she managed to move forward and break the connection.

As she found herself coming closer to the box that Hawk had brought in, and when she saw a giant pink tag on it with the name Mary Pascal, she gulped. Mary was a sweet child who had just moved to the area with her parents. They were living with the child's grandparents, and the family had hardly a dime to their name. Had he brought the little girl gifts?

"Oh, please, no," she murmured.

She was already falling for this man, though she'd continue to fight it for as long as she had the strength to do so. It was just that even though he tried so hard to act tough, he was actually very kind and amazing with the children. She understood why everyone valued his volunteer work at the pageant so highly. Not once had she seen him lose his temper or even get the slightest bit irritated as child after child clung to him or jumped on his back.

He seemed to have never-ending patience, and if he wasn't the fire chief, she could easily see him as a schoolteacher. In fact, she could *really* see him as the gym teacher, preferably in a tight shirt and a nice pair of shorts. Nope. She was going to push that image right out of her mind this *second*.

Natalie got busy, and she was very happy that she was able, for once, to avoid Hawk for the whole evening. He didn't make it easy, but she was discovering that if she kept a tracking beacon on the man, she could anticipate his moves and counter them.

But if his hand brushed hers one more time, she couldn't be held responsible for anything she might do. And if she did what she *wanted* to do, the local sheriff was going to be hauling her in for public indecency.

"Evening, Natalie."

Startled, Natalie jumped, then relaxed when she saw Bethel walking up to her.

"Evening, Bethel. The mountain scene is looking wonderful."

"You are too kind, darling. We should be all set up and ready to go within a few days."

"Yes. It's moving fast. Could I ask you something?"

"Anything, darling," Bethel replied.

"There's a box over there with Mary's name on it, and . . ."

"Oh, that's a secret Santa gift," Bethel said, beaming.

"Secret Santa?"

"Yes. Each year the community members pick families that may need a little something extra. Whoever participates is very secretive and the boxes are always left where the children are sure not to miss them. Mary was one of the children chosen this year."

"That's amazing," Natalie said, thinking back to her childhood. How much would it have meant to her to receive a gift from Santa?

"Her parents should be here soon, and then you'll see Mary's face light up. That's always the best part. The other children love to be a part of it, too. The nice thing with living here is that we do truly love the people in our community."

The two of them spoke for a few more moments, but fell silent when Mary's parents walked into the gym. One of the kids quickly took them over to the box that the little girl had been waiting to open. There was so much pride in the set of both parents' shoulders, and so much obvious love for their daughter shining in their eyes.

"Can I open it?" Mary asked eagerly.

"It appears to be for you," her mother whispered softly.

Hawk was moving across the stage, cleaning up the endless line of crumbs from snacks the kids had just finished, but watching out of the corner of his eye. Natalie's eyes darted between him and Mary as the child opened the box.

When Mary pulled out a warm winter coat, a brand-new pair of boots, and several outfits, her eyes welled up with tears. "Is this all for me?" she asked as her small fingers caressed the soft down jacket and took in the pretty black boots with small purple flowers at the top. She also brought out some presents wrapped in bright paper with labels saying Don't Open Till Christmas Morning.

"I think it is," her mother said, and a tear slipped from her eye.

An envelope was tucked discreetly inside the box, and Natalie had no doubt it contained some money so the parents could get something for themselves. Hawk's generosity was choking her up. Damn his hide.

"Who's this from?" asked Mary's mother, Stacy.

"It's from Santa," Bethel replied, but her eyes strayed to the stage where Hawk was still sweeping away.

Without a word, Stacy began to move, slowly approaching Hawk. Placing her hand on his arm, she said something that stopped him from what he was doing. Although Natalie was too far away to hear the words whispered between the two of them, there was no mistaking the shine in his eyes as Mary's mother wrapped her arms around him and gave him a grateful hug. When she let go, he bowed his head, nodded, and vanished through the back door. Mary's mother returned from the stage and spoke quietly.

"He won't admit it was him, but he said that Mary is a sweet child who has the voice of an angel."

Natalie didn't even realize tears were falling down her own cheeks as Stacy spoke.

"He's a pretty spectacular man," Maggie murmured as she stepped up and hugged Mary's family.

"Yes he is," Stacy said quietly.

Soon the group walked from the gym together, leaving Natalie there all alone with her thoughts. Natalie realized that she'd learned more about this man in a few days' time than most people learned about anyone in a lifetime. He was good and kind, with a heart the size of Texas. She'd have said the size of Montana, but that was too small.

If she wasn't careful, this man would change her entire future, whether he was willing to or not. She needed to avoid him. She had a feeling that she was going to become too attached, that he was going to want to have a casual affair, and that she was going to give him her heart. That just couldn't happen. So what came next?

She honestly didn't know.

chapter 10

Why aren't you ready?"

Natalie stood in her doorway looking at Maggie, Bethel, and Eileen, all wearing thick coats, thicker hats, scarves, and high boots.

"Ready for what?"

"The big party!" Bethel said, looking at her as if she'd lost her mind.

"Party?" Natalie vaguely remembered some of the other teachers speaking about it the day before at school, but it was Saturday, and after a long week, she was looking forward to curling up in bed and sinking into a good book.

Okay, if she was to admit her true feelings, she wasn't exactly pumped about her big plans, but she was trying to avoid Hawk, and she knew if she went to the only café in town, she would most certainly run into him.

"Yes. Tonight we light the Christmas tree and then go to the fire hall for a party," Eileen said with anticipation.

"Brrr. Invite us in and we'll wait while you get dressed," Maggie said, leaving Natalie no choice but to open her door wide for the three bundled-up women to enter her toasty little house.

"Don't take too long. I don't want to strip down just to put all these clothes back on," Bethel said as she looked around. "You really need some decorations in here . . ."

"Oh, you leave her be, Bethel," Maggie scolded her friend. "She's only been here for about two weeks. Some people need more time than that to make their mark on a place."

"Ha! When I moved into my home, it was all good to go in three days," Bethel said.

Not used to such friendly people—heck, not used to visitors, period—Natalie couldn't move. She just watched the three women make themselves comfortable looking around, or, more accurately, snooping into just about everything.

"Go on, girl. I'm getting warmer by the minute," Eileen said when she turned to find Natalie still standing just on the inside of her front door.

Defeated, Natalie slunk to her bedroom and began pulling out clothes. It looked as if she was heading to a party. Her stomach churned because she knew there was no way that she wouldn't run smack-dab into Hawk.

And the part that frightened her the most? That she wasn't as upset about this as she should be. The man had run into her life with a steamroller—or at least with his gargantuan truck—and though she told herself she wanted to avoid him, in reality her heart rate spiked at even the sight of him. It was pathetic. It was wrong. It wasn't the right time.

But it was much easier to know what she should do than to actually do it.

After changing clothes, she went to her bathroom and looked into the mirror. Between the way her blood was racing through her veins and the prospect of the cold she'd be enduring the next hour or so, she certainly didn't need any blush. With a quick layer of mascara and some lip gloss, she figured she was as ready as the three women out there would allow her to get.

When she stepped back into the living room, she couldn't help but smile. Maggie was absolutely grinning over a knitting project on the coffee table. And when Hawk's mother looked up, her expression almost proud, Natalie felt a warmth in her chest she hadn't felt since . . . She actually couldn't remember.

"This is beautiful, Natalie. You have a real talent," Maggie said before putting the knitting down and walking over to her. "I don't know what it is about you, but I just want to bring you home and take care of you."

The sincerity in her voice, the glimmer in her eyes—it was all too much. Natalie had to turn away before her own eyes followed suit.

"If you ever need someone to talk to," Maggie said, "you know where I live. I feel as if there's a lot inside of you that wants to be free."

Sometimes the pain of always being alone was overwhelming, and now she had this woman before her who was asking for nothing but offering her the most precious gift of all—love.

Before Natalie could respond, Maggie wrapped her arms around her and gave her a hug. Natalie was grateful when Bethel and Eileen joined them, breaking up the moment. She had to get out of there. If she gave in to her emotions, she wouldn't be able to stop crying—not for a long, long time. Too much had been buried deep inside for too long, and she knew that it would be disastrous to let it out.

"Oh, almost forgot," Eileen said. "Here's your candle." She handed Natalie a long candle with a shield surrounding the bottom. "We'll wait to light it until we reach the next block over."

Natalie had no idea what Eileen was talking about until they turned the corner and saw a line of her neighbors walking down the street, all of them holding candles as they sang Christmas carols. Bethel pulled out a lighter and lit all their candles, and they merged with the crowd as more people appeared from their houses and joined them.

A light snow began falling as they marched toward the town center, sweet voices all around them singing "Silent Night." So much nostalgia filled the air. It was more touching than anything Natalie had ever experienced before.

As she walked with her candle in her shaking hand, she was barely able to sing. She was surprised that the small flakes of snow didn't extinguish the light, but it seemed that nothing, not even a winter storm, could stop the magic of this evening.

They reached the little park in the center of town, where a huge tree stood proudly with a stage to the left of it. The newcomers saw a small crowd of town residents already waiting for more people to arrive, and for the next twenty minutes, the festive caroling continued as more and more people joined in the celebration.

When the songs stopped, the mayor stepped up to a microphone and gave a short speech about the magic of the season and the blessings of living in a small community. Then another man stepped forward and the crowd clapped noisily.

"This year we've been blessed more than ever before. Our town continues to stay strong while other places struggle. And why? Because we genuinely care about each other, and because we know how to treat our neighbors. I expect each and every one of you to come and give me a kiss beneath the mistletoe." He finished his remarks with a saucy wink at the crowd. Natalie found herself laughing along with everyone else.

"I'm sure Eileen will be the first person in that line," Bethel said, making Eileen blush.

Eileen bristled. "That's just not polite, Bethel."

But Natalie noticed that Eileen was still gazing at the man who'd just left the lectern and microphone.

"Who is he?" Natalie asked.

"That's Martin Whitman," Maggie said. "He employs

most of the people in this town at his oil plant. Has four very sexy sons, and they're each just waiting for a woman to tame them."

"Oh." Natalie didn't know what else to say to that.

"You'll pretty much meet the entire town tonight," Bethel told her, and for some reason Natalie found her own cheeks taking on major color. Just because she was meeting people, it didn't mean that these nice women were trying to match her up with anyone. It wouldn't do them any good anyway, as it seemed she couldn't think of anyone other than the town's sexy fire chief.

The talking stopped when Martin stepped over to a large box and pushed a button. The tree lit up instantly, and the crowd gave out a collective sigh.

"Come on, darling. Time to find that mistletoe," Maggie said, and she took Natalie's arm in hers as everyone began moving toward the fire station.

Natalie's stomach dropped. Yes, because she could so easily picture kissing a certain person beneath the bunch of leaves and berries. And she'd be mortified if his mother knew the less than strictly religious thoughts that were running through her head. When they walked through the doors, there was barely room to move, let alone seek anyone out.

Yet somehow Natalie found herself beneath the mistletoe. And even more amazingly, she was standing right in front of the man she couldn't stop thinking about.

"I've never been able to resist a beautiful woman beneath the mistletoe."

That was all the warning she received before Hawk bent down and captured her lips. As festive partyers merged around them, Natalie saw no one, heard no one, and thought of nothing but Hawk and the way she felt with his lips caressing hers.

Why again did she try so desperately to avoid this man? Because when she was actually in his arms, all her insecurities faded and all she could think about was that this was perfect, it was right.

When he finally released her lips, he looked down into her eyes, and she knew she was his for the taking. It was too late for her to turn around this thing between them, because she wanted to get lost in his arms, and whether he wanted her for a day, or a maximum of three as the ladies at school were so fond of saying, then that's what she'd give him.

Walking away at this point just wasn't an option. "Wow," she finally whispered and his lips turned up in a sexy grin.

"I was about to say the same thing. Want to go find all the places mistletoe is hung?"

"I was thinking that you could at least offer me a glass of eggnog first," she replied, trying to rein in her passion. After all, they were surrounded by most of the town of Sterling.

"I think I can arrange that," he said, freeing her from his arms but quickly capturing her hand and maybe capturing a little bit of her soul . . .

chapter 11

Way too much eggnog!

The party was over and her head was beyond fuzzy, but Natalie walked about the nearly empty firehouse with the other volunteers who'd offered to stay for cleanup. She wasn't capable of doing much to help them, but she could at least say she was *trying* to help.

After a couple of dances with Hawk, the two of them had been separated, so here she was, trying to decide whether to go home alone or to wait him out. She knew she would rather wait, but on the other hand, she didn't want to seem desperate. The alcohol was messing with her rational mind.

Music was playing softly over the speakers, smooth country tunes, mellow, relaxing. She felt her eyes grow heavy, and she spread herself out on the front of the near est fire engine. The step was wide enough for her to get just a little rest.

No one would notice if she lay down for just a moment . . .

Before she knew it, she was asleep.

❄   ❄   ❄

"See ya later, chief!"

Hawk watched as the last people trickled from the fire station. They'd done such a great job of cleaning, it didn't even look like there'd been a party. Good. He liked it when things were all in order. He valued a job well done. Only one problem remained.

He'd been separated from Natalie too soon. He hadn't been ready for their night to end, and he still wasn't. And now as he turned out the lights and did his final walk-through of the station, he felt an odd emptiness settle inside him.

It was ludicrous. Hawk didn't need to be around a woman to find fulfillment. He didn't have to have companionship. But in the space of a couple of weeks, he'd found himself counting down the hours until he got to see Natalie again. The highlight of his day was when he walked into that gym and found her there, speaking with the children, smiling, gifting them with her laughter.

This was so far beyond anything he'd ever experienced before that he couldn't even identify what exactly he was feeling. One thing he knew for sure, though—he wasn't going to wait until Monday to see her again.

He couldn't. He had to see her. Tonight.

Walking around the front of his line of fire engines, Hawk stopped in his tracks.

"What happened?" Natalie's voice came out huskily as she began sitting up on the front bumper of the fire engine before him.

So Hawk didn't have to go anywhere to find Natalie. She was within grasping distance. At the sight of her sleepy eyes and tousled hair, he could think only of taking her, right now.

"Everyone's gone," he said, his voice a low growl.

Her eyes widened, and then, even under the dim lights, he could see the change in her expression. She knew what came next. They both did.

He stopped trying to fight himself. This was inevitable from the moment he'd caught her in his arms that first day on the cold front porch of his rental property. He stepped forward, grasped her hands, and pulled her to her feet before kissing her, knowing this time he wasn't going to be interrupted.

Urgently, almost frantic, Hawk reached for the hem of her sweater and yanked it over her head. He had to see her body, had to feel her naked skin against his as soon as his own clothes came off.

Her moans of pent-up desire encouraged him, and he grabbed her wool slacks and slid the zipper down. Within minutes she was standing before him in nothing but a lacy bra and matching fire-engine-red panties. Whoever had invented women's underclothing should be thanked profusely, he told himself.

He'd get on that. Well, maybe not right now. He'd get on her instead.

"Let's go inside," he said, feeling a sudden urge to take her in his favorite fire engine. Yes, he knew that some of his men, just for the thrill of it, brought women to the fire department for a night of sex, but Hawk hadn't even thought once about doing such a fantastical thing.

He doubted it was a great idea now—he'd never walk through these doors again without thinking of her—but they were hurtling forward at breakneck speed, and there was no reverse for the ride they were on.

He opened the door to the fire truck, and Natalie wobbled in that direction. She reached the first step on the truck, leaving her bent over with half her body inside the truck while her luscious behind presented itself right in front of his face, hanging outside the door.

Gripping her hips to stop her from going any farther, he ran his fingers along the smooth skin of her thighs, delighting in the panties that barely hid anything from his view. Her pleased gasp encouraged him to continue.

Spreading her thighs, he moved his fingers along the seam of those delectable panties, touching her moist folds and reveling in the slow purr she gave in response.

"So ready," he whispered, wondering how he'd managed to wait this long to make love to this woman. Passion like this didn't burn out. No. The only way to extinguish the fire burning within them both was by coming together in a blaze unlike anything he'd ever battled before.

As Natalie arched her back, lifting her derriere higher into the air, her hands clutching at the diamond-patterned floorboard of his truck, Hawk leaned forward and caressed the smooth skin of her behind with his tongue. He took a slight nip at one perfectly round cheek, and she wiggled her hips in return, wanting more. So much more.

He was more than willing to give it to her. Running his tongue down and around toward what he wanted so badly, he pulled on her hips so he could get a taste of her sweet, boiling-hot core.

So wet.

So willing.

The fabric of her panties was no barrier against his tongue or fingers. He slid them effortlessly out of his way so he could pay homage to her womanhood. He built her pleasure higher and higher until they were both ready to explode, and she was writhing beneath his expert tongue.

When he pulled back, she moaned in protest, but after a moment, she slowly climbed the rest of the way into the truck. Without any guidance from Hawk, Natalie bent forward over one of the jump seats and grabbed ahold of a hanging strap.

Hawk took his time. How could he not look his fill at the sweet image of her flushed skin, of her ass in the air, of her moist folds peeking out at him? Tempting him. He could gaze at her curvaceous body all night and be a happy man. Well, maybe gaze at her *after* he'd satisfied both of them.

Leaning forward, he unhooked her bra, freeing her beautifully round breasts, perfectly proportioned to fit in his hands. Reaching around while the softness of her backside cradled his still-clothed arousal, he squeezed her nipples with expert pressure, making her cry out. When her nipples hardened beneath his touch, he so wanted to flip her around and take the luscious tips inside his mouth.

But he had plenty of time for that. He had all night long to make love to her. Right now he had to feel himself sliding against her core. Pulling back a few inches, he shed his pants, allowing his arousal to spring free, and then he gripped himself before pushing forward toward his goal. He wanted so desperately to sink deep inside her hot body, but he didn't want this exquisite moment ever to end.

So he ran the tip of his manhood against her wet heat, and he pushed the head against her provocatively. She pushed back against him. Her moans were his primary clue to her desires, and the clue was an unmistakable *yes*.

Hawk had never received so much pleasure from teasing a woman in this way, but he was throbbing as he ran his erection along the outside of her folds. The more she moaned, the more he wanted to prolong everything that was happening and not happening between the two of them.

But she had other ideas. She wiggled her behind, and he felt his engorged tip sink inside her tight heat. And then he was lost. With a hard thrust, Hawk was finally buried inside her, and he felt his world spin as she gripped him like a vise and pulsed around his staff.

Her groan reminded him to move, and he was soon thrusting in and out of her, clasping her hips as he pushed harder and faster, searching for release.

When she cried out and contracted tightly around him, he nearly let go, but as he slowed his movement to draw out her pleasure, he knew he needed to look into her eyes, needed to see her face when he came.

When her orgasm had run its course he pulled free, then gently turned her over to face him. She sighed in pleasure, her eyes half slits of satisfaction.

Leaning down, he enveloped the pink bud of one luscious nipple in the warmth of his mouth, sucking gently and placing light pressure with his teeth to draw out her afterglow, the taste even more exquisite than he'd imagined.

When he looked up at her face, he could see that she was already anticipating more. He felt her slick folds, and then he was done with foreplay. Neither of them needed it now. He pushed her back against the seat, lifted up one of her legs, rested her foot on the crossbar of the cab door, and spread the other leg to the center console. She was wide open for him, and he drove inside.

After the first thrust, Hawk had to take a second to breathe and regain something like control. But when he looked down and saw her body quivering with the need for another release, he managed to establish a quick rhythm in their holiday dance.

This time, when her body convulsed around him, he let go, filling her with his pleasure while he delighted in watching her eyes as the final shudders passed through both of them. One night wouldn't be enough. He knew that beyond a shadow of a doubt. He opened his mouth to say something.

And the fire alarm went off.

Natalie's eyes widened with panic as the lights of the fire station filled the room as if it were midday. She jumped from the truck, then tugged her sweater over those perfect breasts and stuffed her bra into her pocket. They barely had time to finish dressing and scamper out of the fire truck before the first men rushed through the bay doors. And before Hawk could stop her, Natalie slipped out into the night, leaving him standing there with a body that didn't realize their lovemaking was over.

The two of them needed to talk, and they would, as soon as the fire call was over. But right now, he had a job to focus on . . .

chapter 12

. . . .

She knew she was a chicken. She didn't even care. Let Hawk think what he wanted, but when he'd come to her door on Sunday, no, she didn't answer it and yes, she'd been hiding.

It was now Monday, and today was the day of the fire station field trip. Just her luck. How was she possibly going to avoid Hawk at his place of work? She'd seriously considered calling in sick, but she had too solid a work ethic to give that idea much more than a passing thought. So here she was, entering the same fire hall she'd been in two nights before—naked.

"Ms. Duncan, do we get to hear the sirens?"

"Of course you do, Bobby." She could do this. She'd just focus on the kids.

"Hello, future firefighters!"

Natalie turned to find a larger-than-life Hawk Winchester standing in front of the same fire engine where he'd taken her to the highest reaches of pleasure and passion. His eyes bored into hers for a full three seconds before he turned his attention back to the kids. That look alone nearly had her sagging to the floor. It was more than clear that he had a lot to say to her. She was grateful there were about thirty small chaperones with her to keep her safe.

From the look he was shooting her way, it was apparent that Hawk Winchester didn't like being ignored.

The tour began and Natalie did her best to not stare at the man of the hour, but their eyes kept meeting over the heads of the kids, and the smoldering look in his deep brown depths was enough to fry her insides. This man would barely have to lift a finger to get her back into the truck that he seemed to be spending so much time showing the kids. Her imagination went wild as she pictured herself leaning back . . .

Nope. Not the place. And *really* not the time.

When the schedule called for snacks and Natalie turned to follow the other teachers and kids into the break room, a hand caught her arm in a punishing grip.

Uh-oh!

"You're not hiding from me anymore. Not a chance."

Natalie felt herself being dragged away from the crowd, and then she found herself alone with Hawk, leaning against the very truck she'd been focusing on all weekend. No one else was in the main garage—the other firemen were helping to entertain the kids inside the lounge—and Natalie felt exposed and raw as she looked up at Hawk.

"This isn't the place or time," she whispered, praying that no one wandered in and saw the two of them.

"I agree. Sunday would have been a great time for us to have this conversation, but you wouldn't answer either your door or your phone."

His eyebrows rose as he waited for her response.

She gathered her courage and spoke sternly, though it wasn't her style. "A wise person would have figured out that I had nothing to say to you."

"I don't think that's it at all, Natalie. I think what happened between us was pretty damn spectacular, and now you're running away scared instead of facing it like an adult."

Such unmitigated arrogance irritated the hell out of her. It didn't matter that he was right; what ticked her off was the fact that he *knew* he was right. No one should be that sure of himself. She certainly wasn't of herself. How could he know how she felt? He couldn't.

"You can think whatever you want, Hawk. I don't care. We had sex. It ended. Get over it, and get over yourself." She tugged against the hold he had on her.

"Nope. I don't think so. You know what, Natalie?"

His pause was painful. They stared each other down for several edgy seconds.

"What?" she practically shouted.

"I've decided I like being with you. I've decided that we make quite a great couple. This weekend we'll have a real date."

"I don't think so, Hawk." She tugged against his hold but it did her zero good.

"Why?"

His now cold eyes wouldn't release her from their hold, just as his hand still gripped her tight. How could she continue fighting him while fighting herself as well? Somehow she dug down deep and found the will to resist him.

"Because you're not what I want, Hawk. You aren't good enough for me to change my plans," she said as coldly as she could manage.

That did the trick a little bit better than she wanted it to. Releasing her quickly, he took a step back, his expression blank as he gazed down at her, making her stomach clench with both remorse and hating that she'd just been so cruel. She instantly wanted to take the words back.

"Hawk . . ."

"Save it. I think you've said all you need to say." Hawk turned and left her standing there. Natalie wanted to run, wanted to flee the station as quickly as she could, but she was in the middle of a field trip.

She reminded herself that she'd been through far worse times than this, and she'd most likely go through far worse in the future. Squaring her shoulders, she took a breath and walked to the lounge where she found the other teachers and the students as they asked questions and gobbled down goodies.

She did just fine until they got ready to leave and her eyes met Hawk's. Trying desperately not to show weakness, she turned away, but feared it was too late. If he'd seen the tears in her eyes, he would know she was a liar. She just hoped he hadn't, because if he came to her again, she knew she wouldn't have the strength to turn him down a second time.

chapter 13

. . . .

$\mathcal{E}$mptying the box of the last tissue, Natalie blew her nose and decided enough was enough. She'd cried for days and it was insane. She wasn't the kind of girl to lay around crying over a guy.

She barely knew the man for goodness' sake. A few hot kisses, a couple of visits at his parents', and the hottest sex known to man did not make for a lasting relation-ship. Looking down she realized she was holding her little notebook, the evil, ridiculous notebook with her stupid goals.

Suddenly, she was furious with herself, her mother, her life. She threw the notebook across the room, feeling immensely good when it hit the wall. Why was she so determined to hide?

What would be the problem with going out on a real date with Hawk? Hadn't she decided it would be nice to be with him, even if it was only temporary? Why did she have to analyze the whole thing, map it out, and deny herself what she wanted?

Just because the idea of going out with him on a real date didn't fit in with her nice little plans didn't mean it was wrong. Why keep fighting this when she knew it was a losing battle? Besides, this man was the last thing she thought about before falling asleep. He was the one she dreamed of, and he was the first thought on her mind in the morning.

But would she even get a choice to go out with him now? The look he'd shot her after she'd told him he wasn't good enough hadn't been too kind. She may have blown her shot with the man. Wouldn't that make this all so much easier?

She was a chicken! That's what she was. She wanted him to hate her because then she wouldn't have to choose between her own happiness and her goals. She was also a fool. With determination, she stood up.

She'd overheard the teachers talk about how Hawk liked to ice-skate with the kids on some Saturdays. Though it had been years since she'd gone ice-skating, and though she hadn't been good at it back then, she decided she should give it another try.

Before she could change her mind, she washed her face, bundled up, and left her house. Practically shaking because she was so nervous, she made her way down to the outdoor skating rink, and just hoped he was against public humiliation.

Not that she wouldn't deserve a good tongue lashing from him, but that would really be a bad end to an already bad day. It didn't take her long to get there, and there was no sign of Hawk, so she rented skates and got ready to go out on the ice.

When she looked up and saw Hawk moving toward her, an odd sense of excitement began to build. This was going to go one way or the other, and from the look in his eyes she really didn't know which way, but she decided to paste a smile on her lips and hope for the best.

"What are you doing here, Natalie?" Still no expression to give her the slightest hint of what he was thinking or feeling.

"I thought I'd go ice-skating," she said, glad when her voice didn't wobble, at least not too badly.

"Alone?"

"I was hoping to not be alone." His eyes widened at that and then narrowed as he looked down at her.

"What game are you playing?"

"It's not a game . . ." She trailed off, because if she was in his shoes she'd ask the same thing.

"Isn't it better to be alone, than to hang around a man who isn't good enough for you?" His voice was deadpan, his eyes cold, making her shiver even more than the icy coldness of the Montana weather.

"I was wrong to say that. It's just that . . . well, it's just that I mapped out a certain life for myself, and for the longest time I thought I had to stay with that plan. Then you came along, and I didn't know what to think. Everything became chaotic, but I like it . . . sort of."

His eyebrows rose at her fumbled explanation, and

he didn't help her out at all with letting her know what he was thinking. She shifted on the bench, wondering if he was going to make her beg. It sure looked as if he was.

"I wrote down goals, and I haven't achieved hardly any of them," she said.

"And I don't fit into those goals?"

"It's not that you don't fit into them," she began, when she decided to be honest. "No. I wanted to have a career established, a house. I don't want to be like my mother. I want . . ." What did she even want anymore? She didn't know.

"Ah . . ."

"That's it? Ah? Really. I'm trying here. I swear I'm not playing with you. It's not a game. I just . . . like being with you." She felt her cheeks flush, but with the cold outside, he wouldn't know that.

Silence greeted her statement and she was about to give up. This was hopeless. She'd insulted his pride, so why should he forgive her? Wouldn't that make it all easier, anyway? She wouldn't have this internal struggle because she'd have no choice but to stay away from him.

"I don't think you're acting," he finally said. The two of them faced off for several moments before he shocked her by smiling. What did it mean?

"Um . . ." She wasn't sure what she wanted to ask.

"Fine. You say you aren't playing a game. I believe you. Argument over." Then he sat down and took off his shoes and began putting on his ice skates.

"So . . . We're okay?" She didn't know how to define

what the two of them had been before their little tiff, so she didn't know what to ask him about them now.

"Yep. We're now officially on our first date."

"Just like that?"

"Yep. Why hold a grudge?"

Turning, he placed an arm behind her and gave her that simmering look that had made her fall for him in the first place. No grudge. No holding it over her head. This was something Natalie was in no way used to. When she'd been growing up, if she'd done something to upset her mother, she wouldn't hear the end of it for months to come.

What if this was his idea of a joke? What if she made a complete fool of herself? What if she fell on her face, which was more than likely, considering she'd never been graceful—face it, she'd always been a real klutz.

There were plenty of what-ifs, but the bottom line was that she was here and their fight was over, and it was their first *real* date. She would breathe and she would get through it. So, taking her cue from him, she decided to act casual and pretend they hadn't fought. If he could do it then so could she.

"I'm warning you now, Hawk, I'm not going to be graceful."

"Don't worry about it. I'll be there to catch you when you slip."

"Oh? *When* I slip?"

"Yeah, we both know it *will* happen. I think you enjoy falling into my arms. I know I certainly like it."

Before she could stop herself, she blurted out her

thoughts. "You have killer eyes. Seriously! Does anyone ever deny you anything you want?"

Hawk looked startled. Then he laughed. "I can honestly say that no one has asked me that before." He leaned closer and whispered in her ear. "But, if I had known it was that easy . . ."

He didn't have to finish that sentence to make her thighs press tighter together in a semisatisfying squeeze. This man was making her shiver and heating her up all at once, and Natalie had to confess she liked the wild sensations running through her body.

Natalie jumped up, needing to move, to displace the sudden energy burning through her. She had gone through a myriad of emotions over the last few days, and right now she felt joy. It just felt right when she was in Hawk's presence. Smiling, she stood and made her way to the rink.

It didn't take Hawk long to follow her, and soon, Natalie was laughing as Hawk lifted her into his arms and spun her around as he glided seamlessly in and out of the other couples on the ice. She was out of breath by the time he set her back on her wobbly feet.

"How in the heck did you get so good at ice-skating?" she gasped.

"I play ice hockey every year," he said smugly.

"Mmm. Now, that's something I have to see."

After another hour on the ice, she was growing more confident, taking longer strides, and even spinning a few times with a few of her students who happened to be there. She wasn't even cold anymore—in fact, with all the activity, she was a little warm. In Montana, of all places!

When she fell against the wall and then felt solid arms cage her in, she didn't hesitate to turn around. She forgot all about the crowd when Hawk's lips captured hers and she found herself lost in his embrace.

❄ ❄ ❄

Bethel lifted a cup of steaming cider to her lips and took a sip. "I know I should be a lot happier about this. But those two kids are leaving us with nothing to do," she groused from the sidelines of the ice-skating rink.

"I know. I thought we'd surely have to do a little more meddling," Eileen said with a grumble of her own.

"Yes. They appear to be falling in love," Maggie sighed, too happy to be grumpy about it.

"What are you ladies up to?"

The three women turned guilty stares to their friend Martin Whitman.

"Oh, just enjoying watching the kids skate," Bethel said. Unfortunately, she'd never been good at telling a fib and she flushed, but she hoped he thought it was from the cold.

His eyes narrowed and he looked out at the ice. It didn't take long for him to home in on Hawk and Natalie, who were still locked in a passionate embrace.

"Enjoying the show, huh?" he said as he sat down.

"Yes. The kids are really getting good," Eileen said with a nervous giggle.

"Somehow I don't think it's the *little* kids you're watching," Martin said with a laugh. "You know, you'd better spill everything to me right now, or I might have to figure it out on my own and tell other people what you're up to."

Maggie's outrage showed only too clearly. "Martin Whitman, you wouldn't dare."

"I'm sure your husband wouldn't be too pleased if he learns that you're meddling in the kids' lives," Martin said with a self-satisfied grin.

"All right. Fine, then," Maggie snapped, and she gave a nod to her two best friends.

They spilled the whole story. They would be pleased to know that their meddling was putting some ideas into Martin's head about his own stubborn sons, who still refused to settle down . . .

chapter 14

. . . .

The stage filled with children in red, white, and green, and even a few in traditional costumes associated with the Near East and Africa. The young performers giggled as they looked out upon the audience, searching for their parents and waving excitedly.

Natalie felt like she was going to be sick. They weren't ready! She was going to prove herself a failure—had she taught them well, given them good direction? Or would they choke out there?

The last week of rehearsals had zipped right by. The only things she could remember about the time were the looks that Hawk threw her from across the gym, making her forget her voice as she tried to sing along with the kids. Now Natalie was standing in the wings, shaking in her nice slacks as the auditorium filled with parents all expecting to see a show as good as the one put on last year.

"Calm down. It'll be fine."

Hawk was standing beside her, a reassuring smile on his lips. But instead of calming down, she felt her heart pick up speed while she remembered that twelve short hours ago he hadn't been telling her to calm down. He'd been making her cry out.

"I can't do this," she said in a hushed wail.

"Not only *can* you do this, but you *will* do it, and you'll do it well. I've been here with you the entire time. You're amazing with the kids. They love you. And so they'll perform their little hearts out for you." He rested a hand on her shoulder.

The gesture settled her down, finally. Hawk believed in her, and if this man, a man she was falling so deeply for, believed in her, how could she go wrong?

"You'll save me if I freeze?" Funny question to ask a fire chief . . .

"I won't need to rescue you, Natalie. You're confident, beautiful, and more than capable of hosting a pageant. Go and knock the socks off these parents."

He nudged her forward, and Natalie had no choice but to step from behind the curtain and face the entire town. Feeling her cheeks turn as bright as the lights she was under, Natalie nevertheless walked to the microphone with what she hoped appeared to be confidence. A hush fell over the crowd as the children behind her continued to giggle and wave.

"Thank you all for coming out this snowy evening." Natalie felt her throat tighten. These people didn't want her to fail. They just wanted to enjoy their children. If only she'd realized this sooner, she wouldn't have been such a wreck.

"I have to admit that when I first arrived in Sterling and walked out of those airport doors, I was in shock. When I saw the one lone street of businesses, I didn't know how I'd survive." No one said anything as she paused to swallow her emotions. "But during this last month, I've fallen in love with this town. How could I not when my neighbors have brought me goodies and cheer, when my classroom is full of beautiful, talented students, all eager to learn, and when every time I step from my home there is always someone passing by with a wave and a *good morning*? All I wanted to do in the beginning was to run far away to somewhere bigger and warmer, but now I can't imagine teaching anywhere else. Thank you for trusting me with your children, and for believing in me to give you a good pageant. I can guarantee the children are ready. As for me, on the other hand . . ." She trailed off with a laugh that had the audience doing the same.

"I can't promise perfection, but I can guarantee I'll always put in a thousand percent effort. Enough about me and my silly emotions. It's time to watch the show!"

Natalie knelt down in front of the kids, and they took over, singing their songs in celebration of Christmas, completely off tune and with full delight.

During the last number, five children stepped forward, and while the kids behind them sang "Silent Night," they signed the words for a mother in the audience who was deaf. It had been something one of her young students had asked to do for her mother, and Natalie had been touched immeasurably by the request. Standing next to the kids, she signed along with them, looking down and smiling at the woman they were doing it for.

When the song ended, the audience maintained a reverential silence for a few moments, and then several people lifted their hands and waved, the universal sign language for applause. The children were glowing with pride as they walked offstage, and as Natalie prepared to thank everyone and call an end to the pageant, Martin Whitman stood up and walked to the microphone.

"The parents would like to extend a very special thank-you to our newest teacher, Ms. Natalie Duncan, for directing another beautiful pageant. You were thrown in at the last minute, and you've done a spectacular job.

"And we'd also like to present an award to our very own fire chief, Mr. Hawk Winchester. This year marks his tenth pageant, and his help with building sets, moving equipment, bringing in the other firefighters to set it all up, and coordinating the necessary fund-raising has always been invaluable. Would you come out here and join us, Hawk?"

The audience burst into applause, and Natalie found herself standing next to Martin as Hawk approached. Their gazes connected and even a room full of people was unable to tear her eyes from him until he turned toward the audience with his most winning smile.

"Thanks, Martin," Hawk said. "I love these pageants, and I feel that I'm getting far more from it than the help I'm giving. I hope you keep me around helping for at least another ten years."

"We're not going to let you go that soon, son," Martin joked.

"Not a chance," someone in the audience called out.

Then Hawk placed an arm around Natalie's shoulders and turned them both to allow photographs to be taken. But instead of facing the camera, she looked up into Hawk's eyes, instantly feeling lost in their deep brown depths. And then, right there in front of the entire town, Hawk claimed her lips and at the same time captured the rest of her heart.

chapter 15

· · · · · · · · · · · · · · · ·

I can't come with your family!"

Natalie was standing in her living room, still wearing her pajamas and looking at Hawk as if he were insane. There was no way she would intrude on his family at Christmas. It was bad enough she'd been thrust upon them on Thanksgiving.

"You're coming," he said with the same sickeningly confident smile he'd been sporting since he'd walked in the front door.

"No, I'm not, Hawk. Christmas is family time."

"And you have no other family, so my mother has decided to adopt you," he told her. "Besides, she's invited a few other friends. The holidays are about more than just family being together. It's a time to leave no one out."

Natalie turned away, pretending to wipe dust from the spotless end table as tears forced their way into her eyes. Dammit, she was always crying now, like some sappy twit, and she sure as sin didn't want to expose her vulnerability where family was concerned. Her relationship with Hawk had been moving at the speed of light, and she felt overwhelmed.

To hear him say so casually that his mother had adopted her choked her up. But she was never going to admit to anyone how badly she wanted to be part of a real family. It would make her sound too desperate, too pathetic.

"Hey? What's wrong?"

Hawk came up behind her, slipped his arms around her waist, and tugged her against him. Great. Having him touch her certainly wouldn't help her gain control over her wretched emotions.

Despite all her efforts, a damned tear fell. They hadn't spoken of the future. They hadn't talked about a happily-ever-after. She hadn't told him how she felt about him.

"Nothing. I'm just . . ." She was just what? She had no freaking idea.

"I'm not demanding that you come with us," he said softly, his breath washing across her cheek. "I'm asking you to please make this Christmas my best one ever, and join us."

How could she tell him no after that? "Okay," she whispered.

"Why is this so hard on you?" he asked again, this time making her face him.

Natalie suddenly needed to speak about it, needed to release the weight from her shoulders. He said nothing more as he waited, his hands caressing her arms and back. She could do this.

"I . . . it was always just me and my mother while I was growing up. She had me when she was only fifteen, and I grew up in shelters, and then she worked hard and got us a little apartment. Mom worked all the time, I mean like seven days a week. Even working so much, we never had enough—not enough food, clothes, not enough to pay the bills. Mom told me over and over again not to mess up like she'd done, not to fall for a guy who would walk away at the first sign of trouble. She told me to go to school, get an education, and get a good job. She was bitter a lot, but she did love me."

"I'm sure she loved you very much," he whispered when she paused for too long.

"She did," Natalie sighed. "She did the best she could. But I had no family, Hawk. I had no one but her and she was gone so much. We didn't do holidays; we didn't celebrate much. I feel like I'm betraying her by enjoying my life."

"You feel that way because you are kind and caring. But, Natalie, if she truly loved you, she would want you to be happy. Don't all parents want better for their children than what they had for themselves?"

"I don't know, Hawk . . ." Would her mom forgive her for straying from her goals? She honestly didn't know.

"I know I want my kids to be happy," he said.

"Do you have some secret children you've been hiding from me, Hawk?" She smiled up at him, trying so hard to quit her self-pity party.

"It's not that easy to divert my attention, Natalie. Let my family love you. Don't feel guilt about it, and don't feel sadness. Just let us love you."

When he said *us*, her heart leapt with joy. But what exactly did he mean by it? The question was on the tip of her tongue, but she wasn't brave enough to ask—not yet, not now. After an extended silence, Natalie was relieved when he asked whether she needed help packing. Their talk was over for now, and she'd survived it. She'd shared something with him, and he hadn't turned away in disgust. There was hope, after all, that the two of them would make this relationship last longer than his three-date maximum.

As they moved through the house, he looked up and smiled. "My family has a cabin up in the woods where we spend Christmas every year," he told her.

"I've never seen a white Christmas," Natalie admitted, not that she'd ever gotten to celebrate Christmas, not really. "I'm kind of excited, though I still hate the idea of snow on every day other than Christmas."

"Let's get your bags in the truck and get up there. You will never miss California again after spending Christmas at our family cabin."

"I already don't miss it, Hawk."

The smile he sent her as he helped her into his truck almost made her heart stop. "Natalie Duncan, I'm not letting you escape." With that, he closed her door and moved around to the driver's side, leaving Natalie to wonder exactly what he meant by that.

When they arrived at the cabin a couple of hours

later, she learned that her idea of a cabin and Hawk's idea were completely different. Yes, the building was made from logs, but this place wasn't some rustic little cabin in the woods. It was enormous! Large enough to house several families *and* all their friends.

That was a good thing, because when they walked in the door, Natalie found what appeared to be half the town inside. Several dozen people were gathered in the spacious living room, their voices carrying with its high vaulted ceilings. Christmas decorations adorned the walls and eggnog sloshed in everyone's cup.

No one made a big deal when she and Hawk arrived, for which Natalie was grateful. They just greeted the two of them with eggnog and spoke with Natalie like she *belonged*. It didn't take too long for her to grow comfortable and realize this wasn't a dream. When it came time to go hunting for a Christmas tree, she was thankful she didn't miss out on joining Hawk and his family and their many friends.

"Are you too cold?"

Natalie entwined her arm with Hawk's and snuggled a little closer. "A bit, but it's refreshing. I still can't believe I'm going to have my very first Christmas with snow!"

"Tell me more about your life in California, more about your life with your mom."

She'd finally opened up to someone, finally shared a small piece of her past, and now she found herself wanting to share it all. But if he knew the truth, the full truth, wouldn't that frighten him away? Even with that thought she couldn't seem to stop herself from speaking. Now that he'd opened the floodgates to her past, the words came rushing out.

"You know that it was just me and my mother and that she worked a lot. So, from the time I was little, I was on my own most of the time. That's why I loved school, because then I was with other people."

"Was it miserable?" Hawk stopped and leaned against a large tree, pulling her into the cradle of his arms as he rubbed his hands up and down her back.

"No. The thing was that even though we didn't have a whole heck of a lot, I wasn't unhappy. I loved my mom, even during the bad times. I loved what little time we got to spend together. I didn't need to have the newest pair of jeans, or to go to summer camp. When she died, I was devastated. It took me a lot of years before I felt like I could live again. She did the best she could. . . ."

"You impress me, Natalie."

"Why?"

"Because you don't dwell on the bad memories. You even manage to find a way to turn the tough times into positive experiences. You humble me with your attitude."

"I'm not that noble, Hawk," she said with an uncomfortable laugh.

"We'll have to just agree to disagree," he said before giving her a kiss that melted the snow that was covering them.

chapter 16

· · · · · · · · · · · · · · ·

"I love my family, but they're a bit overwhelming," Hawk said later that night as he and Natalie strolled outside, hand in hand.

"Yes, but I honestly enjoy spending time with them. I think your mother and I baked at least five hundred Christmas cookies today," Natalie said with a laugh as they approached a large red barn.

"Want to see something really cool?"

"Always."

He opened the barn door and they stepped inside. She didn't see him turn around and engage the latch.

"Over here," he said, and he led her through the *ginormous* building.

They entered a large room behind another door, and before her was an old cherry-red fire truck.

"It's seventy years old and my dad and I spent ten

summers bringing her back into mint condition. I love this engine." He couldn't contain his excitement when he ran his hand along the shiny bumper. That small gesture had her stomach clenching as she thought back to the other fire engine and the first night they'd made love.

It had been several days since they'd last been intimate, and now that her body knew how incredible sex between them was, she didn't want to miss out on the feel of his hands and his . . . never mind . . . for even a single second more.

Without much sound, Hawk was suddenly behind her, wrapping his arms around her waist and tugging her close. "Want to see where I had my first kiss?"

Natalie tensed at the thought of Hawk ever kissing anyone else.

"Hawk!" she snapped, no longer wanting to play as she had ten seconds before.

"Awww, come on. The place is really cool."

"I seriously have no desire to see where you kissed some trashy girl."

"Well, can you really be trashy at five years old?"

"Five? Really?" she asked suspiciously.

"Yep. I was five and kissed JoBeth up in the hayloft," he stated proudly.

"And how many other girls did you kiss in the hayloft as the years passed?" Natalie had no intention of being just one of many.

"I kissed lots of girls in lots of haylofts, but, alas, only JoBeth in this one," he replied.

"Fine. Show me this loft, but if you think you're

going to get any kisses out of me, then you will be very disappointed."

They climbed a ladder and then Hawk was right behind Natalie, nuzzling her neck. "I'm not kissing you, Hawk," she said again, but her voice came out breathy because his hands were slipping beneath her shirt and touching the bare skin of her stomach.

"Why? Don't you like my secret hideaway?" he murmured as he gently nipped her shoulder while his fingers climbed higher, lightly brushing across her breasts.

"No," she replied, though they both knew she was lying, especially when she pushed back against him and rolled her hips so she could better feel his arousal.

He lowered his fingers across her abs and reached for the zipper of her jeans, taking his time in releasing the material that was binding her. Natalie gave up even the smallest pretense that she didn't want this.

"Yes, Hawk. Faster."

He didn't disappoint her. He slid his hands inside the denim and gave a good push, and then her jeans were pooling at her feet, landing on the hay to provide a nice barrier between their bare skin and the dry grass when they became horizontal.

With her back still to him, Hawk pushed her legs apart, leaned in, and sucked on her neck while he slipped a hand inside the silk of her panties and found her core more than ready for his touch.

"I love how you respond to me," he groaned in her ear, causing a shudder to rip through her.

"You make me catch fire, Hawk."

"You inspire me, Natalie."

He took her shirt away, adding it to the pile beside them, then flung her bra aside, leaving her gasping while his hands wandered all over her.

"More," she begged, moaning as he pinched her hard nipples.

Dropping them both to their knees, he turned her around and kissed her before edging back just a couple of inches so he could remove his shirt, revealing his incredible abs and disgracefully hard pecs. With sure fingers, he undid the buttons on his jeans and pushed the denim down his muscular legs. When he unveiled her favorite part of his body, she gasped in anticipation. Soon, very soon, that pulsing arousal would take her to new heights of pleasure.

Natalie pushed him backward, and he lost his balance. She crawled up his legs, her tongue licking along the sweet muscles of his thighs until she reached his manhood. Without hesitation, she grabbed his hardness and took her first taste of him. *Oh my . . .*

"Natalie," he groaned.

She didn't answer him; she just moved her hand up and down his throbbing arousal while she sucked on it. After a couple of minutes, he pushed her back, his face crimson, his eyes wild.

"Your turn," he growled, easily flipping her over onto her back. "Hold on!"

Hold on to what? she wondered before she couldn't think anymore, because he'd slid his hands beneath her thighs and was taking his turn at tasting her. Natalie cried out as his masterful tongue stroked her pulsing flesh, taking her higher and higher as she strove for release. His low moans mingled with her cries in such beautiful music that Natalie felt tears sting her eyes.

When the first explosion of pleasure raced through her, she rode the wave, loving how he drew it out, loving the perfect way he played her body. He slowed his touch, murmuring his approval of her response to him. Then he shifted, his eyes hungry, almost starving, as he looked down at her flushed skin. Without another word, Hawk climbed up her sated body and then plunged inside her, making her cry out again at such a welcome invasion.

"More," she practically sobbed as he moved back and then thrust forward again, and she dug her nails into the slick skin of his back.

"Yes, Natalie. Give me your pleasure . . . Let it go," he demanded.

How could she possibly refuse him? Her body knew what it wanted, and when he thrust forward again, she gripped him tightly as a violent wave of ecstasy rushed through her. Hawk's shout of joy followed quickly.

"I could make love to you all night," Hawk said as he kissed her slowly, tenderly, making her stomach start to flutter again.

She giggled. "You wouldn't hear any complaints from me."

Her lips parted when she felt him growing hard against her thigh. *Whoa. Impossible.* Hawk proceeded to prove to her that he wasn't just offering up empty promises . . .

chapter 17

· · · · · · · · · · · · · · ·

*N*atalie shot straight up in bed, clutching the comforter to her chest as her heart pounded.

"What's wrong?" Hawk slowly sat up beside her with blurry eyes. They couldn't have been asleep for more than a couple of hours.

"What was that?" she asked as she tried to calm herself.

"What was *what*?" He still wasn't awake.

"How in the heck can you wake up at a tiny little beep from your pager, but then sleep through what sounds like a bomb exploding?"

"I don't know. You just learn to tune out certain noises," he said with a crooked smile as he began rubbing a hand along her thigh.

Natalie jumped again as the door was thrust open and Hawk's sister gazed in at them, her face going from excited to impish at finding Natalie in her brother's room.

"Go away, brat!" Hawk said as Natalie tried to hide beneath the covers. Dang. She wished that he hadn't insisted she spend a little time in his bedroom last night.

"Not a chance, Hawk," Taylor said. "It's Christmas morning and I want to open my presents." She crossed her arms against her chest and stamped her foot, a mutinous scowl on her face.

"You're not five anymore, Taylor. You're twenty-three," he pointed out.

"And you're well past five, old enough to have set your alarm for the big family celebration. Anyway, I don't care how old a person gets. If you're not excited about Christmas morning, you just aren't human. By the way, hi, Natalie!"

Smoked out. Natalie peeked over the covers, her face scarlet. "Hi, Taylor. Please don't tell your mom," she whispered, mortified at the thought of Maggie knowing she was in Hawk's room, even if they were adults.

"Then you'd better get downstairs fast," Taylor said with a satisfied grin.

Natalie was more than willing to agree to the demand, but the two stubborn siblings remained in a deadlock for several tense moments while Natalie's head whipped back and forth between them. Finally, Hawk let out a disgusted sigh.

"Fine. We're coming," he said. "Turn around for just a moment, my darling sister." He threw off the covers, yanked on the pair of sweats that he'd discarded nearby, and rose from the bed.

Natalie's mouth dropped open at the sight of his naked back. It didn't help that the sweatpants rode so low on his amazing hips. No matter how many times she saw this man half dressed, he still awed her.

"Close your mouth, Natalie, before you let in some flies," Taylor said with a mischievous grin as she turned back to face them.

"I swear I'm not going to give you your presents if you don't go away right now," Hawk said, and he moved threateningly toward the door.

"Fine. But if you aren't down in five minutes, I'm coming back," Taylor said, before adding, "and I'm bringing Mom!"

Hawk shut the door in her face. He turned and winked at Natalie. "I can set up a barricade."

"It's tempting . . ." And she actually considered it. But the sound of more footsteps thundering down the stairs caused her to sigh and climb from the bed. "Nope. We better get moving," she said as she floated to the en-suite bathroom after grabbing her clothes from the floor.

It was going to be tricky enough sneaking back to her room without being seen. No way was she doing it without a quick shower first. When she came out, Hawk grabbed her around the waist and hoisted her into his arms, letting her feet dangle in the air. "I love it when your cheeks are all rosy."

"It's been well over five minutes," Natalie reminded him with a giggle. "We'd better go before they send out a search party."

He kissed her and then set her back on her feet. Hand

in hand, they went to the door. And right there on the other side was Taylor with a perturbed look that made Natalie laugh in spite of herself.

"I'm sorry, Taylor. I took a really quick shower."

"Most people wait till after the presents are opened to shower," Taylor grumbled, but as it was Christmas morning, she forgave them both. Still, she wedged herself in between them to lead them down the stairs.

Natalie couldn't help but grow excited herself when she found Hawk's entire family and several other family friends all sitting around the giant living room with a huge tree taking center stage and so many gifts that it looked like a department store had exploded.

Soon, laughter filled the cabin as paper tore and thank-yous rang out. Natalie had to fight emotion as present upon present was thrust her way. She took her time with each one, not wanting to ruin the paper, and not wanting this moment ever to end.

She had never, ever received so many gifts before, and she felt guilty because she hadn't been able to do nearly as much for this wonderful family as they were doing for her. She hadn't expected to spend Christmas with them, but she'd still purchased a few items she'd planned on giving them after Christmas. What did you get a family that obviously had so much? When a tiny package was thrust at her, she was concentrating so hard on not ruining the paper that she didn't notice how quiet the room had become.

She found a small jewelers' box inside the wrapping, and the thought that she was about to get a pretty new trinket made her absolutely gleeful. No one in the room could have missed the brilliance of that smile. But when she opened the case and found a magnificent diamond ring inside, she almost dropped it.

Lifting her face, she saw Hawk staring intently at her with a look of love so tender that she was grateful to be sitting cross-legged on the floor already.

"Natalie, I know this has been quick. I know that you're probably terrified right now, and I know I should have done this more privately so you could tell me to take a flying leap if you wanted. But I love my family and I want them to be a part of this moment, because up until meeting you, I didn't think there could ever be another person in my life who would make me feel the things you make me feel. Even though it's only been a month, I know you better than any other person could, and I love that. I feel like what we have together is one hundred times stronger than anything I've ever felt before. I never thought anyone could make me as happy as you do. Everything that's stressful in my life disappears the second I see your smile. I can say with one hundred percent certainty that you are my soul mate. There is a plan for everyone and I know that you are my only future. I will never let you go no matter what your answer is. Please marry me and make me the happiest man alive."

He didn't break the connection of their eyes, and though he'd shown her day after day that he wanted to be with her, this was something she would have never expected from him, not because he wasn't perfect, but because she wasn't. At least she wasn't in her own eyes. Natalie didn't know what to say.

Yes, this had moved quickly, and yes, she should try to think logically, but running over the last month in her head, she knew that she was happiest when with him, whether at the school, or in the gym, or just sitting and playing a board game at his parents' place. Their love would only grow stronger from this day forward.

This wasn't a part of her plans. This wasn't even on the table, but love didn't care. They had found each other and there was nothing that would change how they felt. Nothing.

"I love you, too, Hawk," she whispered. And she didn't even notice that her voice had wobbled. "I love that you care about me, insecurities and all. I love that you see me differently than I see myself, and I love that family is so important to you. I want a family; I've just always been afraid to ask for one. I thought I had a plan I needed to follow, but what you've taught me is that the best things in life aren't planned—they're discovered."

"Will you marry me, Natalie?"

"Right this minute if I could," she told him.

Soft sighs echoed through the room as Hawk moved forward, pulled Natalie to her feet, and drew her gently into his arms, where he sealed their promises to each other with a tender kiss. Love had found them this holiday season, and it had taken hold of both of their hearts. And it wasn't about to let go.

epilogue

· · · · · · · · · · · ·

Valentine's Day

Well, what do we do now?" Eileen asked.

"I don't know," Bethel said with a sniffle. "We should be a heck of a lot more happy. That was a wonderful wedding."

Maggie's answering smile was accompanied by watery eyes. "Yes, I think Hawk and Natalie are going to make each other very happy."

"Yes, they will," Martin said. "They were meant to be." Even he sounded a bit choked up.

Still, Bethel pouted. "But I'm bored now."

"Well, Hawk isn't the only single man in this town," Eileen said.

Bethel perked up instantly. "That's *very* true."

"My boys are way past their time to find their brides," Martin reminded them.

"I couldn't agree with you more, Martin," Maggie replied with a painful level of excitement.

"I just don't know where to even begin," Martin said.

"I know. It worked out really well with Natalie, but we don't need any more schoolteachers," Eileen said.

The four of them sat at a large table and watched Hawk and Natalie hold each other tight while dancing to Lonestar's rendition of the song "Amazed."

"I know that I've been more than ready for Jackson to settle down, but that boy avoids commitment like it's a double-headed snake," Martin groused.

"What do we do to change his mind?" Bethel asked.

Martin said, "I'm at a loss. I just don't know . . ."

"Well, he does have that trip to Paris coming up. Any chances of a romance there?" Eileen asked.

"It *is* the city of love," Maggie said.

"We need help!" Bethel insisted.

Martin grinned. "Maybe it's time to call Joseph."

"That old rascal hasn't visited in too long," Eileen said. "What is Joseph Anderson up to these days?"

"I know that he's managed to create a large family for himself. He's told me a little about how it all happened, so I know he had his hand involved," Martin told them.

"Well, then. Let's give the man a call!" Eileen pulled out her cell phone and punched his number from the contacts list.

"Hello?"

Joseph Anderson's voice boomed across the line, and the meddling was only just beginning . . .

Rekindle the Flame

....

KATE MEADER

chapter 1

. . . .

Last Christmas, I gave you my heart . . ."

Eyeing the crush of cheerfully wasted humanity as they sang along to the soppiest Christmas song ever, Beck Rivera let go of a frustrated sigh. It turned into a growl midway through.

"If one more idiot in a red suit breathes his fumes on me, I'm going holiday nuclear."

His brother Luke laughed at Beck's out-of-character dramatics. Normally the least excitable one in the family—except for their oldest, Wyatt, who wouldn't know drama if it upchucked in his face—Beck was clearly teetering on the brink tonight. Three weeks to Christmas and the annual Santa Shuffle Pub Crawl, a staple of the Chicago holiday scene, had stalled in his bar.

Ho-dee-ho-ho.

"So how is holiday nuclear different from regular

nuclear?" Luke asked. He pulled gently on the Guinness tap to complete the shamrock imprint in the stout's foamy head.

"With holiday nuclear, I'll go ballistic—with an elfish smile."

Pint safely delivered to a thirsty customer, Luke laid a strong hand on Beck's shoulder. "Stay cool, psycho. You'll be back in bunker gear before you know it."

Before he knew it couldn't come soon enough. Put on leave after his recent brush with death and the brass at the Chicago Fire Department, Beck was itching to return to firehouse duty. Sitting around all day making an ass-shaped dent in his sofa was killing him slowly and, but for the fact he was pulling extra shifts at his family's bar, Dempsey's on Damen, he'd probably lose his mind. Along with the love of his foster siblings—three guys, one gal—who held no truck with his moodiness over the last month.

At least he was alive, for Christ's sake. And so was the poor kid he'd managed to haul free before the roof of that South Side crack house caved in Old Testament style. So *maybe* he'd disobeyed his lieutenant's orders—Beck's MO had always been of the act-now-beg-forgiveness-later variety. But where usually the head honchos liked how the heroics looked for the papers, this time it had landed him in deep shit.

Now, with at least another month until his disciplinary hearing—because God forbid anyone at HQ make a decision over the holidays—Beck had plenty of time on his hands to brood and shine up a new rash of apologies.

"Hey, amigo," Beck heard behind him. One of the red-suited troublemakers, a downtown professional type. With Puerto Rican skin darker than most of the pasty-faced Chicago Irish set who propped up the bar at Dempsey's, Beck supposed he might look like someone's amigo, but he sure as hell didn't appreciate this stranger bandying the word about. Red Suit leaned forward and, in his eagerness for a drink, blindly elbowed a cute blonde out of the way.

So, not looking to get laid, then.

"Careful, now," Beck said.

"What's that, amigo?"

F'real, dude? "I said you need to be careful." Beck enunciated each word, then turned to the blonde. "You okay?"

"Fine, thanks." She shot a hostile look at Red Suit, who chose that moment to bare his teeth in an approximation of a grin that went thoroughly unreturned. Nice.

Beck directed his attention back to the loser. "What'll it be?"

"Chivas, neat, twice over." Red Suit glanced over his shoulder to where his rowdy friends stood, making a lot of noise. A spilled beer on a woman's dress earlier had been the first hint these guys were trouble. Two more rounds until they were cut off, Beck estimated. "A bottle of Bud and a Goose Island. Whatever the holiday ale crap is."

"Sure," Beck said. "How about I add it to your tab and bring it along?" Red Suit blinked his acceptance, adjusted his padding, and loped off.

"Hey, Rivera, how's life sitting around eating bon-bons all day?"

Beck slowed while pouring the Chivas, then rearranged his expression and his bones to neutral for Frank Gilligan, a CPD detective with a mouth as big as his ego. He happened to be a friend, but more often a pain in Beck's ass.

"Detective, the moment I met you I knew we'd get along."

Gilligan smiled that crugly grin, the one he gifted drug dealers before he gifted them his fists in a pretty red bow. "I'm touched, Rivera. Really."

"Yeah, because cops and firefighters have so much in common." Beck worked the pause for a beat. "They both want to be firefighters."

An oldie but a goodie, it pulled a guffaw from Gilligan, who enjoyed the semiserious rivalry between the city's first responders. But the detective's words had pinched a nerve all the same. Beck would be hard-pressed to think of a worse time to be sidelined than the holidays. Burst pipes, electrical fires, Christmas tree combustions, and hot girls in skimpy Santa outfits usually kept the team at Engine 6 busy, a state of affairs he was not alone in enjoying. Since their foster parents and brother, Logan, had died, the rest of the family preferred camping out at the firehouse over the holidays. Anything to feel useful and honor their loved ones' memories.

Hard to feel useful kickin' back on the sofa. Christ on a crutch, he wanted to hit something.

Raucous shouts whooped from the corner followed

by a distinctly female complaint of "Hey, watch it, dick-head." Beck sent up a brief acknowledgment to the Big Guy. Ask and you shall receive. In seconds, he was out from behind the bar and halfway toward the corner pocket of Santas.

"Beck," Luke called after him in a voice edged with warning. Beck raised a hand to say he had this. Damn it, he needed this.

"Want help, Smokeater?" asked Gilligan.

Beck threw a smirk over his shoulder. "Watch and learn, Mr. Policeman." As the saying went, God created firefighters so cops could have heroes, too.

His fists balled of their own volition, and Beck could almost feel the tape wrapped taut over his knuckles. Three-time winner of the Battle of the Badges, the charity boxing match between fire and police, he was as at home wearing gloves as not. But there was something eminently more satisfying about delivering a pounding bare-knuckled. Definitely more primal.

"Boys, we can do this the hard way or the easy way."

Red Suit turned, wearing the gaze of a man not quite so wasted that Beck would have reservations about kicking ass.

Cue elfish smile. Hello, holiday nuclear.

"But I'll warn you, amigo," Beck said. "The hard way is my favorite."

❄ ❄ ❄

"It's like the Justice League of hot bartenders."

Mel's hazel eyes shone as bright as the red-suited Santas on a zombified trail down Milwaukee Avenue. "And I've got my eye on Thor."

Gingerly, Darcy planted her high-heeled boots on the treacherous sidewalk outside the wine bar where they had spent the night dishing. Soft, nonthreatening flakes melted as soon as they made landfall on her cashmere coat, but with five more inches forecast tonight, Darcy was unimpressed with the peaceful snow globe vibe. Native Chicagoans knew better.

"You have your superhero mythology mixed up. Thor's part of the Avengers, not the Justice League. Maybe you've got your lusty eye on Aquaman or Green Lantern, both of whom are generally acknowledged as inferior in the superhero pantheon."

"You would know that, nerdette."

"It's my job to," Darcy said. "I get so many requests for bulging men in tights, I could write a thesis on it."

Mel grasped Darcy's arm so forcefully she almost hit the deck on her Michael Kors–covered butt.

"You've got to come with me! The last time I was there, Thor—"

"Or Aquaman."

She waved the hand not death-gripping the sleeve of Darcy's coat. "—made his interest very clear. I'm sure tonight's the night. My womb's feeling all tingly."

"Might want to check that out with your doctor," Darcy retorted.

Mel made a face beneath her dirty blond curls. Piqued looked super cute on her.

"Here I am," Darcy announced as they drew alongside the '96 Volvo jalopy her friend Brady had lent her for what was supposed to be a fleeting visit to Chicago. The month she had taken out of her life to shepherd Grams through her recovery from a stroke had stretched to three, but now the old girl was almost back to her crotchety, razor-tongued self. By the time the last New Year's Eve firework had exploded over Navy Pier, the spectacular Chicago skyline would be perfectly framed in Darcy's rearview mirror. Next stop, Austin, Texas, and that spanking new job.

"Always be moving" was her motto.

"This town isn't big enough for me and my father" was a close second.

She would miss Mel, though, who had kept her entertained through the fall with dating horror stories that made Darcy laugh-pee every time. The woman was a magnet for every panty-sniffing mouth breather in Chicagoland.

Darcy hugged her girl. "Thanks for hanging and listening to me whine about my family." The Cochrane holiday photo shoot that afternoon, first in a number of dreaded family events dotting her schedule over the next couple of weeks, had left Darcy more than a little on edge.

"Ah, those little shits I teach have primed me well. But you know what's the perfect antidote to whining? Drooling. Panting. Moaning." Mel squeezed Darcy's arm tighter as she punctuated each huskily spoken word. "It's hard to whine when your mouth's filled with a sexy bartender's tongue or other interesting body parts."

Darcy considered her friend's arguments. She had to admit that chilling with the walker-and-Jell-O set at Grams's upscale nursing home had put a decided crimp in her love life. "My sex point average *is* at an all-time low."

"Which is why you should be coming to this bar with me." Mel linked Darcy's arm like it was a done deal. "I can't believe you're all dressed up like a North Shore princess—"

"Watch your mouth, bitch. It's Gold Coast. Higher property values," Darcy said, referring to the tony Chicago enclave where she'd spent her formative years.

Her friend flashed a toothy grin. "And you don't want to use those pearls to flirt with a little rough? Come on, help this J.Crew–clad pleb out."

"You know I only got trussed up like this so I wouldn't scare Grams with my usual threads." Actually, Grams would have taken Darcy's biker chic threads and all they revealed in stride. Not so the rest of the Cochranes. The glare her father daggered her way a few hours ago was evidence enough that she was still a crushing disappointment to him. And as much as she would have loved to grace the shoot in ripped jeans and a tank, it would have smacked of a tad too much teenage rebellion for a twenty-five-year-old woman. Instead, she'd donned the designer twinset of boring to keep the peace.

"Just a half hour playing my wing girl," Mel pleaded. "I can't go in alone. What would that look like?"

Sighing, Darcy inched away from the car. In truth, she didn't want the night to be over quite yet. With the holidays just around the corner, her chances to hang with Mel were diminishing rapidly.

"Lead the way to bartender nirvana."

Holding on to each other as they walked a couple of blocks, they managed to remain upright on the slippery walk, no mean feat for women sporting weather-inappropriate footwear.

They were laughing so hard at the sight of yet another drunken Santa lurching down the street, this one with a healthy serving of chalky butt cheek on display—"Shrinkage alert!" yelled Mel—that it took Darcy a moment to realize they'd turned a corner. This bite of Damen Avenue was hopping with a steady stream of bar crawlers, suburbanites, and friends meeting for pre-holiday drinks. It was also achingly familiar. With each crunch of hard-packed snow underfoot, icicles of dread jabbed Darcy's chest.

"What's the name of this bar, Mel?"

"I dunno. Something Irish, Dennehy's or Donnelly's."

What was the likelihood there were two Irish bars on the same block?

Oh, balls.

"Dempsey's," Mel announced. The muted strains of the Pogues' holiday classic "Fairytale of New York" pulsed against the bar's heavy oak door.

Dempsey's. Darcy had driven by it a few times since her return, and on each pass she had floored it. Ridiculous, she knew. It was just a bar and he was just a boy. A man, now.

He might not work here.

It might be under new management.

But the kick of her heart to her ribs said nothing had changed. The Dempseys still ruled this little corner of green in Chicago just like the boy she once knew still took up valuable mental real estate. A spot that ignited whenever Darcy saw firefighters or boxers or Irishmen or . . . *damn* . . . Suddenly curiosity overruled her dread. Benevolent gods would ensure he had grown into a pot-bellied troll with a receding hairline and bad skin from a diet of Portillo's hot dogs and deep-dish pizza. A girl could hope, anyway.

Didn't she owe it to herself to find out? If he was behind that door, didn't she owe it to herself to show him what he had missed by walking away from her all those years ago?

Bring it on.

Letting determination flavored with old-fashioned payback fuel her steps, Darcy reached for the wrought-iron handle. But before she could get a grip, the door crashed open and *Bam!* a large red blur filled her vision—and dropped her on her ass. Her ankle twisted as she hit the cold, punishing street.

The blur—more of a sack, really—rolled off her leg.

Then it spoke.

"Christ, I'm sorry," it slurred through a beer-stained slash of white cotton. "I didn't mean to—"

Whatever it didn't mean to do, she would never know. Red Sack was violently wrenched aside. Huge hands settled on her shoulders and pulled her to a sitting position.

Oh, God. Time and space contracted with her heart, bringing an onslaught of sensation in its wake. He smelled the same—a clean, male spice that made her light-headed. Seven years, and he still smelled like the boy she had held tight inside her soul all this time.

He spoke, the exact words inaudible above the beat of her silly heart. The timbre of his voice was deeper, huskier, but its power to ripple through her and set her quivering with need had in no way diminished. Or perhaps it was just the frigid temperatures. Yes, that had to be it. Her coat had fallen open except for one precariously fastened button; her wool skirt had ridden up to midthigh. She looked ridiculous, and not just because she was lying on a snowy street thanks to what she realized now was yet another wasted Santa. Seriously, there ought to be a law against that sort of thing.

With a bolstering breath, she lifted her eyelids to meet the gaze of Beck Rivera.

Who was not looking at her.

His unstinting focus was on her limbs, his sure hands tracing over her extremities, seeking out injuries. Weaknesses. Her heart cranked out a few more beats than were safe. Her mind scrambled for Zen. While it was startling to have him touching her so intimately, at least the moment gave her a chance to examine *him* unnoticed.

Scimitar-curved cheekbones, a nose broken several (more) times, and, mother of God, a scruffy lumberjack beard. That was so damn hot and not in the least bit troll like. He looked as serious as ever, but the gravity seemed more intensified on his twenty-six-year-old face. That dark hair, formerly a wavy handful of sin she loved tunneling her fingers through, was now close-cropped and split, not by a parting, but by a scar. Recent, by the looks of its raw, pink anger. He had cracked open his skull.

Idiot.

"What an asshole!" Mel shot a death glare at the Santa who had fallen—or more likely, was pushed—on Darcy. A trio of men in red were hauling up the troublemaker as he muttered something about a lawsuit that'd "send your Mick bar back to the Stone Age." Ignoring the threat, Beck kept up his thorough damage assessment, hot hands moving over soft knees and trembling thighs.

"Are you hurt?" he asked, now treating her to a full proton blast of the Beck Rivera gaze. More navy than blue, the shade used to shift often with his variable moods. But now those eyes registered distant, polite. Was she hurt? Not physically. Just incredibly pissed that the boy she had adored for two years in a previous lifetime had blocked her from his mind.

For God's sake, the shit head didn't recognize her!

"I don't think so," she said in a clipped tone.

"Can you stand?" He was already dragging her up with those arms as thick as her calves.

Agh! Sharp pain lanced through her ankle. He caught her as she crumpled, sweeping her into his arms and moving toward the pub in one sinuous, catlike movement. She had no choice but to loop her hands around his neck, his body heat the perfect counterbalance to her freezing butt cheeks.

"Should we call an ambulance?" Mel asked, concern coloring her voice.

"No," he said sternly. "Get the door."

Mel jumped forward and pulled the handle. A gush of warmth, spiced with memories, escaped the bar, and Darcy realized that she really needed to speak up.

"Beck, it's Darcy." She mentally cringed at having to reintroduce herself after all they had meant to each other, or as was now becoming painfully obvious, all she had *not* meant to him. Her face heated despite her best efforts to stay chill. "Darcy Cochrane."

Staring straight ahead, Beck's lips twitched.

"I know, *princesa*."

chapter 2

. . . .

With alarming ease, Beck plowed through the candy cane–colored haze to the far end of the bar, where he pointedly glared at the expansive backs of two men sitting on stools.

"McElroy," Beck said impatiently.

The men turned, took one look at Beck, another at Darcy, and immediately stood.

"Here you go, miss," one of them said deferentially, while the other made way for Mel.

"Oh, I'm quite all right. You don't need to do that."

Beck set her down on one of the vacated seats and popped the last hold-out button on her coat. It parted, almost indecently, and *ta da!* was whipped from her body like a magician's tablecloth trick. He hung it on a convenient coat hook.

Whoa, that was hot. Flushing at this potent demonstration of his sharp movements and impressive reflexes, along with all the erotic memories they conjured, she caught Mel's eye. Or her jaw, really, which was grazing the floor.

"Shut it," Darcy muttered to her friend, who promptly closed her mouth and eyed the rather gorgeous African American hunk who had surrendered his seat. The logo of the Chicago Fire Department popped above a pec that rivaled The Rock's.

"So, are you a firefighter?" Mel asked, eyelashes batting vehemently, all blond innocence.

CFD Beefcake opened his mouth, but Beck spoke first. "Lieutenant McElroy's got fourteen years on the job, twelve of them blissfully married."

A sheepish McElroy shrugged his broad shoulders. "Guilty."

Mel sighed good-naturedly and climbed onto the next stool. "No worries, my hormones are invested elsewhere." Once settled comfortably, she turned to Darcy. "Good seats, girl. How we doing?"

"Not bad. Think I just turned my ankle."

"Do you mind if I look?" Beck asked in a low voice that made her uncomfortably warm.

"I'm sure it's fine." Beck's version of "looking" would invariably involve touching, and she readily admitted that she had enjoyed the previews a little too much out on the street. Determined to prove her well-being, she placed her right foot on the floor with purpose.

Bad move. There was no hiding the grimace that screwed up her face.

"Stop being so brave and let him take a look," Mel said, giving Beck an appreciative twice-over. "Qualified EMT along with those firefighter chops, I assume?"

"Uh-huh."

Darcy chewed on her lower lip while Beck waited. He was good at waiting, always had been.

"If you don't mind," she said primly, channeling her grandmother.

He hunkered down and held her booted foot with astonishing reverence, as if trying to determine the best access point for a tricky rescue. Almost leisurely, he unzipped the soft suede and slipped it from her foot. *Zing!* Another sizzle of sensation snaked through her insides.

Opaque tights covered her legs and the evidence of how she had been spending her time all these years. He moved his hands knowledgeably over her ankle, testing with his thumbs, rolling the joint.

"Anything?" he asked, looking up with those serious blue eyes.

Could she plead the Fifth? The truth would be so damn incriminating. An acutely pleasurable ache settled between her thighs, accompanied by an acutely pleasurable dampness.

"It's just a twinge." Darcy's gaze dropped to the top of Beck's head, her heart throbbing as much as her ankle. That scar . . . what had he done?

"No swelling, from what I can see," he murmured.

In the ankle area, no. Other areas, however, swelled like a tidal surge. Her breasts, the sensitive area between her legs as she tried not to squirm against the bar stool.

He stood, leaving her foot bootless and her chest strangely empty.

"Hands."

"Excuse me?"

"Show me your hands."

When she failed to react quickly enough to his order, he took her hands and examined the palms. They were raw from her fall but the skin was intact. However, instead of letting them go, he curled his long, sensuous fingers around hers and squeezed. Unexpected tears of surprise stung the backs of her eyelids at his gentle touch.

"Darcy."

"Beck."

"How do you want to do this?"

She fought a smile. Barely won. Beck had never been one to waste words. "Seven years in a hundred and forty characters or less? Let's see. College in Boston, traveled the world, returned to Chicago when Grams had a stroke three months ago. She's on the mend."

His eyes softened. "Sorry to hear about your grandmother. She's a nice lady."

At Darcy's eyebrow lift calling bullshit, Beck's wicked lips shaded a hint of a smile. "Okay, she's crazy as a loon with a tongue that could slice prune cans, but I always liked her. Do you still draw?"

The lie came easily. "No."

"And the rest of the family?"

"My parents finally divorced, which was really for the best. Jack's running my father's empire in London." Unlike Darcy, her brother was never subjected to the same pressures to fulfill some grander role in the Cochrane dynasty. No need, when he was fast becoming a clone of her father.

Her turn. "How about you?"

"With CFD for seven years as of last September. That and this place keep me busy."

So, barely a month after he dumped her, he got his wish and joined his brothers in the service. A small surge of jealousy pinched her. She wasn't proud of it.

"Your family good?" With difficulty, she dragged her gaze away from his ruggedly compelling face to drink in the sausage fest behind the bar. Luke, with mink brown waves framing his handsome features, was not all that changed except for a slight hardness around his eyes. The tall blond must be Gage; he'd been barely sixteen when she saw him last at Sean and Logan's funeral. Now he rocked a Hemsworth brother vibe as he impressed a gaggle of girls with a cocktail shaker at the other end of the bar. Mel's Thor, Darcy assumed.

"They're great," he said. "All in. Even Alexandra."

"Your father would be proud. Logan, too."

Those shocking blue eyes flashed, and remembrance of that night flooded the space between them. The night they both lost something, and everything changed.

He angled his thumbs to stroke her pulse in tight, erotic circles. Unadulterated lust slammed through her. The power he had over her still . . . it electrified her to the core. Just one look stripped her bare and stunned her with want.

An attention-grabbing cough sliced through the loaded silence.

"Hi, I'm Mel." Her friend thrust out her hand.

Beck released Darcy's hands, shook Mel's, and had already redirected his burning focus back to Darcy before he spoke his name. "Beck Rivera."

Okay, this has been awesome. "We should go," Darcy said.

"After you've rested that ankle and we've had a drink," Mel chimed in. "A couple of G and Ts, please. Heavy on the G."

"Sure, coming right up." Beck wrapped Darcy in an all-encompassing look that left her feeling she'd been touched in an intimate way—and enjoyed it far too much. "Leave your boot off in case the ankle swells. I'll check back on it later."

He lifted a wooden flap at the end of the bar and went back to work.

"Okay, spill the juicy deets," Mel intoned. "Now."

"Well, my ankle really hurts when I put any weight—"

Mel cut her off with an exaggerated eye roll. "When and where did you do Wolverine?" She gestured violently to Beck just in case there was some confusion about which bearded sex god was under discussion.

"We were kids."

Mel gave her the don't-even look, which she had honed to eviscerating sharpness in the years since they had first met at Harvard.

"Popped your cherry?"

Darcy sighed heavily, caught between annoyance it

was so obvious and relief her friend knew her well enough to guess. "Popped it, then popped a cap in my heart."

"Ooh, you so ghetto, girl."

Funny, that. Maybe if she had been, things might have been different between the Gold Coast *princesa* and the dangerous, furious boy who had lit her soul on fire. Before he doused it with an ice cold vat of adios.

Mel's eyes widened in a way Darcy was sure she would not appreciate in three, two, one . . .

"He's the one you cried your eyes out over all freshman year. The guy your father hated because he was a gangbanger."

Ex-gangbanger, saved by the Dempsey fostering machine when his biological father died during a drug deal gone bad. Not that she had learned those details from Beck, who shared nothing. Jack had filled her in, trying to scare her away from him.

"How do you remember this stuff?"

Mel tapped her temple. "Mind like a steel trap. Other body parts as well, which I hope to be demonstrating before the night is through." She waggled her eyebrows and directed a sexy pout in Gage's direction. "So we have firefighting, bartending brothers—"

"Foster brothers, taken in by Sean and Mary Dempsey. They couldn't have children of their own so they were big on spreading the love to kids who needed it, five boys and a girl. Sean was a big-time fire chief who died on the job just over seven years ago. The oldest son, Logan, died in the same fire."

"Holy shit."

"A couple of them—" She nodded at Luke behind the bar. Intimidating Wyatt was nowhere to be seen. "—did a stint in the Marines first."

Mel's twisted expression depicted a battle between sympathy for the city's fallen and imminent collapse into a puddle of lust. "Hot ex-marine Chirish firefighters. Jesus, my panties are going to melt."

The lust option. Excellent choice, madam.

"Not Irish, just raised that way. And your panties melted about five minutes ago, you dirty bird."

Mel grinned. "True to the last drop. What's the skinny on my man, Thor?"

There was something about him, something different that teased the cold edges of Darcy's mind and refused to come in to the open. "That's Gage and from here, he fills out his shirt and jeans *reeeeal* nice. What else do you need to know?"

"Too fucking right," Mel said, laughing that girlish tinkle, step one of her slide into flirt mode.

"That shit's wasted on me, you know."

She giggled inanely. "Just warming the pipes. And I think from the look the cherry popper is giving you, things will be getting nice and warm in Darcyland very soon."

Lifting her eyes to Beck took effort, as did meeting the unerringly scorching look he was laying on her. So much for benevolent gods. He had to go and grow hotter over the years. Strong arms corded with sculpted muscles stretched his tee sleeves to the limits, walking temptation in a six-foot-two package. Virile, warrior-like, and a beard to boot! Hot damn, she loved a good smattering of facial hair.

Concern lined Mel's brow. "What happened, exactly? I know you met in high school, but all I can really recall is the ugly crying before the inevitable graduation to 'guys suck.'"

"If they're any good, they will," they said in unison, drumming the bar with a quick one-two. *Ba-boom.*

Darcy's laughter gave way to a sigh. "He was a friend of my brother's. They used to train together at a boxing gym."

That look came over Mel again, the one where her brain might disintegrate to lust-mush any second.

"Yes, Melanie, he was a boxer. Control yourself." Admittedly, it had been verra, verra sexy.

"And?"

"For a year"—*and two months, one week, three days*—"he didn't breathe a word to me. He'd come over to play video games with Jack and I'd try to get him to open up, but it was like talking to a brick wall. An unbelievably sexy brick wall. I thought he hated me. He'd get this crimp between his eyebrows every time he looked at me like he'd smelled rotten eggs. Or was trying to solve a really difficult math problem."

"Kind of like how he's looking at you now?"

No need to lift her gaze to verify that his eyes were still trained on her. Her skin sizzled with his penetrating heat.

A patchwork of sensual images grabbed hold. Their first kiss during a winter festival at Lincoln Park Zoo, her hot chocolate cooling while his lips kept her warm. A yearlong diet of sexy smooches and teenage exploration, stopping short of home base because Beck refused to take full advantage.

"I begged him to do the deed, but he said I was too young. Finally, when I turned eighteen, he—" She stopped as memories of Beck's blunt prizefighter hands on her body, seeking out erotic flash points and bringing her to blistering release, assaulted her senses.

"Did you good?"

"So good," she said, lowering her voice though the bar's noisy hum provided adequate cover. "I was gaga about him and I thought it was mutual until he sent me packing."

Darcy still remembered his final words to her all those years ago, spoken in that graveled voice, dripping with sex and menace. Only a month after he had made her a full-fledged woman and claimed every part of her.

Forget you ever met me, Darcy.

And she had, after a year—or five. She stowed the boy in her brain's basement and went on to a new life, one she chose for herself instead of following the gated path her father had insisted she travel. Underneath this designer sweater and perfectly cut skirt was the project she had been working on for years. A well-traveled, well-adjusted, reinvented woman.

"You're not a kid anymore," Mel said. Despite only seeing each other a few times a year, her friend could always intuit when Darcy was about to send out invites to the pity party. "You should go for it."

"Go for what?"

"School the cherry popper. Make him beg. Milk. Him. Dry."

Though Darcy had been on that very wavelength before actually coming face-to-face with Beck, now that he was in her immediate orbit, looking hot as sin and twice as dangerous, doubts assailed her. "Hooking up with the old flame who took my virginity and cast me aside quicker than the used condom? That seems a bit—"

"—revengey," Mel finished with a smug grin.

"Sad. It seems sad. I'm not looking for revenge. Revenge is for people who care." She most definitely did not care about Beck Rivera and his soulful eyes. Nor did she care about that livid scar on his head or how he came by it. And no way in hell did she care about how good his ass looked in denim. Those trim, tight glutes were the natural resting point for a gaze that started at the broad triangle of his shoulders and traveled down his solid back, tapering waist, and slim hips. Even from behind, the man was painfully beautiful.

Did not care.

"You lied to him," Mel said, her brows veed. "About your art."

So she had. Explaining how her life had turned out would open a can of worms and invite unwanted scrutiny. While wearing the costume of her alter ego, the Gold Coast princess, she could keep her true identity hidden. She didn't owe him any explanations. She didn't owe him a thing.

"Like I said, don't care."

"So bang that hot firefightin' ass and don't care," Mel said. "And hope to God he's better at that than he is at tending bar. I'm parched over here."

Bang him and don't care. Not revenge, necessarily, just raising her sex point average. And if, in the process, she happened to remind him of everything he had given up by casting her aside? Well, that was just extra credit.

Forget you ever met me, Darcy.

Maybe it was time to ensure Beck Rivera never forgot he met her.

chapter 3

. . . .

*O*f all the bars in all the world, she had to be tackled to the ground outside his. And she had hardly changed. Beck's man card required he knew subshit about designer duds, but even he could tell those fancy fabrics clinging fondly to her curves and the pearls around her swanlike neck were the real deal. The *princesa* still oozed money, class, and keep-the-fuck-away.

"She looks familiar," Luke said as Beck poured shots of gin.

"Darcy Cochrane. Another lifetime."

Luke's mouth tightened in recognition. "She was at the funeral. Her father owns the *Trib*?"

"And *Chicago* magazine, a slice of the Cubs, part of the United Center."

"She's grown up fine," Luke mused.

True that. The prettiest girl Beck had ever known was

now a knockout on an epic scale. Sleek hair pulled tight off her face in a swishy ebony fall. High, haughty cheekbones, ruby pink lips, a chin as stubborn as her father's. The feel of her curves beneath his searching hands left the impression of a heaven-formed, amazingly built woman.

"She's been traveling the world," he said, because Luke seemed to expect something more. She had skipped any mention of her marriage from the catch-up checklist, though he noticed she wore no ring. Admittedly not compelling evidence, and that it spiked his pulse annoyed the bejesus out of him. The day Luke had pointed out the engagement notice in her father's paper, eighteen months after they had split, Beck had punched a wall so hard he broke his hand. Whatever Darcy's situation now, apparently she could drop her jet-setting life for three months to help her grandmother.

"Well, now she's back," Luke said. "Whatcha gonna do about it?"

Beck's heart hitched and tripped out a ragged beat. She was the cliché, the one who got away, and now she was here, a glowing second chance. A do-over.

Except she was still so far out of his league that she may as well be crater hopping on the moon. And oh yeah, he had dumped her without explanation in the name of doing her a favor.

Right.

"It's not quite so simp—"

"Jesus Christ, ladies, could you put a plug in your hourly gossip and help me out here?" Gage threw his hands up dramatically in case the caps-lock delivery didn't reflect sufficiently *The Real Housewives of New Jersey* vibe.

"You're doing fine, Short Stack," Luke returned, clearly amused. "Think of all the tips you're making."

"Tips I'm sharing with you dickheads. When I should be keeping them because I'm so fucking awesome."

With both hands in perpetual motion, Gage deftly added vodka shots to a couple of metal shakers, then got busy squeezing lime halves into the mix. His T-shirt advised his fans to Feel Safe at Night: Sleep with a Firefighter.

A group of enthusiastic female customers cheered Gage on and slammed a couple of twenties down on the bar. Their youngest brother had read an article on mixology last year and introduced a special cocktail menu that no one could get right the nights he was on shift at Engine 6. His grand pretentions were a menace, but they loved him all the same.

It had taken Beck awhile to get on that page. By the time he was pulled out of the foster care system into Waif and Stray Central at the Dempseys, he was thirteen years old, and the rest of the kids had been part of the family for years. A well-established unit with rituals and connections and nuances he could never hope to understand. He spoke to no one for the first six months, just nodded to Mary when she asked if he'd had enough to eat and grunted at Sean for everything else. Unfortunately, he had to share a room with a ten-year-old Gage, and the kid would not shut up.

Want to read my Spider-Man *comics?* Gage was obsessed with *Spider-Man.* The transformation from wimp to superhero really appealed to him.

Beck had ignored him. Not there to make friends, he'd already been kicked out of two families because of his "emotional dissociation," which apparently meant he wasn't emotional enough. Like he was a robot. He'd show them robot. Because if he showed them anything else— the rage inside him, the fury spitting for a target—they would return him as defective, anyway. The Dempseys had five foster kids already, and he was the last one in. Even a fucked-up junior banger like him knew what that meant.

Last in, first out.

But Gage would not give up. His sunny disposition bugged the shit out of Beck until one day he threw the little runt's latest peace offering, a Game Boy, against a wall. And then he called him names. Queer. Fag. Words that filled Beck with shame to this day. While waiting for Gage to rat him out to Sean, just in from his shift at the firehouse and pounding his steel-toed boots up the stairs, Beck refused to look at Gage. Refused to give him the satisfaction. But as his heart galloped in time with Sean's heavy tread, two piercing realizations smacked him upside the head.

He was so frickin' tired.

And he wanted to stay.

He wanted to stop fighting, but his mouth couldn't shape the words in his heart, and now it was too late.

Sean curved his head around the door and, after ten mind-blurring seconds, pulled back with a mere nod. Gage hadn't snitched. Though he didn't fully understand why, Beck was overwhelmed with a gratitude that warmed his cold, neglected heart. His little brother, more annoying than all get out and one of the best people Beck knew, had smiled like he'd won a prize and dropped the latest issue of *Spider-Man* on Beck's bed.

Gage and Beck had been on the same page ever since, and it opened the floodgates with the rest of them. When Logan took Beck to the gym to try his hands at boxing, Beck knew he was in the right place and with the right people at last.

But growing up Dempsey was a double-edged sword. If not for them, he might have been content with an ordinary girl instead of an upper-crust babe like Darcy. The problem with being a Dempsey is that they made you believe anything was possible.

"You need to talk to her," Luke said, jolting Beck back to the present.

Beck shrugged his response, all those old insecurities coming back to bite his neck. Talking had never worked for him. And what could he say after all these years? *I was crazy about you, but I let you go for your own good.* Because that shit would fly. Women just loved being told what was good for them.

Luke took an order from the adorable blonde who'd been manhandled by Red Suit. Clearly interested in more than a rum and Coke, her face fell when his brother didn't respond to her overt flirting. With his divorce recently finalized, Luke had yet to reach the bang-his-way-out-of-his-misery step. It would come.

Beck remembered it well.

Gin and tonics in hand, he ambled over to the side of the bar, frowning when he found no sign of Darcy. Her coat still hung on the hook but her boot was gone. Darcy's friend was groping the bicep of Jacob Scott, one of Beck's coworkers on the truck, but paused to thumb over her shoulder. "Little leprechaunette's room."

"Think I'll take that break now," he said to Luke, who smirked at that.

Smug bastard.

"Sure, Becky. Take all the time you need."

Not even Luke's use of the girly nickname Beck had been plagued with as a kid could quell the anticipation thrumming through him. Sort of like the energy sparking his blood before a run or a fight. He didn't want to punch anyone, but he wouldn't say no to stoking a fire. First, though, he wanted to talk more. Find out what she'd been up to all these years.

And touch her. Definitely touch her.

He found her in the corridor heading to the restrooms, and covertly he watched as she tentatively tested out her ankle with brief stops to flex her foot. Satisfied she was back in business, she leaned her back against the wall, and he took a blessed moment to admire the curved wave of her body as she texted on her phone with quick, supple fingers. He used to love how fast those fingers moved, creating portraits in charcoal, quick sketches that she would later develop into masterpieces. It was their only communication during that first year of nonversation. She, trying to capture his mood while he sat in her family's den. He, biding his time, scheming to capture her heart.

"How's the ankle?"

She lifted her tilty-green gaze, but there was no surprise at seeing him. "I'll live."

He stared, the need in him rising more quickly than expected as every cell in his body clamored for action and release. A fiery blush crept up her neck. When the sweep of heat tagged her cheekbones, she made a disgruntled noise in the back of her throat, and knowing he still had that effect on her had his dick at attention in an instant.

"Some things don't change, I see," she said as she slipped her phone into a purse slung over her shoulder. "You've not become a sparkling conversationalist in the intervening years, Beck."

"We never needed to talk, *princesa*."

Man, how she used to hate that endearment, though in days past, using it had sparked some of their most pleasurable moments together. He would goad her until her cheeks flushed and his cock swelled and relief could only come from sinking his fingers in her hair, her mouth, her slick-for-him sex.

Now, on a razor's edge, the moment lived, then deflated when she gave him a nervy smile. She looked unsure, vulnerable, not at all like the girl he knew.

"What are you up to these days?" he asked.

Thoughts ran circles over her face as she geared up to . . . *huh*. Lie her sweet ass off.

"This and that. Mostly helping with Grams's recovery and organizing the charity fund-raiser for the homeless she hosts each year. Big party in a couple of weeks."

Maybe *this* was a boyfriend or *that* was a husband.

"How's Preston Collins III?"

Her composure took another hit, but on the beat of three she picked herself right back up and smoothed her expression to a cool slate.

"I've no idea."

"So your marriage didn't work out?"

"I never got married. That was something my father wanted, not me."

There was no time to enjoy the sweet balm of relief those words created in his chest. Something else was going on here, a restlessness about her that matched his own edgy mood. The tell in her eyes piqued his interest. Time to double down.

"So how mad at me are you right now?"

She sucked in a breath. "Mad? At you? Why would I be mad at you?"

"Oh, I dunno." Because he had dropped her like a bad habit. "You seem uncomfortable at seeing me again. Pissy."

"Beck," she said in the tone of one about to explain something to a dimwit. "When I was eighteen years old, you broke my heart. Stomped on it. Pulverized it into a mess I thought would be irreparable. I cried for two months, cut my hair and dyed it a really awful blond, let it grow out, made friends in college. I even had a boy-friend, a hot linebacker who was excellent in bed. But every day since, I've wished I was here with a guy who voluntarily runs into burning buildings. I wanted to be waiting at home with my heart stuck to the roof of my mouth, hoping he'd text me whenever a warehouse fire was splashed all over the local news. I longed to be getting into arguments about whether it was okay to use my family's money to get us a better apartment because my man was so proud he insisted on supporting us on his city salary."

"So, still mad."

She angled her head, taking him in like he was a bug not worthy of her attention. And then she gave him a huge-ass smile.

Fuckin' A! Hell, fuckin' B, C, D, *and* E. He felt like he'd been pumped with a triple dose of tropical sunshine.

"Sorry, just needed to get it out," she said. "You dumped me a month after we had sex for the first time and that kind of thing is enough to give a girl a complex. I had it in my head that I must have been god-awful in the sack."

Mierda. Surely she had not been living with that?

She stayed the tip-of-his-tongue protest with a hand, and that she still had the imperious thing going on put his groin on serious notice.

"But I realized fairly quickly that it was for the best. We were from different worlds, Beck. I don't harbor any grudges."

Listening to her mature and measured assessment

should have put him at ease. Should have. But his body did not feel loose. His mind did not accept this.

"It's okay to be a little ticked off," he said, strangely ticked off himself at her self-possession. "I treated you pretty shabbily."

She arched a dark eyebrow, its delicate upward curve a message in itself. "After all this time, you'd rather I was angry. You'd rather I kept you in here"—she touched a clenched fist to the soft swell of her breast—"because it would mean I still care and you still have some power over me."

Yes, a million times, yes. He hooked her pearls to bring her closer and then, very deliberately, placed one palm against the hallway's wall inches from her heat-stained cheek.

"I'd rather you were mad because then I could make it better. Remember what I used to do to calm you down? Your dad would piss you off and then I would piss you off more and before you knew it, you were coming apart, screaming my name."

A muscle ticked at the corner of her mouth, begging for his thumb to soothe it.

So he did.

"Kissing you, touching you, every hurried fumble in my car, every time we explored each other's bodies—it was all amazing. And when after months, years of waiting, I finally drove deep inside you where I belonged, that was also amazing, Darcy. Sex had nothing to do with why we didn't work out."

There. He'd said it. As for the reasons for their split—

the real reasons—now was neither the time nor the place. Might never be, but she needed to know she was not to blame.

The soft thud of a closing door signaled that someone was exiting the restroom around the corner. A guy weaved by on his way back to the bar, and with each passing second, Beck's heart thundered in his ears.

He turned back to Darcy in time to catch her blinking away an intrusive thought. "Thank you for setting the record straight and letting me know my sexual inexperience was not a contributing factor."

Uh-oh. Sarcastic, if his snark-o-meter was calibrated right. "You said you had a complex."

"I said it was enough to give a girl a complex." She rubbed a tuft of his coarse beard between her finger and thumb, like she was testing the quality of fabric in a high-end store. "But I figured out quickly that I'm rather awesome, both in and out of the bedroom. Lots of hot college guys helped with my sexual awakening."

"Your what?"

"My sexual awakening. Those first few months of school, I jumped right in with all the zeal of a frat boy at a kegger. Discovered what I like." She tugged on his beard and it felt surprisingly good, despite the fact he was half-past pissed at the words spilling from her pert, kissable mouth. "What I don't like."

A tight band of steel squeezed around his chest, and the pounding in his ears grew louder. *He* had been the one to nurture her sex-starved body, not some Dockers-wearing college boy. Beck's nineteenth year had been one of the most painful of his life. A year of stiff sheets and balled-up tissues, every cock-stroking fantasy filled with sweet, sexy Darcy begging him to touch her, take her.

Own her.

Denying his raging needs for months, he made sure to take care of hers until finally he surrendered to her tight, virginal body the night of the funeral, in the boxing ring at the gym where he had made Sean and Logan proud so many times. Not how he had planned it at all. It was too rough, too raw, too damn visceral. But he had needed her desperately, the only drug that could numb his soul-splitting pain.

He scrubbed a hand across the scruff on his jaw. "You like the beard, *princesa*."

"It disgusts me," she deadpanned, but there was no missing the wisp of a smile on her lips. Teenage Darcy was a fiery creature, spoiled and perpetually indignant, and the ability to laugh at herself was not part of her makeup. Somewhere along the way, she had developed a sense of humor, and damn if that wasn't sexier than every one of her soft, womanly curves.

"What else about me disgusts you?"

"How long have you got?"

"Ten good inches."

She snorted. "See? Dirty mouth."

Covering her body with his, he nuzzled his raggedy jaw against her cheek and absorbed her shiver into his own. "You used to like my dirty mouth and all the magical things I could do with it."

"Teenage hormones have a lot to answer for."

"Adult ones, too." Though it killed him a little, he put a few painful inches between them and trailed a finger along her jaw, noting with satisfaction that she trembled under his touch. "It was good to see you again. Have a nice holiday."

Her expressive brow told him she liked what he'd done there. "When did you get funny, Beck Rivera?"

"Around about the time you got a sense of humor, *querida*."

There it was, that fire-bright smile. He felt like he'd swallowed the sun.

"Your shtick needs work."

"Then show me how it's done. *Bésame*." Kiss me.

She laughed, right in his face. "*Bésame el culo*."

Kiss my ass? Oh, it was *on*. Leaning in, he caged her with palms on the wall. The air around them shook with sex and need. Her lush body damn near vibrated with it.

"So demanding, *princesa*. How about I start with your mouth, then work down to your breasts, your belly, your thighs? Plenty of country to rediscover before I get to your sweet *culo*."

But before he could kiss her, she kissed him. Unexpectedly, like the Darcy of old, and expertly, like this new Darcy he liked very, very much. Her lips claimed one corner of his mouth, then the other, and he parted to let her in. An invitation she accepted with joy. He'd always loved how she approached kissing, like she approached everything—with a single-mindedness that bordered on pathological. Over the years, she had probably honed her technique with a ton of guys. He hated every fucking one of them.

His arms snaked around her involuntarily; his body had always known what it wanted where she was concerned. By the time his mind caught up, he was a goner. He gathered her closer, perversely pleased that she didn't soften immediately. He deserved to suffer. As their tongues tangled, realization shocked him stupid: no one else affected him like this, sent his heart soaring into the stratosphere and his cock punching against his zipper. A kiss, that's all it took with Darcy who had once been his fantasy girl, and was fast becoming his fantasy woman. It was like someone had opened a bottle of good lovin' wine. Vintage, seven years ago.

She had closed her eyes and the fact that she still did that during a kiss made his heart ache so sweetly. Slowly, she opened them as if waking from a dream.

"*Te necesito*, Darcy," he murmured. So strange, only with her did his first language—one he barely spoke anymore—come out. She unlocked that primal part of him.

Their lips met again in a rush of heat and desire, and this time he abandoned his misguided attempt at coolness. It had never been a game with her. She clutched his shoulders, digging into his skin, and he couldn't get enough of the bite of her. Her soft mouth, her clawing fingers, the fight in her body. She let loose a groan he felt all the way to his balls.

Crowd noise filtered through from the bar, reminding him that they were in far too public a place. Lifting her, he headed a few short feet to the back office and pushed his way through, kicking the door shut behind him. Too small for anything, it was perfect for this. He sat her on the desk, on top of a pile of invoices. Her purse hit the floor. She was breathing heavily, the swells of her breasts lifting her pearls.

"Is there someone else?" he asked, needing to know for a million reasons, none of them good for his sanity.

"Not at the moment." She reached for his belt and undid the buckle while he pushed her skirt up her thighs. Thick woolen tights covered her legs, and the memory of her peaches-and-cream skin made his mouth water.

"Hurry," she said, her eyes wild. "Please."

This was moving at lightning speed, but she'd get no complaints from him. Next time—and yes, there would be a next time—he'd take it slow. Right now, he needed to be inside her, feel the clutch of her silken folds around his cock, find the pleasure he craved after a shitty couple of months. After far too long without her.

Quickly, he produced a condom and rolled it on while she watched approvingly. His hands shot up her skirt, seeking out the top of her tights so he could yank them south, but the snugness of the fabric over her hips made it difficult to get purchase.

"I think we need to—"

"Rip it, Beck," she whispered.

"What?"

"Rip it." She dragged his hand between her thighs, and he could feel her pulsing with want right there. A throaty moan escaped her lips as he applied more pressure. "Please. Now."

Rip it. Get inside her. No waiting, no seduction, no

fucking games. Just Darcy with that hot brew of pleading
and ordering that destroyed him every time. He pulled
the thick wool away from her body and, after a couple of
tries, tore it down the seam. Slipping his fingers inside, he
pushed aside her panties and found her soaked.

"Jesus, Darcy. You're—"

"Yes, yes, I am," she said, grinding her pliant heat on
his hand. She hooked a finger in his jeans pocket and
drew him toward her. "Do something about it."

Yes, ma'am.

His mouth crushed hers, and then it was all hot hands
and slick tongues. His on her, hers on him. Stroking with
velvet licks inside her demanding mouth. Taking time-
outs to watch as her pale hands pumped his cock, dark
and pulsing even while sheathed. Memories he'd locked
down broke through and added an indescribably sweet
edge. Darcy giving her body to him the night he buried
the two men he loved the most. Darcy making it better
before he made it worse.

She felt it, too, he could tell. Remembrance flickered
through her green eyes and he entered her just then, like
that one action could seal the bond between past and
present. He held still for untold heartbeats, ostensibly letting her adjust to his expanding size, but really because he
needed to grasp onto this for a few seconds longer before
the tethers of his waning control snapped.

One, two, ah . . . He cupped her jaw, enjoying immensely the delicate feel of her bones and how the softness of her skin churned something inside him. He
plundered her mouth and mapped it with his tongue,

giving her what she wanted, taking what he needed. A wave of clenching pleasure slammed into his midsection. Only then did he withdraw and plunge deep.

So damn good.

With his hands on her wool-covered ass, he urged her closer, tighter, the claustrophobic binding of their clothing adding another layer to the pleasure. It wasn't enough. He jerked at the hem of her sweater, anxious to see the changes time had wrought on her body, only to be met with resistance. She pushed his hand away.

"No—no—we don't have time." A shocking vulnerability shone from her eyes. Was she unsure of being naked? Because he would not allow it. "Just take me there, Beck."

Take me there. The same words she would beg when they were too young to even know their significance. It might have meant simple pleasure or outright oblivion. He had hoped it meant forever.

He did as he was told. Fucked her harder, got lost in the feel of her, took her to that place. Slick suction where their bodies joined fell into a hot rhythm with their fevered pants. Desperate thrusts and pulls ramped up his desire so fast he had to actively slow it down to make sure he lasted. This woman was so hot. And Christ, he wanted to burn.

Her moans got louder, the clench of her silken muscles tighter.

"Come for me, Darcy. *Sé mía.*" Be mine.

"Beck," she whispered. Her tight channel clamped around his cock, and in every cell he felt the shatter of her orgasm as it unraveled through her body. It triggered his own release, and he let go with a roar, pumping every last ounce of tension and need into her.

Un-fucking-real.

"Hmm," she hummed after a couple of minutes spent panting their way back to even breathing levels.

"*Sí*," he managed.

She laughed. "That Spanish gets me every time."

How lucky was he to have found her, right here, right now, as if he'd wished for it? Kissing her softly, he worked the condom off and disposed of it. She kissed him back, caressing his mouth with sexy kitten licks that melted his insides and hardened him everywhere else.

"I can't leave the bar now," he said, "but I can see you later."

Keeping her gaze low, she adjusted her skirt to cover the ripped tights, like she could hide the glorious sleaziness of what they had just done. "I . . . I don't think so."

"It wasn't a request, *princesa*."

Her head snapped back and a flash of the old Darcy sparked in her sea-green eyes. "I don't follow orders anymore. Not my father's, not yours, not any man's." Standing tall, she gave his dick a gentle tug. "It was great seeing you again, Beck. *Feliz Navidad*."

And before he could muster an argument or shove his still aching dick in his pants, she was out the door, moving astonishingly fast for someone who had twisted her ankle not half an hour ago.

Five seconds passed in disbelief, another ten in outright awe. He forced himself to swallow this devastating dose of reality: he had just been wham-bammed by Darcy Cochrane and then she had said good-bye with a dick shake.

A dick shake!

The door flapped open and his heart boosted in hope before plummeting to the floor, along with his flagging cock. It was only Luke with that well-worn smirk on his face.

"For fuck's sake, Becky, how about you put your dick back in your pants and come help us out here?"

chapter 4

· · · · · · · · · · · · ·

Something was off here.

Beck strummed the steering wheel of his truck and
peered up at the gray, nondescript building on this in-
dustrial stretch of Clybourn. A construction site a half
block down instilled hope that the area might be up-and-
coming, though that claim had been made about this
neighborhood before. Not that "neighborhood" really
applied—it was no neighbors, all hood.

He checked the torn-off slip of paper in his hand,
covered in Gage's loopy writing. The snooty butler at the
Cochrane mansion in the Gold Coast said Miss Cochrane
was not residing there, which left Beck to tap his usual
sources. Marcy at the DMV had turned up mothereffin'
zilch, and he still owed her sister a date. Finally Gage had
come through with a call to Darcy's drinking buddy—
Melissa or Paula or something.

He needed to see her again. Her taste still coated his mouth, honey-sweet, exactly as he remembered it from all those years ago. How could she taste the same and how could his body still react like that? Even now, the memory of her eager lips and that surrendering sigh as she came gave him pleasure he had no right to enjoy. Not after how he had let her down, treated her as no better than something stuck to the bottom of his boots.

But lust makes monsters of us all, and this monster was greedy for more.

Sucking a sharp breath of snow-tinged air, he pressed each label-less button on the intercom panel in turn. The metallic buzz echoed in the quiet, broken only by the intermittent whoosh of traffic behind him. He let a minute tick by. Tried again. Nothing. Looked like the friend had sent him on a wild goose chase, maybe under orders from the *princesa* herself. Which wouldn't surprise him, given how fast Darcy had bolted from his bar last night.

Out of the corner of his eye, he caught a ghostly flicker. At the gable of the building, a wall-mounted neon sign read Skin Candy Ink, the *S* struggling to stay lit, the *K* in *Ink* extending to an arrow that pointed to a spot out of sight. Maybe someone there could provide the answers.

Decided, he stepped between the buildings, half expecting the gap to close behind him and explode into a fantasy world like something out of *Harry Potter*. If someone were to approach from the shadowy bowels at the end of the tight passage, they'd both have to flatten their backs against the walls and slither by to avoid contact.

Ten seconds and a hundred heartbeats later, the passage opened out into a small clearing. Like a dirty beacon, the tattoo parlor shone, its glass windows darkly tinted except for another neon sign affirming he'd reached the right place and a large banner proclaiming "We reserve the right to refuse service to any asshole."

Better keep his asshole tendencies in check, then.

He pushed the door open and his body thanked him for the warm blast. The gratitude did not extend to his ears, however. Classical music assaulted them where something hard edged with a booming bass would have been more welcome. The feeling of having stepped into a strange new world washed over him.

"Be with you in a second," a muffled voice came from the back.

Moving farther in, Beck scanned the surroundings, first looking for exits. Nothing marked, which was against code. He tripped his gaze over the walls. Every inch advertised the shop's craft: cartoon figures, superheroes, skulls, half skulls/half devils, half skulls/half Marilyns, winged hearts, arrowed hearts, hearts inset with *Mom*. The whole gamut.

Another few steps brought a whole other level of artistry into view. A raven-haired woman bent over a client, a tattoo machine poised in her gloved hand. On her exposed shoulder blade, a flock of birds gathered low before taking flight at the base of her slender neck. Inked cuffs laced her toned biceps, a shocking contrast to her porcelain skin and the white tank top barely covering purple bra straps. One of them fell in dishevelment off her rounded shoulder, the kind of messiness that always stirred him up. Pretty damn sexy.

As was the rest of her. Slim, with full hips that flared and kept her short black skirt snugly in place. The ink picked up along her left thigh, a vine of blue roses that disappeared into her biker boot. Sexy *and* badass.

Beck felt a ping in his chest—perhaps more of the strange new world effect, but something was off. All firemen learned to recognize that whisper, that gut check, and shit if he wasn't feeling it now. Seeking his bearings, he scoured the walls and let his eyes rest on signs that broke up the images:

"Love lasts forever but a tattoo lasts six months longer."

"Tattoos hurt. No bitching, whining, or passing out."

"A man without tattoos is invisible to the gods."

Were the gods looking down on him now, laughing at his torment? Giving him a taste of Darcy and what might have been, only to snatch her away from him again? He'd spent his whole life defying those fuckers' plans for him. The gods could go screw themselves.

Something glanced by his legs, and he dropped his gaze to an obese tabby cat that reminded him of another place and a time long gone. It rubbed against his jeans affectionately.

Then it hissed.

Beck's eyes widened in recognition. That cat had always hated him.

No way. No. Fucking. Way.

"I'm looking for someone who lives around here," he said, but he already knew he'd found her.

She straightened, every muscle in her curvaceous body locking up tight. Carefully, she raised the machine from her client's arm and placed it down on a tray like it was loaded. As she turned, hints of color peeked out above the edge of her left bra cup.

The blinding realization that had crashed over him about ten seconds ago was just now catching up to make his skin buzz. Still, it was nowhere near enough time to adjust to this new information. He had known she loved to draw, but he never imagined this. Could never have connected the neurons to even dream it. Darcy Cochrane, tatted and dressed like she belonged here. Like this was her world.

The Earth had flipped on its axis, dragging his brain along for the crazy ride.

"How did you find me?" she asked, cool as the other side of the pillow.

"I have my ways, *princesa*."

Long denim-clad legs swung off the chair behind her, and combat boots thumped the ground. A beast of a man towered over Darcy's shoulder, boasting raw scar tissue on the right side of his face that gave the impression he'd road tripped to hell and made a few friends there. His protective stance sent a surge of fury through Beck.

Darcy and . . . *nah-ah*.

"It's okay," she said, looking up into her protector's smoke-dark eyes. "Beck's an old friend."

Old friend? Hell yeah, he was.

With care and a slightly unsteady hand, she placed a wrap over her recent work, which looked like—was that a habanero pepper? Both of the guy's arms were blanketed in ink, barely room to spare for a postage stamp.

"I'll stay while you lock up," the brute said, one eye on Darcy, the other on Beck.

"I've got this, Brady."

Brady crossed his arms resolutely and planted his feet.

Seeming to arrive at a decision, Darcy pushed out a noisy breath. "Brady, Beck. Beck, Brady."

This dude was clearly important to her, not in a romantic sense, because if he was her man there would be zero debate about leaving her solo with another guy. But he was important on some other level, a realization that did not put Beck at ease. Darcy seemed A-okay with the situation, though. Her worlds had collided and she was figuring it out—with a lot more mental agility than Beck.

Beck stepped forward and held out his hand, half amused because the situation had the ring of a hostage handoff in Berlin circa 1985. *She's safe with me, new scary friend.* Brady acknowledged Beck's outstretched hand with a look but refused to take it. Alrighty, then.

Without further pleasantries, not even a "later" for Darcy, Brady headed out into the Chiberian night in short sleeves, ink as armor. Watch out, darkness.

Beck turned back to Darcy, his surprise momentarily giving way to blatant curiosity. "Where'd you find him?"

"Paris. Don't take the handshake thing personally. He doesn't like to be touched." She clicked off the music with a remote control, and then with nimble fingers unhooked the needles from the tattoo machine and placed the apparatus in a box like a cube-shaped microwave. Entranced, he watched her, waiting for the wavy lines in front of his eyes to clear. On the off chance he was stuck in a crazy fever dream, he shut his lids, counted to three, and opened them again.

Nope, still there.

Darcy Cochrane, heiress, charity doyenne, and one of Chicago's elite, had turned into a tattooed biker chick. So, no motorcycle as far as he knew, but she had the boots and the 'tude and the fucking ink. This was a million times removed from old Darcy with her pink, fuzzy sweater that used to have him in fits. And not even on the same planet as Darcy 2.0 from last night with the designer clothes and the pearls.

"Think I'm gonna need the non-Twitter version, Darcy."

"Oh, but we never needed words, *querido*."

Throwing his own smooth line back in his face? Nicely done, *princesa*.

He leaned on the counter, making it abundantly clear he was settling in for the long haul. In the bruising silence, he raked his gaze over her from head to toe, trying to craft his own story of what her body art meant. Last night she hinted at bad blood between her and Daddy, but hell if this wasn't one head-kicking case of rebellion. Those images were etched into her skin for a reason.

"So paint me a picture."

❄   ❄   ❄

Oh, he looked good. Grumpy and annoyed that he didn't have all the information, sure, but surly had always looked like sex on him. All that heart-wrenching intensity, and when it had been focused on her as he moved inside her, it was so easy to believe they were the last two people on Earth.

Mr. Miggins, her crusty old kitty, snaked a figure eight through Darcy's legs and scratched out a plaintive mewl. Evidently, already feeling the tension.

May as well start with the easy stuff. "I'm filling in for the owner who heads to Florida this time every year. Snowbird. I do this during the downtime when Grams can't bear the sight of me fussing around her. I'm staying in the apartment upstairs."

"That covers the last three months."

Needing to do something, anything, to escape his visual dissection, she turned the knob to the high setting on the autoclave so the tattoo iron would be sterilized in fifteen minutes, then set about tidying up her work area. Always be moving.

"I've been in Paris for the last couple of years, working with François Bernet. He's a well-known tattoo artist and he's taught me a lot." Both in and out of the sack, when he wasn't being a controlling French jerk, but Beck didn't need to hear that.

Too late. The crimp creasing his forehead said he'd read between the lines and come away with "Darcy did Paris" in more ways than one.

After some first-rate glowering, he found his voice again. "I knew you loved art, but . . ."

"You had no idea how much?"

"I'm pretty sure Skin Ink 101 is not an elective at Harvard."

She sighed. "I dropped out my sophomore year. The expectations . . . well, they got to be too much."

"Was your engagement part of those expectations?"

She had wanted to study art, but there was no room in her father's plans for a foolish girl's dreams. A Chicago media and real estate tycoon, Sam Cochrane had a rather feudal attitude when it came to the family's fortunes. For years he had treated his children as cogs in a plan to consolidate power without dirtying his hands with outright politicking. The front lines were of no interest to him, not when playing puppet master suited him better. The Collinses were a wealthy Connecticut family where everyone over the age of thirty was a U.S. congressman and had numbers after their names. Preston was the dynasty's most eligible bachelor.

"I met Preston at a political fund-raiser my father encouraged me to attend. We dated for a few months and he asked me to marry him. I was only nineteen. I thought it was what I wanted, but every day closer to the wedding I became more panicked. I bailed two weeks before the big day."

Darcy had stared down a lifetime of bruncheons and getting her hair ombréd, and realized this was not how she was supposed to go out. Finding out that Preston and her father held regular powwows with agenda items covering everything from how many children she should push out in the next five years to whether a political wife actually *needed* a college degree had woken her up from the *Matrix*-like life she'd been sleepwalking through. When she asked for her father's help canceling the wedding, he told her to play ball or be cut off.

"Let's just say I didn't want my life to be mapped out for me."

On a grunt, Beck flipped open one of the flash books, the shop's equivalent of clip art for people who wanted a tattoo but had no imagination beyond the initial impulse.

"Last night you ran out on me," he murmured.

"You ran first."

Electric eyes snapped to hers. Jaw muscles bunched. She longed to bite back the hastily spoken words. *Not supposed to care, Darcy.*

"Ancient history, *princesa.*"

"And you can cut that *princesa* shit out, for a start." For a start? No, no, no. Nothing was starting here because he was right. They were ancient history and dredging up the *whys* and *whats* was about as useful as Matthew McConaughey's shirt collection.

"Why are you here, Beck?"

"You ran out on me," he repeated, the edge in his voice hitting the hollow between her lungs. He shut the flash book, the sound a brutal echo in the tense silence, and skirted the counter, devouring the ground with long, measured strides. She backed up into the remaining inches available until her butt met the chair.

"And now I've found you."

She took those words as more than mere acknowledgment that he had located her at this point in time, in this particular place. The underlying meaning, that she had been rediscovered and would be at his mercy, thrilled through her despite her best intentions not to be aroused.

"And now you can be on your way."

He placed a big palm on either side of her, hemming her in against the chair's armrest with his feral, male heat. So sexy, so dangerous. That damn pirate's jaw!

"Do you think I'm stupid?" he rasped.

"Well—"

"Let me rephrase, because right now you might have something there. Standing this close to you makes me feel incredibly stupid." He sucked in a hissed breath. "Do you think I'm going to let you go now that we've reconnected?"

Her heart thudded insanely fast. "I'm thinking you don't have a say in the matter, Beck Rivera."

Shit. She needed to stop using his last name like that. Or his first name. It smacked of a lover's familiarity and a level of comfort she did not want to indulge in. Last night, the ease between them as they teased and flirted had filled aching gaps in the cold corners of her mind. Not to mention what had come after. All day, she had savored X-rated visuals of his hard body fusing to hers, that in-out rhythm as he entered her so deeply she felt him clear to her heart. Tasting him had been such a bone-headed move she wondered how she was still standing. Shouldn't her brain matter have squeezed out of her ears? Shouldn't she be collapsed somewhere in a fetal heap of regret?

He inched closer, invading, conquering her body and soul with his quiet intensity.

God*damn* him.

One thick finger traced along her collarbone and down, down, down over the inky flora blooming above her tank top's neckline. He tracked the motion with his somber gaze. It was unbearably erotic.

"Last night, you were covered up. Looked like you'd come from one of your grandmother's fancy parties."

Her breathing came in short tugs. "The Cochrane holiday photo. Just playing the part for my father."

"*Rip it, Beck*," he whispered hotly against her ear, mimicking her desperate plea from the night before. "You didn't want me to see your body. You chose to hide this shiny new version of yourself from me. Why?"

The edge in his tone boosted her pulse precipitously, and not just the one that supplied oxygen to the troublesome muscle in her chest. Between her legs, another heart beat a chant to the one man she had loved like no other. Her labored breathing smashed her breasts against his chest, the friction turning her nipples to aching points of need.

Those Beck blues flashed. "Why did you insist on hiding this beautiful body from me, Darcy?"

"It seemed easier to . . ." Her mind flailed like a dying fish. ". . . to pretend."

"That you're something you're not?"

Perhaps she had been playing the part for more than just her father. She'd taken enough *Cosmo* quizzes to know that walling up her essence and falling back on the old was a classic defense mechanism. This way, she controlled the situation. She stayed in charge. No need to complicate sex with something as inconvenient as the truth.

"People have certain expectations of me. Even you. You wanted to relive the good old times with the Gold Coast princess, and that's what you got."

He swiped her lower lip with the thick pad of his thumb. "Think I got a whole lot more, *querida*. Think I haven't even begun to scratch the surface of this fascinating, new woman you've become."

The shock of that almost undid her. She was so much more than Darcy Cochrane, the painted rebel or her father's pawn. The way Beck held her gaze captive completely unnerved her. She wanted to be seen so badly. She wanted to be seen by this man.

Why him? Why the man who had cast her aside like day-old bread? His arrogance made her muscles seethe. Men like that were welcome in her bed, but not in her heart.

Stark evidence of his arousal pressed against her hip, hard and thick, sending a message to her clenching sex. *Soaking wet,* it shot back like a Morse code throb. If she shifted a couple of inches, it would be an invitation for him to lift her skirt and thrust into her. She suppressed a groan. If she stayed still, what did that say? He could wait her out forever with the patience of a feline predator.

So color her surprised when he withdrew his granite body from her personal space, the loss of it so shocking she almost whimpered.

"Do you have a portfolio?"

"What?"

"An album of work, demonstrating what you can do."

Irritation frayed her patience. Might have had something to do with the chill his body's removal left on her sensitive skin. "I know what a portfolio is, Beck. And it just walked out the door."

"That guy?"

"Yeah, I've inked most of his body. Even parts you can't see." She plastered on a saccharine smile, enjoying his disquiet and especially getting a kick out of how she had hauled the power back to her side of the room. Because now he was thinking about what other ink lay beneath *her* clothes—and whose hands she had permitted on her body. "Why do you want to see my work?"

"Because if I'm going to let you brand me, I'd like to know it's worthy of forever."

Her breath caught. Power shift, activate.

"Brand you?" *Forever?*

Their gazes locked. Held. Warmth unfurled in her blood.

"Yes, Darcy. I want you to design a tattoo for me and brand it on my skin."

The way he said that, the way he owned it, made her wetter. Word that she was in town had filtered out, guaranteeing her dance card was full through the end of the year. She didn't need new business. She didn't need *this* business. But hell, she needed something.

"What did you have in mind?"

"Something for Sean and Logan. To commemorate them."

"That's beautiful, Beck."

He coughed out a mirthless laugh at her compliment. "It's a typical reason to get a tattoo, isn't it? Remembering people."

The air was charged with memory and want. Dangerously so. The past held risk, the present just as much. She needed to claw her way back to the safety of the future.

"I'm only in town for another couple of weeks. I'm moving to Texas for a job after the holidays." It was best to get it out there, establish the parameters of the transaction. An old friend had offered her a job in his parlor, and Austin was on her never-ending bucket list of places to live.

Nothing on his face indicated whether he cared about that. The pang of disappointment in her chest pissed her off to no end.

"Will you have time?" For the tattoo, he meant.

"Yes, I will." But Darcy meant something else. Time enough to flush Beck Rivera out of her system once and for all before she headed to warmer climes—and a fresh start.

chapter 5

· · · · · · · · · · · · · ·

The pots of money invested in Sunnyvale couldn't quite mask the astringent smell of disinfectant, marking it a place where old people went to pass on to the other side. Sort of morbid, Darcy admitted as she quickly navigated the slick floors of the lavish care facility, where her grandmother was camping out while she recovered from her stroke. The old girl was richer than God and could have afforded around-the-clock care at the mansion, but the docs had recommended she spend her rehab here. Something about socializing her way back into regular life.

Lord help the other residents, was Darcy's answer to that.

Darcy entered her grandmother's room without knocking. "Hey, Grams, how's it hangin'?"

Eleanor Cochrane's regal gaze landed with a thud on Darcy's bustier-molded cleavage.

"You trying to catch a cold or a man in that outfit?"

"Oh, a man. Most definitely a man."

She'd gone leather today from the waist down, and maybe it was too sexy for her grandmother, but it sure as hell wasn't for Beck Rivera. For that man on fire, it was the perfect temperature. She had plans for him later.

Bending over Grams, Darcy kissed the wax-papery skin of her cheek. The woman had aged so much in the last three months it scared the shit out of Darcy, which is why she loved when her grandmother showed flashes of spirit—even if that spirit was laced with acid.

Darcy plopped down into a comfy armchair near the bed. "Looks like you might be on the hunt yourself, Grams. In that nightie, you're flashing enough bosom to send the boys here to their graves with big smiles and bigger hard-ons."

"It's a peignoir, Darcy. Your expensive education was clearly wasted on you." She inhaled a breath with difficulty, causing Darcy some difficult breathing of her own. "But at least you're here. Not a single visit from the rest of them. All waiting for the call that I've croaked and my money is ready for distribution." Them, meaning her cousins. The rest of the Cochranes found it hard to fit tongue lashings from the family matriarch into their busy schedules.

"I'm only here in the hopes you'll change the will and drop it all on me," Darcy said with a grin, knowing that despite Grams's diatribes against the younger generation, she would never do such an outrageous thing. *Blood is king* was her mantra when she wasn't damning the lot of them to hell.

"He'll cut you out for good if you're not careful."

At the mention of her father, Darcy stiffened in the plush chair, but recovered with a wave. "Guess I should continue to be careless, then. I don't want it. Any of it." Her father's cash-rich approval came with strings so tight they made the bustier she was wearing feel roomy. Since she had dropped out of college and became her own person, she had felt free. Rootless, a little lonely, but liberated. She loved Chicago, but there wasn't an umbrella big enough to weather her father's toxic rain.

"He misses you," Grams said, and Darcy's heart melted. Not because she believed Sam Cochrane truly missed his daughter, but because Grams sounded so forlorn.

"I miss you, too." That earned Darcy a geriatric scowl. Gaudy shows of emotion were unacceptable from a Cochrane.

They spent ten minutes chatting about the upcoming fund-raising gala for homeless women that Grams organized each holiday season. Darcy was playing proxy for her grandmother, and had discovered that ordering people about in the name of Madam Cochrane was the ultimate power trip.

Her grandmother turned on the dowager countess stink eye once more. "So who are you flashing all that skin for?"

Heat scalded Darcy's cheeks. "Do you remember Jack's friend? The boxer from about seven or eight years ago?"

Grams screwed up her pinched face, calling deep on her memory reserves, and Darcy held her breath. Just how much damage had that stroke done to her?

"Serious boy. Broken nose."

Phew. "That's him. Beck."

"Ah, my favorite ladies."

Darcy's muscles locked up as the deep, resonant tone of her father both warmed and chilled the room. Sam Cochrane had a marvelous speaking voice, which he used to great effect encouraging his employees Trump-style—and crushing their dreams, when any of them dared step out of line. It was the same tactic he used to control his family.

Self-pity, thy name is Darcy Cochrane.

She turned in her seat, "displaying her wares" as he had once described her body art and revealing clothing. Petty satisfaction warmed her gut at watching his lips form a grim seal.

Tall and urbane, with graying hair winging his temples, her father had aged exceedingly well. Tori, his third wife, was a health nut and she made sure to keep him active, both in the gym and in the bedroom. A between-the-sheets exercise regimen with women who weren't his wife had always been his go-to before the latest Mrs. Cochrane.

He had married Darcy's mother, a former beauty queen and daughter of a wealthy man, for seed money. And then he left her to a boozy rot in their Gold Coast mansion while he screwed his secretaries and figured out ways to contort everyone around him into knots. Darcy had seen the effects of her father's manipulations on her mother. It dragged her down, made her small. But she had eventually wised up and was now happily remarried, living in South Beach.

"Well, Grams, I've got to go seduce that man. I'll check back in later." Darcy sprang up and gave her grandmother a kiss good-bye along with a gentle squeeze, netting for her trouble a disapproving *hmph* at her mawkish display.

Bypassing her father, she headed to the corridor with a parting nod of acknowledgment. "Dad."

"Darcy," he said, following her out. "Stop behaving like a child."

She halted and let the fury work through her body for a gratifying moment before she spun on her boot heels and drew herself taller. He made it so easy to hate him. "In another two weeks, I'll be out of your hair. I'm only here for Grams."

"What about the fund-raiser?"

"Like I said, I'll be there for her. Not for you."

"Dressing appropriately, I hope," he said, his dark gaze skimming her outfit. "Your stepmother would appreciate it."

Instinctively, she drew the lapels of her jacket together, hiding what made her individual, different. Not Cochrane. Her ink felt like a huge X over her heart, an invitation to her father to take his best shot. Every battle in this war between them left her diminished and bruised, and now she dug deep for ammo.

"Dad, do you still have it in mind to trot me out as

meat for one of your screw-someone-over schemes? Who is it this time? The scion of a Swiss banking dynasty? The geek founder of some start-up you want to buy out? Or is Preston Collins back on the market looking for Wife Number Two?"

Her father scoffed. "Well, now that you've made yourself look like a barrio mural, no one of use to me would want you."

Shock sliced through her, not at his words, but that they could still sting so much. Her usefulness to him had vanished with every *screw you* she embedded in her skin. She could feel her body curling up, her heart shrinking in his outsize presence.

"I'm more than what you choose to see, Dad. I always have been."

Subtlety was not part of her father's skill set, but in that moment, he seemed to realize his faux pas in cutting her so deeply. His mouth softened.

"Darcy, you're still my daughter and I love you. Come home."

"It doesn't feel like home anymore, Dad."

"Even with one of the city's finest at your *beck* and call?"

Rage boiled up. "For God's sake, Dad, have you been following me?" His keeping tabs should not have surprised her. Given some of his past stunts and his preference for gold jewelry, he had more in common with an old-school Mafioso than with the upper echelons of power he so wanted to control.

"He's not worthy of you, Darcy. He never was." He

stared her down for a moment, then turned and walked into Grams's room.

❄   ❄   ❄

"Keep your fists up," Wyatt said.

Shoulders back, Beck adjusted his stance, putting more weight on his back foot, and delivered a one-two to the bag with his chin down and fists proud. Only three weeks since he'd started his leave, and his muscles bitched at every unfamiliar motion. Sweat rolled off his neck, soaking his tee, the impurities of his body sloughing away with every punch. Not the impurities of his mind, though. He held on to those like a drowning man whose life flashed before his eyes in bursts with each desperate second above water.

Darcy writhing under him, encouraging him to take her harder, do her right. Darcy's hands exploring his chest and rasping his nipples. Hell, sexy shit she hadn't even done!

The bag hit his head so hard that his ears popped and rang.

"The fuck?"

"You're distracted," Wyatt said as he steadied the bag he had just used as a weapon to usher Beck back to reality. If reality meant the cramped gym at Engine 6 on Chicago's North Side, he'd take his fantasy life, thanks. The old quarters could do with a face-lift, which given the city's budget woes and the fact CFD came last on their good mayor's list of priorities, would not be happening in any Dempsey's lifetime.

Wyatt cleared his throat. "Keep that shit up and you'll get your head bashed in by the Five-Oh."

"It's not until April," Beck said, referring to the annual Battle of the Badges. "Plenty of time to get undistracted." Two more weeks should do it. She'd be gone, off to Texas and some cowboy hick who would learn every inch of her tattooed body, and what each image meant.

"So you are."

"Are what?"

Wyatt's flinty expression said Beck shouldn't even bother playing it cool.

"Yeah, I'm distracted." He had Darcy on his mind. Then. Now. The future with a heaping side of regret if he didn't act and lock her down. She'd lied to him about this amazing woman she had become while he lodged his body deep within hers. But as mad as that made him, he understood that deficit of trust on her side. Maybe she was right to keep the real Darcy from him; maybe he didn't deserve to see the woman behind the ink, not while past mistakes were milling around in his brain.

Beck knew he was going to rue the next words out of his mouth because Wyatt was the worst sounding board ever, but sometimes talking to a human wall was better than a lady-feelings exchange with Gage or Luke.

"There's this girl."

Wyatt hoisted an eyebrow. Already overseas with the Marines when Beck and Darcy had started dating, his oldest brother had missed out on all the drama from back in the day.

"I cut her loose years ago and now she's on my radar again. She was this big bright light that made me feel like I could do anything, y'know?"

"I know," Wyatt said with uncharacteristic feeling. Guy was completely cryptic when it came to his sex life, so that was about as effusive as Beck had ever heard him.

"Keeping her close would have been the best thing for me, but it would've dragged her down, dimmed all that radiance. She had college and this golden life ahead of her, and she would have given it up to stay with me." She knew he couldn't leave Chicago, not when his future involved suiting up in CFD bunker gear. Which left the option of a long-distance relationship, or Darcy staying put and possibly giving up her dreams—for him.

He threw a punch at the heavy bag, keeping his top knuckles centered in the glove to absorb the shock. "I needed to be a firefighter, to honor Sean and Logan and everything they had done for this family, this city. My life was here, but hers . . ." Another solid blow to the bag kept him focused on getting out words that had never before found air. "Not sure I could have lived with what a life with me would have turned her into."

For a start, her father would have cut her off for hooking up with a punk-ass street kid. Staying in Chicago with her wings clipped, living on the fumes of teenage love that might not pass the test after a year or two of real life—no way did Beck want to shoulder the blame for that cluster.

"Love someone, set them free. That your angle?"

"I s'pose." Beck landed a hard, yet unsatisfying one-two-punch on the bag. "She's turned into this amazing woman, Wy. Strong, beautiful, independent." As for what Beck brought to the table, the jury was still out. He knew one thing, though, with a clarity that cut him to the core.

He wanted her.

"Becky, you've got a visitor," Luke called out from the gym's entrance.

"Are you decent?" a sultry voice crooned. Speak of the green-eyed temptress herself . . .

Darcy peeked around Luke's shoulder, her palm caging her eyes inadequately as she scoped out the gym. She dropped her hand dramatically. "Oh, that's disappointing. I was hoping for more sweaty men."

Beck's heart punched his ribs with all the force of an attack hose pumping out water at 400 psi. Just when he thought he'd have to chase her down, here she was, and holy shit, she had dressed up for her Engine 6 debut.

Leather molded to her curves like it had been painted on with a brush—or tattooed with her gun. High-heeled boots brought her up to Luke's chin, and he was taller than all of them. The jacket she wore was unbuttoned, revealing that revolt of colorful florals on the rise of her breast. All she was missing was a frickin' crossbow.

"Hey," he said. Wow, positively Shakespearean.

"Hey, yourself," she said back, a smile in her voice. "Can I have a word?"

That should have been enough of a hint for Beck's nosy brothers to clear off, but from their assorted smirks and raised brows, no one was budging. Fuckers. Hurriedly, he made introductions and was about to quickstep her out of there when Gage strutted in.

"Hey, it's Darcy, isn't it?" Gage asked. "Hot damn, I love your ink!" Never one for boundaries, baby bro nudged the lapel of her jacket aside and scrutinized her cleavage. "Heard you're a big-time tattoo artist now."

"I wouldn't go that far," she said, a becoming watercolor bloom of pink suffusing her cheeks.

Gage threaded his muscled arms over his chest. Today's T-shirt slogan announced: I'm a Firefighter—What's Your Superpower?

"Beck's been stalking you on the Web, trying to piece it all together Sherlock-style. Those pics . . . Darcy Cochrane, you are a stone-cold fox!"

"Sometimes I wonder if this gay thing is just a phase," Beck muttered, drawing Wyatt's low huff of laughter.

"Oh!" Surprise perked up Darcy's face, and she considered Gage with renewed interest. "That's right, you're gay. Mel is going to be stricken with grief."

Gage winked. "Yeah, I get that a lot."

As he stripped off his gloves, Beck recalled the details of his investigations on Darcy, which had turned up far-flung locations like London, Paris, and LA. She lived a nomadic lifestyle, always leaving her clients—and no doubt her many admirers—wanting more. In the tattoo world, Darcy Cochrane was a big fucking deal. She had won contests, displayed her art at something called the Body Expo, was a respected force in the business of drilling pigment into the skin. She'd even inked a well-known rock star, and there were rumors of a brief, combustible relationship, if TMZ was to be believed.

Gage was still gabbing. Jesus. "I couldn't believe that in all this time, he's never once looked you up. I mean, that's what the Internet is for."

"I thought it was for cat videos and porn," Darcy deadpanned, catching Beck's eye with a glint in her own.

"But it's also for snooping," Gage said with authority. "I'm always checking up on my exes, usually with my fingers crossed that one of them has made it onto some revenge porn site or that they take a really bad mug shot."

Amusement curved Luke's lips. "Does anyone take a good mug shot, idiot?"

Gage double thumbed in the direction of his head. "This face is incapable of having a bad day."

Darcy laughed warmly, just like Beck remembered, not that he had ever given her much reason. As a kid, he was too nervous around her, his skin so tight he felt like it would snap right off his bones. He liked to think he had lightened up in his old age, but he would never have Luke's innate charm or Gage's easy good humor.

Jealousy of his gay brother gnawed his innards. These two would be fast friends before the day was out; tequila and pillow fights would cement the deal. Still, another part of him enjoyed that she dug his family. He wanted her to be part of this thing that was so important to him.

"What did you need to talk about?" Beck asked, cutting in on the *Gage and Darcy Show*.

"Oh, right." She opened the big-ass purse on her shoulder and extracted a piece of paper. "I wanted to show you the design for the tattoo."

Her moss-green eyes were alight with a brew of fire and apprehension as she handed it to him. The names of Sean and Logan in Celtic lettering hit him like a right hook out of yesterday. Even after all this time, he felt it. The void they had left.

"The black script is a bit hard on the eyes," Darcy said, "so I thought I'd soften it with a shamrock on one side for Sean and the CFD logo on the other for Logan."

Beck struggled to get the words out. "Two separate tattoos, then?"

She placed her hand on his bicep. "One for each gun," she said softly, her fingers cool to the touch from being outdoors. He felt the sizzle as the heat between them expanded, and for a moment everything fell away and it was just him and Darcy, eyes fusing like their bodies had two nights ago.

Several heartbeats later, she lowered her eyes, then her hand. "I can do something else. Just tell me what you need."

Everyone stared at the design, trapped in their own vortex of memories and pain.

"It's awesome. We're in," Luke pronounced, breaking the heavy silence. "Unless you want this just for yourself." He held Beck's gaze, worry that he had spoken out of turn clouding his eyes.

The unabashed rightness of this struck Beck squarely. It was for them all.

"If you guys want to be a part of it and Darcy can manage the work, then that's fine by me. She's in high demand and . . ." He trailed off as the memory of how long she'd be around sucker punched him in the solar plexus. She was planning to skip town by year's end, and shit on a hot dog, that sucked.

"I can do you all." She bit down on her lip and took in the ring of Dempseys staring at her avidly. "Well, you know what I mean."

"If I was gonna turn, Darcy, you'd be first on my hetero bucket list," Gage said, ever the outrageous flirt. He added to Beck with a wink, "CPF, man."

Beck's scowl at that was cut off as the alarm sounded, the mechanical voice of dispatch echoing its siren call through the firehouse. "Engine 6, Truck 43, Ambulance 70 . . ."

"Time to get smoked," said Luke. "Later, bro." He nodded, doing an admirable job of reining in the pity that they all got to speed off while Beck was forced to stay behind, but Beck saw it all the same and his heart bled a little. In a clatter of thudding boots and organized chaos, they headed out, leaving Beck alone with Darcy.

Bewilderment creased a line between her pretty dark eyebrows. "You don't have to go with them?"

"No."

"Day off?"

Lots of days off. "I'm on admin leave." He huffed out a breath. "I almost killed my brother."

chapter 6

. . . .

A cold gush flared and froze to a block of ice in Darcy's chest. "What happened?"

Beck's face crusted over like a rusty lock, the tumbler click, click, clicking into place. Damn, she had a nanosecond to grasp at it before he shut down completely.

So she grabbed his sweaty T-shirt and fisted it.

"Jesus, Darcy. That's skin you've got."

"Oh, sorry. I just wanted your attention." She loosened her grip, but still held on.

He gave her a bemused look. "You always have my attention. When you're in the room, you're my sun."

Those words battered her breathless, and it was a moment before she could draw enough air to fuel what she said next. "Tell me what happened. It was on a call?"

"A month ago. Fire at a crack house on the South Side that started on the second level. The place was in dire straits when we got there, but it hadn't reached the first floor yet."

He paused, so she rubbed his chest over the skin she'd grabbed. Encouraged, or perhaps just resigned to honesty now that he'd opened the floodgate, he went on.

"Another company had arrived before us. Typically the first on site makes the calls and they said the second floor was clear, so Luke and I swept the first. It was empty, but on the way out I heard something on the landing. Someone was trying to get out. I raced up the stairs but the heat was too intense. I could feel it through my hood, fighting to take control of my mask. Luke was calling behind me to get back. My lieutenant was on the radio screaming at me to pull out, but this kid . . ." He laid his head against her forehead. "Darcy, he was just gang fodder, caught in a bad place, pulled in by all the shit. I managed to haul him free for the handoff to Gage, but before I could get clear, the ceiling crashed in on top of me. Luke dragged me out."

"You saved that kid's life."

He nodded. "And almost got my brother killed trying to save me. The boys at HQ don't look kindly on behavior that endangers your fellow firefighters. It's just—" He took a breath. "This kid has probably gone his whole life with no one on his side. But I could do that for him. Come storming out of my corner, gloves on, fists raised. 'Cause if not me, then who?"

"There but for the grace of God," she whispered.

In his eyes, she saw his relief that she understood. In another lifetime, that kid could have—no, *would have*—

been him, and Beck needed this save to honor the people who had saved him. Coming from gang-infested streets, Beck had always known how blessed he was to be taken in by the Dempseys. Paying it forward was a given.

She recalled the scar on his head, that raw rift of pain. "How long were you in the hospital?"

"A week. They induced a coma and then brought me out of it after a couple of days. But they won't sign off on me from a disciplinary standpoint. I'm on suspension until they schedule a hearing, probably not until after the holidays. Waiting around for the sword to drop is killing me."

"Following orders keeps people alive," she said, not wanting to pile on the scoldings but so, so angry with him for putting his beautiful self in danger like that.

"Thanks, Luke," he muttered.

She pressed her palm to the vee of sweat branding his gray tee. The musky scent of man wafted into her nostrils, giving her a contact high, making her knees and heart go soft. Beneath her fingertips, she felt his thrumming vitality and the emotion that he had always done such a good job of reining in until he buried his body inside hers and took them both to a place she hadn't known existed before she met him. A place she wanted to get back to—with the only man who had the power to affect her on a soul-deep level.

"Don't be mad at me," she teased. "Unless it makes the sex better. Then continue with your emo posturing."

That won her a rare laugh, a glorious sound. He snaked an arm around her waist and pulled her so close they shared their next breaths. Life-giving, yet making her weak.

"Can't get mad at you, Darcy. You're the only one who can take me out of myself." He tightened his hand over hers and entwined their fingers in a target over his heart. "I did not deserve you."

That was not what she wanted to hear, talk of the past invading the pleasure of the present. Much too serious.

"I'm glad you're not dead, Beck," she clarified, aiming to cut the tension thick as the lump in her throat. "Better, baby?"

He flashed a so-help-her-God smile. "I'm glad you're glad, *querida*."

The intense heat of him along with his masculine scent intoxicated her, and she drew back to get a much-needed influx of Beck-free oxygen.

"How about you give me the tour?" she asked. And give her a chance to catch her breath.

"Step this way, m'lady."

He squired her around the quarters, mostly empty except for a too-cute-and-blond secretary in the back office and a couple of firefighters playing cards at a table out in the truck bay. After stifling her giggles at the hose tower (*where they dried their hoses*), followed by the equipment room housing couplings (*for hand jacking hydrants—um, dying here*), profound disappointment set in when she learned she could not take a slide down the fireman's pole. (*We don't have one. No, really, Darcy, we don't.*)

Watching him walk ahead of her in his damp shorts and tee, his powerful legs making her light-headed with desire, she was reminded of the first time she had seen him in that dingy boxing gym nine years ago. The place had scared her breathless with its floor ossified with decades of loogies, its walls propping up granite-faced men who stared right through her. And the smell! Like someone had dipped sweaty sneakers in a fondue of sewage and offered them up for their dining pleasure.

She was only there because her best friend, Shaz, had it bad for Darcy's brother and wanted to see him in shorts. At seventeen, Jack was almost as tall as Darcy's dad, and had at least six inches on the other guy standing in the boxing ring, who hopped back and forth like a bunny playing with an invisible jump rope. Darcy found her gaze magnetized to those feet before it slid north over the rest of him. Strong, gleaming, cocoa-skinned legs maintained her interest on the upward journey until—

It was the first time she had noticed a guy's butt.

Tight and trim, it filled out his shiny black shorts in a way that brought heat to her cheeks. *Turn around,* her blitzed brain urged. *Turn. Ah. Round.*

He obliged, fighting the air with jabbing punches as he went. Posturing, she would have assumed if it were anyone else, but this was different. He was different. This was a boy who played sports, not games. CFD was stamped in large letters on his broad chest. The Chicago Fire Department. The boy, his shock of black hair already damp with exertion, stared at Jack, his opponent for the upcoming bout. Barely leashed rage radiated from every dark pore.

Then he turned, his burning blue focus rewired on her.

The floor dropped beneath her feet, her heart plummeted into the void. Every moment in her sixteen years on Earth had been building to this. A malodorous gym and a serious boy's blue gaze. He saw into her, through her, out the other side, and she felt like one world ended and another began. Teenage dramatics, she knew now, but at the time it had felt so important. So cell-shockingly real. On the germ-ridden chair where she had planted her butt, she squirmed, the chill of the metal a bite on the underside of her soft thigh, and all she could think was: *I want him to win.*

That's when Jack coldcocked him with such force he dropped like a stone to the mat.

Oh crap!

It took every inch of her willpower to hold on to the rim of the chair with her clawed fists. Shaz jumped to her feet, cheering her crushing heart out for Jack, who had taken a couple of proud steps back to assess the damage. A cocky smile spread over his reddening face. In that moment, Darcy hated her brother because he was so like their father. Sneakily striking at the good, reveling in the havoc he wreaked.

The boy stood while the referee checked his face, shaking his head somberly. Blood blanketed his mouth; the word *broken* filtered through to her consciousness. Disappointment rose up to freeze her chest. It was over. One strike and it was over.

An older man about her father's age said something and threw a soaking rag into the ring. The boy picked it up, wiped his broken nose, and lobbed the rag over his shoulder, past the ropes. Pretty hard-core. Darcy's heart pounded wildly as the referee stepped back, looking shocked, but his retreat an unspoken agreement that the fight would go on. For twenty-three seconds, the boy let loose on Jack, a whirl of flying fists and unmoored fury until the referee was forced to stop it. Her brother lay on the floor, stunned, grudging admiration for his conqueror in his eyes. Darcy had wished like hell she'd had her sketch pad.

"That guy's an animal!" Shaz said, railing with indignation. Darcy wanted to sigh at that, but her skin felt too tight for something so casual.

The animal wiped his bloodied, smashed nose with the back of his glove and speared her with another unstinting stare. There was no pride on his face, no joy in his brutal achievement. She wondered why he bothered and hated that she cared. Then he hooked one corner of his bloodstained mouth up, sending her stomach into a wriggle. Lower, too.

Nine years on, and nothing had changed. Beck Rivera was still the boy who heated her from the inside out and forced her to hold on to a germ-ridden folding chair for the ride of her life. He excited her like no one else.

Raise that sex point average, Darcy. Show him what he's been missing, Darcy.

You're a grade A idiot, Darcy.

"Last stop," he said, yanking her back to the present and Engine 6's shower room. Over the door a sign proclaimed "Old firemen never die, their nozzles just rust away." Cute.

She arced her gaze over the trio of single-use shower stalls. Not quite the stuff of her filthy fantasies, which were more on the level of communal showers with hordes of hot men soaping up and getting sexy-slick.

"Is this where a fireman keeps his etchings?" Darcy joked, nodding at the tattoo sketch he still held clenched in his fist.

Beck set the drawing on a side ledge. "Nah, it's where this fireman learns about his girl's."

His girl's. Stepping in, he moved his palm over her collarbone, down over the crest of her breast to trace the cherry blossoms budding above her bustier. She quivered under his touch.

"I want in you, Darcy. I want to feel you tight and hot and wet around me. But first I want to know every one of these tattoos, all the stories. Where you've been. Where you're going."

And she wanted to tell him. Everything. She dropped her purse and shrugged off her jacket, the soft sounds of leather hitting the floor loudly resonant in the tiled shower room. Her bustier showcased her breasts to *how ya doin'* levels, but the true beauty lay below the fold. His hands wandered to her back, seeking access.

"Here, let me," she said, unzipping at the side with trembling fingers. Her breasts spilled free, revealing the vibrant blossoms painted down the left side of her body, each stem ending in flames.

With his lust-stoked gaze, Beck tracked the motions of his hands down her breasts to her hips. When his eyes fell on the stems, the licks of heat on her skin came alive under his laser-like scrutiny.

"Fire," he said, one finger tracing the orange curls of flame on her hip. "Beautiful. Dangerous."

He coasted his hands up her sides and rested a finger above her breastbone, the gentle motion enough to make the blossoms on her skin bloom brighter. Beck's touch, the sun and the rain.

"Tell me about them."

"This one I got in San Francisco about four years ago. In Chinese culture, cherry blossoms are a symbol of life and love, as well as sexual power."

"Hmm." Gently, he turned her and glanced his knuckles along her shoulder blades. "And the birds?"

"I know a guy in Madrid."

"Sounds like you know guys everywhere."

There was no snark in his tone. That wasn't Beck's style, but nonetheless Darcy imagined an undercurrent of jealousy. Reveled in it a little, if she was being honest.

"The birds represent freedom."

He hooked a finger in the waistband of her leather pants and pulled her forward so her breasts grazed his chest. Her nipples tightened to pleasurably painful buds. Slowly—so damn slowly—he unsnapped the button and inched the zipper down, the scrape sending her pulse rate into overdrive and her core into a flood. Only when her bare skin met the tiled wall outside the shower stall did she realize he had walked her back.

"Did you ever think of me, Darcy? When you were traveling the world? When someone drew this on you?"

Her first tattoo at the age of nineteen was of a heart in flames, its trite symbolism cringe-worthy years later. Poor-grade artwork, it served as an introduction to a weird new world and sparked her interest in body art. Later she covered it up with the spectacular elaboration of blooms and fire along her torso—not for Beck, but for her. Still, he had always been there, a part of her she could never deny.

"No, I didn't think of you." *Liar, liar, thong on fire.*

He slipped a thick finger under her lacy underwear, through her damp curls, until he found what he needed. Right at the spot where she needed.

"Good," he whispered. "I told you to forget and you did. That's all I could have wished for, *querida.*"

Oh, Beck. Unbearably touched by the words that had once broken her heart, she gripped his shoulders and dug her nails into his skin, needing an anchor. The staccato of her beating heart thudded in her ears and telegraphed an unnamed need for more.

She moaned deep as his finger rubbed through her seam, every return hitting her clit with the perfect amount of pressure. Two fingers breached her body and found a hot, steamy haven. Heat coiled tight in her belly. He was watching her, waiting for her to go over, so she held on desperately because the longer he trapped her in his intense gaze, the better the release would be. His other hand curled around her neck in a possessive, wildly sensual spread.

"More, Beck. Please."

A finger soaked in her slick heat circled the nerve-packed nub of her clit, just like before, just how she liked it, and she shattered. His hand cupping her sex and the wall at her back were the only things keeping her upright.

And then his hand was gone.

Which left the cool tile. Slumped against it, she watched in a daze as he did that one-hand-over-the-head thing with his tee and reached in to turn on the shower. The tightly loomed muscles of his back moved like cogs under chocolate silk. Everything about him screamed pleasure.

Her spine had dissolved, leaving her useless, so thank God he took over. Holding her steady, he pulled off her boots and socks, divested her of her pants, sinking to his knees as he pulled them down. On the journey back up, he kissed the blue roses along her calf, languidly running his tongue over her damp, heated flesh.

"Where did you get this one?"

"Wh-what?"

"The roses. Where?" He christened the cerulean flowers with scorching hot kisses.

"London," she panted. "It was the first big piece I got. The first one I was brave enough to get."

He rewarded her bravery with more brain-destroying flicks of his tongue.

"Beck," she whispered into the vapor, feeling like she had entered a fevered dream. Feeling a reckless abandon she had never before experienced.

No, wait, she had. With him. Only with him.

Nudging her thighs apart, he splayed those blunt hands over her soft skin. Oh, God, oh, God. The throb built inexorably the closer he moved to the well of her sex.

"Just a little taste, Darcy. You always tasted so sweet."

As if she could deny him a single thing.

Mouth set to torture, he tongued her blooming folds, scooping up the intimate moisture, creating more with every luxurious sweep. She was flagging, her legs weak as the steam, her body a quivering mess. Any moment now, she would be knocked out of time—

Damn. He stood, giving her a chance to catch her breath (not necessarily a good thing) and appreciate his glistening mahogany chest (most assuredly a good thing). Dark hair arrowed down to his groin, blazing a trail she yearned to follow with her fingers, her lips, her tongue. He was perfectly formed, all steel flesh, so beautiful that it simply hurt to look at him. But she suspected it would hurt more when she no longer could.

"I need a condom. I need to be inside you when you come again." He stepped back with the intent to grab protection, leaving her boneless against the wall.

"My purse," she pushed out. Now wasn't the time for coy.

"Atta girl." He handed over her purse and she rummaged for the three-pack among the rest of her crap. After what seemed like an eternity, not helped by Beck sucking the delicate juncture where her neck met her shoulder, she found the Trojans.

Within two seconds, he had shucked his shorts,

smoothed the condom on, and lifted her off the floor with little effort apparent in his raw, fireman strength.

Then he dawdled.

Teased and rubbed.

Drove her mad with anticipation.

Only when she begged did he enter her slowly in one consuming thrust. Their united groan reverberated against the tile, such a satisfying sound.

Such a *loud*, satisfying sound.

Panic about how public this was warred with bone-melting desire. "Beck, someone might come."

"I guarantee it." He stroked her long and deep, massaging her swollen clit with every return of his thick, sleek length.

"I mean—"

His mouth fitted over hers, choking off her words. A brutal, uncivilized kiss. The steam from the shower— the one they were *not* taking—added a skin of moisture that made her hands slip off his shoulders. But she never doubted his ability to hold her safe as he took her higher and made good on that guarantee for both of them.

After her world had been rocked—two more times— Beck still held her close, protectively and possessively, wedged deep inside her.

"We just had hot shower sex outside the shower," she said with a giggle.

"Find 'em hot, leave 'em wet," he murmured. "Well-known firefighter maxim."

A stray thought cut through her mind fog. "What's CPF? Gage said it before he left."

His grin was wry and about the sexiest thing she had ever seen. "City Property Fuckable. It's against the rules, so if you're going to do it, you need to make sure it's worth losing your job over."

"And I'm CPF?"

"You know it, *querida*. You're my first."

His first, just like he had been hers all those years ago.

There was that rare smile on his lips but, also, in his lake-blue eyes she saw his determination: the inner strength that helped him survive those early, dangerous years in a life he hadn't chosen. The same strength that powered him in the ring and on every call in this life he had made his own.

Maybe it was delayed shock, or the power of the O, or the fact she was standing in a firehouse shower room with her hot Latin lover impaling her to the tile, but it suddenly hit her like a two-by-four.

He could have died.

And she would never have known.

She would have popped into Dempsey's bar with Mel and assumed it was his night off. Might even have silently cheered the bullet she had dodged by not running into him. Only two days later, the idea of a world without him—*her* world without him—turned her blood to ice.

Tears sprang into her eyes. Goddamn him.

"Darcy, what's wrong? Am I hurting you?" He made to withdraw, and she clasped his perfect, tight ass to preserve the physical connection as if it could minimize the emotional.

"You're a good man, Beck Rivera."

He looked unconvinced. "I'm not. I'm selfish and greedy."

"No, no." She kissed the knotted bridge of his nose. "Look at what you do, at what you've become. I'm so proud of you."

He drew back with the expression of a stern angel, and when he spoke it was like he gouged each word from a deep, dark place.

"This won't be enough for me."

Thoughts toppled like dominoes, and her heart seized in her chest, not unpleasantly. But her walls had walls, so she said the first thing that popped into her scrambled brain.

"Let's not complicate it."

"No, Darcy. Let's."

His kiss cut off all argument, making her blood pound, her heart soar, and consuming her utterly and completely whole.

chapter 7

. . . .

"Have I told you lately how sexy you are?" Darcy tip-toed up to kiss him, then moved her lips along the edge of his ear, eliciting a shiver.

"You're just sayin' that 'cause it's true, *querida*."

Damn, she looked fine in a long coat and cream scarf, like a pristine present he wanted to unwrap slowly. And the backdrop could not be more perfect. All around them, the twinkling trees and festive atmosphere at Zoo Lights in Lincoln Park painted the scene in the brushstrokes of a fairy tale. Each year, the zoo and ComEd—draped the trees in colored lights, blasted tunes from the sound system, and scared the shit out of the animals. A most excellent Chicago holiday tradition.

Darcy had said she didn't want to complicate what was happening between them, but Beck had quickly ki-boshed that idea. Knowing that shock-and-awe tactics were needed to break down her barriers, he had planned a romantic date with holiday lights and hot chocolate and frickin' polar bears, followed by a horse-drawn carriage ride down Michigan Avenue where he'd hoped to cop a feel under a warm tartan blanket. The fact that this magical space was home to their first kiss years ago made it just that much sweeter.

It had all gone terribly wrong.

"I want to see the gorillas next," an imperious voice rang out from below. The third wheel, on wheels. Darcy's grandmother had invited herself along when Darcy let slip their plans during a visit to the nursing home.

"Probably looking for a new husband," Darcy muttered, not unkindly. She pushed her grandmother's wheelchair along the tarmac path toward the monkey house with ease. The old lady couldn't have weighed more than eighty pounds soaking wet.

"I heard that," Mrs. Cochrane snapped back. "Two of my three husbands had more hair than any of the brutes in the cages here. I like them well covered."

Darcy shot Beck a sidelong glance, barely suppressing her laughter. The cold brought color to her pale cheeks, making her appear fresh-faced and younger than her twenty-five years. She looked happy, and that brought out his happy.

"How about some hot chocolate, Mrs. C?" Beck asked. "Warm those crabby old bones of yours."

"Let's hope you're hung, young man, because you're certainly not charming."

Darcy broke into shocked laughter. "Grams, be nice.

Beck didn't have to bring you," she said, adding a sly smile for Beck that sent his lungs on hiatus.

"Extra whipped cream," the old bag muttered.

Beck winked at his girl and hustled off to get the hot drinks, but as he stood in line at the kiosk, his smile melted away. In less than two weeks, she'd be outta here, winging her way to the Lone Star State and this new job she seemed excited about. He could make sacrifices to the gods of Chicago—the Bulls, the Bears, whoever people prayed to on the I-90—but it would be useless. It was like wishing he could hold back the sunrise.

Feeling glum, he delivered the hot chocolates and took over pushing duties so Darcy could have her hands free to drink. After a spin around the monkey house and a pop in to see the giraffes, they watched the light displays choreographed to holiday tunes, followed by the ice sculpting. Or Darcy and her grandmother watched.

Beck watched Darcy.

The lights danced over her delicate features and picked up flecks of gold in her big, expressive eyes. She had traveled all over the world, lived a cosmopolitan life most people could only dream of, and here she was with him, impressed by a crappy light show and a kid with a chain saw. In that instant, all her passion and beauty overwhelmed him.

It was time to lace up the gloves and step into the ring.

"Stop staring," she murmured out of the side of her gorgeously mobile mouth.

"Never."

Blushing, she snagged her plump lower lip with her teeth. So damn pretty. He noticed with approval her breathing had picked up, so he leaned in and buried his cold nose in the warm, fragrant skin of neck.

"Problem catching a breath, miss? I can help. Qualified EMT."

"You're evil, Beck Rivera. And freezing."

"I want you to stay in Chicago."

She lowered her eyelids, and the twinkling lights on her dark lashes made them sparkle like decorative fans. "What are you doing to me?" she breathed, and when she opened her eyes again, they shone glossy with emotion.

"I refuse to believe you entered my life again only to walk right out a few weeks later. The gods couldn't be that cruel." His lips brushed hers, gentle, teasing, then a stronger press that made his intent clear. She was his.

Then. Now. Forever.

She sniffed and pulled a tissue from her pocket, then scowled at his inevitable smile. "Shut it, Rivera. I always get sniffly in winter."

Her father had done a number on her, made it so she had a hard time letting anyone in. Now Beck was insinuating his way into the emotional nooks and crannies, finding those hard-to-reach places, shining a light. And just like he practiced out on the battleground of fire, no one would get left behind.

Over the sound system, a holiday classic filled the air with its smooth, velvet croon.

"I really can't stay . . . But baby, it's cold outside."

"Gotta stop running sometime, Darcy."

❊ ❊ ❊

Darcy held Beck's stark blue gaze and let the words sink in. Soured by her near-miss marriage and her father's formerly tyrannical grip on her life, funereal bells tolled in her brain as soon as any guy started dictating the terms. "Always be moving" had served her well so far. Free agency suited her.

Beck might be different, but was it enough? He had dumped her once with no explanation, no apology, nothing. Of course, she refused to delve deeper. Asking implied caring.

So she did what terrified, fragile, in-denial girls everywhere did—she fronted with her stock answer. "Chicago's not big enough for me and Dad."

"Oh, I dunno. Third largest city in the United States. And you have other reasons for sticking around."

"Such as?"

"Meddling friends. Terrifying, tatted guys who care about you. Evil grandmothers." That one he mimed, unnecessarily as it happened, because Grams had nodded off. "A business you can do anywhere because you rock at it." Pause. "Burn-the-sheets sex."

Considering they'd never made it to a bed, that particular claim was not entirely legit. She turned into his chest to keep her voice from carrying in the clear night air—and oh hell, because she fit perfectly under his strong jaw—and sucked in a heady lungful of him. "Hmm, you might have something there. The pickings for burn-the-sheets sex are bound to be better in the third largest city in the United States."

He gentled the back of her neck and kissed her, sweet and slow. His sexy jaw scruff conjured up a wash of sensation and sensual memories of how it had rasped her thighs during their steamy not-shower.

Gettin' so warm inside . . .

"Let's keep it PG, handsome," she said, when he let her up for air.

"Pretty good? Think I can manage that."

Another press of his lips, and the addition of his wickedly effective tongue, lifted her to a higher plane. This man of hers could kiss away every doubt, make her believe anything was possible. Even that she could live in the same metropolitan area as her father.

She was a much-sought-after body artist who loved her job and the freedom it gave her. She had built a good life, yet the idea of letting someone in—someone who might seem perfect on the surface, but could end up as manipulating and controlling as Sam Cochrane—seized her heart in a fist.

"Tell me why bustin' out of Dodge is so important," he whispered. "Because the way I see it, you have more reasons to stay than go."

"I didn't turn out how he wanted. The pliable daughter, the budding trophy wife. If I stick around in Chicago, he'll find a way back into my life, and before I know it I'll feel small again, just another cog in his machine. Look at how he tried to marry me off."

"You should be thanking him."

She gulped, unsure she'd heard that right. "Excuse me?"

He cupped his ear. "Do you hear what I hear?"

"You mean Mariah Carey warbling her way through one of my favorite holiday songs?"

"No, I mean the sound of your brass balls clanging, Darcy Cochrane. You've grown from a dependent girl into a self-reliant woman. And you have your father to thank because his dick moves set this great life of yours in motion." He curled his hand around her neck and tunneled those rough-cast fingers through her hair, his tactile strength unbelievably sensual against her scalp. "Look at what he unleashed on the world. Look at you takin' names, *querida*."

God, this man's support just slayed her. But as encouraging as that sounded, Beck was taking the product-of-her-environment argument a little too far. She owed nothing to her father. He had no say in how she turned out, yet . . . they were alike in so many ways. Stubborn, unyielding, hardheaded. She wanted to heal the rift between them, not go through life with this ball of negativity like a dead weight in her chest.

They were silent for a few moments, the air heavy with their thoughts and the chain saw's whine as it cut through the ice.

"You're pretty good at this," she finally murmured.

"Uh-huh. PG."

Her scarf was moved aside to reveal skin for a sensual nip of her neck. So not PG.

"I meant that you're good at seeing the silver lining, making the best of any situation."

"It's the foster kid code. We live in the now, take the scraps, and hope to God some miracle can turn it into a five-course meal. Shifting your perception, choosing to take a situation that makes you afraid or hurt or angry, and see it differently—that's the best way to move forward."

Her Beck had become quite chatty over the years. Insightful, too. "Look at you being all wise and shit," she said.

He grinned. "I know, right?"

"You own a suit, Mexican Dempsey?" Grams piped up, having just woken from her power nap.

"Does a birthday suit count?"

"Get one. Darcy needs a date to the fund-raiser."

Darcy mimicked strangling her grandmother. "Grams, I can get my own dates, thanks very much! Also, his name is Beck Javier Rivera and he's Puerto Rican, not Mexican, which you well know." With an embarrassed head shake, she turned to find him beaming a sexy grin. Yum. "Friday at the Drake. You in?"

Surprise lit up his eyes like stones in a stream. "As my hearing has yet to be scheduled and I've already finished Grand Theft Auto—twice—I'm all yours."

Waiting around for the call on his hearing was driving the poor guy screwy, but Darcy was reaping the benefit while he spent his free time with her. As for the fund-raiser, it would be a fitting punctuation to what had been an unexpectedly wonderful couple of weeks.

Something lurched in her chest at that.

He nuzzled her cold nose. "I'm all yours, not just on Friday night, but every night you want me."

"Beck . . ."

Another kiss swallowed her protest, an invasive sweep of his tongue as he breathed his promise into her lungs.

And she let him, because it was just easier to give him his way in this. For now.

chapter 8

· · · · · · · · · · · · ·

*T*he next afternoon, Darcy shifted her weight back on the tattoo parlor's stool and snapped a few mental candids for her memories. No one filled out the chair quite like Beck. Those beefy arms, strapping thighs, and well-built shoulders—he was every inch the powerful fighting machine.

"Can't believe that fur ball of piss 'n' vinegar is still around," he said, jerking a chin in the direction of her cat, Mr. Miggins, who was curled up in a sated ball near the hissing radiator. The two had never been fans of each other.

"He's like Grams. He continues out of spite."

Smiling, Beck returned his gaze to his arm and scrutinized Darcy's work. The green shamrock, like a pulsing Irish heart, bloomed on his bicep above the name of his foster father, Sean. Relatively simple in design, it might not impress her usual clientele, but pride swelled her chest at the thought of helping this amazing man commemorate his fallen heroes.

"You like?"

"I love." He raised his eyes to snag hers as he said that. Intense, blue, romantic—and a hundred times steadier than her heartbeat.

I love.

And she did. Completely, utterly, and . . . she was not happy about it. Not at all. Every day with Beck dragged her deeper and tore her under a powerful current until she could barely breathe for wanting him.

Happy Frickin' Holidays, Darcy!

Occupying her hands would be her best play here, and though they itched to meander south and stroke the perma-boner Beck always seemed to sport around her, she reined in her inner minx and reached for a bandage.

Beck was staring again. "How are you fixed for Christmas Day?"

One more week to the holiday, and then a few days later, *bye-bye, Chicago.*

Bye-bye, Beck.

"I'll drive Grams over to Dad's, we'll scarf turkey while Tori tries to chitchat through the awkward silences, and then I'll drop Grams back off at prison—I mean rehab."

He cocked his head. "You want to come hang at the firehouse after? Gage is gonna Martha Stewart the hell out of the dinner. He's already making paper plate angels for all the place settings. An inordinate amount of glitter is involved."

She stood and tidied up her station, extracting ink needles and lobbing soiled tissues into the trash.

"I'll be so busy with getting Grams settled and tying up loose ends." Such as loading up her piece-of-shit car. Steeling herself for the journey ahead to the job she wasn't sure she cared about anymore. Holding her ribs while her heart broke into icy shards.

Her body stilled as his masculine heat blanketed her from behind. "*Querida,* it doesn't have to end."

"We'll have the fund-raiser on Christmas Eve, Beck. It'll be a nice way to say good-bye."

With a strong hand on her shoulder he turned her to face him. Those eyes blazed hard and furious, shining like bullets.

"Is that why you invited me? So you could say adios in a room full of blinged-out strangers. We'd eat some rubbery chicken and dance a sad old waltz, though God knows I'll be crap at that. Maybe you'd get a final fuck-you in at your dad because you brought that guy he hated, then you'd wave to me as you wheeled Eleanor out the door."

Burning emotion snarled beneath her breastbone. Damn him for making it so hard. "I was never going to stay, Beck. You knew that. I just can't make a life for myself in the same place as my father."

Storm clouds brewed in his eyes, myriad emotions battling beneath his usually calm surface. Kinetic energy seemed to bounce off the walls, in her chest, between their bodies.

"That's just an excuse. So he screwed you over and

you're still pissed. Time to grow up, *princesa,* and figure out where you're going instead of dwelling on where you've been." He scrubbed a hand over his close-cropped skull. "You can't deny what's happening here with us."

"Of course not. But it's just chemistry, lust, nostalgia, whatever you want to call it—" She carved the air with her hand, seeking the right words to minimize the outrageous potency of what existed between them. "I've come too far in my career and my life to throw it all up for the special feelings caused by a return to the good old days. Besides, you had no problem letting me go before."

"That was different."

"How? How was it different?" She had never pried about his reasons—he hadn't given her any insight at the time, and she had always ascribed it to the bad space he was in after Sean and Logan made the greatest sacrifice. Preferring not to know, if she was being honest.

"We were kids," he murmured. "Now we're all grown up."

"You got over me, Beck." A lot more easily than she recovered from the onslaught of him, she might add. "You threw me away seven years ago. It hurt. It really fucking hurt."

Empathy laced with pain shone back in those terrible blue eyes.

"It was for the best. You know that."

"I don't know anything. Why was it for the best?"

He looked like he was weighing his options for evasion, when something clicked in his expression. Resignation. "I wasn't good enough for you, Darcy. I was a street punk who wanted nothing more than to follow in my foster dad's footsteps. Honest, hard, backbreaking work. Seeing you was like being blinded by a goddess. Touching your skin with my callused hands felt like sacrilege. Look at where you came from, at your people. How would I take care of you right?"

"So you did care about me—"

"I fucking loved you!"

All strength fled her legs and she gripped the edge of the counter behind her. Hearing those words spoken with such passion, even in the past tense, made her woozy.

Then, angry.

"Yet you dumped me."

"For your own good."

Outrage rushed through her. "You—you decided that I would be better off without you. You made that decision. Not us."

He snorted. He may as well have said *duh*. "Look at how it all worked out."

God*damn* him. "You think this is all because of you? That because you threw me away, it allowed me to flower into the woman I am today?"

Silence. Oh, the arrogant prick.

"How does your big fat head not fall off?"

A hint of a smile on his lips greeted that. "I think getting out from under your father's thumb was good for you. We were kids, half formed, clueless about who we were. You needed to experience the world. Earn your ink." He waved a hand around the shop, the supposed fulfillment of all her dreams. "If we'd stayed together, what would have happened? You were talking about switching to a college in Chicago or taking a year off. Already compromising yourself, maybe your future, for nothing."

Nothing? She would have had *him*, her serious boy with the shocking blue eyes. Beck was all she had needed back then.

"It wasn't your choice to make," she gritted out.

"Get real, Darcy. With me, you'd have been making happy noises while shriveling up inside because you didn't get out there. Travel, learn, be. I was never going to leave Chicago. You would have hated me eventually."

"And I hated you anyway."

"Yep," he said, and then he smiled again, a little sadly.

Confusion swirled in her chest, stopping to grasp at her heart with icy fingers. Since reconnecting with Beck, she had shied away from thinking about how they parted. Really thinking about it. Because if she truly gave that awful time the mental space it deserved, she'd remember the heartache and how it felt to be pushed aside.

Now to hear that he played the ultimate decider on this—his trust in her so negligible that her opinion never entered the equation—sliced through her like a blade. She had loved him so much, but his version held no respect.

Only a need for control.

"So what's changed? Don't say you're suddenly good enough for me now that I'm not the Gold Coast princess anymore." She held up her palms, stained from the tools of her trade. "Have my manual labor hands knocked me off that lofty pedestal, Beck?"

He glowered. "Stop twisting what I'm saying. It's not how you start, it's where you end up. This is where we are now and it's worth fighting for."

She drew herself taller, which was surprisingly difficult when your heart had stopped working properly. Thanks to her father, she had been there, done that, bought the I ♥ Assholes mug. She had almost collapsed under the weight of Sam Cochrane's controlling hand—and damned if she'd let any man do that to her again.

"Make sure you put Bacitracin on that tattoo. Every day for a week."

He stared at her, the notch between his brows deeply pronounced. "Darcy, don't shut down on me now. Not when we're so close."

"Tell me this," she whispered. "If you had to do it all over again, would you make the same choice?"

"In a heartbeat." No hesitation, not a moment to consider. Of course, swift, brutal decisions were his bread and butter on the job. Why would his life be any different?

She could barely push the words through her rapidly constricting throat. "Just forget you ever met me, Beck."

"That's not likely now, is it? And not just because of this." He touched the bandage over his tat, then grasped her hand and targeted his heart with their tangled fingers. "You're in here, *princesa*. It broke me to give you up but I stand by it. You left scorch marks that never healed. And I don't want them to."

She extracted her hand from the heated cocoon of his. Stepped back. Inhaled . . . a shallow breath, because deep at this moment was impossible.

"Just go," she choked out, turning her back on him like she had on her father, on her whole charmed life, all those years ago. Only back then, taking a stand had been the first step in Darcy becoming strong. Now, when ten seconds later the door to the parlor clicked shut, she couldn't remember the last time she had felt so weak.

chapter 9

. . . .

"Coffee shops. The last resort of the desperately single."
Mel cast her critical gaze around the busy Starbucks in
Lincoln Square. "They used to be so promising. Now
they're filled with aspiring writers and wannabe day trad-
ers, frankly, the worst collection of talent I've come across
in years." Sighing, she sipped her skinny latte and eyed
Darcy from beneath her golden lashes. "But that's not
why we're here, is it."

Darcy poked at the chocolate croissant she had
bought in a fit of pessimism five minutes ago. Her third
since walking into the aromatic, supposedly calming
interior of the popular coffee place with Mel. Between
the holiday excess and this Beck business, it looked like
she'd be making her grand exit from the city ten pounds
chunkier than when she arrived three months ago.

Or maybe all that extra weight could be attributed to her heavy heart.

"Well, I'd love to see you settled before I leave Chicago," Darcy said with fake cheer. Her disinterested gaze drifted to a salt-and-pepper-haired professorial type reading an actual newspaper. "Elbow Patches seems nice."

"Lives with his mother."

Undeterred, Darcy tried again. "That guy with the hipster hat and the sideburns is cute."

"There are only so many microbrewery tours and ironic T-shirt shopping trips I can fit into my schedule." Mel's pixie features turned kindhearted. "Quit stalling. Time to discuss the man of the hour—or should I say the decade?"

Darcy gave her most Continental shoulder shrug, perfected during her time in Paris. "There's nothing to discuss."

"Right." Mel stared Darcy down. "So how's this going to end, D?"

The end was a done deal. Seven years ago. Again, two days before when she discovered Beck had cut her out of the decision to take the road to Splitsville. More men taking care of business for their women. Her father, Preston Collins, François, every guy she'd ever dated, really, and now Beck. She almost rolled her eyes at the canyon of self-pity his actions had opened up. Her heart was set to deluded, and now she wanted to wallow in her own stupidity for a while.

"It's not going to end with me forgiving him."

"Hmm. Men are just manipulating douche canoes," Mel said in sympathy.

"Testify."

"They leave the toilet seat up, can barely walk and chew gum at the same time—"

"Act like they know best," Darcy cut in, getting warmed up.

"That's their problem. They think they know best, but in this case . . . I have to agree."

Darcy was stunned. "I can't believe you're taking his side."

Mel blew out an oh-girlfriend sigh. "It was a long time ago and he was crazy about you. That's gotta count for something."

Darcy didn't doubt Beck's feelings for her all those years ago, but it was tainted, corrupted, *ruined*, by his high-handed behavior. What gave him the right to ride solo on such an important decision?

"I've spent the last few years building myself up. I can't be with someone who doesn't respect me. Who pays lip service to the notion of my strength but wants to pull the lever behind the curtain."

"Like your dad."

"What?"

"You know."

She did. Every man who crossed her path was assessed with the checklist: was he bossy, manipulative, demanding, in any way like Sam Cochrane? One tick was enough to scuttle any potential relationship. But at the same time, she was drawn to decisive, confident men. Men like

Beck who knew what they wanted and fought with gloves on, fists raised, to make it a reality.

So sue her for being a girly mass of contradictions.

"You had to give him my address," she said faintly, not quite ready to capitulate to common sense.

"Gage extracted it from me under false pretenses," Mel said, as if Thor-lust could excuse her guilt. "Still can't believe that hot piece of ass is gay. I weep for my fellow Vagina Americans."

"I really loved him, Mel."

"When?"

That pulled her up short. She had fallen in love with a serious boy that day in the boxing ring, and two weeks ago, fell right back into the Beck Rivera groove. The *when* wasn't a fixed point in time. Her feelings for this man existed on a continuum.

She had never stopped loving him. Not for one second.

Mel gave a short nod as if Darcy had spoken that aloud. "You said you were over him. That you'd moved on and this was just a fling, revenge, whatever, to see you through the holidays. But you never got over him. Not really. And now you want to punish him for breaking your heart all those years ago instead of just accepting that shit happens, people make decisions for good or bad—" Darcy opened her mouth to object but Mel countered with the hand. "And that now he's a different person. You're a different person. He wanted the best for you, to make you happy in the long term because he was nuts about you. Best intentions, so-so methods."

"You think I overreacted?"

Mel broke off a piece of Darcy's croissant and popped it into her mouth. "Is that what you call it when you pick a fight?" she asked around her chewing. "'Cause that's what you did, babe. All this time you didn't want to know why he dumped you, but the minute it comes down to the wire, as soon as he pushes you to be brave, *now* you start channeling Countess Curiosity? You knew you wouldn't like the answer, and it gave you the perfect out."

Darcy hated that Mel was right. Damn her.

"I guess I panicked."

"*Yeah*, you did. Loving this man is going to turn your life upside down and make you question everything. That's a lot to take in if you're not ready for it. I tell my students all the time that fear is often a good pointer to what we really want and need. If it's outside your comfort zone, it's going to be so much more rewarding when you pull it off. You have to feel it to heal it."

Darcy knew that what Mel said made sense, but making sense never made it easier. Bringing her fears front and center was supposed to make the hurt of facing the truth worth the pain, all shit that sounded great on paper. She thought back to Beck's words, how she needed to figure out where she was going instead of dwelling on where she had been.

Gotta stop running sometime, Darcy.

Was she ready to let down her guard, expose her soft underbelly, and give this man free reign over her heart?

❄ ❄ ❄

Beck tore off his mask and gulped the cold, pine-scented nighttime air. Even mixed with the acrid smell of smoke and burned wood, it was the second best scent ever because it told him he was back in the thick of it. The best scent . . . damn, thinking of that, thinking of *her*, would only drive him mad.

"Good job, Rivera," Lieutenant McElroy said with a clap on Beck's back as they gathered for the debrief by the pumper outside the four-story walk-up on Sheridan. "You didn't screw up once."

Two kids with minor smoke inhalation, mom with first-degree burns on her hands, and Fluffy the family dog would survive this holiday season. The same could not be said for the Douglas fir that had once stood proud in their living room—or the oodles of presents beneath it.

"Any idea how you pulled this one out of your ass?"

Beck turned to find Luke squinting at him through black-rimmed eyes. He shook his head, still bewildered by the turn of events over the last twelve hours, starting with this morning's 6 a.m. wake-up call from the deputy fire commissioner.

Your hearing's been scheduled. Get your ass in gear, now.

Four hours later, witnesses had been called, testimony had been given, and Beck was in the clear with a warning to "not be so eff'n impetuous" and an order to report for immediate duty. His captain said it was a done deal and, while Beck appreciated being back in the fray, he appreciated less the helpless feeling that the strings were being yanked from above.

Decisions made by big men in small rooms.

A little like how Darcy must have felt, when she realized Beck had made a unilateral ruling that affected the course of their entire lives. How her father always made her feel. Growing up as he did, Beck knew the helplessness of having no control over your life. One day you're on the streets, the next you're inhaling Irish stew with a bunch of wild foster kids.

Regret at how things had ended with Darcy constricted his chest like he had choked down black smoke. Sure, he could see her point, how cutting her out of the loop minimized her agency—but to use it now to bail on this great thing they had going?

Unacceptable.

He knocked back a half bottle of water to cool his parched throat and raised his gaze to take in Luke. "I never said thank you."

His brother frowned. "For what?"

"For saving my life."

Luke gave a desultory sniff. "I won a packet on you at the last Battle of the Badges. You think I'm going to let my meal ticket get incinerated?"

"Screw you, then."

"You know, Becky," Luke said in that parental tone that signaled a major speech was about to go down. "Maybe it's middle-child syndrome, but sometimes I think you forget that we are your family and there is nothing—and I mean nothing—we would not do for you. Walking into a burning building to drag your dumb boricua ass out? It's just part of the deal. Of course, I'd appreciate it if you didn't try to upstage me with the heroics on every frickin' run. I am older, after all." With a smile in his eyes, he laid his gloved hand on Beck's shoulder. "Semper fraternus."

Forever brothers. Made a man feel good to know he had these people in his corner. But there was someone else who had always been rooting for him, right from the moment their eyes clashed over a boxing ring's ropes.

"Lock and load, boys," McElroy called out, his heavy boot on the sideboard of the pumper's cab. "Back to the house we go."

"We need to make a stop, Big Mac," Beck shot back.

The lieutenant's face lifted, flashing white teeth bright against ebony skin. "Burritos as big as your head? You're speaking my language, Rivera."

Luke threw his helmet into the cab and climbed up. "You can stuff your face later. Our boy needs to take care of important business."

Beck stared past the truck, down the snowy street, and all the way to the merry band of red and green lighting up the hundredth floor of the Hancock on Michigan Avenue. With no time to shower or change, she'd just have to take him as he was. As Sean used to say, you can't fall off the floor, boy, the only way is up.

The count was not over. He could still haul himself off the mat.

And this time, Beck would fight to win.

chapter 10

. . . .

With its gold-leafed pillars and crystal chandeliers, the grand ballroom at the Drake Hotel might seem like an odd choice for a charity gala aimed at helping the homeless, but such was the way of big-time philanthropy, Cochrane-style. Opulence always made people feel important, and the decadent surroundings were intended to inspire subconscious counting of blessings and deeper digging into Benjamin-lined pockets.

"They're more fake than a three-dollar bill."

"What are?" Darcy asked her grandmother, and immediately regretted it.

"Her tits," Grams pronounced in a loud whisper, lifting a bony finger in the direction of Darcy's stepmother, Tori, who admittedly did have a very fake and very fine pair of girls, bought and paid for by Darcy's father.

Tori and her gravity-defying breasts were currently in

deep conversation with Mayor Eli Cooper, who looked like he was hitting those puppies up for a campaign donation. He caught Darcy's eye and winked. Chicago's youngest-ever mayor, and undoubtedly its most handsome, Eli was an old friend of the family. Since his election three years ago, he had kept the female voters in a perpetual state of hormonal frenzy.

"You covered up," Grams remarked in a voice flavored with disapproval.

She had. Darcy could have walked in, tats—and tits—blazing, but frankly she was over it. So she had worn an LBD, though the L stood for *long*, the B stood for *boring*, and she looked like she was auditioning for Morticia in the *Addams Family* musical. Masking every inch of her offensive skin, the dress and matching jacket made her invisible, which was just how her father liked her.

Two tables over, Sam Cochrane sat glad-handing the governor, but raised his head when the low murmur of moneyed voices went from a burble to a babble toward the back of the room.

Darcy turned in the direction of the commotion, and her heart stuttered, stalled, and stopped. Striding toward her in full firefighter regalia, and looking so hot she half expected the sprinklers to go off any second, was Beck. His expression blazed a path of fire to her table, sizzling all the way up her spine. The clucking of the well-heeled crowd increased with every sure step.

He halted, huge and potent above her, and the smell of smoke and man hit her hard.

"Darcy."

"Beck." Using the edge of the table, she hauled her wilting body upright. "You shaved."

"Had to. Back to work."

She wasn't sure how she felt about that. Clean and smooth-jawed, he stared at her for interminable moments. This infuriating man!

"What are you doing here?"

"You said you needed a date. Sorry I'm late. Had to save Christmas first."

"Nice suit, Pancho Dempsey," Grams chimed in, her voice echoing in the now eerily quiet room. The clucking had stopped, only to be replaced with silence ten times as deafening.

"Thanks, Mrs. C." He turned back to Darcy. "I had a big speech planned. Something about fighting for you and claiming what's mine." He frowned. "But this is all wrong."

Panic flared in Darcy's chest. "It is?"

"What the hell are you wearing?"

"Um, a dress."

"You look like someone died." He curved his blunt hands around her hips. "This isn't you, Darcy. This isn't the woman I love."

"I . . ." She slid a sidelong glance to her grandmother, who was not paying attention to her, but had her beady eyes trained on Beck. Unsurprisingly, no demographic was unaffected by his particular brand of sexy.

And he had just said he loved her. Not only in the past, but in the present. Right here, right now.

"I don't want to make a fuss," she said, trying to make that sound like it was a good thing.

"Why not?"

He had a point. Why was she lying low until she could slink away unseen into the cold, starless night? This was not the girl who had waited tables in a Boston diner and pulled pints in a Covent Garden pub when her father cut her off. This was not the woman she had worked so hard to become.

She was Darcy Fucking Cochrane, kick-ass body artist, and lover of the brave man who was currently eating her alive with his eyes.

With shaky fingers, she reached for the button on her high-necked jacket and unfastened it. The fabric's silky slide against her skin as she slipped it off her shoulders felt sensual. Liberating. It floated to the table behind her, likely smack dab in the middle of her five-thousand-dollar-a-plate dinner.

Not a problem. The only sustenance she needed stood before her. In Beck's eyes, she saw appreciation for her body, respect for her choices. She saw . . . everything.

He laid a soft kiss on the sleeve of ink she had revealed, blessing it and her. "Darcy, I've loved you from the first day you distracted me in that boxing ring." He switched his talented mouth to her other shoulder, cutting a path of sweet devastation along her newly bared collarbone on the way. "The result? A broken nose and the crap beaten out of your brother. Which I know you wanted me to do, by the way."

"I did not—".

"Yes, you did." Unwavering, unflinching, those blue-on-blue eyes held her captive. "From that first minute you were in my corner, Darcy, and I'm sorry I wasn't always in yours. I was careless with your heart and I didn't trust you to make the important decisions for yourself. *No más.*" No more.

No more hiding.

No more running.

No more denying.

"I'm yours, *mi reina*. Always have been, always will be."

Her apparent promotion from princess to queen sent a surge of power through Darcy, making her so heady she white-knuckled the table's edge.

"Then I guess you'd better kneel, Beck Rivera."

A brief flash of *fuck, really?* tweaked his mouth before it curved up into that do-me grin. He jackknifed to his knees before her, his hands coasting down her thighs over the acre of fabric as he felt a path to her ankles. Checking for injuries just like the first night he rescued her outside Dempsey's. Only this time, he would find her strong and whole.

Girl walked into a bar, hooked up with her destiny.

Gently, he raised her foot and kissed the visible skin with hot, purposeful lips, transferring his intimate heat to her body. The sight of him in supplication unraveled her like a loose thread on a sweater.

Lifting his head, he held her gaze boldly. "You're strong and sexy and I love you. I need you to breathe, but I need to make sure my woman can breathe first. What do you say, *querida*?"

He delivered the Rivera smile, the same crooked one he wooed her with that day in the ring after he had taken down one Cochrane and set his sights on conquering another. He captured her heart then, and had held it in his iron fist ever since. Beck saw her. He truly did. She could spend the rest of her life looking at him looking at her.

There was only one thing she could say.

"Rip it, Beck."

A quicker-than-the-human-eye move, and he tore her dress from the hem all the way to midthigh. Gasps hissed though the stultifying air at the sight of her skin shining in glorious Technicolor under the harsh ballroom lights.

Unfolding to his full, staggering height, he stood back, an expression of plain relish on his face at what he had created.

"Now give me your mouth, Darcy."

She launched like a heat-seeking missile and kissed him with everything she had.

"About time," Grams muttered, though she sounded a little choked up, the old softie.

"Right on, Mrs. C," Beck said, once he broke their kiss. "Now if you don't mind, I'd like to take my girl away from all this. Think you can hold down the fort here?"

"Go, go!" Grams flapped her birdlike hands. "I need to do the rounds and squeeze more money out of these clam-fisted tightwads."

On ramshackle legs, Darcy leaned down and kissed Grams on the cheek. "You sure you can manage?" She motioned to her ripped dress and bared shoulders. "I might look like a walking middle finger to your donors, but I can stay if you need me."

"Be gone, girl. Someone else can put in the work for

a change." Grams curved her regal gaze behind Darcy. "Tori! Get your plastic butt over here and push."

Beck was already half carrying, half dragging Darcy to the exit. Past Chicago's glitterati. Past a parade of shocked, pursed mouths. Past her stone-faced father.

She stopped and pivoted. "Just a second."

"You sure?" Beck asked, concern bracketing his mouth.

Her father stood, age and disappointment sketched in craggy lines on his face. "Darcy."

Looping her arms around his neck, she hugged him for the first time in so long it brought tears to her eyes.

"Thank you, Dad. Thank you for pissing me off so much that it made me strong and beautiful." She smiled up at his flinty gaze. "Call me when you're ready to talk."

Sometimes you forgive people simply because you still want them in your life, but if her father wanted more, he would need to meet her halfway. She refused to allow another bead of toxicity to burn her skin. Taking Beck's hand, she led him from the ballroom and didn't look back.

In the Drake's foyer, Beck placed his fireman's jacket over her exposed shoulders, and the protective gesture loosened that painful knot beneath her breastbone and activated the waterworks. He crushed her to his strong chest and gave her a few precious moments to lose it. The tension sloughed away with every jerky sob until she rested, boneless and spent in his arms.

"Happy?" he murmured.

"Ecstatic," she said thickly into his neck. Peeking up, she met the serious blue gaze of her first and last love. "I love you, Beck."

"I know." He pressed a soft kiss to her lips that turned ferocious in seconds. A soul kiss that went on forever, but was still over too soon.

Behind her, she heard an interrupting cough. The mayor stood with a smirk on his face, a redhead on his arm, and a security team bringing up the rear.

"Nice exit, monkey," Eli said, kissing her damp cheek. "Very colorful."

She sniffed, not quite ready or willing to pull it together. "Watch out, Mr. Mayor. Standing too close to me, you might lose some voters."

"Or attract the youth base. If they actually voted." He shifted his sharp gaze to Beck and back to Darcy. "Surely you have better manners than your grandmother, Darcy Cochrane."

She rolled her eyes. For years, Eli Cooper had teased her like an older brother and his ascent up the political ladder had made him only more insufferable. "This is Beck Rivera, one of your bravest at Engine 6."

"Rivera?" The mayor's lips firmed. As the official boss of the CFD, part of Eli's job was keeping tabs on the firemen, and with his antics, Beck had clearly not eluded the mayor's notice. "Incident back in November. Tough situation all around, but I hear you acquitted yourself well. On the mend?"

Beck nodded.

"You're one of Sean Dempsey's foster sons. You lost me a shitload of money at the Battle of the Badges."

"I'm one of his sons. And I recommend that next time you don't bet against a Dempsey."

Eli's mouth hooked up in appreciation of Beck's snappish correction. He parted his lips to say more, but checked it when one of his lackeys whispered in his ear.

"Have to go kiss some rich donor asses. Good to see you, monkey." Man-to-man nod at Beck.

As the mayor and his entourage left, Beck drew a callused finger over her jaw. "Since when are you on such good terms with our fearless leader?"

"Oh, didn't I tell you he was an old friend? I had the nicest chat with him last night about bureaucracy and red tape and how absolutely nothing gets done at city hall over the holidays. He's trying to put a stop to all that lollygagging. Part of his platform, you know." She shot him a wicked grin.

Beck grasped the lapels of the jacket he had caped her with and drew her flush, his eyes dark with molten hunger. "You didn't have to do that. But thank you."

"What use is the Cochrane name if I can't pull in a favor every now and then?" She dropped a kiss on his sensuous lips. "Besides," she whispered, a teasing glint in her eye, "I was only doing what's best for you."

Beck drew back and studied her playful smile. "*Querida*," he chided, "too soon."

She laughed. "I'm just getting started, Beck Rivera. The next step? Branding you as mine."

That earned her a sexy Beck growl. "I like the sound of that, *mi amor*. Think of me as a new canvas for your portfolio. This heart, this soul, this body . . ." He held her hand over his chest and the wild *th-thunk* of his heart. "Use me, Darcy."

She planned to. Just imagining the artistry she could create with this man filled her heart to bursting with love, life, and magic.

"I already know how I want to ink you next, Beck. Something old school, maybe a heart with my name." She lowered her palm to his tight, trim ass, that part of him she had noticed first in a dingy CFD gym all those years ago, and gave it a healthy squeeze.

"Right. About. Here."